I0823858

To Kill a Cook

ALSO BY W. M. AKERS

Westside

Westside Saints

Westside Lights

Critical Hit

Pocket Full of Stars

W. M. AKERS

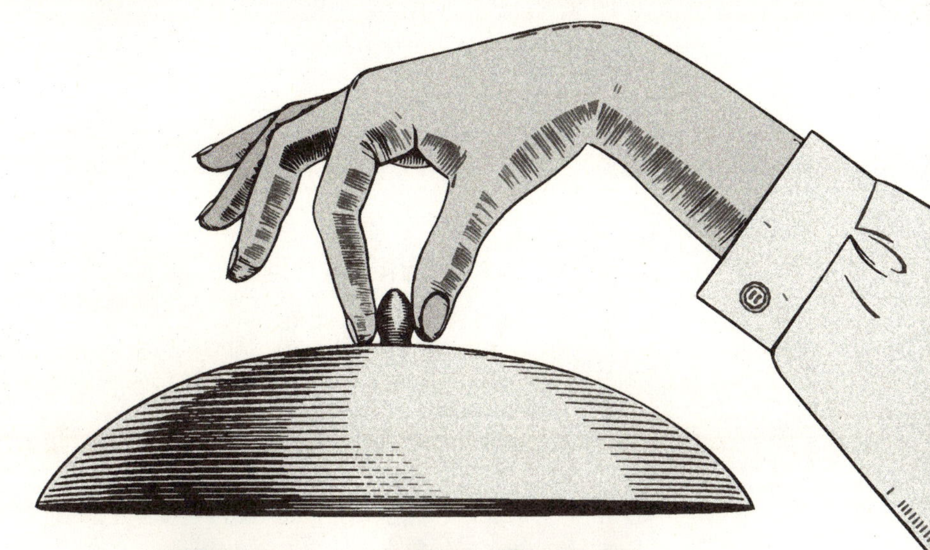

To Kill a Cook

G. P. Putnam's Sons
New York

PUTNAM
— EST. 1838 —
G. P. PUTNAM'S SONS
Publishers Since 1838
An imprint of Penguin Random House LLC
1745 Broadway, New York, NY 10019
penguinrandomhouse.com

Book design by Laura K. Corless
Title page art: Hands holding a cloche © Maisei Raman/Shutterstock

LIBRARY OF CONGRESS CATALOGING-IN-PUBLICATION DATA

Names: Akers, W. M. author.
Title: To kill a cook / W. M. Akers.
Description: New York: G. P. Putnam's Sons, 2025.
Identifiers: LCCN 2025025775 (print) | LCCN 2025025776 (ebook) | ISBN 9798217044863 hardcover | ISBN 9798217044870 ebook
Subjects: LCGFT: Fiction. | Detective and mystery fiction. | Novels.
Classification: LCC PS3601.K482 T6 2025 (print) | LCC PS3601.K482 (ebook)
LC record available at https://lccn.loc.gov/2025025775
LC ebook record available at https://lccn.loc.gov/2025025776

Printed in the United States of America
1st Printing

The authorized representative in the EU for product safety and compliance is Penguin Random House Ireland, Morrison Chambers, 32 Nassau Street, Dublin D02 YH68, Ireland, https://eu-contact.penguin.ie.

For Annie, whose kitchen
smelled like garlic and hot oil

For Mom,
who taught me how to cook

And for my father-in-law,
a very cool guy

Most cooks, it would seem, are misunderstood wretches, ill-housed, dyspeptic, with aching broken arches. They turn more eagerly than any other artists to the bottle, the needle, and more vicious pleasures; they grow irritable; finally they seize upon the nearest weapon, which if they are worth their salt is a long knife kept sharp as lightning.

—M. F. K. FISHER

To Kill a Cook

One

• Tuesday •

So it started with a severed head.

Well, not really—nothing ever *starts* with a severed head. It started at seven A.M., I guess, when the kids woke up screaming like they were being stabbed in the spine. I'd been living with my fiancé and his boys for about a year but I hadn't acclimated to the furious inefficiency of a morning with children, so even before I got out of the house I was running late. I skipped breakfast because I was headed for Laurent's, on Fifty-Fourth and Madison, only half a block from a nasty little deli that does the most exquisitely greasy pastrami, egg, and cheese, so I stomped through Central Park toward my destiny or, at the very least, something to eat.

It was a bright blue morning in early April and the sun was shining like a freshly unwrapped toy. It should have been beautiful, yeah, but this was New York in 1972, so getting out of the park meant navigating a four-foot smear of human waste. Shit doesn't bother me—you step around it, it's not a hassle—but being late makes my jaw ache. Toru had the kids, which meant it was my turn to work. I had a column to write and nothing to say, so I needed to do some eating and some thinking, and unless I stuck to my schedule, there was no way I'd have time for both. By the time I hit Mad the coffee had turned to bile and I was dying for a cigarette and it would have been fine if I'd gotten that sandwich, but when I neared the deli there was smoke on the wind. Somebody had smashed a wood-paneled Torino wagon through the front window, and I definitely wasn't getting anything to eat.

Still, I felt better when I got to Laurent's because I always do. I turned at the faded green awning, took four steps down from the sidewalk, and pulled the handle of the famous rust-red door. It was locked, which was annoying because Laurent had promised to leave it open, but you don't get to be a genius by remembering to unlock doors. I thumped a few times and I guess I looked unhinged because a family of tourists outside the hotel next door stared at me like I was a rabid dog. I peeked through the window.

"If he's not here I'm gonna kill him," I said.

Two huge ferns flanked the front door, older than the dinosaurs. I played a quick game of eenie, meenie, miney, moe, chose the left one, buried my hand in damp dirt, and felt around for the spare key. The tourists continued to gawk. They were refugees from the Sears catalog. The mom looked like a Creamsicle—orange minidress over orange slacks, all dripping white fringe—and the boys had matching bowl cuts, green polos, plaid pants, and expressions of stupor. The only thing spoiling the picture was the dad, who was wearing a puffy winter coat even though it was, I don't know, sixty-five degrees? He had one of those three-martini faces, twisted into sweaty fear.

"The concierge said it isn't safe," he said.

"Bert," sighed the woman, "he said it was safe after eight."

"It's 7:54," said one of the kids, staring intently at his Mickey Mouse watch. "No. 7:55."

"We're going back inside," said Dad.

"I did not cross half the country to sit in the hotel," answered Mom.

"And I didn't come here to get stabbed."

Tourists really do get worse every year. Sure, plenty of people get killed in this town, but the odds are decent that on any given day it won't be you. So I pulled my arm out of the planter and yelled something encouraging: "Get breakfast!"

They froze. Which I guess is understandable because I was a stranger with a dirty arm but they were gonna benefit from my expertise whether they liked it or not.

"You're three blocks from Cohen's, they do amazing potato pancakes. On Madison and Fifty-Second there's this pastry shop called Antoine's, I think, and they've got éclairs and croissants that ooze butter, or if you want something good for kids, go left on Lex and walk until you see this big chrome clock—that's Shepherd's Diner, which is cheap and the food comes fast and the waiters flirt but not too much."

As far as I was concerned, this was all very helpful—free advice from a professional eater—but I guess I was kind of shrieking because with each word they inched closer toward the door. The man tried to answer.

"The concierge said—"

"The concierge wants you inside all week eating room service. Where you from?"

His mouth flapped. No words came out.

I yelled louder: "I said where are you from?"

"New Harmony," said one boy.

"Indiana," clarified the other. The parents hugged them closer, afraid that any more information would be enough for me to murder them in their beds. I plunged my arm into the second planter and dug for the key that, damn it, just had to be there. I kept my eyes on the family, though—I'm coordinated enough that I can shout and rummage at the same time.

"And you didn't haul yourselves all the way from Indiana to sit on a hotel bedspread eating rubber eggs and watching *Captain Kangaroo.* Don't be a coward. Eat!"

Y'know when Daffy Duck runs away so fast that he leaves behind a little cloud of duck-shaped dust? That's how they bolted back into the hotel.

"Their loss."

My hand closed on the chill metal key. I put New Harmony out of my mind, brushed off the dirt, and opened the door.

It was dark in there. That was part of the charm. At night it was a place of shadows and golden light where everyone looked a little bit beautiful. In the morning, it was a big room with the lights off. I waited for my eyes to adjust. When they didn't, I felt for the switch and tried to ignore how threadbare everything looked under the glare.

"Laurent?" I called. "César?"

My voice crashed into the soft beige tablecloths and died. I passed the maître d's stand and climbed to the bar, jaw-clenchingly aware that I had roughly fifteen minutes before I had to head downtown. I filled a rocks glass with something called "pub mix." Once Laurent's bar snacks had been toasted almonds and cured olives, but the belt had been tightened until only canned mix was left. It was stale, yeah, but salty too and exactly what my body required. I bit through the pale brown crunch and eyed the old pictures of Laurent posing with all the favorite post-war celebrities: Lee Dixon and Walter Pidgeon, Tommy Dorsey and this blonde whose name I couldn't remember but whom I considered deeply glamorous when I was a child. They looked bleached and tanned and sweaty with gin, smiling like the party was never gonna end. I found it terribly unfair that they were allowed to smoke while I was not.

Time passed, like it usually does. After thirteen minutes, I grabbed the bar phone and dialed. Judy Grich, my editor, answered mid-inhale. I could smell her from here.

"Yeah?" she said.

"It's Bernice."

"Not like you to be running late."

My back got hot. The only thing worse than being late is being called out. I twisted the phone's pale blue exoskeleton in my fist.

"It's Toru's birthday party Friday. We're having it at Laurent's."

"Sure is nice to have fancy friends."

"Except he called with the menu and it was, I don't know. Bland."

"Like what?" She sounded hungry. I flipped open my notepad and read what Laurent gave me on Sunday night.

"Cruise ship food. Chilled hearts of celery. Something called 'petite Alaska shrimp cocktail gourmet.' Yorkshire pudding, garden peas, Carolina rice, all wrapped up with fruit compote and lychee nut ice cream."

"Not very French."

"That's what I said! I told him to serve the fucking classics, right? Caviar and champagne and orange duck and chocolate mousse."

“And what’d he say?”

“He said come by before they open and he’d show me something special. So I figured I’d squeeze it in before our meeting but he’s running late, so maybe I come by next week instead?”

“Yeah . . .” Another long drag. “Nah, sorry, I gotta see you today.”

“What about?”

“Nothing really. Just gotta see you.”

“Can we do it on the phone?”

“I’d rather not.”

Shit, I thought. Shit shit shit. It’s lovely having a sociable editor—it’s a good way to get lunch on the magazine’s tab—but when she insists on meeting, well, either it’s because my cover story on “The New Spaghetti” won a Pulitzer or something’s wrong.

“How about ten-thirty?” I said, with an irritating note of fear.

“That’s just fine.”

She hung up. I popped another piece of pub mix and found I had no spit. I hung my elbows on the bar and scowled at the room. I don’t like being in restaurants when they’re empty. It’s improper, like catching Helen Hayes in her curlers. The chairs were upside down and the air was crisp with Pine-Sol. The mirrored columns looked foggy; the banquettes sagged; the seaside murals of Calais looked cheap. And the clock was still ticking. Soon I’d be late again.

I remembered some awful show the kids watched where this fresh-faced ersatz hippie whispered about how, “When we’re angry or upset, when we’re feeling scared, all we need to do is *breeeeeeeeathe.*” I tried to *breeeeeeeeathe,* which made me cough, which made me want a cigarette. I was tempted to root around to see if C.J. had a pack stashed, but instead I closed my eyes and tried to find my happy place and remembered that, fuck, I was already there.

I fell in love with Laurent's long before I ever passed through its door. I found out about it through *Our World*, one of those full-color magazines that were such a big deal back when the whole world was black and white. They dubbed him "King of the Butter Boys" in 1955, which would've made me, Christ, about twelve years old. He got the cover and an eight-page spread and the declaration that his place was "the first great restaurant New York has ever seen." Which sounds impressive, yeah, but you've gotta understand how little competition he'd had. Back then American fine dining meant ham steak and boiled potatoes with a cup of terrapin soup. Our fruit was mushy; our veggies canned; our meat indistinguishable from asphalt. Laurent was different. He preached green salads and red steak, hand-whipped mayo and icy champagne, brackish caviar and creme pâtisserie so sweet it made your heart pound. *Our World* showed him at the red door, smiling wide, one hand in the pocket of his double-breasted suit, the other clutching a thick cigar. He was stout and cheerful, with thick black glasses and a gap between his front teeth, and he talked with the confidence of Moses, commandments in hand.

"Americans believe French food must be luxurious, and yes, sometimes it is. But luxury should not inspire fear. Good food—really good food—is a painting by Vermeer, a beautiful woman, an impeccable sunset. It requires no expertise. All you need is an appetite."

Well, that and a bankroll—the prices *Our World* quoted made clear that, despite his republican chatter, Laurent's was no soup kitchen. But it was expensive because caviar is expensive, because truffles have to be dug out of the damn ground by pigs. He was dishing up pigeonneau de Bresse! Goujonnette de sole with sauce tartare! Médaillons de ris de veau à la maréchale! I didn't know what it meant but it sounded like heaven on a plate. The restaurant and the celebrities who roosted there were beautiful but the prettiest picture in the article was of the orange duck, which I cut out and taped to my dresser. It cost $6.50—a fortune—and the price only made me want it more.

Because let me tell you, my family didn't eat like that. I was born in Brooklyn—don't snicker, it wasn't my idea—to an Anglo-Irish sandhog named Barton Black and a woman born Annie Giolitti who was the only Italian in the borough who hated Italian food. I grew up in a house where garlic and onions were prohibited, where tomatoes were unwelcome, where even salt was barely tolerated. Mom tried like hell to be English or Irish or anything but Italian, so instead of being raised on tortellini and parm, I got her interpretation of British cookery: boiled meat and boiled veg and tough little rolls that the NHL sometimes used as pucks. That meant it was Dad who taught me and my sister to eat. The subway still cost a dime then, so on his day off we'd ride all over town to sample hot dogs at Coney Island, borscht at Brighton Beach, pastrami up and down Flatbush, and spicy sausage closer to home. I'm not nostalgic for old Brooklyn—the trolleys were slower than walking, stickball is boring, egg creams are worse than milkshakes, and Ebbets Field stank of piss. But those afternoons on the train with Dad, I think about a lot.

So when I went off to college at good ol' CUNY–Forest Hills—let's go Seagulls, rah rah rah!—I was determined to eat the city whole. I started by finding the best Chinese takeout, pizzerias, and diners near campus, then expanded across Queens, eating Greek and Puerto Rican and West Indian and anything else I could find. All of it was beautiful and I learned a hell of a lot, but at night I still dreamed about Laurent's. By then he was probably the most famous chef in America. He'd turned out some cookbooks and he had a cooking show that was broadcast pretty widely across the Northeast, where he'd pull housewives out of the audience and teach them to flip omelettes and use their blenders to whizz up mayonnaise. But the restaurant remained his home and I still dreamed about it often enough that I figured it was time to get a taste.

I took a job at the school library microfilming back issues of the *New York Clarion*, where I got wicked headaches squinting at ads for Dort motor cars and Palamino cigarettes—"You Can't Help But Love Them!," yeah, no shit. They paid me pennies and I saved every one. By winter break, just before the end of 1961, I had enough socked away. I broke out my prom dress, a scarlet number heaped with ruffles and flared to kingdom come, paid too much to have my hair teased, and talked my roommate, a skittish aspiring model named Lucy Rogers, into coming with me. We dropped our tokens in the turnstiles, rumbled under the East River, and emerged into a world of white lights, perfume, and fur. As soon as we crossed Park Avenue, Lucy got twitchy. I could feel her hand sweating through her glove.

"We look like dopes," she said.

"We look phenomenal. Everybody thinks I'm some eastern European princess and you're a movie star just in from the coast."

"I'm from Jersey, Bernice. Not even one of the high-class suburbs. I'm from the shore."

"So fucking what?"

The light changed. I tugged on her hand. She quivered like a tightrope.

"Can we skip it? Find some red sauce place and eat spaghetti and go home?"

"We're doing this."

"I'll treat. Cheesecake, even. Just please let's go somewhere we belong."

"We belong wherever the hell we say."

So I basically dragged her over to Fifty-Fourth and her legs got heavier with every step. I think I could have muscled her inside if it weren't for the limousines. As soon as she saw them—eight coal-black Cadillacs, like some mobster's funeral—she let out this little yip and ran.

"God damn it!" I shouted.

"I'm sorry!"

"It's only food, y'know? You've had it before."

"I'm getting pizza and I am going back to Queens. You coming or what?"

I looked at Lucy, shivering in her mother's clothes. She was dressed like a pineapple and still looked better than me. But I hadn't eaten since breakfast and when my stomach's growling nothing stands in my way. So I strolled down the steps like I owned the building and reached for the door. The doorman got there first.

"Oh yeah," I said. "Thanks."

I gave an asinine curtsy and tried to remember what fearless looked like as I shuffled into another world. You know *The Lion, the Witch and the Wardrobe*? It was basically that except instead of being about Jesus it was food and sex and instead of stepping into a magic forest I tumbled into a fog of smoke, Shalimar, and sizzling fat. The lights were dimmed down to nothing. Every candle glimmered like its own little star, its glare dancing off the mirrored columns and the dangerously low-hanging chandeliers and a few million dollars' worth of rubies and emeralds and diamonds, diamonds, diamonds.

Everyone looked so gorgeous that it took me a moment to notice the actual famous people perched on Olympus—the five prime tables on the raised platform that overlooked the door, which I'd been seeing in my dreams ever since *Our World* taught me its name. Merle Oberon piled a toast point with caviar. Casey Stengel and Yogi Berra fenced with their cigars. Burt Lancaster told Gregory Peck, "Shut the fuck up, I'm paying," while Mort Sahl gawked at the legs of Cyd Charisse, whose dress was pale blue and studded with lace flowers so delicate they made me feel like I was wearing a barn.

I wanted to run. I figured I had about fifteen seconds before they grabbed me and trussed me and hurled me into fancy-people jail. But then a waiter swirled past carrying mussels and scallops and crisp striped bass and I knew there was nowhere else I belonged.

I tore my eyes off Olympus—let me tell you, it's hard to stop looking at Cyd Charisse—and strode up to the maître d', a plush-bodied man who'd been born in his tuxedo. He was shorter than me but his eyebrows had been teased toward the heavens, giving him a look of incredulity that only grew more severe as he watched me approach. His name, if my research was correct—and, folks, it always is—was César Lerond.

"Bernice Black," I said. I'd never hated my voice so much. "Seven-thirty."

He dropped his eyes. He found my name. He looked surprised.

"A table for two."

"That's me."

He gestured at a pair of pink velvet chairs.

"You may wait here until your date arrives."

"I don't have a date."

"Oh?"

"My friend Lucy, she, well . . . It's just me."

His eyes were little red marbles. I expected the glasses to tumble off his nose, but somehow they held on.

"That is not possible."

"And yet here I am."

"But a young woman unattended . . . even at the bar . . . you understand how it would *appear*."

I blinked. He didn't. Berra jabbed his cigar at Stengel's chest, sending his erstwhile manager tumbling into his chair. Beside them I spotted a sad-eyed woman with a halo of blond hair staring listlessly into her soup, absolutely alone.

"What about her?" I said. "She's unattended—nobody thinks she's a whore."

"Because that is Princess Grace."

"Of Monaco?" I gulped.

"The same."

He lit a cigarette. I'd never had anyone light a cigarette *at* me before, but that's how he did it—like he was putting a bullet in my skull.

Garbage stink wafted through the front door. A cackling couple tumbled through with it.

"Excuse me," said César. "There are other guests."

He waved his hand and I stepped aside. I wanted to sob but I had no interest in letting Grace Kelly see me cry. Instead I waited, metal in my mouth and acid in my gut, thinking how hideous it would feel to get back to the subway and find Lucy waiting on the platform with pizza grease on her chin and no slice for me. I'd starve to death before we made it back to Queens.

I'd rather die here.

So I sank into one of the pink chairs, which smelled exactly like your grandmother, and watched for an opening. Through the mob I spotted a table in the back where a heavyset Ivy Leaguer stared blankly at an empty bottle of champagne while his date worked her way through the biggest piece of cake I'd ever seen. A brace of busboys hovered above her shoulder, waiting for the last crumb to tumble across her lacquered lips. When it did, everything happened all at once.

The girl stood. It took him a couple of tries, but her man did too.

The busboys reached for the plates.

And César lit another cigarette.

As his eyes crossed over the Zippo's flame, I darted onto the floor. Daffy, I know—what'd I think, he wouldn't notice?—but I had this twisted feeling that once I sat down, once I crossed my legs and ordered my wine and demonstrated that I knew exactly which fork was which, they'd see that I belonged. My heart pounded, my palms sweated, my feet screamed *RUN*, but I forced myself to proceed as sedately as the lady I was pretending to be. I had nearly reached my freshly cleared table when a plump little hand closed on my arm.

"Mademoiselle."

Shit, shit, shit!

César had caught me and whatever he did was gonna be worse than pizza on the subway. It was gonna be an all-time humiliation and I'd be banned forever and I'd never have the nerve to go into a restaurant again. I'd die. In Brooklyn. Hungry and alone.

Except it wasn't César.

It was the man himself.

Laurent Tirel.

My first thought on meeting the chef whose genius I'd been admiring since I was in bobby socks was that *Our World* must have taken his picture with him standing on a stool. He was at least two inches shorter than me and I have never been mistaken for tall. His teeth were crooked and his glasses made his eyes look like full moons, but something about his smile told me that once, long ago, this guy was a dish.

"You are?" He smiled like the words tickled his mouth.

"Bernice Black. I'm not famous or anything, I go to CUNY–Forest Hills, I grew up in Brooklyn and I have a reservation for seven-thirty and it was a table for two but . . ."

"Why?"

"What?"

"Why did you make a reservation at my restaurant?"

"To eat."

"To eat *what*?"

"Everything you have."

He chuckled—the best department store Santa in the world didn't have so warm a laugh—then let go of my wrist and offered his arm.

"If you need a date, my dear, perhaps you would accept me?"

Two

Swear to Christ, I thought he was joking, but his arm kept dangling, so finally I took it. I was so dizzy, all I could see were the flowers: yellow roses and purple hyacinths, lilacs and larkspurs and pansies striped with every color nature ever dreamed up. Their smell was intoxicating but it couldn't compete with the food.

"Twenty thousand a year, just on flowers," said Laurent. "My owners think I'm mad but beauty is worth spending for."

"Especially if it's not your money."

I regretted it as soon as I said it—I've never been good at keeping my mouth shut—but he smiled bigger and said, "Ah! You understand!"

At the back of the dining room, swinging padded doors opened onto a flight of stairs. Framed menus hung above the banister, each bearing the signature of a distinguished guest. I was too lightheaded—from hunger, from celebrity, from the sensation of a dream about to come true—to decipher their names. Anyway, who cared? Lucy was the starfucker. I was here for roast duck.

The stairs took us to a windowless room with four tables, each shrouded by a Japanese screen. Another pair of swinging doors led to the kitchen. There were no bold-faced names here—just deeply rich bastards. Laurent sat us down at the only empty table and said:

"Thankfully, Mayor Wagner is in Washington tonight."

I cracked up. I mean, Burt Lancaster was one thing but the mayor's table was too much to bear. I tried to explain.

"So yesterday I had dinner in the school cafeteria. Salisbury steak, real gritty, with boiled broccoli and flaccid fries. Just me and a couple of magazines. And now I'm here."

A cork popped. A glass appeared. I took a long sip. The champagne was sharp like medicine.

"Hey, my mother would shrivel up and die if I didn't say this—we're just pals, right? Nobody's getting any ideas?"

He blushed. Probably I blushed too.

"I assure you, Miss Black, that I am always a gentleman. At least at work."

"Fabulous."

"And you really wish to eat everything?"

"Goddamned right."

He laughed like a backfiring Buick.

"Then that is what we'll have!"

So he ordered the whole menu. Started me off with my first caviar—like eating the ocean—then a crystal-clear consommé, which I mistook for chicken soup, and a mousse of sole with truffles that tasted like dirt with whipped cream except in a good way. Every unfamiliar thing made my palms sweat and my heart pound, but I ate like I'd been raised on it. We killed one bottle and he didn't ask before opening another—just kept pouring while he told me everything he missed about France, which he'd escaped in 1943.

"There a tomato is a tomato. A squash is a squash—delicate and fine. Here tomatoes are basketballs and a squash is big enough to use as a canoe. Everything is enormous and nothing has any taste. We make do."

Next came tête de veau—pink and tender, dotted with parsley and ringed with crispy potatoes—and when he asked if I liked it, I said it was the best thing I'd eaten since the caviar.

"Would it change your opinion if I told you it was boiled head of calf?"

"Nah. In Brooklyn we cook the cow's ass."

That got another cackle and I'm not going to say it didn't feel good—not just to make this guy laugh but to do it by being Bernice. But there was something worrying me, something minor, something I wouldn't even have brought up except that once I've got something to say, I basically can't function until I get it out of my brain.

"How about the duck?"

"The duck?"

"I saw it in this magazine, I guess, like, five or six years ago? And I maybe cut out the picture and taped it to my dresser, y'know, where other girls put Elvis. The caneton—I'm sorry, that's probably not how you're supposed to say it—the caneton à l'orange."

"We took it off the menu. My backers insisted. Too complicated, too expensive. We lost one dollar and ninety-eight cents on every one."

I sagged. He dragged on his cigar and gave me the smile you'd use on a kid with a busted balloon. I forced a smile and took another couple bites of the calf's head—it really was something, creamy and chewy at the same time, with just enough lemon juice to sting the back of your throat—and he shook his head in a way I didn't understand. We were quiet for a minute and then he wiggled his cigar in the air, summoning the head waiter. The guy's name, I'd learn down the line, was Jean-Louis. A veteran of the French resistance and Indochina, he'd quit soldiering after taking a bullet to the hip and washed up here. He was six foot and change, hair cropped, with a pencil-thin mustache that said less "Madam, may I have this dance?" and more "Madam, I shall break your neck silently and hide your body where it will never be found." He stared, mouth flat, as Laurent chattered. I'd learn later that, like all of Laurent's staff, Jean-Louis spoke excellent English but stuck to French during service for the sake of mystique.

Jean-Louis gave a curt nod and marched into the kitchen. My eyes strained to glimpse the place where the magic was made. What I saw reminded me of an operating room—cold and white and clean, a place of spotless order where decadence was born.

"What'd you tell him?" I said.

"To put in an order for caneton à l'orange."

I blinked. It still didn't make sense, so I tried blinking some more.

"But you said . . ."

"I say all sorts of things. Truth is, we always keep a few ducks in the freezer. For friends."

Friends. Can you believe that? I floated to the ceiling while he refilled my glass.

The caneton took long enough that by the time it showed up, I was hungry again. It was two ducks, actually, tiny and crisp and snuggled tight on a silver tray, swimming in a sauce spiked with brandy and caramel, surrounded by little boats of carved orange peel. It looked exactly like it had in *Our World*, only better because it was mine.

It was the first thing I'd ever eaten where it smelled so good, I tasted it before it hit my mouth. The skin cracked like spring ice. The flesh was almost too salty, almost too sweet, but instead it was perfect—so tender, I didn't even want to swallow. I just wanted to hold it in my mouth and let it melt.

I ate both ducks and knew I'd never be the same.

By then I was drunk on butter and salt. But when Jean-Louis brought out a frosted tureen of chocolate mousse, I didn't think of saying no. He slapped it onto my plate like a mason laying down mortar and topped it with a dollop of whipped cream. I licked my plate clean. I didn't think I could stand and was very grateful when, instead of asking me to haul myself out of there, Laurent poured me a little glass of crème de cassis.

"Before you barged in here," he said, "you were scared?"

"To death."

"Didn't show. You have excellent taste, Miss Black. Follow it. It will take you far."

As I rattled home on the IND, those words bounced around my brain like a Spaldeen. Call me corny, but that meal changed my life. I wrote a twelve-hundred-word story about the dinner—"Roast Duck, Chocolate Mousse, and My French Chef"—and shopped it around. The *Clarion* bit. That was a big goddamned deal. My dad had been reading the *Clarion* my whole life and when he saw my byline he called and said, "Okay, kid, I guess this writing stuff is going to work out." Of course, it wasn't that easy. The $24 they paid me vanished in a week—naturally, I spent it on food—and when I graduated they steadfastly ignored my requests for a job. But I used the clip to catch on at the *Select,* a shithouse rag that paid like hell and had absolutely no respect for its reporters. It folded in '65 and after that I bounced between broadsheets and tabloids, covering absolutely anything they'd pay me for. I learned to hit deadlines, to curse like a professional, when to flatter my editors and when to make their lives hell. I wrote about crime and I wrote about Wall Street, I interviewed actors and ballplayers and one incredibly flatulent Met Opera soprano, but food was always my goal. When I heard the *Sentinel* mag wanted someone to cover restaurants, I never looked back.

Food's the most important thing in the world because it's something everybody has in common. My rule is, I'll eat anything twice. Upscale French, downtown vegetarian, Indian or Chinese or Mexican or Thai or Vietnamese or three hot dogs with relish from the cart on the corner of Forty-Fourth and Sixth—I don't care. I'm not saying I don't have standards—if I didn't, I'd be out of a job—but I'll give anything a shot except for lima beans—and if you put enough butter on, hell, I'd probably eat them too. What I can't stand is cooks who waste my time. I don't bitch about price—between the recession and inflation, I accept that the thirty-dollar lunch is here to stay. But I expect everybody in the place to bust their ass for every hungry bastard that comes through the door, to take their work as seriously as I take mine. Every time I sit down to eat—or stand, New Yorkers often stand—I'm expecting the best meal I've ever had. Usually I'm disappointed but I don't let it get me down—there's always the next one.

As far as I'm concerned, I've got the best job in the world. I eat out five nights a week and most afternoons and the magazine picks up the tab. Even the Rockefellers don't eat so well, I swear. And none of it would have been possible if it weren't for Laurent. Turns out that once you're invited downstairs, you're a regular. I took full advantage, coming back whenever I had the cash and hanging around the kitchen when I didn't. Some people thought he was an asshole, a snob, but I saw the truth, which was that he had standards and he expected the same from the people who cooked his food and the people who ate it too. He taught me how to cook and how to eat, and even though the cooking lessons never stuck, I was grateful for them. He took me to the Fulton Fish Market at five in the morning and showed me how to buy turbot and bream and merlan and other fish I'd never even heard of. He told me that pigeonneau was just what it sounded like—pigeon—that goujonnette de sole was a four-dollar plate of fish sticks, that médaillon meant medallion—who'd've thought, right?—and ris de veau was pancreas, which tastes better than it sounds. But mostly he gave me confidence and there's no better gift.

I opened my eyes, and to my horror, it was still 1972. I looked at the famous faces above the bar. It had been years since there'd been any new additions. Classic French was beyond passé. It was shunned. People wanted exotic cooking—Lebanese, Indian, Ethiopian, Brazilian—or else they wanted low cal, low sugar, low everything. Butter and cream were pariahs. Even champagne had lost its allure. The rest of the Butter Boys were dead or retired or simply gone. Laurent's hung on, yeah, but the menu wasn't what it used to be—he couldn't throw around truffles like he once had—and the limousines rarely came by. César no longer refused anyone. Even the seats at Olympus were up for grabs. And the flowers, oh boy, the flowers. In '69 the restaurant's ownership passed from Conrad Blount to his son, Oswald, a bitterly humorless theatrical agent who understood Broadway and nothing else, and the first thing he did was kill the flower budget. Now every table sported these shameful bouquets of paper daisies, which had looked cheap when he bought them and looked worse now.

But Laurent remained Laurent. He wore the same thick glasses, the same laughably old-fashioned double-breasted suits. He still smiled and laughed and told every lady she was beautiful. He still did favors for his favorites. He still made New York a more delicious place. I was lucky to know him—but right now I was pissed that he was late.

The clock said 9:17. My stomach felt like a deflated football. Little tendrils of pain stretched from my eyes down my neck. I was hungry, is what I'm saying, and I hate that even more than I hate waiting around.

"It's a restaurant, isn't it?" I muttered to my pub mix. "So how about something to eat?"

Downstairs was deserted. I called for Laurent, for César, for Jean-Louis or Oswald but nobody said a thing. I pushed into the kitchen. Something fluttered in my stomach. Nerves? Impossible. This was my second home. There was nothing to fear.

The lights were off. I fixed that. Blinding white fluorescents flared on. The air was pregnant with fat. The counters of the long double galley were clean. The stoves were bare, save for one mammoth stockpot. I followed my nose, peeking in the pot to see if there was something to nibble. I found stock—veal, probably—that had been reduced to the consistency of cold blood.

Aspic.

So this was Laurent's surprise.

You're familiar with aspic. A jelly made from reduced stock

that's so thick with fat it stands up on its own. It's just like the Jell-O mold you brought to your last weenie roast, except instead of being studded with marshmallows and maraschino cherries, it's filled with the most delicately cooked fish or meat or eggs. It's hell to make—I've botched it half a dozen times—and it takes forever, especially if you resist the temptation of commercial gelatin, which Laurent surely did. I'd wanted something special for Toru's party. This was a hell of a lot more grand than I'd had in mind.

I wanted to see the finished product, so I poked my head into the walk-in.

No aspic.

I looked in the low boy. Same thing.

So I opened the fridge at the end of the prep area—avocado green with double doors—the one the pastry crew reserved for special desserts. The aspic was there. And it was gorgeous.

You ever look through the glass in a really old house and it seems perfectly clear until you tilt your head and see it's warping the world on the other side? That's how this jelly looked. It was tinted pale amber and striped with thin pieces of pimento and white cabbage, woven as tight as a medieval tapestry to create hypnotic swirls. I'd have eaten it with a spoon and savored every bite except the decorative veggies weren't the only thing inside.

There was also the head.

Laurent's head.

My friend's head.

Cut off at the neck, trapped in the jelly, eyes wide, mouth curled in a look of twisted horror.

The best chef New York had ever seen.

Dead, dead, dead.

Three

I called the police and they sent a detective called Donati. He was the least dynamic cop I'd ever seen. A sniffling lump of around forty-five, he moved like he was terrified of bumping into something. He wore stiffly pressed tweed, single breasted with immense lapels, and a green tie whose enormous Windsor emphasized his alarmingly skinny neck.

We sat upstairs and I gave him the whole story—who Laurent was, why his restaurant was so important, why I was here—while he stared at my nose. I finally called him on it and he said it was a trick his rabbi taught him—that it's supposed to put people at ease. I told him his rabbi was a dope and to look me in the eye, but apparently that was beyond his power because he just stared at his scuffed leather shoes and asked if I could show him the head.

So I took him to the kitchen. I wasn't sure what time it was but I was deeply late for my meeting with Judy. I'd gotten a filling the week before and it was aching like I'd been chewing rocks. My heart was hammering and the pub mix was stubbornly refusing to settle. I was pretty sure another look at Laurent would send me over the edge, so when the detective yanked open the fridge I turned away.

"Yep," he said. "That's a head. And whaddaya call the goo?"

"Aspic. Can I leave?"

"Not yet."

Donati stared at the aspic. Didn't talk, didn't take notes, just gaped. Beside him was a strapping young patrolman who had a square jaw and a flat expression. He looked camera-ready for *Adam-12*. I wished, vaguely, that he would stop eyeing my ass.

I kept trying to *breeeeeeeeathe* but every expansion of my chest made my stomach clench, so I sucked air through my nose and hoped it might keep me from passing out. I wandered away, ignored, and opened cabinets and closed cabinets and stole a nice-looking tin of bacalao. I took in the gleaming counters and blackened old stoves, the skyline of stacked pots, the tidy piles of fresh rags. And then I looked at the butcher's station, where the serious knives were nestled inside of a heavy wooden block—all save one.

"The cleaver is missing," I said.

This made no impression on Donati, who smeared his handkerchief across his brow and mumbled, "You gotta stop killing each other."

"What?"

"Not you personally, lady. New Yorkers generally. Murders are up to five a day and my blood pressure's, like, one thousand over one thousand. Every time the call comes in, I pray—I swear I honestly pray to god—for a simple killing. Like a wife stabs her husband and we find her holding the knife. Or a hack kills a fare for stiffing him and he shoots himself out of guilt and both bodies are waiting, nice and still, when we get on the scene."

"I take it you don't expect this to be simple?"

"This one has the feeling of being—what's the word? Baroque. Baroque murders get me yelled at."

"And that's why I can't leave?"

He gave a mournful nod and started taking notes. I let my eyes drift past the fryer, past the grill, past the saucier's fiefdom and the cold room for the pastry chef and the guys who did garde manger. A scarred wooden door with a frosted window led to the repurposed storage closet that served as Laurent's office. Right in front of it there was a little mark on the tile. Laurent ran a clean kitchen. He took particular pride in spotless floors. I took a step toward the spot and Adam-12 whistled like he was correcting a dog.

"There's something over there," I said.

"So what? Stay."

"Fine. But if you whistle at me again, I'll rip out your tongue and cook it with onions."

After that, he didn't talk anymore.

Donati looked at the head for a long time. Finally he shut the fridge.

"I took a date here once. Typist from the precinct. Made a fool of myself trying to order in French, and when the food showed up, she said she can't taste a thing. So add salt, I told her, but she said no, she can't taste anything. Ever. Brother hit her in the head with a foul ball when she was a kid and now everything tastes like wet grass. So there's fifty bucks down the drain."

"I'm sorry, okay, but this has been the worst morning of my entire life and I'd like it to end now, you understand?"

"Yeah. Except there's one thing bugging me . . ."

I waited for him to finish but the sentence dangled like a hanged man. I'm a human being, okay, and that means I love *Columbo*, but the schtick is less cute when it's your time being pissed down the drain.

So finally I said: "And the thing that's bugging you is . . ."

"There's no body."

"You just noticed that?"

"I mean obviously the head has been, y'know, detached. But the rest of the body ought to be somewhere close by."

"Am I allowed to move?"

"Who said you couldn't move?"

I shot a look at Adam-12. He answered with a cold smile.

"There's a spot on the floor," I said.

"I don't see it," said Donati.

I crossed the tile, stomach tighter with every step. I bent over the spot, praying that it would be a scuff or spilled sauce or anything but what I knew it would be.

"Blood," I said. Well, tried to say. When I drew in my breath to speak I caught a smell creeping through the office door. Sweet and sharp like garbage in July.

"What?" said Donati.

"I said blood." I held back a retch and waved a limp hand at the office door. "I think he's in there."

Donati straightened, vertebrae popping like firecrackers.

"I guess I'd better go inside."

He didn't sound any more excited about it than I was. I got out of his way. He wiggled the knob but it was locked, so he smashed his shoulder against the wood. I shut my eyes so I wouldn't see what was behind the door, but that didn't protect me from the full stench of death. It poured over me, filling mouth and nose and pores with a stink that was grimy and round and pulsating with everything life hates most.

Folks, let's just say I wasn't sorry when Donati shut the door. I slumped against the counter, neck sweating and stomach churning. I grabbed a head of garlic and breathed in that wonderful papery funk until my sinuses were clear. Adam-12 scratched his mustache. His uniform shirt was baby blue. It was supposed to make cops less threatening but I'd watched enough of the footage from Chicago to know that no color, no matter how cute, would stop him from cracking my skull.

"Can I get out of here or what?" I said.

"Not till the detective says so."

So I strolled, hands behind my back, wondering when this nightmare would end. I'd visited this kitchen countless times. I'd been here during service, when it was sweaty and greasy and profane. I'd been here taking lessons from Laurent, when it was the most inviting place in the world. A couple of times, I'd been splayed out on the prep table, dress bunched above my hips, alone with . . . well, he's not important right now. This was the only time that I'd ever been here when it felt cold.

A photographer entered—a gray man in a gray suit—and asked, "Where's the stiff?"

Adam-12 pointed at the fridge.

"Some in there . . ."

He pointed at the office.

"And some in there."

The photographer opened the avocado-green fridge and snapped pictures. I kept my eyes on the floor. Then the photographer opened the office door. I tried not to look. I mean I swear to god I tried. But my eyes darted sideways just long enough for a glimpse of Laurent's plump body on the floor beside his little metal desk, his neck a gory stump.

The room was painted with blood.

Donati lurched out. He was as white as a chef's toque, and I was pretty sure I was a shade or two paler than that. I squeezed the cold metal of the counter, wishing I had something frozen to press against my neck. I was very close to throwing up.

"Was Tirel a heroin addict?" said Donati.

"Excuse me?"

"There was a little wooden box on his desk. A couple thousand bucks' worth of horse inside, plus needles, everything. Was it his?"

"Fucking of course not."

He smirked like I was being naïve.

"Then whose was it?"

"I don't know. How about you let me leave?"

"Yeah, yeah, of course. Just a couple questions first."

I squeezed the counter with both hands. The metal wasn't cold anymore.

"Tirel have any enemies?" said Donati.

"No."

"Financial difficulties? Owning a place like this comes with a lot of headaches."

"He wasn't the owner. Just the face—the executive chef. The owner's a Broadway agent named Oswald Blount. Inherited it from his dad."

"Restaurant doing okay?"

"Not like the fifties, but it did business. Can I go now?"

"Sure, sure . . . I just, I know I'm forgetting something. Heck, what is it?"

Vomit rose in my throat.

"You'd like to know where I was when Laurent died."

"That's it! Where were you yesterday?"

Deep breath.

"The kids woke me up early. I fixed them breakfast—Cap'n Crunch, in case you're curious—and then Toru, my fiancé, took the oldest one to school. It was my day with the four-year-old, so I took him to the library and spent a while running around Central Park. I picked Peter up at school, we hung at home for a while, and then I went to dinner at this awful new Italian restaurant, just under the Fifty-Ninth Street Bridge. Marinara's."

He nodded pointlessly. "I saw that place. It's no good?"

"Gluey noodles, scaloppine like mud flaps."

"That's a crime."

"No, Detective. Murder is a crime. Perhaps I should leave you to it?"

"Sure. Only I'm still hung up on this aspic."

My stomach clenched like a middleweight's fist. "What about it?"

"You writing about this?"

"I don't think so."

"Okay, so then you can help. Starting with, does food really taste better if you cover it in meat Jell-O?"

Deeper breath.

"In the right hands, yeah. A good aspic melts in your mouth and tastes like a dream. Plus it's beautiful. Like a display case, y'know, for world-class food."

He pulled open the avocado fridge. Laurent's dead eyes stared at me. I spun on my heels.

"This one here," said Donati, "you'd call it world class?"

"Yeah."

"How can you tell if you're not looking at it?"

Adam-12 snickered.

"I want your professional opinion," said Donati, "and then I'll let you go. Promise."

"Okay."

I drew the deepest breath I could manage without throwing up. I squatted so I could be level with Laurent—a strange vantage, since I always had a couple of inches on him when he was alive. Cool air bathed my face, and to my surprise, my mind cleared. My stomach halfway settled. I tried to tell myself this wasn't murder. This wasn't my dead friend. This was food.

Food I understand.

"This is the prettiest aspic I've ever seen," I said.

"Except for the head."

"Yeah."

"What makes it good?"

"The jelly is crystal clear, which means the killer reduced their stock nice and slow. Never let it boil."

I realized I was basically quoting Laurent. Some tribute.

"How long would something like that take?" said Donati.

"Christ. A while. If you're making the stock from scratch, that's three hours right there. The jelly reduces for a couple hours, then you have to let it cool before you put the whole thing together in the mold."

"So we're looking at what . . ."

"Close to twelve hours, start to finish."

Donati let out a whistle.

"And they cleaned the head up nice before they put it in," he said. "That cut's real tidy. There's not much blood. As far as murder scenes go, this is as classy as it gets."

It's sick but he was right. *Classy* was the word for it. It even smelled good. I was breathing as shallow as I could and I was still getting this round, warm aroma—like the best chicken soup your mother ever made—studded with pepper and nutmeg and this sweet, fruity something that I couldn't place. I had a twisted urge to crook my finger and scoop out a bite—a thought so vile that my nausea roared back stronger than ever. Donati shut the fridge. I stood up and the blood rushed to my head and I leaned on the wall, not sure if I was going to throw up or faint.

"I don't get it," said Donati.

"What do you mean?" I mumbled.

"Murder is the ultimate shortcut, y'know? Your average killer is a lazy so-and-so. Putting in all this work just doesn't fit."

"Some people have standards."

"Excuse me?"

"Only a professional could make an aspic that nice. And to make it as a professional cook in Manhattan, you have to make shit perfect. Your killer is the kind of person who, once they start something, is gonna see it through all the way to the end. Even if it's completely fucking insane."

Donati stared at the ceiling with his mouth open and his tongue digging between his two front teeth, failing to dislodge a speck of bread.

"You don't have to do that, y'know," he said.

"Do what?"

"Curse. I work with some pretty tough customers but I keep it clean. Would it kill you to be a little more ladylike?"

"Go to hell, Detective."

His eyes got big. They looked like Ping-Pong balls.

"You've been very helpful, Miss Black, but I gotta tell you—I do not like your vibe. Now, get the heck out. We're done."

I felt Adam-12's eyes burning into me as I shoved through the kitchen doors. I hustled up the stairs and back to the street. I had just made it to the sidewalk when the morning came down on my stomach like a guillotine. I knelt, concrete scratching my knees, pulled my hair out of my face, and vomited into the gutter. Three big heaves and I slumped onto my ass, leaning on a mailbox, enjoying the cold through my shirt. Laughter opened my eyes.

It was the kids from New Harmony, giggling like a lady puking was the funniest thing they'd ever seen. Their parents dragged them back into the hotel by their little white necks.

Four

So here's a stupid question: What do you lose when somebody dies?

You lose their laugh, their smile. You lose every joke they were going to tell you and every stupid story you were going to tell them. You lose every fight you were gonna have, every birthday, every morsel of unsolicited advice. All of that's deeply general because grief is general—it's the most general thing in the world—but the stuff I'd lost with Laurent was bitterly specific, and every time I thought of something else, it was another knife in my spine.

The way he'd call me sometimes on Monday mornings—the restaurant was always closed on Mondays—and announce we were going to lunch or an art gallery or an old screwball comedy at the theater he liked in Kips Bay.

The crumbs of strange gossip he'd drop whenever we spoke. For a professional snob, he hated artifice. He sneered at toupees and falsies and whitened teeth. If he noticed a man with lifts in his shoes, he'd call me immediately. "What's wrong with being short?" he'd grumble. "God knows I'm not tall enough to open half the cabinets in the kitchen. If it doesn't bother me, it shouldn't bother anyone else. The only defect that cannot be overcome, you know, is shame."

Oh, he was full of those little pearls. If people were honest, he'd build them up. If not, he'd cut them down. And even the people he called out never complained—not only because he'd been right, but because any humiliation was worth the food. In his hands, something as cheap and humble as a potato was gold. Give him a pound of the saddest, scraggliest corner-store spuds and he'd whip them into a soufflé that was crisped desert brown on top and feather light all the way down. Everything he cooked was perfect.

But what I'd miss most was the madeleines. When he discovered my weakness for those squishy little cakes, he had the pastry guy start making them just for me. Every time I ate there, he'd bid me goodbye by slipping one into my palm, like we were spies doing a handoff. It was a moment of connection, of approval, of consistency in a city where change was religion.

And I'd never taste it again.

Nothing to do about that, now or ever. So I took a breath and closed my eyes and slunk into the cold, dark basement that lives deep inside my mind. On the wall was a shelf of jars full of shit I didn't want to deal with. I filled up a fresh one, labeled it "Grief," and slammed it onto the shelf, right between "Fear of Death" and "Oh Shit My Parents Are Getting Old," underneath "What If Toru's Kids Hate Me?" and a thirty-two-ounce jar of sexual neurosis that, frankly, I couldn't even stand to look at. Then I dragged myself back to reality.

It was time to start my day.

Past time, in fact. The drugstore down the block had a clock out front, and Jesus Christ, it was after eleven. So I stomped back to the corner, where the fire department was hauling the Ford Torino out of my deli's window, and ducked into the pay phone. There was shit on the floor and the receiver was smashed to pieces. I checked two more phones, both of which had gum in the coin slot, and by the time I found one that worked, I was nearly an hour late. Punctuality is something I take seriously—as in, being late causes me physical pain—so I was aching when Judy picked up the phone.

"I don't like waiting, B.B."

"Even for a scoop?"

"Weekly magazines don't do scoops."

"But the paper does. So let the city room know that Laurent Tirel is dead."

"What kind of dead? Heart attack dead? Hit-and-run?"

"Murder."

She lit a cigarette. It sounded delectable.

"Shit."

"Yeah."

"Wanna write something about it? We could use your column for a little memorial."

"I don't know. No. I'd better go home to grieve."

"You're probably right. But . . ." A long drag. "I still need you to come down."

Suddenly I knew why. A few weeks prior, Judy and I were downing embarrassingly expensive stingers at a finance bar down the street from *Sentinel* HQ when a mad impulse drove me to ask for a raise. Inflation had nearly doubled the grocery bill and Toru's last advance was long gone and I figured there was nothing wrong with asking for a bump. She said she'd let me know. If she needed to do it in person, the answer couldn't be good.

"You make it sound like I'm in trouble," I said.

"You're not. But there're some things we've gotta talk through. Today."

The receiver felt greasy against my palm.

"All right. I'll be there in forty-five."

My dad always told me it's dumb to be upset and hungry at the same time, so I stopped at the hot dog cart on the corner and treated myself to a pair with mustard and relish. They tasted like they're supposed to—hot and rubbery—and they calmed me, stomach and soul. The buns were so crunchy that at first I thought they were toasted, but nah, they were just really stale. Whatever, I thought. It's not the worst thing that's happened to me today.

By the time I stomped into the IRT, my tooth was still killing me but otherwise I was almost feeling human. The local came before the express and I got on because I was desperate to sit down, but the car was beat to shit and all the seats had been ripped out, so I had to content myself with slumping against the window, hoping I looked alert enough that nobody would grab my purse. The rumble of the train soothed me, like it always does, and I was starting to think I could get through this morning intact when one of my fellow passengers put her hand on my shoulder. She was short and heavy, maybe forty, with a round face and thick lips and bright green eyes and a granite bob. She wore a belted, long-sleeved jumpsuit with elastic around the wrists and ankles that made her look like an astronaut. Her perfume wrapped me up like a sleeping bag. The sight of her made me want to panic for reasons that I was not equipped to explore.

"Kleenex?" she said.

"Why?"

"You're crying."

"I am?"

"For the last six stops."

"No joke."

She tucked the Kleenex into my hand. I wiped my eyes and honked my nose and jammed the tissue out the window.

"You shouldn't litter," she said.

"Track fires, right?"

"Track fires."

She smiled a very warm smile. Like, extremely warm. Like, center-of-the-earth warm. The lights flickered and the wheels screamed and when the darkness was over she was still right there.

"You okay?" she asked.

"Not in the slightest."

"Wanna tell a stranger?"

The train slowed. The conductor mumbled something about Canal Street. My new friend rested her hand on my elbow—a meaningless gesture that scared me to death.

"I have to find a caterer," I blathered.

"Excuse me?"

"My fiancé's birthday party. Our chef is dead and his restaurant is a crime scene, so I need a caterer and an event space too."

She cocked her head like a baffled puppy. The train slammed to a stop and I kept my footing because no matter how dazed we may be, New Yorkers never slip on the train. The doors screeched and I tumbled off even though Canal was extremely not my stop. I was gone before she could say goodbye.

The *New York Sentinel* occupied half of a grimy building on Park Row, overlooking the seedy wasteland of City Hall Park. The sidewalk was a wreckage of crushed beer cans and shredded pizza and yesterday's newspapers matted with this morning's piss and shit. The lobby had been transformed into what we called Fort Sentinel—an austere marble hall lately jammed with pistol-toting security guards staring slackly at flickering TVs. It had been this way since a pair of bomb threats and a bag of dog-shit tossed into the publisher's limo put the paper on a war footing. I signed in and was pleasantly surprised to avoid a frisk.

I was slouching in the elevator, staring at a poster that read, HOW WILL YOU AVOID BEING MUGGED TODAY?, when the groaning doors were interrupted by a jeweled fist. In swanned Elma Zumwalt—she swanned everywhere, even elevators whose floors were heaped with wet cardboard—and a stench of Estée so powerful I nearly fainted. An aggressively fashionable widow, widely suspected of talking her husband to death, Elma split her days between flitting around Upper East Side society and writing a gossip column so insidery I couldn't even begin to understand it. But she considered me a friend and I never fought back—the woman knew everybody and people who know everybody are handy to know. She was only a few years older than me but everything about her, from her Pat Nixon bouffant to her aggressive tan, made her look like a well-preserved fifty-five. Her stare made me feel like a mink she was about to skin.

"You and Toru are still coming to dinner Thursday," she said—less a question than a threat.

"That's the plan."

"It's going to be quite the affair. I've been taking cooking classes from your friend Ambrose. He's a wizard, you know. Helped me curate an authentic menu for a Chinese dinner party."

"Oh . . . god."

"Yes! All the classics. Watercress and meatball soup. Oriental rice. Hot spiced beef with orange flavor. Doesn't it just sound divine?"

"Hot spiced beef, huh?"

"With orange flavor! Toru will feel right at home."

"You realize he's Japanese-American, don't you?"

"Right. At. Home."

And I swear to god, reader, on those final words she booped me on the nose. It was enough to make me lose my breakfast, but I try to avoid puking twice before noon. So I nodded and murmured, "I'll stop eating now. Hate to spoil my appetite."

"Ha ha ha," said Elma, who never actually laughed—she simply performed laughter. "As if you could ever really be full, darling. But speaking of fine dining—oh my lord, it's awful—you heard what happened to poor Laurent Tirel?"

"I found the head."

Elma pouted, disappointed to be scooped.

"How did you hear so fast?" I said.

"People talk—even the girls on the police switchboard. Is it true they found a pound of cocaine in his desk drawer?"

"It was heroin. But it didn't belong to Laurent."

"You never know, dear, you never know. You remember my friend Deb McGlothlin? The interior designer?"

Of course I didn't.

"Of course I do."

"She redid my entire front parlor in orange. Tangerine wallpaper and shag carpet, a mandarin settee and these rock-hard plastic chairs, and she painted the ceiling the color of a basketball.

She swore it was 'the next thing' and I believed her, I honestly did, but it turned out she was utterly stewed on LSD. She's dead now, I think, or on the city council."

I just smiled. Talking with Elma wasn't a conversation—it was a hurricane.

"What did you do with the parlor?" I said.

"What could I do? I loaded up on orange kaftans."

The elevator opened and she followed me into the smoky chaos of the city room, which occupied a grand Beaux Arts chamber with twenty-foot ceilings decorated with tar-blackened murals of Hermes. We wove through the desks, stepping over mounds of paper and outstretched legs.

"I suppose the $64,000 question," said Elma, "is who's taking Laurent's place?"

With gossip columnists there's no such thing as off the record, so I chose my words with unaccustomed care.

"I'm not sure anyone can."

"But someone must. Laurent's has fallen off, certainly, but it's an institution."

"Oswald Blount owns it. Ask him."

"You know I will. I love Ozzie—I always see him in Southampton wearing the funniest little red shorts. You can trace every vein on his testicles—it's a scream. I'll give him a call. But I must say the natural candidate—the one I'm already hearing whispers about—is your old beau."

"Henri? He'd never take it."

"Principles tend to wither when there's money on the line. Are you dead set on marrying him?"

I stared at her, waiting to see if what she'd said might start making sense. It didn't.

"I'm not marrying Henri. I'm marrying Toru."

"Naturally. But you're sure it's the right move?"

"Why wouldn't it be?"

"It's not that he's Japanese—these days, so many people are—or even that he's older than you. Mr. Zumwalt was desiccated when we met and that worked out nicely for me. But he's a writer, isn't he, so he's poor. And two kids! Why saddle yourself with all that?"

It occurred to me that part of what made Elma both irritating and impossible to ignore was how much she reminded me of my mother. Mom had been hammering me with those sorts of questions ever since Toru and I announced our engagement. I'd tried explaining that I loved him, that the kids were charming, that having children without enduring pregnancy seemed like a magnificent shortcut to the next phase of my life, but Mom hadn't heard any of it and Elma wouldn't either. So I gave the only explanation she might understand.

"His apartment is two bedrooms, two blocks from the park. One hundred and forty-eight dollars a month."

"Rent controlled?"

"You know it."

She tapped the side of her nose and gave a nod.

"I shouldn't have underestimated you, dearie." She lit a thin blue cigarette. "Returning to gloomier subjects, will you be writing a tribute to poor Monsieur Tirel for this week's magazine?"

"I'm not sure I have the strength."

"Are you kidding, Bernie? You're the strongest person I know."

I left her in the city room with that unexpected compliment ringing in my ears. It wasn't even lunchtime and I'd already been spotted crying on the subway and puking on the street. I was surprised by how much it meant to hear that somebody, even someone as ridiculous as Elma, thought I was worth a damn.

I followed the dim hallway that led to the converted maintenance area that held the Sunday magazine. Here the ceilings were low-hanging asbestos tile and the light was blackened fluorescent. But it was quiet, at least, with none of the seething panic that comes from daily deadlines. There were too many desks and most of them were piled with back issues and weird swag—books and ball caps and a gross of pencils advertising the revival of *A Funny Thing Happened on the Way to the Forum*. I grabbed a couple of pencils, figuring that if Judy was gonna shoot down my raise, I was entitled to steal.

The *Sentinel* magazine had been founded in 1968, as a response to a survey that suggested youngsters—that was the word, *youngsters*—found daily newspapers "a drag." It was an incoherent publication known for splashy cover stories with titles like "The Future of Tomorrow" and "How Will the '70s Smell?" Based on the advertising, its true purpose was to sell cheap scotch, and it must have been selling enough of it because my paychecks, however pitiful, kept coming.

My editor, Judy, was the most deeply stressed woman in New York. She was passionate about two things—losing weight and smoking cigarettes—and that morning I found her with a Marlboro in one hand and four WeightWatchers cards in the other. She spread the cards across the table like she was giving me the world's grimmest tarot reading and said, "Okay, B.B. What's for dinner?"

I scanned the cards. There was a melon mousse that looked like blanched brain, a chilled celery log that appeared to have been the victim of a car wreck, a gelled fruit and cheese mold, and something called "crown roast of frankfurters," which was—and I am *not* making this up—a dozen halved hot dogs braced against a mound of shredded cabbage. I tapped the fruit and cheese mold—I suppose I had aspic on the brain. Judy swept the cards into her drawer.

"Sorry about Tirel," she said. I was already sick of condolences. This was going to be a long week.

"Me too. It's disappointing when your friends get killed. What am I doing here?"

"Smoke?"

"I'm stopping."

"Oh yeah. Good for you."

"Listen, if you can't give me the raise, you can't give me the raise. You didn't need to make a big thing out of it."

Judy rubbed her neck. I got a hit of her perfume, which she must have bought a lifetime supply of back in 1962. It smelled like coconut and leather and vanilla and about fifty other things. It was called "Occur!," and baby, that's just what it did.

"What raise?" she said.

Fuck.

"We were at that bar on Liberty Street drinking stingers—"

"Honey, I never remember *anything* after stingers."

"Then what am I doing here?"

Her lips tightened around the Marlboro and I realized that ever since I came in, she hadn't looked me in the eye. I dragged my fingernails down the arm of the chair, peeling up little spirals of paint. Through the cloud of Occur!, I smelled doom.

"Are you firing me?" I said. I wasn't used to hearing my voice so soft. I hated it. "In the middle of a recession? Judy, I don't need this."

"Calm down, okay?"

"Not until you explain."

She stubbed out her cigarette and stared at the ash.

"You're not fired," she said. I was about to exhale but then she kept talking. "Well, you are. But I'm not the one who's doing it because I'm fired too. The magazine is winding down."

"The hell does that mean?"

"Those were the publisher's words: 'winding down.' He said the magazine is a wonderful publication, exciting and challenging and ahead of its time. He also said it's a money pit. Advertising is in the toilet and so many people have left the city and when they flee to Long Island or Westchester the *Sentinel* isn't a subscription they keep. Says the money he's spending on the magazine would be better spent on the paper's core mission."

"Which is?"

"Covering every mugging and murder in the city like it's the Lindbergh baby. Scaring the shit out of tourists. Making the mayor look like an asshole. Our work doesn't rate."

Judy looked brittle. I'd never felt sorry for her before but she deserved better than this bullshit. So did I. So did everyone. I sucked down some air and tried to remember that I was a pro.

"How long do we have?" I said.

"Four issues. You'll stay on salary and you'll get some kind of severance, but I'd start looking for a new job, like, now."

"Who's hiring?"

"Nobody."

"That's what I thought."

She picked up another cigarette, started to light it, said, "Sorry," then lit it anyway. She got up to open her window, I guess to spare me the smell, but it was painted shut. She strained until she started coughing and then she sat down.

"You okay?" she said.

"I'm . . . dazed, I guess."

She nodded like, *Yeah, that checks out.*

"You've had some morning," she said.

"An all-timer. When the magazine folds, what happens to you?"

"I go back to the paper. Style section, same gig as before. Half my current pay. Or fuck it, maybe I go into advertising. It'd be nice to have a job that lets me buy steak more than once a month."

"Can I tag along?"

"To Madison Avenue?"

"Hell no. To the main paper. They cover food, don't they?"

"They want reporters to cover busboy strikes and health department violations. If the restaurant in the Hyperion Hotel had rats, they'd write about that. They don't print reviews."

"So forget reviews. I'll cover whatever the fuck they want."

"There's not enough work for a full-time food writer."

"What about Ambrose? They've been running his column for decades."

"Which means they don't have room for you. I'm sorry."

She stared like we were on a life raft and she was waiting for me to ask to be eaten. I wasn't having it.

"Ask them," I said.

"What?"

"Call the publisher and ask. I need this job, Judy. Toru and I are supposed to get married. He's got two kids and a landlord who likes when we pay rent."

"He brings in money, doesn't he?"

"Not steady. If I'm out of work we're living on his book advances and those aren't reliable. We'd have to leave the West Side. We'd have to . . ." I gulped. "We'd have to move back to Brooklyn."

"The next time I speak to the publisher, I'll ask."

She smiled limply as her smoke tickled my nose. I could tell she wanted me to leave. Instead I got up, braced myself against the sill, and wrenched open the window. I let the breeze dry the sweat on my neck. I'd been fired before. It used to be a lark, an excuse for a bender and a change of scenery, but since I moved in with Toru and his boys, unemployment wasn't so funny. If I scraped for it, I could probably land another job but I'd never have the freedom that I'd found here.

"What about Laurent's murder?" I said.

"They'll give it a few inches in tomorrow's paper."

"But what if there's more?"

"Like what?"

"I don't know. But say I get the whole story, top to bottom."

"I thought you needed to grieve."

"I grieved on the train. I'm ready to work."

She laughed until she saw I was serious. She waved her hand above her head. Her smoke carved circles in the air.

"The city room can handle it."

"Not like me. I was at the crime scene. I'm tight with the detective—you should have seen how much this guy loved me—and I know every possible suspect in every relevant kitchen in New York. I can get you a five-thousand-word feature on the life and death of Laurent Tirel."

"That's fine, but—"

"And I can get you his killer too."

"Don't be silly."

"Four more issues, right? That's plenty of time."

"You're not a detective."

"I'm better. I'm a reporter."

The breeze picked up, carrying a magnificent whiff of garbage across my back. Judy killed her cigarette, gnawed on her lip, then lit one more.

"All right," she said. "Look into it. But you keep writing your regular column and you don't expect shit."

"Naturally."

"Because my pull in the city room is very, very limited right now. You could write *In Cold Blood: 1972* and it wouldn't guarantee a job on the paper."

"But it'd help."

"I guess it would."

And that was good enough for me. I said thanks three or four times, then got out of there. My tooth didn't hurt anymore. I felt like a Saturn rocket. This was the story of a lifetime and I was gonna nail it to the wall.

Five

I got halfway across the city room before I remembered I didn't know anything about investigating murder. So I grabbed a desk that was old and wobbly and scarred by years of journalistic graffiti. It was scattered with pamphlets for local union chapters—teamsters, pipe fitters, the International Brotherhood of Electrical Workers—which suggested the occupant was either a labor reporter or was looking for a new gig.

"Smart guy," I muttered as I shoved his shit out of the way, sharpened my new pencils, and got to work.

I've always been a planner. As a kid I kept schedules for myself in fifteen-minute chunks, with everything from playtime to bathroom breaks carefully plotted out. When I went to college I trapped my advisor for three hours and forced her to draw up six different courses of study—one for every major I was considering. I'd spent the last year plotting out different versions of my wedding, and if Toru and I ever got around to setting a date, it would be perfection. So naturally I plan the hell out of my reporting—figuring who I'm gonna talk to and what I'm gonna ask and how

I'll press 'em if they bullshit. I update the plan every night, copying choice details from my notebook to the looseleaf binder that I work from when it's time to write. Maybe that sounds nuts but since I moved in with Toru and the kids, my methods have kept me sane. The only way I could work *and* watch the kids *and* find time for socializing or fucking or exercising or, God forbid, sleeping is if I scheduled myself to death. It works for me, okay? That's all you need to know.

So I started with a list of twenty or thirty people I'd need to talk to. I'd come at them like I was just writing a feature about Laurent but really I'd be looking for whoever wanted him dead. I'd talk to chefs and suppliers and waiters and everybody I knew who'd ever worked a shift at the restaurant. I gave myself two weeks for reporting, a week for writing, and another for edits, with follow-up interviews sprinkled in as needed. I'd have to start by formally interviewing Donati, of course, and anybody else I could get ahold of at the NYPD. Maybe one of Elma's blabby switchboard girls, I thought, as I dialed Centre Street. A sad little man drifted into my peripheral vision, twisting a kaiser roll in his hands and waiting for me to leave. I held up a finger and he nodded wearily, as though women were always stealing his desk and it was simply his cross to bear. I got connected to the detectives' bureau, where a suspiciously friendly desk sergeant told me Detective Donati had planned a press conference on the Tirel homicide for that afternoon.

"When?" I said.

"Five minutes ago."

I slammed down the phone and swept my notes into my bag. The man whose desk I'd borrowed was about to say something but honestly I didn't have time, so I gave him one of my new pencils, patted his thinning hair, and scooted on out.

I booked it across City Hall Park, dodging drunks and tourists and drug dealers and a couple of particularly shady characters who I figured must be mayoral aides. I pounded past the ugly bulk of the future police headquarters, which wasn't even done yet and was already showing its age. I hurried through Chinatown, resisting the urge to grab dumplings, and Little Italy, where I didn't even stop for carbonara. When the cake shops gave way to gun stores and bail bondsmen, I knew I was almost there.

NYPD headquarters was a scruffy old beauty on an irregular block that had been wasted on the NYPD since before I was born. I took the grand marble steps two at a time, hustled through security, and got lost trying to find the press room. The hallways were filled with files to be transferred to One Police Plaza. They smelled like 1909. By the time I straightened myself out, the press conference was over. Donati almost flattened me coming out of the briefing room, but stopped his apology short when he remembered he didn't like my vibe.

"What are you doing here?" he spluttered.

"I came for the press conference. I guess you didn't wait?"

He got close enough for me to smell his aftershave. It was mint. Not bad.

"You said you weren't writing about this."

"Then I wasn't. Now I am."

"It is entirely inappropriate for a witness to a murder—"

"I found the head, I didn't witness anything."

"—to even think about reporting on the investigation!"

"Is that supposed to slow me down?"

"If you were a lady, it might."

I guess that was supposed to hurt my feelings, but I quit trying to be ladylike sometime around first grade. I just stood there, waiting for him to get out of my way.

"Aren't you leaving?" he said.

"First Amendment says no. I thought I'd talk to my colleagues. See if I can crib from their notes."

"Fine." His voice dropped to a whisper. "But keep mum about the aspic."

"Why?"

"We're holding that back, okay? That way, anybody who knows about it, they killed him. Voilà."

He looked very pleased with that little bit of French.

"How am I supposed to write about this murder if I can't talk about the single most important detail?"

"Who says the aspic's important? It's a coincidence. A frippery. The heroin is what counts. We figure the killer was whacked out on speedballs and spotted the jelly on the stove and figured, 'What the hell?'"

"For twelve hours he said, 'What the hell?'"

"That's right. And don't breathe a word or I'll have you arrested."

"For what?"

"For ruining my day."

And with that, the leading light of the NYPD strolled off. I shouldered my way into the cramped confines of the press room. It stank like the kids' bedroom after a farting contest. Inside were reps from most of the reputable dailies and a few of the disreputable ones too. I perched at the elbow of Merv Karp, the *Sentinel*'s man, who I knew vaguely from my days on the blotter at the *Select*.

"What'd I miss?"

He stared with rheumy eyes and spoke around the stubby cigar that had been lodged in his mouth since before the Giants left town.

"I don't know, girlie. Who are you?"

"Bernice Black. The *Sentinel*."

He couldn't have looked more confused if I'd told him my name was Merv Karp.

"Like hell," he said. "I'm the *Sentinel*. I have been since fifty-two. Or did they retire me without letting me know?"

"You're the paper. I'm the magazine."

"The *Sentinel* has a magazine?"

"For the next four weeks. Fill me in."

He snapped his notebook shut. His eyes twinkled with what I guess he thought was wit.

"Sorry, baby. I don't help the competition, even when they're on my team."

He left. I guess I looked lost or helpless or just pissed off because before I could get up, a woman sat down. She had coarse gray hair and handsome wrinkles and a bulky skirt in honey gold with white pinstripes. She stuck out her hand and shook mine hard.

"Pat Humphrey. The *Clarion*. Don't mind Merv—his main issue is he's a total piece of shit."

"I gathered."

"You're the woman who found the chef."

"Yep. Did Donati say anything interesting?"

"Hard to say. Got a quote for the *Clarion*?"

I smiled. This was business and business I understood. I thought for a moment before I spoke.

"Laurent Tirel taught New York to eat. He was the first serious chef in the city and he forced everybody else to up their game. If you've ever had a decent dinner in this city, he's why. He could be a pain in the neck but that's what happens when you have standards. I'm gonna miss him, I think, more than I can say."

I started to tear up when I said it, so I guess it was true. Pat flipped out a handkerchief and I dabbed my eyes and when I gave it back, she filled me in on everything Donati had said.

"ME's best guess is he was killed yesterday between noon and two o'clock."

"Cause of death was, I guess, decapitation?"

"Think again. He'd been dead a few hours when the head came off." She dragged her finger across the highest part of her neck. I shuddered. "The head came off here, right? Well, a couple inches below that was a nice long slash across the throat. Deep but not nearly enough to knock off the head. That's what killed him."

My stomach was getting tight again. I told it to knock it off. I was absolutely not throwing up again today.

"That's, uh . . . that's gruesome," I said.

"No kidding. They figure Mob hit."

"Laurent Tirel wasn't connected to the Mob."

"Donati said his books showed a $137,000 debt to an outfit called South Side Hauling."

"His garbagemen?"

"Yeah. Either he was producing, like, a million pounds of trash a week or he had some other shit going on. Plus, there was the heroin. You do the math."

"So who's South Side Hauling?"

She checked her notes.

"A Brooklyn hood named Tom Motisi."

I cackled. The sound startled Pat, like laughter was something she was unfamiliar with.

"Ducky Motisi!" I said.

"You know him?"

"My dad had stories about him from when he was growing up. Said he was an old-fashioned psychopath."

"The type to cut off his customers' heads?"

"Maybe. But he'd be seventy or eighty years old by now."

"Must be drinking his V8."

"Yeah. Cops talked to him yet?"

"They've gotta find him first."

I thanked her and cleared out, pondering Ducky Motisi as I stepped back into the bright blue sunshine. Getting to the bottom of this was going to be a living goddamned nightmare but I was grateful that the work allowed me to ignore my grief. I headed for the train, feeling cautiously optimistic because I apparently knew one thing the NYPD did not.

The fastest way to a mobster's heart is through his stomach.

He's never said it explicitly, but I think my dad has a thing for Italian girls. He grew up Anglo-Irish in a mostly Italian neighborhood—Park Slope, north of Union Street—where his friends were Italian, his dates were Italian, and his absolute favorite food in the entire world was polenta with melted gorgonzola stirred right in. When he stumbled into marriage with an Italian girl who hated all things to do with her mother country, he leaned in further, cultivating what I guess you'd call a fetish that he passed on to me.

So it was in the old Italian restaurants by the Gowanus Canal where I learned to use a knife and fork, where I learned the difference between fusilli and gemelli, where I had my first sips of plonk. These were places where my dad enjoyed nodding acquaintance with men who had "connections." As a kid I figured that meant they had lots of phone lines. At some point, I learned better.

When I went to college my parents quit Brooklyn for Long Island—no, I don't want to talk about it—and since then my visits had been irregular. I'd grown up thinking Brooklyn was like the emergency room: a place you only went when there was no other choice. Yeah, there's food there—the red sauce places and the steak belt on Bedford Ave and all those beautiful Middle Eastern cafés and spice shops on Atlantic—but there was food in Manhattan too and for that I didn't have to ride the train. Brooklyn was best appreciated in the past tense. The only good thing about it was that it never, ever changed.

Except lately it had. I got off at Pacific and walked the old blocks to the soundtrack of hammers and saws and Creedence Clearwater Revival. I passed bright-eyed white people with growing beards and growing families bounding in and out of the hardware stores that had sprouted on every corner. I saw hundreds of stubby little trees growing where once there'd been cracked sidewalks and hopscotch and trash. An earnest Harvard type wearing a Nehru jacket and a beret handed me a flyer asking me to help save Park Slope and I resisted the urge to say, "From you?"

This had been going on for a while. I still wasn't used to it. My family had lived here for decades, bopping from shitty apartment to shitty apartment on tenement streets like Baltic and Berkeley and Dean. This place was ours, but not in any way you could put on a deed. And now the back-to-the-city movement was carrying optimistic young professionals to Park Slope and Brooklyn Heights and bullshit neighborhoods like Boerum Hill—which is flat—and Carroll Gardens—where nothing grows but weeds. I don't want to act like it was just the Italian and Irish blocks that were getting warped—the same thing was happening to the Puerto Ricans south of Union Street and to the Black neighborhoods in Bedford-Stuyvesant. The whole of South Brooklyn was "being revitalized," it was "on the upswing"—phrases I loathed because they suggested that I'd grown up on the downswing in a place that was dead.

But the thing I really couldn't wrap my head around was the food. People were opening restaurants in Brooklyn—on Court Street and Seventh Ave and up and down Atlantic—and the brownstoners simply would not shut up about them. Their food was light, modern, slimming. Diet conscious and health conscious and consciousness conscious. They were pickling and preserving, experimenting and evolving, and acting like they were the first cooks in history to consider fresh produce a good thing. I'd eaten at a lot of these places and I'd written about a handful of them and when they were good I said so but I found it impossible to really love them. Maybe I just can't find happiness without butter and salt. Maybe chewing brown rice takes so long that after the third mouthful I'm ready to go to bed. Maybe I'm just a pill. All I know is, when I pushed through the curtained door at Angelo's on Third Ave, which was close enough to the canal for the fumes to stain the concrete, it felt like home.

It's the kind of restaurant you've been to. Red-checked tablecloths and black and white tiles and a pressed-tin ceiling that they've kept not because it's historic but because it's already there. The walls covered with group photographs of guys who'd been dead fifty years, the air heavy with bread and garlic and plastic and wine. Every table was set, even though you could tell from the dust on the glasses that only the front three ever got used. A chalkboard advertised daily specials—YOUNG CHICKEN LIVERS W/ MUSHROOMS BROCHETTE, $2; PROSCIUTTO & FRESH MELON, $1.75—that hadn't been updated since 1959. Hardly welcoming, yeah, but the smells drifting out of the kitchen gave me hope.

There were a couple of old dudes in the corner wrapping up lunch—or maybe they'd just been there all day—and a skinny bartender in a loose apron whose teeth and fingers were stained nicotine brown. He was older than my dad and I thought I remembered him but there was no way to be sure. So I ordered an espresso and leaned on the counter and while I was stirring in the sugar I said, "I'm looking for Ducky Motisi."

He chortled.

"Fucking why?"

"A friend needs garbage pickup. He heard South Side can't be beat."

The bartender pulled a silver bowl of mints from under the counter. He popped two in his mouth and offered none to me.

"Your friend should know garbage collection goes block by block. Whoever shows up is his guy. And anyway, Ducky's retired."

"Then who's in charge?"

His eyes narrowed to the width of an envelope.

"A nephew. Tiny Tommy."

"Let him know I'm looking for him?"

"I don't know who you are."

"Barton Black's kid." No recognition. "An Irish guy, a sandhog. Used to come in here all the time."

"A lot of people used to come in here."

"I ate my first oyster here."

He sucked his mints until they cracked. I pointed at the far end of the bar.

"We were on those stools. Dad ate two dozen oysters and ordered a dozen more. I wanted to go home but he said we couldn't until I tried one."

"What'd you do?"

"I slurped down the oyster. And then I puked it up all over the bar."

The bartender smacked the counter.

"Puke girl! You're the puke girl! I been telling that story twenty-five years."

"Well, here I am."

"Still eating oysters?"

"Every chance I get."

"How 'bout a dozen on the house?"

It was a little late in the season for me, but how could I refuse? He dished 'em up and I slurped 'em down. They were cold and salty and fine, the lemon juice sharp, the horseradish kicking hard. I could have eaten thirty more. Instead I told the bartender I was from the *Sentinel* and that Tiny Tommy would do well to talk to me before the police got to him.

"I don't actually know Tommy Motisi," said the bartender, tough-guy routine discarded.

"But maybe you know somebody who knows somebody who does. Anyway, put the word around. Is Martino's Bakery still open?"

"Yeah, thank god."

"I'll be there later in case Tommy wants to come say hi."

So I called Toru and he answered with such a cheerful, "How's your day?" that for a moment I was offended and then I remembered, shit, he doesn't know about Laurent.

I gave a nauseous laugh and said, "Not great!" I gave him the whole thing as quick as I could—my friend was dead and my job was on the line—and when I asked if he'd be all right picking Peter up from school, he said, "Of course."

"Are you sure? Because it's my day, y'know, and the schedule is useless unless we stick to it and—"

"You're dealing with serious shit. I'm on the couch in my underwear watching Nicky throw blocks. It's fine."

His voice was deep and sturdy, calm in a way I couldn't even aspire to. I knew he didn't mind—he'd handled both boys just fine before I moved in—but I was auditioning for World's Greatest Stepmom and you don't get to be World's Greatest by taking time to work or grieve. But my mom always told me that parenting means feeling guilty no matter what, so I said the only thing I could:

"Thank you. And I've got Nicky tomorrow, plus Peter's pickup."

"If you say so. Love you, babe."

"I love you too."

I got off the phone, nerves tingling with affection and regret, and tried to be grateful that I had a lead. I spent the rest of the afternoon hauling myself up the slope and down the slope and up the slope again. I went into a dozen places that were functionally identical to Angelo's, and even when I didn't have vomit stories to break the ice, I got my message across. I watched their eyes go wide when I mentioned Tiny Tommy; I nodded politely while they said a number of astonishingly racist things about Puerto Ricans; I nibbled sundry antipasti. When I plopped down at the long marble counter inside Martino's on Fifth Ave and Degraw and ordered my third espresso and my first plate of cannoli, I was reasonably certain the prime suspect would drop by.

Martino's hadn't changed much—I'm pretty sure the wedding cake in the window had been there since 1945—but it was dead. I remembered when it was a hangout for dirtbag teens with greased hair and greasy faces and dirty white shirts with sleeves rolled up to show off skinny arms. They'd flick cigarettes on the floor and tell every girl in there, "Suck my cock, mama!" like it was the cleverest thing anybody had ever heard. Now the air was stale and the floors were clean. I kind of missed the hoods.

The cannoli shell was fried oak brown, blistered and brittle and overflowing with filling that was creamy and tart but not too sweet. I could have had seconds but instead I bought a postcard of Paul VI and a cookie decorated with the flag of San Marino, then popped into the phone booth and made some calls. This time it wasn't a mobster I was looking for—it was a caterer, and it turns out they're much harder to find. I called the best in the city, most of the middling ones, and a few of the worst. When I said I needed food for two dozen on Friday night—and that I didn't know where the party was happening—most of them cursed and all of them laughed. No one cared that the World's Greatest Stepmom needs to be able to work full-time and raise charming children and plan impeccable parties without one hair out of place. Everybody was booked, it seemed, until the end of time.

So I grabbed a paper—the *Brownstoner's Gazette*—and an outside table and tried to lose myself in city council meetings and mortgage adjustments and DIY tips about restoring the single-family houses that past owners had rudely sliced into apartments so little kids like Bernice Black could have a home, but it was impossible, and it wasn't just the leaden prose or the way the caffeine pounding through my system was making it impossible to sit still.

It was the playground across the street that had my eye.

There was nothing special about it. Just a little patch of concrete tucked between an old boardinghouse and an empty lot. There were swings and a basketball hoop and one of those creaky metal things that spin around and give kids tetanus. A half dozen kids, mostly toddlers, screamed like they were being murdered en masse. Them I ignored. I was watching their moms.

They looked like all the girls my dad dated when he was growing up. Probably they were their daughters. They had big eyes, big shoulders, and big hair, and they barked at their kids in sullen Brooklynese. There was one in particular I couldn't stop staring at—a woman probably five or six years younger than me who had one eye on her daughter and another on a magazine. Her friends were sweating in housecoats and quilted robes but she had on this incredible purple tunic with a stripe down the middle and white pants that fluttered in the wind. Her legs looked as strong as the statues that surrounded Grand Army Plaza and her feet were planted so solid, it was like she'd taken root.

And if I'm gonna explain why I was staring at her, I'm gonna have to go down into the mental basement and open that thirty-two-ounce jar. The one I really, really don't want to touch.

I'm a lesbian.

Sort of.

I like guys, right? I mean, I really like guys, only lately I can't get women out of my head. And I feel like a fraud, kind of, because I've never kissed a woman much less, like, made it with one. But a few months ago I read an article in *Week* called "The Guys & Girls Who Like Guys & Girls" that was pretty stupid, frankly, but it said people like that—people like me, I'm trying to get in the habit of saying people like *me*—are calling themselves bisexuals now and I like that word.

It sounds like a bicycle.

But sexy.

Bisexual. Biiiiiiisexual. Sometimes I say it to myself on the subway, when the train is so loud nobody else can hear.

"I am bisexual."

Try it. It's fun.

I think it took me this long to pick up on it because the kind of women who are supposed to be sexy—models or actors or whatever—don't register with me. Turns out I've got it bad for girls with heavy features and dark hair and loud voices, girls with big legs and big asses and opinions on *everything*. Girls who can destroy you with a smirk, who check you like a hockey player if you're slow on the subway steps. Girls like the ones I grew up with. And the more I see the more it gets me thinking, and the more I think the worse it gets, and it turns out that when you're turned on by Italian girls and Jewish girls and Black girls and Puerto Rican girls, New York City is a minefield.

I told my analyst about it and he laughed—said I was engaging in "a regressive adolescent fantasy" that could only be resolved through group sessions with my husband—so I told him to fuck off and quit going altogether. Instead of dropping forty bucks for fifty minutes twice a week, I started haunting the used bookstores on Fourth Avenue, combing the stacks for trashy lesbian pulps—stuff like *Sorority Sweethearts* or *Her Lying Lips*. They're stupid and cheesy and horny as hell, and I swear to god, they're the best therapy I ever had.

But the smut's only half of it and lately it's not even the big half. I think about what it's like when I'm alone with my female friends—the one or two I grew up with that I can still stand and all the battle-of-the-sexes bullshit just falls away. Sometimes it feels like my whole life I've been wearing shoes two sizes too small and I can't even imagine what it would feel like to try on a pair that fits. I imagine—

Safety.

Comfort.

Understanding.

No longer needing to pretend that I'm never afraid.

Toru gives me a lot of that a lot of the time, don't get me wrong. But I haven't told him any of this because I figure it's not worth maybe blowing up my entire life until I've got a grip on how much of this is fantasy and how much is real. For now, it stays locked in my head, keeping me safe even as it drives me insane.

Anyway, so I watched those moms for thirty or forty minutes. I was dipping into an alarmingly specific fantasy about me and the woman in the purple tunic on Martino's tiled floor, when I was rescued, thank god, by the big red Lincoln that drove onto the sidewalk and the two ugly bastards who spilled out. The one in front had shaggy curls, bright blue eyes, and a long red leather coat that he must have been absolutely boiling in. His face was as flat as a cast-iron skillet and his plump red tongue dangled as he grabbed my arm.

"The fuck!" I said.

He yanked me out of my seat. My hip slammed into the table and my demitasse smashed on the pavement. He shoved me toward the car. I splayed out my legs and stiffened my spine, like the cat when we're jamming him in the carrier. Hands closed on my ankles. They lifted me into the air.

"God damn it," I screamed, "let me go!"

I don't think I made it easy on them. I kicked and screamed and scratched and spit. But there were two of them, and well, they were always going to win. I sort of thought that if I hollered loud enough somebody might help, but the guy in Martino's, the people watching from their windows—none even pretended to care. When they finally managed to shove me into the back seat, my eyes locked on the mom in the purple tunic and I screamed for help and she gave me a look like, *Fuck off and die, wouldja? My kids are trying to play.*

And then the doors slammed and the engine roared and, baby, we were *gone*.

Brooklyn, Christ.

You can keep it.

Six

I let them drive. I'm a New Yorker, all right, so I know how to get mugged. I'd caught it three times in the last five years and even though one was very much "My First Mugging"—a kid who muttered, "Gimme your money," took the two bucks in my pocket, and didn't even bother to snatch my handbag—I still followed the rules.

No eye contact.

No chitchat.

Do what the man says.

But this was different. Because I was pretty sure I was about to die.

It's something I had experience imagining. Maybe this is everybody, maybe just me. Put me at Forty-Second Street and Broadway. While everybody else is dazzled by the neon, I'm thinking about how it would feel if one of the buses jumped the curb and squashed me into Bolognese. I'm smelling the flowers at my funeral. I'm watching tears stream down Toru's face. I'm hearing his kids scream. I see Toru boxing up my clothes, trying to hold it together while he haggles with the consignment ladies on Amsterdam. The kids drawing pictures of me at school and breaking their teachers' hearts. The cat not giving a damn. My analyst, back before I fired the bastard, assured me this was "a perfectly healthy expression of the death wish," but it left me feeling ill. Anyway, it meant that as we trundled out of Park Slope toward whatever darkened alley these gentlemen liked for their murders, I felt right at home.

"She scratched me, Blue," said the hood beside me. He had thick black curls and a long jaw—Elliott Gould if Elliott Gould weren't cute. A pistol rested on his knee. He stroked it compulsively, in a way that might have been amusing if the gun weren't pointed at me. "All down my arm."

"So what?" said Blue—the man in the red leather coat.

"So I want to hurt her."

"Stones?"

"Yeah?"

"Shut the fuck up."

Stones shut up. For about three seconds. When he spoke again he was surly—like Nicky when he asks for another cookie and I tell him, for the fifth time, no.

"I'd just like to maybe break her jaw."

"No," said Blue with a finality that would have been encouraging if he didn't follow it with: "Not yet."

The car rolled onto Flatbush and we crawled past wig shops and butchers, Middle Eastern grocery stores and bail bondsmen, gun shops and pawnshops, women who told fortunes and men who offered extortionate payday loans. I scratched my forehead as casually as a person can, then let my hand drift onto the door handle. One quick yank to open the door, then I'd hurl myself out. I'd probably get my skull crushed by an unlicensed cab but at least I'd have given it a shot.

I took a deep breath and was about to make my play when Stones tapped his gunsight on my knee.

"How 'bout if she opens the door?" he said. "Then I can shoot, right?"

"Oh yeah," said Blue. "Naturally."

I let my hand drop.

Blue drummed his fingers as he shuffled through the late afternoon traffic. I assumed we were heading for Manhattan but instead he eased us onto the BQE toward North Brooklyn. The traffic blurred. Blue tapped a cigarette out of a soft pack of Luckies and let it dangle from his lips while the car lighter got hot.

"Do I get to know where you're taking me?" I said.

"Nope," said Blue.

"How 'bout what's going to happen when we get there?"

He shook his head. The lighter went *pop.* Driving with his knees, he filled the car with sweet blue smoke. My jaw was clenched so tight I was seeing streaks.

"It's a bad idea to kill me," I said.

"Why?" said Stones.

"About fifty people heard me asking about your boss today. If I disappear, they'll know who did it."

Blue jabbed the radio. The sickly sweet voices of the Bee Gees filled the car. If he thought that would shut me up, he didn't understand how loud I could talk.

"I'm a reporter, okay? People know my byline. They know my face. If you kill me, you'll fucking fry."

He turned the radio louder. I put my face in my hands.

"Could you at least change the station?"

He cranked the dial a little bit more. My ears screamed.

"Every time you talk," he said, "this gets louder. Get it?"

I nodded. Nobody said anything else until we got to Williamsburg. We spent a few long minutes cruising burnt-out streets, where every window was covered with plywood or tin, and stopped in front of an unmarked warehouse. I was reasonably certain I was going to die in or near that car, and while I wasn't pleased about it, espresso and cannoli from Martino's was a decent last meal and there was some consolation in knowing I'd never have to tell Toru what I was keeping in the thirty-two-ounce jar.

Stones opened the door and said, "Out."

"Fuck you," I said. "You wanna kill me? You're gonna have to spoil your interior."

Stones's cheeks got red. He leaned back and kicked my hip but I was braced pretty firmly against the seat. So he got out, marched around, seized my wrist, and pulled hard, flinging me toward the scarred steel door.

"Inside!" he shouted, waving his pistol like it was a plastic flag.

"Why do you keep thinking I'm going to make this easy for you?"

He pressed his pistol against my chest.

To explain what happened next, I have to tell you how I made my first best friend. Me and Bobbie Piantoni met in junior high but basically didn't notice each other—she was shy and bookish and I was, well, neither. But when the eighth grade took its big trip to an extremely grubby motel on the edge of Washington, D.C., we got paired as roommates. All the other kids stayed up late goofing off but Bobbie and I were wiped from a long hot day tramping up and down the National Mall and when the lights went out, we crashed—until about three in the morning, when

Andy Bruckner, one of our grade's assortment of idiot boys, started banging on every door and screaming, "FBI! FBI! It's J. Edgar Hoover and the FBI!" When he got to us, I let him knock once and then I tore open the door and smacked his face so hard that I sprained my wrist. He shut the fuck up, and Bobbie laughed until she got the hiccups, and for the next few years, we were inseparable.

Anyway, that's how hard I hit Stones.

He crashed to the pavement. His gun went flying and he lunged for it and I was about to kick him in the face when Blue came up behind me. I raised my palm and he backed off.

"There's been a misunderstanding," he said.

"Then how about you explain?"

"Mr. Motisi heard there was a reporter looking for him. He asked us to come get her."

"Why?"

"For dinner."

"Bullshit."

Stones picked up his stupid gun. He was already wearing the imprint of my hand.

"How about you quit torturing us," he said, "and go inside?"

"How about I hit you some more?"

He cocked his pistol. I was about to say something cute but then he pointed the gun at me and I figured the debate was closed.

Blue yanked open the door and shoved me inside. I breathed deep, catching a whiff of garlic in olive oil. It was dark in there, as dim as a tomb, and my eyes adjusted slowly. I don't mind telling you my mouth was dry and my palms were wet. I felt tickles up and down my spine, anticipating the bullet. But then the door closed behind me—with Stones and his pistol on the far side—

and the darkness cleared and I saw waiters and I figured that meant I was safe.

There were three of them, all ancient, hunched over a table in the corner, aprons starched and hair greased, smoking unfiltered cigarettes and trudging through a moody game of three-handed hearts. It was a restaurant the size of an airplane hangar. Spotless white curtains dangled from a curved roof. A low stage occupied one end of the room. In front of it were maybe a hundred tables set with crystal and silverware and tablecloths like virgin snow. And they were empty, except for one.

Even from here I could see Tiny Tommy was neither tiny nor enormous, which was kind of a disappointment. He was just a regular-sized guy sipping a cocktail and staring like he was impatient for me to sit down. Good, I thought. Let him wait.

I leaned on the bar and admired myself in the mirror. I looked as tired as potato salad that's been left out in the sun. I smoothed my hair. It didn't help.

There was no bartender, which meant a long wait while one of the waiters ambled across the floor. I didn't mind. It gave my hands a chance to stop shaking. I couldn't believe I hadn't pissed myself. Hell, I couldn't believe I was alive at all. When the waiter finally pulled up, I ordered a Campari and let its bitterness take the edge off my fear. This was my territory now. If there's one thing I know, it's how to cross a restaurant floor.

Tiny Tommy was handsome, in a Brylcreem sort of way, with hard-slicked hair, thick black glasses, and the orangest tan I'd ever seen. He wore a precisely tailored orange suit, each lapel as wide as my thigh, and a bright green tie that made my eyes water. I figured he was around thirty-five but the glasses and the tan made him look ten years older. He smelled like a baked cigar.

He slid his chair back and started to get up but I shoved him right back down.

"What's your fucking problem?" I said.

"Ma'am—"

"Absogoddamnlutely not. I'm a human being, you piece of shit. You do not send armed men to grab me off the sidewalk, shove me into a town car, threaten my life, subject me to the Bee Gees, and press a pistol to my chest."

"My boys did what?"

"I'm gonna sue your dick off. I'm gonna have you arrested. And yeah, yeah, I know you've got an army of lawyers and you'll be back on the street in forty-five minutes or whatever the crooks say on *Dragnet*, but it would take your muscle out of commission, and I know a hood is no hood without meat to back him up."

He wiped his mouth. He hadn't been eating, so I figured that meant he was rattled. Good.

"Maybe tell me what you're looking into so we can figure out what kind of problem we have," he said. "My unions? My nephew? Or, shit, it's not the thing in Long Island City?"

"It's Laurent Tirel."

He squinted. Maybe he really had no idea what I was talking about. Maybe he was full of shit. I'd have to treat this like any other interview. I'd start by saying hello.

"I'm not just a reporter, asshole. I'm a food writer. My name is Bernice Black."

He jumped out of his seat too fast for me to even think about shoving him back down. I thought he was going for my windpipe but before I knew what was happening, he had one arm around my shoulders. The other was pumping my right hand.

"Holy hell!" he gasped.

"You're crushing my hand."

"Sorry, sorry, I just can't believe it. B. B. fucking Black!"

"I guess you've heard of me."

"Christ forgive me, I can't believe I didn't recognize you. I read your column like some guys read the *Racing Form*. You're always dead on the money and funny too. Holy shit, if I'd known it was B. B. Black asking for me, I'd have dressed up. Let's eat! We gotta eat!"

A fan. I'd never counted on finding a fan.

"Mr. Motisi, let me go."

He backed off, face even oranger than before.

"Sorry, sorry. When it comes to my friends, I'm a touching kind of guy."

"We are not friends."

"But you're gonna join me, right?"

"I just want to talk."

"Oh, please, Miss Black. You ever been here before? Verucchio is the tops, I'm telling you, best old-school Italian in Williamsburg. And like you say in your column, there's nothing like the promise of an empty plate."

"I don't think you understand the *terror*—"

"I know, I know, and I feel like a heel. Join me for supper—I'll answer every question you have."

Listen, my pride didn't want to let me sit down with this man. But my stomach was growling and my notebook was empty and the place really did smell like heaven by way of Napoli. So I made to sit down and he leapt around the table and yanked out my chair. I took out my notebook and pen.

"So what's new with Laurent?" he said, all smiles.

I sighed. It gets old quick, being the emissary of death.

"How about we order first?"

"Smart, smart. I talk better with food."

He pressed a button in the middle of the table. A buzzer dinged. One of the waiters set down his cards and walked over as slow as a person can. Tiny Tommy ordered for us—Manhattans, gnocchi, osso buco. The waiter didn't bother writing anything down.

"And wine," he said, "we've gotta have wine. We just got in a couple cases of this Burgundy, from a little town called Moraches. Nineteen sixty-one. Sixty-one was good, wasn't it?"

"Sixty-two was better."

"We've got that too!" Motisi clapped his hands. "Open a bottle of the sixty-two!"

The waiter drifted away. Tommy looked at me like he was a teenage girl and I was a shirtless Donny Osmond.

"Why didn't you meet me at Martino's?" I said.

"I don't like going places at the moment. People want to talk to me, this is where we talk."

"Where were you yesterday from noon to two?"

He tilted his head and smiled, a little cute and a little confused.

"That's a cop question. I thought we were going to talk about food. Like, are leeks the breakout star of the onion family?"

"I have no idea what that means."

"I read it in *Epicure*, I think, or maybe *Taste*. They also said chives are the new shallots. What do you think of that?"

"I think it's bullshit. Now, what about yesterday afternoon?"

"Why do you care?"

"That's when Laurent Tirel was murdered."

Tiny Tommy slammed into the back of his chair like the Tin Man into a magnet. His skin had the color and texture of the tablecloth. Manhattans appeared. I took a sip. It was sweet like summer fruit and it was exactly what I needed.

"You're kidding," said Tiny Tommy, loosening his tie.

"No."

"What happened to him?"

I gulped. This part wasn't getting any easier to say.

"Somebody cut off his head."

He drained his cocktail and waved for another like he was dying of thirst. I focused on my notes. It was very comforting, it turned out, to act like I didn't care.

"So you're here because I'm some kind of suspect," he said.

"Let's just say the police are very eager to talk to you."

"That's discrimination, you know that? Anti-Italian. He and I were friends, you get that? Very good friends."

"I thought you hauled his garbage."

"Yeah, sure. Took it over from my uncle. Some restaurant guys get pissy about garbage pickup—they try to negotiate—but he was French, y'know, extremely cool. One night I was in the neighborhood, so I stopped in for a drink and he asked me to eat downstairs with him. Said he wanted to learn more about my business. I thought he was pulling my leg but he really just wanted to understand."

"There wasn't anything about that restaurant that he didn't get, inside and out."

"So he orders me up that orange duck, and my god, the first bite I was hooked. I never knew food could taste that good, y'know?"

"I know."

"That was eight years ago, maybe, and since then I'm eating there three, four nights a week. Gave him a rate on his garbage and he let me run a tab. I like the roast chicken, the grenouilles, and everything he does with mussels or fish. But that orange duck, I'm an addict."

The waiter dropped a couple plates of gnocchi onto our table. They were gorgeous—tender little balls of spinach and parm and I think ricotta too—and they warmed me down to my shoes. Tiny Tommy poured Burgundy. I'm not a wine expert—I was bluffing when I said the '62 was better—but it tasted as good as liquid can.

"Did you loan him money?" I said.

"Here and there."

"One hundred and thirty-seven thousand dollars?"

"A friendly loan. No interest, no repayment schedule. I'd have paid a mil to keep eating that orange duck."

"Did you sell him heroin?"

"Do I look like I sell heroin?"

I stared until he laughed.

"I may have advised him, in a strictly hypothetical way, how a person might obtain such things."

"Why did he want it?"

"Usually people want heroin because they want heroin, y'know? It's not like he was putting it in the soup. But I didn't get junkie vibes off Laurent. Had the feeling it was for a friend."

"Who?"

"People who ask questions like that end up bobbing around the East River."

I finished my glass. He poured me another. The osso buco came, so hot it fogged Motisi's glasses. The veal fell right off the bone. The veggies were mushy but the sauce was thick and nicely seasoned. Motisi sucked the marrow and looked pleased when I did the same.

"You never told me where you were yesterday," I said.

"You're not gonna believe me."

"Veal makes me credulous. Try."

"I was taking a cooking class."

I laughed. He didn't.

"It's the truth," he said.

"Prove it."

"How?"

"They've got a kitchen here, don't they? Let's go."

He thought for a second, then dropped his napkin and pushed back his chair. I followed him across the creaking floor to the frosted glass that divided dining room from kitchen. There was no door—we just rounded a corner and suddenly we were back in 1895. I don't know if you've ever been in a really old kitchen, but they hardly even feel like a place to cook. There was no tile, for starters—it was wood on the walls, the counters, the floors. There was no walk-in—just a pair of antique ceramic iceboxes—and instead of a shiny new stove there was a stubby cast-iron monster that looked like Ben Franklin used it to fry eggs.

Tiny Tommy tied on an apron. He flicked a burner, set out a good-sized saucepan, and tipped in two cups of water, two cups of sugar, and a couple tablespoons of red wine vinegar.

"For bite," he said.

He let it boil, then turned down the heat. He peeled a couple of pears, sliced 'em in half, and slipped them into the bubbling syrup. While they poached, he refilled my wine, rigged up the mixer, and whipped cream.

"When did you start cooking?" I said.

"The day I was born? Most Italian mothers, they'd chase their boys out of the kitchen, like they were gonna turn sissy if you taught them to slice an onion. But from before I could stand, Momma had me on her counter helping her knead dough, beat eggs, stir gravy. So I been cooking my whole life, simple stuff—

chops and potatoes and whatever the guys wanted to eat—and then my uncle died and I took over his business and suddenly I was richer than I'd ever been and I couldn't even go out and spend the money. Half the time I'm laying low, the rest I'm working, and I figured I needed something that was just for me. I wanted to learn to cook high class, like European, so I called up the best instructor in the city. You know who that is?"

"Ambrose Clendenon."

"Correct."

He tested his softening pears with a long knife. His mother had done well—he was very comfortable with a blade.

"You realize Ambrose is one of my closest friends," I said.

"I knew you were both at the *Sentinel*. I didn't want to presume."

"And he's never mentioned you."

"I pay him to be discreet. So yesterday I was at his apartment—"

"Which is where?"

Tiny Tommy smirked like, *You're not gonna get me that easy.*

"The studios on top of Carnegie Hall."

"What was the lesson?"

"Soufflé. Mushroom and leek." He snapped. "Say! He was the one who said leeks are the breakout star of the whaddayacallit."

"Ambrose will confirm this?"

"There's a phone in the corner. Call the man and ask."

The phone was a little wooden box mounted on the wall. I cradled the earpiece and dialed Ambrose. I got his service.

"Mr. Clendenon is out for the night."

"Where?"

Papers shuffled. She attempted French.

"Le Cœur d'Or."

I hung up and watched Tiny Tommy fish out the pears with a slotted spoon. He arranged them neatly on paper-thin china and dressed them with a dainty serving of whipped cream.

"I take extra whipped cream," I said. "Always."

"Why?"

"Life is finite."

He slopped on some more whipped cream and slid the plate my way. I took a couple of bites. He was straining like a racehorse, trying not to ask how they were. I put him out of his misery.

"Very nice," I said. "Tender. In a perfect world you'd let them get down to room temperature—the whipped cream is melting right off—but the vinegar really does add bite. Problem is, poached pears are not a soufflé. And they are definitely not an alibi."

"So what's that mean?"

"I've gotta see Ambrose."

"I'll have my boys give you a ride."

"Only Blue. Stones is a prick. I don't ever want to see him again."

He sliced off the last bite of pear, leaving the core behind like a stripped skeleton, popped it into his mouth, and showed me the door. Ten minutes later I was cruising over the Williamsburg Bridge. I'd never been so grateful to escape Brooklyn. When I was fifteen I was certain I was going to die there—today I nearly had. The thought gave me the shakes, so I jammed it in a jar, banished it to the basement, and tried to lose myself in the view. Manhattan glittered against the river, its lights the only jewels I'd ever need.

Seven

When you entered Le Cœur d'Or, a velvet tunnel birthed you into a room filled with a grating excess of people and noise. The dining room was large, dimly lit, and overwhelmingly green. I mean all of it—floor and ceiling, carpet and tablecloths, the uniforms, the napkins, the glasses, the plates. Even worse, none of the greens quite matched. The chairs were aged copper, the cutlery violent lime, the cocktails every shade of baby poop.

The place was packed—tourists from Texas on one side, junior Wall Street assholes and their shrieking dates on the other—and there was an actual string quartet in the corner doing an impeccable impression of the 6 train as it screams into Union Square. The men wore black suits and white shirts, like undertakers, and the women were dressed like it was 1965. God, I wished Ambrose had been anywhere else. Even on my best days I couldn't handle Cœur.

But Cœur was the scene, so that's where Ambrose had to be. He'd been covering New York's restaurants since before Laurent came over, before they were really worth a damn. He'd spent his entire career at the *Sentinel,* starting as a stringer in high school, and had carved out a niche writing amiable, rambling columns that were half gossip, half food writing, and all fun. He was Yankee Stadium—past its prime, maybe, but not something New York could live without.

When he wasn't writing he used his Carnegie Hall studio as a venue for cooking classes—he'd taught every woman in New York society how to crack an egg—but really he treated the entire city as a classroom. He had a standing offer to Manhattan's chefs: If you're struggling with a dish, I'll help you fix it, free of charge. He was the one who convinced Cal Haney to cut back on the anchovies in Geldorf's Caesar, who helped Griffin Lloyd perfect the bouillabaisse at Perf, who taught the griddle man at the Fifty-Fourth Street deli to get the pastrami hot before adding the cheese. He was known for having the best palate in the city and you could argue—as I often had—that he'd done even more than Laurent to shape how New York ate.

I loved Ambrose for two reasons. The first was that in the mid-fifties he'd found a sideline covering New York restaurants for national magazines, including *Our World,* where he wrote the profile of Laurent that changed my life. The second was that when I joined the *Sentinel,* instead of treating me as a rival, he took me on as a friend. On my first day, he took me to lunch at a Jewish dairy counter because the buttermilk was the only thing, he said, that could quiet his ulcer. Since then we'd eaten together at least a couple hundred times. He introduced me to every chef in the city who was worth a damn, he got me tables that were simply impossible, he encouraged me when I was low and he kept me humble in the rare moments when my quarter teaspoon of celebrity threatened to go to my head. He'd spent years taking care of me. I knew he'd be heartbroken about Laurent and I wasn't sure I was ready to take care of him.

But before I made it to his table I was ambushed by Minnie Anglade—Cœur's co-owner, manager, and enforcer. A woman in her mid-forties who styled herself like a demented seventy-five, she wore a turquoise dress, sea-foam stockings, emerald eye shadow, and mint gloves. Her hair was curled in every direction at once, like she slept with her head in a fan. She looked annoyed to see me and I knew exactly why.

"Miss Black," she said in a voice hauntingly reminiscent of my third-grade teacher, "you know better than to enter my restaurant wearing pants."

You probably think she was kidding. You're wrong. Cœur had the strictest dress code this side of the yacht club. They evicted women for wearing trousers or going braless; they tore McGovern pins off lapels; they once made a huge show out of evicting a Rothschild who had the audacity to order coffee *with* dinner instead of waiting until the meal was done. It was more than snobbery—it was sadism, and the regulars loved it. The more people Minnie tossed, the more grateful were those who got to stay.

"I just need a quick word with Ambrose," I said.

"Do it someplace where your outfit is appropriate. Like the sewer."

"For fuck's sake—"

"Vulgarity will hardly change my mind."

"You need me to make a threat here?"

"Just try."

"Okay. How about, let me into your *fucking* restaurant or I use my next column to expose Cœur as the most retrograde, reactionary, anti-feminist . . ."

Minnie's face twisted into a wicked smile. An angry column was precisely what she had in mind. Something she could hang behind the bar, right beside her prized photo of the time Nixon stopped in for lunch. I sucked in some air and looked around for another angle and noticed that Minnie and her waiters were all wearing armbands: black with green stripes.

"Those for Laurent?" I said.

"They are."

Then she did, somewhere, have a heart. Minnie and Vic—her husband, partner, chef, and punching bag—had both come up through Laurent's. He'd cooked in the kitchen for a hot minute, forming no real ties, but she'd worked the cash register all through the fifties and had been as much a part of the place as the flowers. To alter anything as visible as her waiters' uniforms meant she must be devastated.

"You hear I found him?" I said.

"I did. I'm sorry." She spoke softly, so no one could hear her expressing sympathy to the women's libber. "It must have been a hideous shock."

"Yeah." I chewed my lip. "So how about we do each other a favor? Don't throw me out. Yet. Gimme fifteen minutes with Ambrose and then ask me to leave."

"Why?"

"Don't worry about why. You and I both need a little fun today—this'll be a gas. And it'll be all over the *Sentinel* too."

She took another look at my pants. She scowled. But then she let me pass, smiling very much like a human being.

"Ambrose is at his usual table," she said. "You get fifteen minutes. No more."

"Okay, but don't start the clock until I sit down. I've got a call to make."

I made for the bar and waved for the phone. Toru picked up, first ring. Before he could say hello, I was already apologizing.

"I'm like three hours late, I'm so sorry, but it has been a *day*, let me tell you, and—"

"I can't hear you!"

I shouted into the phone: "I'm sorry for being late!"

"Don't worry about it. The kids were easy. We rode the bus to the Met, then came home and ate TV dinners. They passed out early and I'm heading to bed."

He said it without malice but it carved me right up. The World's Greatest Stepmom doesn't come home stinking of cigarettes after everyone else has gone to bed. She doesn't drop the ball on school pickup. She doesn't let her family eat TV dinners. And she sure as hell doesn't get wrapped up in murders. And yet, here we were.

"Everything's really okay?" I said.

"The cat keeps shitting on things but otherwise life is peachy."

"Thank you. I mean it. And I promise—tomorrow will be less of a disaster. It has to be."

We said goodbye. I hung up and waded back into the crowd, which was as thick and stinking as a swamp. I dodged elbows, cigarettes, and martinis as I wove my way around the edge of the room toward Ambrose's usual table. He preferred sitting in corners—"Like a mafioso," he said—so he could watch the crowd. That meant he saw me coming and even though he gave his warmest grin—and it was very warm—I could see how much work it took to smile. I sank into a wobbly plastic chair and tried to match his labored cheer.

Ambrose was in his mid-sixties. He had the kind of face you

might call cherubic, but in the last couple of years age had hit him hard. His hair, which he still wore swept across his head in a trademark swoop, had gone gray and thin. His massive frame, custom built for a lifetime of professional eating, had hollowed out. His clothes hung loose and his once-proud double chin dangled from his neck like an empty pillowcase. When I asked him about the weight loss he laughed it off, told me that he was on a diet and it was working and would I please refrain from mothering him. But I wasn't convinced. I was afraid he was sick—like, really sick. After the day I'd had, I could hardly stand to lose any more friends.

I offered a hand and he squeezed it tight and said, "Having a nice day?" and we both laughed so hard we started to cry. Christ, it was what I needed. Two minutes of actual grief in the company of someone who simply understood. It didn't solve anything but it knocked the pressure down. When my shoulders stopped shaking I dried my eyes and took out my notepad and said, "I've got to ask something important."

"Can it wait until the food comes? I'm not certain I have the strength."

I glanced at Minnie, who stood by the door, straight as a hatpin, schmoozing with a well-liquored couple dressed like it was casino night at the country club. I'd be lucky if she gave me fifteen minutes. I had to move this along.

"It can't."

He squirmed. Ambrose hated being rushed. Pinning him down would be like corralling the last pea onto your spoon.

"Couldn't we talk about something pleasant instead? The wedding, for instance. Have you set a date?"

"I'm still venue hunting. We're thinking fall but everywhere in the city is too busy or too expensive or both. I've got my mother calling every three days to tell me my father's old union hall is available, but as you can imagine I'd rather die. And now the magazine is folding—"

"I heard, it's awful—"

"And I'm starting to think maybe we just wait till next year but I'm afraid if we don't do it now we'll never do it, only I don't even know if we should until the kids have really accepted me and how the hell do I know when that will be?"

He offered me his water. I drained it—I'd had no idea how thirsty I was—while he twiddled his cravat.

"What if I asked around?" he said. "I know all sorts of people with all sorts of places."

"That would be spectacular. Now let's talk about Tommy Motisi."

Fear snapped across Ambrose's face. Before I could ask more, a plate of scallops fell from the sky. I looked up and saw "French Vic" Anglade, chef and co-owner of Cœur, who somehow combined bad teeth, a crooked nose, and overgrown sideburns into a grimy sex appeal. He was a short guy but strong, with bulging Peter Lorre eyes that always left him looking a little bit sleepy and a little bit sad. He'd come over from France in the early 1950s, did a stint at Laurent's, and then went home for fifteen years. When he came back to open Cœur, the place made a splash. Every dish was bright and fresh, with featherlight sauces and carved bits of garnish that were both adorable and an expression of an extreme, almost monastic technique. People, myself included, started talking him up as the next big thing, a possible successor to Laurent as the leading light of French cooking in Manhattan. But he never quite got there, mainly because Cœur was so damn inconsistent: You could order the same fish three nights in a row and get something totally different every time. The finance boys found this exciting, I guess. For me, it was infuriating.

That night he wore a greasy chef's jacket, unbuttoned to the waist to reveal a stained Jimi Hendrix T-shirt, and he held a bottle of red wine. He pulled a corkscrew from his pocket, filled our glasses, and slumped into an empty chair. He took a long sip and made the face Nicky does when I give him broccoli.

"This wine is disgusting," he said.

I took a sip and told him, "It tastes like wine."

"It's a sixty-eight, you understand? A four-year-old wine is no more fit to go out into the world than a four-year-old child. It is *infanticide.*"

"Then why serve it?"

"It is what my wife provides."

He said *wife* like it was a slur. Deciding not to poke that particular hornet's nest, I nodded at the plate.

"What's with the scallops?" I said. "Should I try them or are they disgusting too?"

"They are *killing me,*" answered Vic. "Minnie got a *deal*—fifty pounds of the things, torn from the sea and frozen solid and dropped on my neck like an albatross. I've tried searing them, grilling them, steaming them, poaching them. They're either rubber or mush. So I call Ambrose and I beg him to come down here and save my ass."

"Could he save your ass later? He and I need to talk."

"Yes, yes, of course. Only if I can't sort this out now, I'll probably die. And I figure one dead chef is enough for a Tuesday."

Ambrose gave an apologetic look, which I guess was him asking permission. I shrugged even though my hip hurt, I had a nasty headache, and I was afraid that if I blinked, I'd fall asleep. Ambrose grabbed the plate—three scallops under a sea of gluey cream—and cut a bite. He chewed and chewed and chewed some more and asked: "How are you defrosting them?"

Vic threw up his hands.

"We've tried them in the fridge overnight. We've tried them under running water, we've tried leaving them on the fucking counter, we've tried chucking them in the pan frozen. *Nothing* works."

"Of course not. They were frozen too slowly. The freezer was overcrowded or set improperly or simply old. When food is frozen without the necessary speed, minute ice crystals form—millions of little knives tearing the flesh to ribbons. When the food cooks, the ice turns to steam. You're left with a soggy wad of inedibility. Is that a word, Bernard? 'Inedibility'?"

"Why don't we go with 'a soggy, inedible wad'?"

"Much better. But no amount of rephrasing will save these, Vic. I'm sorry."

Ambrose took no pleasure from this. More than anyone I know, he hated to see food—even lousy food—go to waste. Vic swished a mouthful of wine like it was Listerine. I speared the remainder of Ambrose's scallop. It was like chewing wet newspaper. I thought Ambrose was being hasty advising him to chuck the whole batch—there had to be something they could do with them—but I didn't bother saying anything. Ambrose had a way of losing his hearing when contradicted. I never bothered anymore.

"How's the rest of the menu?" I said.

"Fucking terrible," said Vic. "We're full every night, making money hand over fist, but what does Minnie give me to cook? Like Ambrose said—garbage."

"Ever consider talking to Minnie instead of bitching about her?"

"Bitching is much more fun."

"Well, save it. I'm on a tight schedule here."

"Yeah, yeah, of course. I should be in the kitchen, right?" He refilled his wine. "God, this tastes like shit."

"She means it," said Ambrose, as gently as he could. "Go."

"I will, I will. Only you remember last month? The grilled chicken?"

Ambrose lit up.

"Did you try it with the béarnaise?"

"Yeah, and it's selling like crazy. But here's the thing . . ."

He didn't actually trail off. I just couldn't stand to listen anymore. There are nights—quite a few of them—when I love my job. When every restaurant is a cathedral, when everyone is beautiful and everything is fun. When I am dizzy with gratitude at the ridiculousness of being paid to eat. And then there are nights when I just want to go home.

I'll let you guess which type of night this was.

So while they chattered about chicken I took another hit of pre-adolescent wine and scanned for Minnie. No sign of her, so I let my eyes drift across the bar. I snagged on a woman who was hunched over a plate of radishes and Irish butter, wearing a belted dress that looked like the striations you see in a geology textbook—reds and browns and oranges and blacks. She had on high red boots and a black crocheted hat that looked like she'd swiped it from somebody's nonna. She turned her neck to look at the clock and my breath caught in my throat.

Shit, I thought. That's Liza Minnelli.

No, it's not.

Yes, it is!

No, it isn't, you idiot—if Liza's in town she's eating at Quint's or Atmosphere or Perf. She is not snacking on salted radishes and butter *by herself* at Cœur d'Or.

But shit, she looked like Liza with curves. She had the big eyes and the chopped black hair and the knowing smirk of Fraulein Sally Bowles. And when she caught me staring I turned so fast I just about fell off my chair. I drained my wine and reached for the bottle but it was empty, so I slapped Vic on the arm and told him to get more. He snapped and another bottle appeared, this one even younger than the first. Vic sighed as he opened it, sighed as he drank, and sighed as he asked me:

"Is it true what Elma Zumwalt told me—that the killer sliced off Laurent's fingers and used them to garnish a Waldorf salad?"

"Not even slightly."

"What a shame."

I slipped my notebook onto the table.

"You weren't fond of him?" I said.

"He was a son of a bitch and I'm glad he's dead. Am I to pretend otherwise?"

"Why'd you hate him?"

"We had a past. I won't say more."

"But you didn't kill him?"

"I'm afraid not. Ask anyone—I was here all day. You're writing about him? Then let me amend my quote. Laurent Tirel was a *despicable* son of a bitch and I am *exquisitely pleased* that he is dead. I don't suppose, Miss Black, that you could get me his job?"

The thought of Vic in Laurent's kitchen filled my gut with broken glass, but Ambrose was amused.

"You may have forgotten," said Ambrose, "but you already have a restaurant."

"This place isn't a restaurant. It's a scene. Laurent's . . . now, that would be a challenge. Can you get me in?"

"You overestimate my power," I said. "I'd be flattered if I weren't so damn tired. Can I have Ambrose now?"

"I'm going."

He didn't. So I kicked him in the shin and he dragged himself up. He waved his glass at his life's work.

"I just wish we had better insurance," he said.

"Why?"

"So I could burn it to the ground."

And then, finally, he left us alone. He was weaving toward the bar when Minnie intercepted him. They embarked on a hushed argument that, I hoped, would give me a little more time.

"Now, about Tommy Motisi," I said.

Ambrose took a shuddering breath. His hand quivered as he prodded one of the remaining scallops, then pushed the plate away.

"Would you choose him?" said Ambrose. "Accepting that Laurent's without Laurent will never be Laurent's, if you could choose any chef in the city to take it over, would you have French Vic?"

I drummed my fingers on the tablecloth.

"Probably not."

"Then who?"

"First explain why Tommy Motisi gives you the shakes."

"I can't . . . you're imagining . . ." A deep breath. "It's not a name I've heard before."

"Then why are you his alibi for Laurent's murder?"

He got a little paler. The word *murder* has that effect. Behind him, French Vic smacked the bar and huffed into the kitchen. Minnie glanced at the clock, saw my time was past up, and started weaving toward me. Liza, I noticed, was gone.

"Our relationship is meant to be secret," said Ambrose, "but if he told you, I suppose I'm at liberty to say our Italian friend visited my apartment for a private lesson."

"What were you cooking?"

"Mushroom and leek soufflé. I apologize for the deception but he swore me to silence and you know how seriously men in his line of work take an oath. It's embarrassing but since I began teaching him, I've been beset by what one might call paranoia. I hear noises in the night; I notice large, unpleasant men staring from parked cars. It's stupid, I mean it's viciously stupid, but when I heard what happened to Laurent, all I could think was, when are they coming for me?"

Minnie loomed over Ambrose's shoulder. I held up a hand, asking for five minutes more. With a sour shake of her head, she backed off.

"How did our Italian friend handle the soufflé?" I said.

"Acceptably. He's inexperienced but fearless and hungry—a promising combination—and good with his hands. But he literally came to our third lesson with blood under his fingernails, Bernard—this is not a man to annoy."

"Precisely how long was he at your apartment?"

"From twelve-thirty to two-thirty."

I scribbled that down. Carnegie Hall was close enough to Fifty-Fourth Street that it was possible for Tommy to have killed Laurent and hoofed it over by twelve-thirty, but it would have been tight and it probably would have required a change of clothes.

"Did you ever teach Motisi to make aspic?" I said.

"No."

"Could he handle it?"

"Perhaps. He's not untalented, you know, and he's almost frighteningly patient. Why?"

God, I wanted to tell him. Not just to get it off my chest but because he'd have insight. Could help me firm up the timeline and figure out whatever was in the aspic that gave it that strange, sweet smell. But at the moment, Ambrose wasn't a friend—he was a source. And he'd already lied once.

"The police think this is about money," I said, "or heroin. I'm not convinced. Laurent was killed in his restaurant with a chef's knife."

"So?"

"So his whole life was about food. I gotta figure his death was too."

"And aspic figures how?"

"I can't say."

He rubbed his head, further tangling his unkempt hair. "Have you considered leaving this investigation to the professionals? I don't . . . Call me silly, Bernard, but I don't want you getting hurt."

"I'd love to. I have enough going on this week—Toru's birthday, plus the kids and the column and every other thing. But if I can't land this story it's my job." I swigged. Maybe Vic was right—this wine got nastier with every sip. "Where do I start?"

"Laurent would tell you to trust your sense of taste."

"And what the hell does that mean?"

He threw up his hands. I rapped my pen until it got annoying, then I flagged down a waiter, who bobbed alongside our table like an eager dolphin, and said: "Got anything in aspic?"

"Oeufs en gelée, ma'am."

"Let's get a plate. And another bottle of red."

The waiter swam away. Minnie saw I'd ordered food. She glared at me. I made a series of half-coherent gestures, trying to explain that it was all Ambrose's fault. She didn't mind humiliating me but Ambrose's approval was important to her, so she threw up her hands and stalked away. No way I could hold her off a third time.

"Who's got the best aspic in the city?" I said.

"You really won't say why?"

"I can't."

"Well . . . Atmosphere's is nice. The Sherbet Room does a respectable parsleyed ham. Aragvi had a few aspics on their old menu but since they moved, I'm not sure."

"Where else?"

"I'm not sure if he's doing an aspic but I'm hearing good things about what Rocky Shanklin's planning at Number 5."

"Oh god. *That* asshole."

"Even if his schtick turns you off, he's a promising young chef. Bite the bullet and say hello."

"Yeah, I will. Anybody else?"

He clicked his fingernail against his glass.

"I know you don't want to hear it, but if you want a classic gelée, you'll have to start at Près du Parc."

"Shit."

"I realize you and Henri have a checkered past, but his father taught him everything. Start there."

"I'll do the other places first. Près can wait."

"If you must start at all. I realize you're having fun, dearest, but there's already one man dead. New York can't afford to lose you too."

The eggs came—gleaming orbs trapped in quivering goo, topped with parsley and blanched leek. I split one with my fork. Yolk oozed in a way that was both disgusting and delightful. We chewed.

"I don't know what you're looking for," he said, "but this is vile."

I tilted my head. *Vile* was harsh. Like so much of what Vic was serving, it wasn't awful. Just . . . pointless. Grainy and underseasoned, with none of the aroma I'd caught at Laurent's. Hardly worth dying for. I pushed the plate away, caught Minnie's eye, and waved her in.

"Sending it back?" said Ambrose.

"Doing our hostess a favor. Watch—this'll be fun."

Maybe it was her dress or maybe she was just uptight, but Minnie walked like a mummy, never bending her knees. When she got to our table she started to say something. I didn't know what it was and I didn't care. I slammed my fist and leapt to my feet and screamed loud enough to be heard on the street.

"Bullshit!"

Everything in the restaurant stopped except for the goddamned string quartet. Minnie stepped back. She was scared. Lovely.

"It is 1972! We have the vote. We have the pill. And we have the right to wear fucking pants."

Her lips broke into that ghoulish smile. She understood.

"We have standards, Miss Black. If you can't change into something more conservative, leave."

"You're throwing out the *New York Sentinel*?"

"I don't think it's good for anything else."

The assembled young conservatives gave their champion a cheer. Gratitude flashed across her narrow eyes. As far as she was concerned, I'd given her a win. But I wanted to give her guests a story they'd remember for the rest of their lives.

So I threw my wine in her face.

She let out a little shriek. Young wine dripped from her nose, her chin, her hair. It spread across her chest like a blooming rose. For a second I thought I'd gone too far but then Ambrose cackled and her customers booed and I strutted out of there with Minnie screaming, "Banned for life! You hear me, Miss Black? You are *banned for life*!"

Eight

I was scanning for a cab when somebody shouted, "That was fucked up!"

It was Liza, stomping down the sidewalk, waving her cigarette like a pitchfork. She was even cuter up close but not in a way I had time for. A rare open cab rumbled down the avenue. I stuck out a hand. The cabbie slowed but Liza waved him off. I could've smacked her.

"What the fuck?" I said.

"We're going back inside. That kind of discrimination is illegal."

"It's actually not."

"When I'm done with that bitch, it will be."

I leaned on the phone booth and crossed my arms and said: "Who *are* you?"

"Oh yeah. I always forget that part." She stuck out a hand. I ignored it. "Susan Gullett. *St. Mark's Arch.*"

I'd never heard of Susan Gullett but I knew the *Arch*. It was a grubby downtown weekly famous for its annual "Surf & Skin" issue, which celebrated the opening of the city's beaches with a multipage spread of "Nude Yorkers" frolicking in the sea. Besides that, they were known for Marxist political coverage, sexually explicit personal ads, and acid-infused horoscopes written by someone called "The Oracle of Stuyvesant Street." I mostly read it in line at Film Forum—once when the ladies' room ran out of toilet paper, it quite literally saved my ass. I'd always written it off as trashy—"cheap words on cheap paper," I'd once told Judy—but at least, unlike the *Sentinel* mag, it had a point of view. And sex ads were lucrative, I guess, because as far as I knew, the paper was in the black and that's more than you could say for my soon-to-be-ex-employer.

"What do you do down there?" I said, staring up the avenue, praying for another cab.

"Editor in chief. It's less impressive than it sounds. We've got fifteen employees and all of us are editors of one sort or another. It's some kind of Maoist management structure?"

"How does it work?"

"It doesn't. You're with the *Sentinel*?"

"Yeah. Well, the magazine. B. B. Black."

Something happened when she heard my name. She got this little smirk, like the universe told a joke that only she could hear.

"I know your byline," she said. "You're good."

"I can't believe you waved off that cab, that's a fucking sin."

"Yeah, well, I'm a degenerate." She sidled up. "Say—you cover restaurants, right? What can you tell me about Laurent Tirel?"

"On the record?"

"Everything I do is on the record."

"Then I've got nothing to say."

She eyed me like beef in a butcher's window. Did I look at sources this way? It was a wonder they told me anything at all.

"I heard the killer chopped him up and used him to make soup," she said. "Can you confirm that?"

I shook my head. The smirk came back. Not like she was kidding, exactly, but like she was . . .

I don't know. And honestly, I was too tired to care. Another cab rounded the corner and I raised my arm. She tried to wave him off but I locked eyes with the cabbie and brought him in like I was directing traffic at JFK.

"You really gotta go?" she said.

"You've got no idea the day I've had."

"So tell me about it. Let me buy you a drink. We don't have to talk about Laurent."

"What the hell else do you and I have to talk about?"

"Anything you want."

And then it clicked—the thing that might be obvious to you, to the cabbie, to any motherfucker on Fifth Avenue.

She was flirting with me.

She opened those big round eyes and they carved me up like an electric knife. My mouth dried out and my palms got clammy and the small of my back went white hot. I was rummaging through my brain for something clever to say when my hand found the cab's door. I yanked it open and was brought back to my senses by the comforting odor of leather, cigarettes, and farts.

"I'm about four hours late for dinner with my fiancé. Goodbye."

I tossed myself in and slammed the door.

"Eighty-Sixth Street, between Amsterdam and Columbus," I said. Through the deep scratches in the bulletproof glass, I saw the driver nod. From the heat on my back I figured Susan was still looking my way.

So by the time I got home I was a little drunk, a little horny, and beyond tired. We only lived on the second floor but I decided to treat myself to an elevator ride. It made my head spin. I wanted to stagger inside and drop my bag and snuggle up on Toru and watch Carson until we fell asleep. I was halfway down the hallway when I heard the screams.

I entered a scene of complete devastation. Peter was in the middle of the floor, flat on his back, bare-ass naked, arms and legs straight, flexing every muscle in his body and screaming as loud as he could, which is goddamned loud. Toru was crouched over him trying to calm him down. He was also naked, testicles swaying like the pendulum in a grandfather clock, and he had the tight-lipped expression he gets when he's trying very hard not to yell. The room was scattered with paper and flags and postcards and tchotchkes. I dropped my bag and figured I might as well tidy up. Toru told me to stop but I didn't respond fast enough, because suddenly Peter was hammering his little fists against me, shouting, "Don't touch it! Don't touch it! Don't touch it!" and still nobody would tell me what in hell was going on.

So, the family. Where should I start?

The first thing you ought to know is, we all had the same haircut. This wasn't by design. When I met Toru his hair was cropped and mine was flowing. Over the last two years, we'd kind of met in the middle, so that by '72 we had matching shaggy mops. Toru cut his own hair and he did the kids' too—up on the roof, where the pigeons distracted them—so they ended up with the same 'do. It was ridiculous but it looked all right and it marked us as a family unit, which was handy since otherwise we don't look alike at all.

Toru was Japanese-American, born in Yorba Linda in 1932, which meant he had the pleasure of experiencing puberty in an internment camp. He hated this country with sincere passion, but he kept it to himself because it turns out white people don't like being told when they've done something wrong. He spoke Japanese fluently and worked translating American fiction for the Japanese market. He also wrote mystery novels, all in Japanese, about a Nisei insurance salesman, based on his father, whose clients kept winding up dead. He had salt in his hair and lines on his face and heavy, strong hands with calluses that never went away because when he wasn't writing he was usually playing guitar. He loved jazz and wine and the New York Mets, all of which I was happy to consume in moderation as long as I wasn't asked to care.

He'd met his first wife, Gert, at UCLA, then followed her to New York when she came for her PhD. They had one of those idyllic academic relationships—always throwing heady vegetarian dinner parties where associate professors drank too much red wine and got into screaming matches about the true meaning of, I don't know, Thomas Hardy. They got married and had kids and would have lived happily ever after except she wasn't happy at all. Her doctorate stalled after the kids were born and she blamed Toru, the children, New York, and herself in equal measure. For the last year of their marriage she was so depressed that she only left the house eight times. When she suggested divorce, Toru accepted gratefully. She went back to California to finish her doctorate and Toru, single and adrift, signed up for a knitting class. That's when his life turned around because that's where he met me. We got serious fast, and before we knew it, we were engaged and I was moving in. It was a weird situation, with the kids and the ex and the age gap, but he never made me feel anything but easy. He was, in short, a good egg.

Peter, the child currently punching me in the ass, was a seven-year-old who liked arithmetic, Spider-Man, and the subway. He was smart and tense and did not take it well when things went awry. Nicky, four, was the youngest. His interests included hiding things in weird places and playing with his penis. He was like me in that, as long as he had snacks, he rarely complained.

The last and most important member of our family was Lexington, a fat old tuxedo cat who spent his time lying on the windowsill, murdering dust bunnies, and staring hungrily at the pigeons outside. He'd been with me since long before Toru and I met, and I treasured him both as an excellent lap warmer and the last connection to my single life.

"Can I go put something on?" said Toru.

I waved him away, dropped to my knees, and stared into Peter's eyes. They were his father's eyes, hard and brown and sturdy enough to build a pretty nice table. I wished I knew what was going on behind them. His brother had been nuts about me since the second time we met, when I gave him half my Danish. Peter had proven tougher to crack. I didn't expect him to love me and god knows I didn't want him to call me Mom. But I'd seen the way he gave Toru what they called "the flying squirrel hug," when he'd get a running jump and hurl himself through the air, forcing his dad to catch him and squeeze him and swing him around. I hoped to earn one someday.

"Okay, kid," I said. "What the heck is wrong?"

He smeared the tears across his cheeks and gulped, "My project is ruined."

I might have known.

Peter was a first grader at P.S. 164, down near Lincoln Center. When he started there we assumed it was an ordinary city school—the same as the ones that taught me to read and, depending on who you ask, write. But because nothing on the Upper West Side makes sense, P.S. 164's principal had recently been replaced with a distinctly fascist ex-Marine who reworked the entire curriculum around "Excellence, Intensity, and Rigor." To prove his dedication to the new regime, Mr. Salas—Peter's teacher—burdened his students with assignments that made the Manhattan Project look straightforward. The latest was "The Great Box of Europe," for which each kid was asked to collect one "unique object" for every country on the continent. In case your geography is rusty, that's thirty-four things Peter had to find. Thirty-four things that had, for the last two weeks, dominated our lives.

We split the list in half. Many hours were spent racing up and down Manhattan—and into Brooklyn and Queens—acquiring objects that would satisfy Peter's idea of what the project required. Toru and I had, at extreme risk to our sanity, cobbled together everything the list demanded. If you think I was overdoing it to impress a child whose approval I desperately craved, well, you're not wrong.

Toru returned wearing my rainbow-striped nylon robe—very cozy—and leaned on the wall, fighting to keep himself awake. I emptied my purse on the ground. I pawed through subway tokens and Tampax and smeared receipts and empty books of matches to produce a postcard of the pope, a slightly squished cookie, and a tin of bacalao.

"We were still looking for Vatican City, San Marino, and Portugal?" I said. "Well, I got 'em. We're good."

"We're not," muttered Toru.

"What happened?"

Peter gulped some more.

"I had a bad dream and I woke up and I came in here and I wanted to check on the project just to make sure it was okay and, and, and, and—"

"Breathe, kid."

"And Lexington was pooping on Andorra!"

Andorra. That was one of Toru's—a particular coup, I recalled. His brother lived in Barcelona and took a special trip to the principality to acquire a duty-free receipt, which he airmailed at great expense. Toru held up the little slip of paper. No question—it was covered in cat shit.

"Who needs Andorra?" I said. "It's a teeny-weeny little country. Mr. Salas won't even notice it."

"He notices everything. That's part of Rigor. Or Intensity. I can't remember right now."

More tears. I waited to see if Toru wanted to intervene but he let me take the lead, so I opened my arms, and to my surprise, Peter leaned hesitantly against my chest. Not a flying squirrel, but not bad. I squeezed as tight as I could, relishing the simple beauty of problems that can be solved—or at least abated—with a firm hug. I tried not to consider that if things had broken different in Williamsburg, I'd have never seen this goofy little kid again.

Peter cried until my shoulder was soaked, and then, without a word, he wandered toward bed. Toru said, "I got him," and I didn't argue. Peter's bed squeaked as they lay down.

I piled the scattered project into the shoebox on which Peter had written EUROPE in meticulous box letters. I found a postcard that I guessed they'd gotten at the Met—a silver plate that the Portuguese had stolen from South America—which meant my bacalao was redundant. I opened the tin and ate.

"Salty," I said.

Lexington crawled out from under the couch—it was amazing he could squeeze himself under there. He hopped on the counter and sniffed the fish. I pointed at the litter box by the radiator.

"There. Cats shit there."

He nodded and I pretended that meant something and I slid the fish his way. I listened to his lips smacking—do cats have lips? Who cares?—and flipped through the schedule I'd slapped together at the office. Thanks to the kidnapping, I'd gotten through basically none of it. I started copying today's unfinished tasks over to tomorrow, but my pencil was sluggish and I finally laid it down. This was a plan for a reporter. I needed a plan for a detective—and I had no idea what that meant.

So instead of worrying about it, I went into the kitchen to make charlotte russe.

Yeah, I know, I said I was beat but walking into a tantrum always left me high-strung, and anyway, sitting still is not one of my strengths. That's why my leg bounces when I type, why I walk out of movies, why the apartment is littered with books I quit on page 75, why I absolutely adored cigarettes. If something grabs me—like *really* grabs me—I'll forget where I am and time will just melt, but otherwise I get twitchy. This is part of what I love about eating in restaurants. Every course is its own adventure, and even when the food is lousy there's always the suspense of what's coming next. So there was no way I was going to relax after the day I had and I figured if I couldn't relax I might as well cook.

If you've never had charlotte russe, well, I pity you. It's a bunch of ladyfingers molded around a very stiff custard and covered with mounds and mounds of whipped cream. My mom made it every Christmas and I'd decided Toru deserved one for his birthday and that meant it had to be perfection. That was the only way I cooked—I'd practice something over and over and over until it was impeccable and only then would I move on. So the one I made that night was another in a string of practices. The real one I'd do Friday.

I separated eggs and beat sugar into the yolks, dissolved the gelatin and got the milk going in the double boiler. By the time I saw bubbles around the edges, I was breathing halfway steady. The smell of warm milk always slows me down.

Toru emerged from the boys' room looking shell-shocked.

"When did he wake up?" I said.

"A half hour before you got home."

While Susan Gullett was flirting with me. For reasons unrelated to that thought, I handed him a scotch and poured one for myself. I was gonna feel weird tomorrow, I thought, but that had been the case ever since I found my friend's head.

"You wanna talk about Laurent?" he said.

"Not tonight."

"Okay. I'm sorry. Like . . . really, really sorry."

"Me too."

"You should call Dr. Leadon tomorrow—I bet he can fit you in for an extra session. Might help."

I grunted meaninglessly. Now was probably not the time to tell him I'd dumped Dr. Leadon. I tempered the eggs with the hot milk, just like Laurent taught me, then dumped everything back into the double boiler and stirred.

"About your party—" I said.

"Forget my party."

"Absolutely not. Laurent's isn't happening, obviously, so I've been calling around for caterers."

"And?"

"I'll be catering it myself."

"You invited like two dozen people."

"I can cook for two dozen people. Okay, no I can't, but I can buy chips for twenty-four and make, I don't know, five gallons of dip."

"You don't have time to make five gallons of dip."

"I'll do it anyway." I kissed him hard. "It's your fortieth birthday, babe. All you gotta do is show up."

"Where?"

"I'm gonna figure that out tomorrow. I'd have taken care of it today except I got a little bit kidnapped."

Toru set his drink down on the little counter that separated living room and kitchenette. It clinked. I focused on my russe. The stirring part, you really don't want to mess up.

"A little bit *what*?" he said.

"It's not a big deal. Is Carson on yet? Let's watch Carson."

"You got kidnapped!"

"Only slightly! And it really wore me out, so can we please let it go?"

I opened the fridge and grabbed the whipping cream. The first carton had gone lumpo—a common occurrence in our fridge—so I swapped it for a fresh one, rigged up the mixer, and started to whip.

"B," said Toru, his lips tight. "I promise I won't be angry."

So while the cream did its whipping I gave the CliffsNotes on my date with Tiny Tommy. Big surprise, Toru flipped—but the kids were sleeping, so he couldn't yell. He just whispered and stomped around extremely quietly, repeating things like, "They pointed guns at you!"

"Just one gun."

"And drove you to *Williamsburg*."

"It's what the BQE is for. What's your point?"

"I don't know! I can't decide what I'm more upset about—that you provoked a mobster into kidnapping you, that you joined him for dinner afterward, or that the whole thing seemed so unimportant that when you were finished being kidnapped you went out and ate dinner again."

"At the second place I mostly had wine."

"I'm calling the police."

"No way. Tiny Tommy is a source."

His eyes, somehow, went wider. I hadn't ever seen him quite so upset. I felt horrible for five or six reasons—most of all, perhaps, that he was still doing such a good job of not waking up the kids.

"A source who tried to kill you," he said.

"If he'd been trying to kill me, I would be thoroughly dead."

"That isn't reassuring!"

I was pacing then, scanning the room for cigarettes, even though I'd put them all in the garbage a few weeks prior. I fantasized about pulling a pack out of the trash—gritty with coffee and half-chewed apples and absolutely divine.

"This is really bad, B."

"I know. I'm not an idiot. I've never been so scared in my entire life. Which is why I need you to stop freaking out."

"What should I do instead?"

“Get into bed and turn on Carson and act like everything is okay.”

A muffled sob came from the boys’ room. Maybe we’d been whispering louder than we thought. We both froze. After a long moment, we started breathing again.

“Is there anything I can do to change your mind?” he said.

“No.”

“Then I guess we might as well watch Carson.”

“That’s what I’ve been saying this whole time.”

I jammed the russe in the fridge and followed him to bed. He made a face when he saw the bruise on my hip but I shook my head and he didn’t ask any more. I snuggled up and I could feel how tense he was—how tense we both were—but Johnny’s monologue was good and soon we were laughing and our anger drifted away. I was dozing off on Toru’s chest when I remembered I had a question for him.

“How does a detective make a plan?”

He swallowed a yawn.

“Depends if you’re asking an American or a Brit.”

“What’s it matter?”

“A British detective plans every minute. They want alibis for everyone and a minute-by-minute timeline of the fateful day. They weigh every ounce of motive, means, and opportunity. They don’t make a move until their case is airtight.”

“That sounds like me. What about an American?”

“They just stir up shit until the killer outs himself.”

“Sloppy.”

“But a lot more fun.”

I was gonna ask more but his eyes were closed. It had been an awful day—perhaps the worst in my life—which meant tomorrow could only go better. My friend was dead and my job was on the line, but my reporting was off to a good start, and as I slipped out of consciousness, I ducked into my basement and found that, yep, all of my jars were shut tight. Everything was fucked but everything was going to turn out fine.

Nine

• Wednesday •

I dreamed I was strapped to a table and George Wallace was scraping out my guts with an ice cream scoop. It was dull, so it hurt like crazy and made a hell of a mess. And he didn't even use what he scooped out—he just flipped my entrails over his shoulder and shook his head. There was more to it, probably, but the nice thing about quitting analysis is you don't have to think too hard about your dreams—they just happen and they're weird and they go away.

I woke up to Nicky crooning, "This is my penis . . . look at my penis . . . it is my penis . . . look at my penis." It wasn't much of a song but he had perfect pitch, so he sold it pretty good. I opened my eyes to find him fiddling with his little acorn-shaped dick about five inches from my face.

"Yep," I said, "that's your penis."

My day had begun.

I fixed breakfast while Toru wrestled the kids into clothes.

Like the cream, the milk was lumpo, which meant dry cereal, which meant cranky children—or would have if I weren't a damn genius and just gave them big plops of charlotte russe instead. We agreed it was excellent but not perfect—the ladyfingers were dry and the whipped cream wasn't on par with what I'd sampled in Williamsburg the night before. After they ate I watched Toru cram Peter's miserable arms through his backpack straps. I felt awful for being kidnapped, for being flirted with, and I wanted to say something to smooth it all over, but the best I could conjure up was:

"When you're done working, grab milk."

"Don't you want me to take Nicky? I can skip work."

"I said I've got him."

"Yeah, but you're on this crazy deadline, so I just figured—"

"Listen, we made a plan and we're sticking to it. I worked yesterday, you work today." I picked Nicky up by his ankles and bounced him like a yo-yo. He guffawed. "This guy and I are gonna watch TV and practice our ladyfingers."

Toru smiled. I still felt the lingering nausea from last night's fight, so I made our traditional peace offering: "Wanna get dinner from China Garden? Pork lo mein, sesame chicken, the whole thing?"

"Hell yes."

I kissed him and things felt halfway better. Peter stood by the door, clutching his incomplete project, his face a death mask. I crouched and put my hand on his shoulder. He shrugged it off. I said: "You're gonna be okay, kid."

"When?"

Ooh that's a big question. This afternoon? Next month? Never? I was fumbling for an answer when he said, "Dad and I have to go, okay? I don't want to be late."

So they got out of there and I had time to take half a breath before Nicky started screaming for reasons I couldn't divine. I looked around for some toys. It didn't take long to find them—they were everywhere. Toru's apartment was the cutest little two-bedroom in the city, outfitted in dark wood and lush white carpet and those European chairs that look like torture but are actually divine. There were books on every wall, eye-catching lamps, a hi-fi he'd built himself, and a subtle scent of sandalwood in every room. It would have felt oppressively adult if it weren't for the stains on the carpet, the bits of baloney jammed inside the radiators that broiled in the winter and made the whole place stink of old ham, the collapsing cardboard rocket ship that took up half the living room and that Peter and Nicky firmly refused to let Toru throw out. I loved its beauty and its mess. I'd only lived there a year but god it felt like home.

I ducked into the rocket ship, grabbed Nicky's peg puzzles and scattered them across the floor.

"Oh no!" I said. "The puzzle monster messed up all your puzzles."

"Again?"

"Again! Can you put them back together?"

"I'm still missing the camel from the desert puzzle."

"Find it, kid. Today is the day!"

Nicky got to work and so did I. Or I would have, anyway, if Judy hadn't chosen that exact moment to blow my morning to shit.

The phone rang and I grabbed it and she didn't even bother saying hello.

"More bad news."

"How is that even possible?"

"The publisher's had a brain wave. He figures if he's killing the magazine, there's no point waiting. Instead of four issues to say goodbye, we get one."

"Just one?"

"Just one."

My heart gave a heavy thud. I tried to talk. Couldn't. My heart thumped again and I answered Judy with the only word I could find.

"Fuck."

Nicky smiled at me and twirled and sang, "Fuck! Fuck fuck fuck fuck fuck!" Not a very nice song, but still, perfect pitch.

"So forget the Tirel story," said Judy. "Just do your last column and make it count."

"I can't forget the Tirel story."

"You can't get it done in under a week."

"Sure I can."

"B.B., come on. Be realistic."

"When's the latest I could file?"

Her lighter snapped.

"Christ. Saturday noon is the absolute latest."

"I can do that."

"One hundred percent no bullshit dead-ass certain?"

"Yes."

Judy sighed. I ached.

"Because I'll be holding the cover for you. If you fuck this up, you won't just be finished at the *Sentinel*. I'll make sure every editor in New York knows Bernice Black can't deliver."

"You'll have it Saturday. And it'll be the best thing you've ever read."

"Goddamn better be."

I hung up and told Nicky to stop cursing and would have quite liked to collapse into a quivering ball of panic but hey!

There was no time! Instead I swept across the apartment, nerves thumping like a bass drum, planning a rapid-fire tour of the city's best aspics. I pulled on my most forgiving clogs and stuffed my biggest bag full of all the junk the World's Greatest Stepmom needs when she's on the go. Toy cars, *Goodnight Moon*, a fistful of blocks, a half-full box of graham crackers, and a couple of changes of clothes because even though Nicky had gotten better at not peeing in his pants, he wasn't going to win any awards. I jammed the kid in the Strollee, and bang, we were ready to go.

"What happened to ladyfingers?" he said as we waited for the elevator.

"B.B. has to work."

He was singing as we cut across the park—something less profane, thankfully—and it was a beautiful damn day and I would have been singing too except my schedule was in tatters. There was no more waiting for Près du Parc. Henri and I were having our reunion *now*.

All right, so before we can proceed we're gonna need a brief history of my supposed heterosexuality. I came of age in the mid-fifties, when girls were expected to swoon over Elvis and James Dean and, I don't know, Marlon Brando. But James Dean was heartbreaking and Elvis was twitchy and Brando made my skin crawl. So while other girls were moaning about how much they wanted to be smooched by rock and roll stars, I was quietly day-dreaming about being pinned to the floor by Gene Kelly's thighs. (If the notion of Gene Kelly's thighs doesn't stir anything in you, you've clearly never seen *The Pirate*.) None of the boys in Park Slope moved like Gene Kelly—no boys anywhere moved like Gene Kelly—so I basically ignored them until I went to Queens. The point is I was a virgin when I got to college and I stayed that way until I met Henri Tirel.

Yeah, Tirel. As in Laurent's kid. And if you're thinking that sounds like a mess, you're not wrong. I was twenty and he was a rakish twenty-five, blue eyed with sunken cheeks and a way of staring like he could see through walls. He snarled French and butchered lambs, he treated his knives like they were holy weapons, he drank too much in a way that seemed mysterious. The first time I heard him say *aubergine,* I was toast. We were together for nine feverish months—nine months in which he snuck me into every great kitchen in Manhattan and introduced me to every hot young chef. We ate and talked and talked and ate and somewhere in there found time for sex. (Remember what I said about being splayed out on the prep table? That was his idea.) Even as a virgin I could tell he was terrible in bed—he was always *apologizing*—but his exceptional mediocrity just made me appreciate his cooking more.

It's romantic, isn't it—I'd think as I scraped another mouthful of pâté onto a piece of toast—he's so dedicated to his art that he forgot how to fuck.

We might have gotten married if it weren't for Laurent's waiters. They went on strike in 1966, complaining the old man didn't pay enough and wouldn't let them rotate stations to spread out their tips. After two months, he fired the lot of them and replaced them with scabs. Henri quit out of solidarity, which was definitely the right thing to do but I was so loyal to Laurent I didn't see it that way. I called Henri ungrateful and he called me a spoiled bitch and after that things fell apart rather quickly.

I hardly thought about him until 1970, when he opened Près du Parc, a cozy bistro on Sixty-First that was homey and authentic and everything Laurent disdained. I didn't have the balls to review it, so I fobbed it off on Ambrose. He said it was mediocre, and while I'm sure he was right, I doubt Henri took it well.

I walked Nicky past the zoo because I thought he'd get a kick out of the sea lions, but he got pissy when I said we couldn't go inside. He was still moaning about how he "wanted to see the polar beeeeeear" when we spilled onto Fifth Ave. At the majestic sandstone apartment building that housed Près du Parc, I disentangled him from the stroller. I tried to fold it but the hinges had rusted, so I just dumped it by the restaurant door, figuring the mothers and nannies of the Upper East Side wouldn't be caught dead stealing that piece of junk. I pulled open the door and was walloped by the smell of crackling chicken skin, rosemary, and salt.

"This place is disgusting," said Nicky.

He was wrong. Près du Parc was picture perfect, long and low, with the passage between the tables just wide enough for a waiter with a really narrow ass. Faded floral curtains covered the windows, blocking out most of the light and giving the place a cozy, nighttime vibe. There was no chintzy crap on the walls—just a long mural of frolicking, Gauguinesque nudes that Henri's sister had flown in from Paris to paint. The rest of the walls were dusky rose; the floors were pale wood and every surface was spotlessly clean.

It would have been enchanting if it weren't for the assholes at the bar.

It was Henri and Oswald Blount—pronounced "Blownt," god knows why—the owner of Laurent's. Henri wore pressed chef's whites and Oswald was squeezed into a powder-blue sports shirt with a collar crisp enough to slice onions. His hair was a shaggy blond mop; his sunglasses covered half his face; his corduroys were painted on.

At first I thought they were dancing but then I realized they were trying to have a fight. They weren't very good at it. Henri was shoving Oswald in the vague direction of the door; Oswald was trying to push Henri into the kitchen using his butt? I think? But then he tripped over a barstool and went sprawling. Henri lifted his foot like he was gonna stomp on Oswald. Oswald dragged him down him by the ankle and they rolled around on the floor, kicking and mewling like ferrets.

"What the hell is going on?" I said.

They didn't answer. So I grabbed a pot of daffodils and emptied it across their backs. They came apart like spent lovers, eyes unfocused, chests heaving. Henri got up first. He'd gotten older, which wasn't a surprise—it happens to most of us—but it bummed me out. His mouth drooped. His jawline had softened. But his eyes were so bright they looked crimson. I wasn't sure I'd ever seen him so mad.

"What's wrong?" I said.

"He came to gloat about Dad's death."

"I came to give condolences," said Oswald, whose voice had the piercing whine of a leaky radiator. "Laurent was a very dear friend—not just to me, to my father and my whole family for god's sake—and I thought we could have an adult conversation about what's next for the restaurant."

"Which is what?"

Oswald broke into the kind of smile that usually gets a man punched in the teeth.

"Laurent's was an institution. Which is a beautiful thing, sure, but it also meant that when it turned to shit nobody dared complain."

"Fuck you," said Henri.

Nicky, amazed that grown-ups could behave so badly, wrapped himself around my leg.

"Hey, assholes," I said. "I've got a kid here. Can we please keep it halfway clean?"

"I just thought Henri deserved to hear that his father's place was fifteen years behind the *doggone* times," said Oswald, smiling bigger than ever. "That I'm in advanced discussions with a prominent local chef—let's call him Vic A.—to come in, modernize the menu, make the food and the décor about fifty pounds lighter, and turn the place around. That's all I said—and this lunatic went for my throat."

"Why?"

Henri pulled a bottle of gin from behind the bar. He poured a shot and downed it in one.

"Because the restaurant is mine," he said. "Maybe not legally—I know Oswald owns it—but spiritually it is *mine*."

"Spiritually doesn't count for shit," said Oswald.

"I mean, that's not wrong," I said.

"Dad wanted me to take it over," said Henri, glaring like he'd caught me trying to steal his kidneys.

"Oh yeah?" said Oswald. "Lemme guess—he told you over a nice bottle of Chateau Who Gives a Shit, some private heart-to-heart that nobody else heard."

Henri sneered. "He wrote it in a letter."

"Bullshit," said Oswald, without much conviction. Nicky squeezed my leg tighter. I rubbed his little head.

"A formal letter," said Henri, almost gloating. "Notarized and everything, saying he wanted me to take it over when he was gone."

"Let's see it," I said.

"No," said Henri. "It's personal."

"You mean it's make-believe!" Oswald's voice was sweaty with relief. He smoothed his already-smooth hair one more time and strolled toward the door, cackling like one of the animals that Nicky and I didn't see at the zoo. "Christ, Tirel, you almost had me scared. I forgot you don't know your ass from an ass-shaped hole in the ground."

"You're not supposed to say that word," said Nicky. Oswald scowled like the kid was a talking rat, then yanked open the door and was gone. Henri took another shot of gin. He wiped his mouth and caught my eye in the mirror and snarled, "What do you want?"

"Well, I came for aspic but now I think I'd like to see that letter."

"Not without a lawyer present."

"Come on, I'm cuter than Oswald. Don't you trust me?"

"Not since the day you walked out."

Had Henri's face always been so red? It was like an old tomato, cracked and wrinkled and sopping wet. He looked ready to drop dead. It was weird to think how recently I'd loved this man.

"There's no letter, is there?" I said.

"Excuse me. I have work to do."

He shoved through the swinging door. Nicky crawled under a table and started mooing, which was lovely but would get old fast. I grabbed the Matchbox cars and hid one under a napkin, one in an upturned wineglass, and left the third out in the open because kids get crabby if games are actually hard.

"There's three cars hidden in this room," I said. "Find 'em all and I'll give you something sweet."

He hopped to it. I pushed into the kitchen, which was cramped and messy and smelled like sizzling fat and fresh herbs, like spilled vinegar and crisp greens. Henri was the only one there. He was in the middle of about eight different things, including seasoning the soup, mincing veg, and prodding something in the oven. His torso was sweating like a cocktail in the sun. He was moving fast but looked like if he sat down for even a second, he'd sleep for a year.

"No staff?" I said.

"Turns out it's cheaper if you do all of the work yourself."

"You'll kill yourself working like that."

"I bring a couple guys in for dinner, okay, and weekends. And don't act concerned, Bernice, like you've thought about me once in the last five years. I'm extremely busy and I absolutely don't have time."

"I found one!" screamed Nicky from the dining room.

"Great, baby. Keep looking!"

"Your kid is cute," said Henri without looking at me.

"He's my fiancé's."

I hit the word *fiancé* as hard as I could. Henri scowled as he tipped a few dozen hard-boiled eggs into an ice water bath. I grabbed one and peeled, enjoying the weird warmth of it pulsing against my palm.

"So about the letter," I said.

"Okay, fine. I don't have it."

"But you've seen it?"

"No."

"Then how do you know it's real?"

"You know C.J. Corrales, Dad's bartender? She was there when he wrote it. She read the whole thing over his shoulder. He wanted the kitchen to go to me."

"But he knew it was Oswald's call."

"Legally, maybe. But morally? My dad built that place. I deserve the job."

"Why?"

He stared, slick with sweat and grief and worry, and somewhere in his face I saw the guy I'd loved like a maniac once upon a time.

"Because I'm his son."

"I found the second one!" shouted Nicky.

"One more, kid!"

Henri seized a goose (dead) and smacked it against the counter until its ankles went *crack*. He reached for a paring knife.

"Wait, did you say you came here for aspic?" he said.

"I'm doing a thing for the magazine, 'Manhattan's Best Aspics.' Thought I'd start with you."

"What is it, 1955? We don't serve it."

"Make one anyway."

"No."

I sighed, steeling myself for what I had to ask next.

"Then let's talk about the other story I'm working on. The death of Laurent Tirel."

He slit the goose's skin and slipped his fingers inside its legs, gripping them like they were the stems of some gruesome bouquet, then squatted on the floor.

"Did you kill him?" I said.

"Go to hell."

"I'll call that a no. Where were you Monday during the day?"

"Here."

"I can't find it!" screamed Nicky. "I can't find it."

My jaw clenched.

"Can anybody vouch for you?" I asked Henri, trying to ignore the kid.

"I talked to the doorman next door when I came in, about seven-thirty. He's an older guy, Black, bald. I don't know his name. And after eleven-thirty there were customers who ate food, which wouldn't have been possible if I'd been out murdering my dad."

He pulled hard, ripping off the goose's feet, tendons and all. It was just like uncorking a bottle—*pop*. He tipped onto his butt, smacking into the oven and sending his hat flying. Beneath was a shining bald dome. Poor bastard. He used to have such beautiful curls. He stood up, slapped the duck onto the cutting board and cut off its head.

Nicky screamed louder: "Why did you make this so hard?" I bit my lip. I was way over time.

"What'd you do the rest of Monday?" I said.

"The whole day? Lunch lasts until two-thirty but the last party was a group of old ladies from Tallahassee and I couldn't get them to fuck off until after three. Normally I grab an hour of sleep in the back room but I was behind on prep, so I just worked until we opened back up at six. My sous, a local kid named Greg Allen, can confirm I was there."

"What time does he show up?"

"Five. I was with him until close."

Henri stepped back from the cutting board, grinning and bloody. Nicky howled like he was getting eaten by a crocodile. I talked louder.

"Question three: Who do you think killed Laurent?"

"Shouldn't you go check on that kid?"

"Answer the question."

"I'd bet everything I own that the killer is on my father's payroll."

"Why?"

"The place was a snake pit. César hated him. Jean-Louis is an ice-cold bastard—he sold out his entire waitstaff during the strike. The new waiters are all burnouts and weirdos. The maintenance guys are creeps. And I don't know what C.J. is about but she steals from the register and I wouldn't be surprised if she sold dope too."

I jotted that down.

"Speaking of dope, was your father a heroin addict?"

He laughed.

"Get out of my kitchen before I lose my damn mind."

He held the door open for me. I stood in the doorway while Nicky glared. His face was red and streaky, his eyes full of contempt.

"Where is the third car!"

I pointed at the table. He'd missed the one I'd left in plain sight. Kids—they're real smart and real dumb at the same time. While he cradled it to his chest, I turned back to Henri.

"Your eggs are overdone."

"That's slander."

"Two minutes, maybe three. The one I ate had that little gray ring around the yolk. Most unsightly."

He tore an egg in half and stared into its soul. He didn't like what he saw. It went in the garbage along with the rest of them—a handy illustration of why Henri was miserable, why he was broke. Just like his dad, the poor bastard had standards.

"Let's say you're able to browbeat Oswald into hiring you," I said. "What would you do with the place?"

"Dad's menu was a mess. He was serving beef stroganoff. Deviled chicken. Minute steak. I'd start from scratch. Cook what French people eat. Not champagne and caviar. Actual food—sweetbreads, kidneys, calf brains, liver, tripe. And I'd never settle for good enough."

"You'd do a good job."

"I *always* do a good job."

"So why are you scared to make me an aspic?"

"Excuse me?"

"Admit it, man. You're stretched so thin, you can't even boil an egg. I don't think you could fix me an aspic if your life depended on it."

He poured another shot of gin. Hell of a breakfast.

"My aspic makes angels weep," he said, "but it takes time."

"Wonderful. I'll come back tomorrow."

"Fuck you. Fine."

Nicky tugged at my dress, smiling like he'd never shed a tear.

"You said I'd get something sweet," he said.

"And you will, darling. At our next stop."

We left Henri to his drink. The stroller was right where we'd parked it. While I got Nicky strapped in, I gabbed with the doorman, who confirmed that, yup, he'd seen Henri come in around seven forty-five on Monday and hadn't seen him leave before his shift ended at three. Child and alibi secured, we marched into the dying morning, noses aimed at Midtown, mouths ready to swallow Manhattan whole.

Ten

The Sherbet Room was a bust, their famous parsleyed ham in aspic cloudy and rubbery and missing the sweet something-or-other that made the one at Laurent's so striking. I got Nicky a gorgeous plate of French fries—thick and crisp, greased flanks sparkling with salt—but he declared them "Way too hot!" and refused to take a bite. His loss.

Nicky alternated between singing the penis song and bitching about his "rumbly tummy" while I strollered us over to Aragvi, a once-proud restaurant at the tail end of a tragic fall from grace. Once the best Russian spot in New York, it had relocated to the basement of the United Nations in 1966 and hadn't been heard from since. Their appetizer cart boasted a staggering array of aspics, inside of which floated boiled chicken and smoked fish, cured meats and steamed veg and fruit the wrong side of brown. I jabbed one. It was like poking a brick wall.

A burly waiter with an improbable mustache appeared behind me. I tried to act like I wasn't doing anything weird.

"You poke it, you buy it," he said, so I gave him three bucks, which was highway robbery, and turned the Strollee around. When it clicked with Nicky that he'd have to keep waiting for his promised sweet, he started crying, so on the way out, we soothed our disappointment by stopping at their scale model of the UN and stealing a fistful of toothpick flags.

A whiny half hour later, we were at Atmosphere, twenty-two floors above Forty-Fifth Street, a sun-blasted dining room that was all shimmering glass and plastic pastels. One hundred lunching ladies in flowing kaftans and bouncing hats flitted table to table like girls in the high school cafeteria, kissing cheeks and fumigating the air with Smirnoff. We'd been waiting for our food for what seemed like an hour. Nicky was edgy and I was feeling the stress of a morning wasted when I spotted Elma Zumwalt flirting with a waiter at the bar and figured that maybe I could get something out of this expedition after all. I caught her eye and she swooped in like a bird of prey. Her sunglasses were so big I could hardly see her face and her perfume was thick enough to choke a goose. I'd spent my adult life surrounded by women like this, I thought—no wonder it took me so long to realize I was bisexual.

"I need your help," I said.

"Burn your wardrobe and cut your hair."

"Easy, girl. I'm not looking for a makeover. It's about Henri Tirel."

"Ah! I heard there was a scuffle at Près du Parc this morning. I thought you might be involved."

I shook my head, genuinely awed.

"How do you get this stuff so fast?"

"My birdies are everywhere, dearie, particularly on the Upper East Side. It just so happens that my chiropodist's psychic has a lover in the building adjoining Près. She was in his lobby when she heard two men shrieking through the walls. Was it about you?"

"Hardly. They were fighting over a letter Laurent supposedly wrote laying out his plans for the restaurant. Know anything about that?"

"I'm ashamed to admit it, but you're far more plugged into the whole eating scene than I. I remember Laurent was close to César, that hateful little maître d' with the impossible eyebrows. Have you spoken to him?"

"He's on my list."

"And what about that bartender? The shaggy, scowling brunette?"

"C.J.? I hear she steals from the till. Maybe sells dope."

"Oh, who cares about dope? This is *sex*, Bernie! It's an open secret—every night Laurent was balling her in the back room." She shot a glance at Nicky, who was squirming miserably in one of New York's least comfortable chairs. "An ugly image, I know, but it's true."

This was only mildly shocking. C.J. was at least thirty years younger than Laurent but she would hardly be the first girl in Midtown to saddle herself to a powerful older man. It wasn't much but it was better than nothing. I was jotting it down when the food arrived: carrot cake for Nicky and a trio of aspics for me—mixed fruit, sliced asparagus, chunked trout. The fruit was tasteless; the trout was like canned tuna and the asparagus was basically raw. The aspic was the same for all three—totally flavorless, like it had been made with water.

"Thin stock," I said. "Not enough salt. I don't even think this qualifies as food."

The carrot cake was worse: a clump of crumbs and cream cheese that looked like it had been stepped on by the entire kitchen. Nicky stared at it like he was about to cry.

"It looks disgusting," he mumbled. My ears twitched, like an old dog detecting a far-off thunderstorm. A tantrum was coming and there was nothing to do but take cover.

"Come on, kid. You might as well try it."

Nicky smeared a fistful of cake into his mouth. He coughed, spraying crumbs across the table. He laid his face down beside the plate.

"It's disgusting," he moaned. I signaled for the check.

"I'm not surprised," said Elma. "Nobody comes to Atmosphere for the food. It's a place to f-u-c-k and get f-u-c-k-ed. But if you're looking for aspics, well, I'm not supposed to be telling anyone this but I met Rocky Shanklin at a party last week and it just so happens that he invited me back to Number 5 for a private sampling of his aspic."

"Was it any good?"

"Everything I tasted was divine."

She winked theatrically and drifted away. Nicky crushed the remainder of the cake with his palm, then wiped his hand on his slacks. His mouth tightened into a scowl. Fuck the check, I thought. Let's try our luck at Number 5.

I threw down some cash and hustled Nicky out of the dining room, hoping I could get us clear before he erupted. I snagged a fistful of pastel mints from the maître d's station to tide him over. He shoved them all in his mouth at once. His face turned purple and he spat them all over the carpet and screamed, "These are also disgusting!" I'd have cleaned them up, I swear, but the elevator doors opened and he bolted inside and I had to leave the slimy mints smeared across Atmosphere's once-immaculate shag.

He screamed the whole way down, his little voice ricocheting off the steel walls and slicing directly through my skull. Three women who were functionally identical to Elma Zumwalt stared at me, smiles thin enough to give papercuts, waiting for me to lose my cool. I felt guilty and embarrassed and generally pissed off, but I didn't let any of that crack my plastic babysitter's smile. When we got downstairs I asked Nicky to get into the stroller and he just screamed louder—"Disgusting! Disgusting!"—so I picked him up and he flexed all his muscles and screamed like he was being dismembered as I wrestled his little arms through the jelly-sticky straps. He just about broke all my fingers but I got him in.

He howled for six blocks but I barely heard it. I was too busy figuring out how I was gonna get the chef of a restaurant that wasn't technically open to make aspic for me and *anything* for Nicky. I guess I got pretty distracted because we were halfway to Central Park when I noticed a miracle.

Nicky's fists were limp in his lap. Little snores tickled his nostrils. The kid was asleep.

Suddenly the sun shone brighter, birds sang better, and flowers bloomed in every crack of the piss-stained sidewalk. It was time for my second interview with the genius behind Number 5.

Nobody knew where Rocky Shanklin came from. He'd materialized the year before out of a fog of hash smoke and killer PR. One day, no one had heard his name. The next day, he was the only thing the city's serious eaters could talk about.

"I hear he taught himself to cook after he had a vision from god."

"Word is he only cooks veggies."

"Word is he only cooks meat."

"Word is he only cooks naked."

"Word is he only cooks high."

"A friend of mine said he fixed a burger so good it made the pope cry."

And then one day last spring, a note appeared in my box at the magazine offices, gold letters on thick stock, like a summons from the queen:

YOU ARE TO APPEAR AT THE FUTURE SITE OF
NUMBER 5 (30 CENTRAL PARK SOUTH)
FOR AN INTERVIEW WITH ROCKFORD SHANKLIN.
MAY 17, 1971. TEN A.M. COME HUNGRY.

I'd have liked to ignore it but interviewing assholes is a big part of my job and this Rockford character seemed like the biggest asshole to come along in a while. If he could cook, well, so much the better. So on the appointed morning, I found myself in a cavern on Central Park South, hungry as hell. I stood and I stood and by the time Rocky showed—ninety-four minutes late—and announced he didn't have "the proper alignment to cook today, so let's just rap, yeah?" it was all I could do not to stab my pen through his eye. He was tall and stoned and gorgeous, with blond locks that tumbled past his shoulders, dreamy green eyes, and pouting Jagger lips. He wore platform heels that had him scraping the ceiling and a paisley top unbuttoned to his navel and everything he said either talked himself up or tore other people down.

"Laurent's a tired old hack," he decreed. "The city doesn't belong to the Butter Boys anymore. They're dead, man, and dead men don't cook."

Judy gave it the cover—"Dead Men Don't Cook!" underneath

a glamour shot of Rocky and a subhead that called him "The Angry Young Chef of Central Park South." I hated him for picking on Laurent and I hated myself for letting it happen. I spent that whole spring dreading the eventual opening of Number 5. I figured it would be a huge hit, that it would make Laurent seem even less relevant, even more pathetic, but spring turned into summer and summer staggered into fall and the howling of his PR flacks dropped to whispers and still the restaurant did not appear. Nobody knew why.

I wasn't even sure how Nicky and I would get into the restaurant, but when we reached the peeling blue concrete wall that marked the entrance to Number Five, I saw that not only was the door not locked, the place didn't even have a door. I backed the stroller over the two-by-four frame, and hey, we were in.

It smelled of wet paint and cured meat. Electrical cords and construction junk clogged the entryway, but the gear was dusty and there was no sound of anybody doing work. I pulled around the corner and found a set of white stairs that wound three levels down to the place where, someday, theoretically, a dining room would be.

It looked like it had been halfway built and halfway demolished and halfway built a few more times. Six types of lamp dangled from the ceiling. The balcony was a graveyard of mismatched chairs. One wall was blue, another blood orange, another painted with a strikingly realistic pornographic mural. There was a bathtub in the middle of the floor with a man curled up inside it. I felt a stab of worry—*another* dead body?—but then he started to snore.

Boy, I thought as I hefted the stroller down the stairs. Things have really started to break my way!

I wrecked my back getting Nicky down the steps but it was

worth it because he didn't stir. I peered into the bathtub—a chipped cast-iron model like you see in old tenements—and discovered a young man with bright orange curls and ostentatious sideburns. He was wearing a shit-brown shirt and holding a bowl of melted ice cream that was dripping steadily across his chest.

This was Shipley Merritt, Number 5's chief backer and PR mastermind—the guy who'd kept me company while his beautiful young genius made me wait, telling me about all the marvelous things Rocky was going to cook for me, none of which I ever got to taste. I considered waking him up but then I remembered that I hated this guy. Let him sleep.

So I slipped into the kitchen, figuring that if Rocky was cooking aspic in between f-u-c-k-ing Elma Zumwalt, there might be some of it lying around. But the kitchen was rancid—moldy vegetables on the floor and rotting meat on the counter, every pot thick with flies and blackened grime—and the walk-in was jammed with six hundred pounds of sweet potatoes and no aspics at all. I opened a cabinet, figuring that if nothing else I might snag something for Lexington the cat or Nicky the kid. I found a piece of paper taped to the inside of the door:

IDEAS FOR #5

American!

English?

Swedish-French!

French but also Indian & Japanese?

Everything fresh

Everything CANNED

Just Beets!

Persian????

New Orleans Minimalism

Florida Maximalism

BYO Vegetables

A Fish for Every Feeling

Pork Pork Pork Lamb & Pork

That was a tenth of it. I was still reading when three things came from the dining room—

A scream.

A thump.

Silence.

I vaulted over the pass-through and landed awkwardly on the unfinished floor. Nicky was fine, thank god—he was still in his stroller—but the scream had woken him and as soon as he saw me he started to howl. Tears rolled down his cheeks like soggy boulders and every part of me wanted to rush to him but first I had to check on the guy lying at the foot of the stairs. He was wearing a skintight canary-yellow turtleneck and a pair of leather jeans with fringe blooming from the crotch. He was lying at a hideous angle: head on the floor, body splayed across the lower steps. Blood gushed from his forehead. My heart was pounding so hard that it took me a minute to realize I knew who he was.

French Vic Anglade.

What the hell was he doing here?

"I need to pee," screeched Nicky.

"Gimme a minute."

"But I need to pee now!"

Was Vic's neck broken? I brushed my fingertips across it—a hell of a joke, as if I could recognize a broken neck by touch. He groaned. That was good, I figured. Dead guys don't groan.

"B.B.!"

"B.B.'s working, baby."

"I'm going to have an *accident*."

And that I really didn't need. So I left Vic to his bleeding and got Nicky out of the stroller and pointed to the corner.

"No way," he said. "I wanna bathroom."

"I know you do, baby, but this guy fell down the stairs and I'm trying to help him and this is a construction site, so just go on the wall."

"Uh . . . I don't really have to pee anymore."

"No kidding."

"But I'm very, very hungry. I'm so hungry, B.B., I think I'll probably die."

I could have brought up the French fries he'd refused earlier, but what was the point? Instead I fished through my bag and came up with a crumbling graham cracker. He accepted it like a martyr and was moaning about how disgusting it tasted when Anglade's eyes fluttered open and he said, "Soup."

"Why are you here?"

"Soup!"

"You need a hospital."

"What I need is fucking soup."

His eyes snapped shut. I thought he'd lost consciousness but then he rolled onto his butt and twisted his neck until it gave a satisfying crack. I stood up, scanning for a phone so I could get this asshole an ambulance. He grabbed my wrist. He smiled so big I could see the blood collecting in the cracks of his teeth.

"If you make me soup, I'll tell you who killed Laurent Tirel."

I stared, trying to figure out if he was totally full of shit or just halfway. But then Nicky started chanting, "Soup! Soup! Soup!"

and I figured tomato soup takes twenty minutes. If I hurried, I could squeeze it in.

So I chucked Nicky a red crayon and told him to draw on the walls. He didn't argue—pissing on the walls is verboten but apparently drawing on them is okay. I slammed into the kitchen, found a pot that wasn't completely filthy, fired up the stove, and chopped an onion and tossed it in oil. I gave it a minute, then dumped in a can of tomatoes and some dried thyme and salt. The smell put life into Vic. He came into the kitchen, blood on his clothes and a cigarette dangling from his lips, and said, "Thanks."

I tossed him a rag.

"Keep that on the wound. You'll probably need stitches but that's your problem, not mine. Now, who killed Laurent?"

"Soup first."

"You don't know a thing, do you?"

He shrugged. French people are so goddamned good at shrugging, I thought. They must learn it in school.

"At least tell me why you're here," I said.

"Rocky and I are pals, you know? I've been trying to help him get this place back on track."

"What's wrong with it?"

"He's a perfectionist, y'know, with too many ideas. Anyway, I guess I've been working too hard, because I tripped down the stairs."

"You're sure you weren't pushed?"

"Yeah. Pretty sure."

He leaned on the wall, eyes closed again. He was lying about something—maybe two or three somethings—but before I could call him on it, more bullshit poured out of his mouth.

"I'm just so broken up about Laurent. He was a great chef, a great man. It's a tragedy, understand?"

I flipped through my notebook.

"Yesterday you said he was 'a despicable son of a bitch.' That you are 'exquisitely pleased that he is dead.'"

"I was in shock."

"You sure it wasn't a call from Oswald Blount that changed your tune?"

His eyes snapped open.

"Why? Did you hear something?"

"I talked to Oswald this morning."

"Did he mention me? Am I getting the job?"

He pulled the cigarette from his mouth and rubbed it so tightly between thumb and forefinger that the paper tore.

"Why do you want it so bad?" I said.

"You think I'm a hypocrite. I get it. But I used to admire Laurent. In France, after the war, we'd lost everything. Maybe Laurent was a prick but that restaurant . . . it gave us hope. What's happened to it is a tragedy. I want to bring it back."

"Inspire the next generation of French kiddos."

"And the ones after that."

He smiled at nothing in particular. It was the first time I'd ever seen him, I think, that he didn't look tired.

"You want it bad enough to kill for?" I said, giving my soup a stir.

His smile switched off. He opened his mouth but didn't get a chance to answer, because that was when the pantry door exploded and Rocky Shanklin stormed onto the scene. He was shirtless, chest matted with golden hair, muscles so shiny that he might have been greased with butter. Viking curls framed his face like chains. His jeans were as tight as a snake's skin and his feet were filthy and bare.

"Don't you touch my fucking stove!"

I stepped back, hands raised. He slapped off the burner and slammed my pot into the back wall, spritzing the steel red.

"I'm wrecked, man," said Vic. "I need that soup."

Rocky smacked him. The sound echoed and died. Vic spent a moment inspecting the ceiling, trying to decide if he should hit back, then flicked his cigarette on the floor and marched into the dining room. As the door swung, I caught a glimpse of Nicky scribbling happily on the wall.

"You good, baby?" I called, increasingly aware that this wasn't the kind of place where the World's Greatest Stepmom brings kids.

"I want soup!"

"It's almost done."

Rocky picked up Vic's cigarette and popped it into his mouth. I probably should have gotten out of there but there were things I needed to ask. His fury seemed to have ebbed, anyway, or he was embarrassed. He pulled my soup toward him like he'd just noticed it.

"Don't you dare ash in my soup," I said.

"Tomato, huh?"

"Very observant."

"You want me to puree it?"

"Sure."

He thumped around for a bamix—a Swiss immersion blender that I'd only seen in magazines. It looked like a torture device—scratch that, a murder device—and I took a step back as he whipped my soup into a bloody foam. He turned the thing off, tasted the soup, and smiled. I reached for it and he shoved my hand away.

"It needs to cool. Your kid likes grilled cheese?"

"Most days."

"I'm not serving tomato soup without grilled cheese."

He yanked a block of cheddar from the walk-in, grabbed a loaf of sourdough and sliced.

"Who are you anyway?"

"Bernice Black." Recognition flickered across his face but it didn't click. "*New York Sentinel.*"

"You interviewed me, huh?"

"Sort of. Mostly you monologued and I wrote it down. That was almost a year ago. You don't look any closer to opening."

"Nope."

"Vic says you've got too many ideas."

He tapped his temple.

"Damn right. I mean, we're operating pretty far past the edge of reason here. I wanna cook things nobody's ever tasted before. Shipley and his buddies are nervy but there's no sense pulling the trigger until we're sure the gun is loaded."

He dropped a skillet onto the burner and flipped in a plug of butter. It screamed. He lowered the sandwiches onto the heat. I did more rummaging. A can of imported brisling sardines made their way happily into my purse.

"I saw your concepts," I said.

"Concepts! Those are more than concepts. They're full menus. Weeks of work on every one. They're all goddamned brilliant."

"Even everything canned?"

"Especially everything canned. You ever eat canned peaches on a hot day? Nothing better. Right now I'm thinking 'Eat with Your Hands.' Y'know, like kids do? Only it's too predictable to do hand-friendly food. We'd serve stews and salads and spaghetti and pudding and, I dunno, soufflés."

"Sounds like a mess."

"Hell yeah! You'd never eat the same again. What we're trying to get at is a whole new universe of flavor and texture and taste. We're not here to suck off Escoffier. We're here to suck off, like, the gods."

"Elma Zumwalt told me you'd been playing around with aspics."

He smirked. It wasn't as cute as he thought it was.

"I made five or ten. Did an applesauce aspic on pork medallions, one jammed full of watercress, another streaked with this boiled vegetable paste I'm screwing around with. They were a scene."

"Got any left?"

"Storage room, spare fridge."

The storage room was a storage room—you've seen 'em—and the spare fridge was an ancient blue model like the one my uncle kept in his garage when I was a kid. The light didn't turn on. It smelled of rot. Inside I found black greens and spoiled pork floating in goo. I stuck a finger into one of the least-rancid-looking mounds and tasted the slop. It wasn't terrible, but at that consistency it was very hard to tell.

"Your fridge is unplugged," I called.

"That explains the stench."

God damn it. All this bullshit and I'd learned zilch. It was like getting kicked in the spine. I wasn't sad, precisely—I was exhausted.

He flipped the sandwiches out of the pan. On their pale brown crust, butter beaded like gold. His knife dropped through, guillotine sharp. He piled them onto a silver tray, ladled out soup, and backed into the dining room. Nicky scurried over. Rocky called for Vic but Vic didn't answer—he'd fallen asleep against the tub. I thought about trying to wake him—he'd promised me a killer's name in exchange for soup—but he was so addled that even if he had known anything useful, I doubt I'd have been able to extract it.

I tasted the soup and was unsurprised to find it perfect—tomato soup was one of the first things I'd mastered, back in college. I took a bite of the sandwich and felt my opinion of Rockford Shanklin soften. It wasn't just that the sandwich was excellent—that was to be expected, the guy was a pro—but it was how simple he'd made it. Chefs were usually embarrassed to cook for children and they'd cover it up by getting cute. Ask 'em for grilled cheese and they'd overload it with homemade mayo or spicy relish or ketchup that tasted like tomatoes instead of wet sugar. The result, invariably, was a pissed-off kid. But Nicky dipped his sandwich in the soup, took a bite, and said, "It's good." As far as kids go, there's no higher praise.

"Thanks, man," said Rocky. "I like your drawing."

"It's Spider-Man farting out spiders."

"Very, very cool."

Nicky wandered away, licking his sandwich.

"What's wrong with Vic?" I asked.

"Heroin. Me and him and Shipley had a little party last night and I guess it takes the old-timers a little longer to bounce back."

I nodded as casually as I could manage, like watching junkies fall down the stairs was something I did every day.

"Is that, like . . . a casual thing?"

"For me, yeah. But Vic, shit, lately he prefers it to salt."

"It's a new habit?"

"Off and on for a long time. Fucked him up pretty bad. It's the reason Laurent fired him in the fifties, the reason he went back to France. But he's been talking a lot about getting clean and I think he's serious."

"Why?"

"Well, you've gotta have motivation, right? For some people it's god. For other people it's their kids. For him it's Laurent's."

"You think he'll get the job?"

"He fucking deserves it. He and Laurent had worked through their old shit. Laurent was planning to retire and wanted Vic to take over. He put it in a letter."

"You seen it?"

"'Course not. He and Vic signed it in blood, like you do, and sealed it up in the restaurant wall."

More bullshit, I thought. Talk to chefs and that's all you get. I crunched another mouthful of sandwich. It's no great revelation but melted cheese tastes good.

"What were you doing Monday between noon and two?" I said.

"Shopping on the Bowery for tablecloths, prep tables, a new grill top."

"Can anybody confirm that?"

"Nope."

"Did you get receipts?"

"Does this place look like I'm tracking how much I spend?" He fondled his chair leg. "Wait a minute! Do you think I killed Laurent?"

"I don't know. Did you?"

"Fuck no! I'm a creature of peace and pleasure and fornication and love. Murder is decidedly not my bag."

Not my bag. I wrote that down and underlined it.

"So who do you think did it?"

"Whatshisname, the maître d'."

"César? Why?"

He jammed the rest of his sandwich into his mouth—the guy

eats just like Nicky, I thought—and sprayed crumbs as he explained.

"Two reasons. First is, he's a professional asshole. Like, that's his whole job. Second, César fucking hates Vic and I bet he'd rather burn the restaurant down than let Vic come in. Third—"

"I thought I was only getting two."

"I wasn't sure I felt comfortable sharing number three. See, I've been getting hypnotized lately, y'know, past lives regression and shit? And last month I found myself in the body of a mouse in Laurent's kitchen, and I was running around the counter looking for crumbs, and then I saw César kick open the door to Laurent's office and he was holding a fucking butcher's knife. And I just froze, man, because that's what mice do, and there were screams and everything and then a little while later César comes out and he's cradling Laurent's head in his arms like a newborn baby, just kissing it on the forehead and petting the hair, and then he trims the gore off the neck like he's gonna serve it for dinner and pops the whole thing in the fridge. I called Laurent and tried to warn him but he just laughed it off and then he died, so who's laughing now?"

I took a thoughtful sip of soup, trying to keep my face from betraying any excitement.

"Left his head in the fridge, huh? I, uh . . . I didn't see that in the papers."

"Sick shit, right?"

"You really think César would do something like that?"

"You'll have to ask him."

From across the room came the distinctive sound of a little boy peeing on the wall. Rocky just about fell out of his chair laughing and I guess I was laughing a little bit too. I offered to clean it up but Rocky told me not to worry and I was late enough that I didn't insist. I pulled up Nicky's shorts and told him it was time to get going. Below the stairs I noticed something I'd missed during my entrance: a chunk of butcher block hanging from the wall with a cleaver buried in the wood. It didn't match the cutlery at Laurent's place, but it was certainly covered in blood.

"Where's it from?" I asked.

"The Bowery. Same as everything else."

"What about the blood?"

"Blood?" said Nicky.

"Don't worry, kid," answered Rocky. "It's corn syrup and food coloring. Thought it added, I don't know, a rustic touch. But it's kind of silly, isn't it?"

"Silly is good."

Rocky cackled. Nicky was being wiggly, so I let him run up the not-entirely-safe-looking stairs all by himself. Watching his little butt bob up and down the steps, I had a weird moment. When I'd met the kid he couldn't walk five steps without falling down. Now he ran like an Olympian. Christ, I thought, they really do grow up so fast.

"You ever want to come by," said Rocky, "get high, fool around, I'm here most of the time."

"No thanks."

"I had to ask. Sometimes chicks say yes."

"I'm engaged. Also, a little bit gay."

"Cool. I was gay for a while. I miss it. Anyway, if this place ever opens up, I hope you'll stop by. The food really will be something else. I might be a flake but I'm working on a secret weapon."

"What is it?"

"Ask your buddy Ambrose."

Before I could dig into that, Nicky started moaning: "Beeeeeeee-beeeeeeee." I trotted up the stairs. As I wrestled him out the door, it occurred to me that Rockford Shanklin was the first person I'd ever given a peek at the thirty-two-ounce jar. It was terrifying to feel so exposed—and rather wonderful too.

Eleven

I motored that stroller through Central Park fast enough that the awning almost popped off. I needed to sit, to digest. But more than anything, I needed an hour—or five—to plan. So I stalked past sunbathers and softball players, pot smokers and screaming children, shredding my schedule in my mind. The plan for tonight had been making calls and arranging interviews, but that was when I was expecting my tour de aspic to yield a suspect. Instead I had bullshit. Instead I was standing still.

The visit to Number 5 had given too much and nothing at the same time.

Rocky knew Laurent's head ended up in the fridge . . . but it was probably a lucky guess.

He had a cleaver . . . but it was the wrong kind.

He had no real alibi . . . and no real motive.

Vic said he knew who'd killed Laurent . . . but he was a drug-addled wreck.

So I walked and walked, brain like a blender, thighs chafing and blisters blooming on both pinkie toes. I couldn't think without silence and a notepad but I had to get the kids home and fix them dinner and make another practice russe for Toru's party and and and—

I stopped. I breathed all the way down to my toes. It didn't do shit. I kept walking.

There was one piece of good news. I had the flags, damn it. I'd stolen them from the goddamned United Nations and I was pretty sure one was Andorra and that was gonna turn Peter's mood around. If I screwed up everything else I did this week, I could at least make the kid smile.

Absolutely hauling ass, I squeaked into the schoolyard just before the bell shrieked. The sun was below the buildings and the only patch of light was occupied by a clutch of moms who all knew Toru but never showed the slightest interest in knowing me. So I shivered in the shade, the dress that felt so fashionable that morning useless against the wind.

Peter trudged out looking shell-shocked, eyes puffy and mouth slack. I waved my arms and jumped and yelled like a dope, failing utterly to cheer him up. When he shuffled over I said, "What's eating you?"

"You know."

"The project?"

"Mr. Salas said it was incomplete."

"Not for long."

Making use of my extremely mediocre sleight of hand—which is just good enough to fool a child—I produced a half dozen toothpick flags from behind his ear. He gave them a sullen once-over. France, West Germany, Spain—each disappointment made his shoulders sag a little more. But then a smile slashed across his face and he pointed at one that was blue, yellow, and red with a golden smudge in the middle.

"Andorra!" he cried. "That's it! That's it!"

And for just a moment, your gal Bernice felt one hundred feet tall.

"Watch your brother," I told him. "I'm turning this in."

I marched across the schoolyard like a conquering general. For once, I didn't mind the glances of the surly third graders or their wretched mothers. I had *won*.

Mr. Salas was the personification of Rigor, a stiffly smiling youth wearing a paisley shirt and sideburns precisely the length considered acceptable for government work. His hair was combed straight forward. His skin was like a boiled egg.

"Whose nanny are you?" He spoke without warmth, the way people do when they're talking to the help. I gave a little chuckle, light and friendly, like I didn't want to punch him in the nose. We'd met at least ten times.

"I'm Bernice Black. I'm picking up Peter Komatsu."

"Oh, of course. You're Mr. Komatsu's new . . . girlfriend?"

"Fiancée."

"Isn't that nice." His smile grew toothier. "What do you need?"

I handed him the flag. He squinted.

"What am I looking at?"

"Oh, see, Peter's project was only missing Andorra. He had it, actually, but the cat threw up on it or shit maybe and anyway that's not important. What matters is I found a replacement. See?"

"Of course I see."

"So he'll get a good grade?"

He handed back the flag. My stomach churned.

“I can’t accept late work.”

“The project was due today. It’s still today, isn’t it?”

“It was due at the start of geography time. That’s ten-fifteen. It is hardly ten-fifteen.”

His voice was greasy with condescension. It reminded me of César, the first time I’d gone to Laurent’s. Today there was no chef to come to the rescue.

“He did the work,” I said. “He did an immense amount of work. Are you really going to be a pain in the ass here?”

“It sounds like you did the work, not him.”

“Because this project is insane! He’s seven! He shouldn’t even have homework. He should be, I don’t know, finger painting and pissing his pants!”

“Those may be your standards for Peter. We set a higher bar.”

“You’re telling me every other kid finished this nonsense on time?”

“Their work has no bearing on Peter’s grade.”

“Take the fucking flag.”

“No.”

It would have been pleasant to rip off his sideburns, but Peter was watching and I could see his tears glinting in the late afternoon sun. I shoved the flag into my purse.

“This isn’t over.”

“It is, Miss Black. It ended this morning at ten-fifteen.”

Peter followed me and Nicky out of the schoolyard. We were silent—well, Peter and I were. Nicky was scream-singing about his dick again and I was too deep in my rage to suggest he lower his voice. I wondered how I’d have handled Mr. Salas if I were still the girl who’d shoved past César into the dining room of the most exclusive restaurant in Manhattan. Had I gone soft or had the city gotten hard?

I got the kids home, dumped a bag of Oreos into a bowl, and told them to go watch TV. Only Peter was too glum to look at the screen, which meant we had to play "find the marshmallow." I scattered eight marshmallows around the living room and made a big deal out of how "I would be soooooo upset if anything happened to my precious marshmallows. I hope you neeeeeever find them." Ten minutes later the kids were stuffed with chemical goo and I'd have gotten to work except they started bitching about what to watch.

"Spider-Man!" screeched Peter.

"*Sesame Street!*" screamed Nicky.

"Spider. Man."

"*Sesame. Street.*"

"Just pick *something*!" I yelled, and I must have been loud because for once they heard me. Embarrassed by the sudden silence, by my idiot temper, I sat with my back to the kids and cracked the sardines I'd liberated from Number 5. *Sesame Street* blared. Lexington hopped onto the table—he can still jump when there's fish on the line—and we shared the tin while I skimmed my notes. For the first time in hours, I formed a coherent thought: I only had sixty-seven hours left. My feet couldn't take another day like today. I needed another angle and I was trying to find it when Toru came home. His legal pad was full, and his shoulders were loose, and I gotta admit, I hated him a little right then.

"Get milk?" I said.

"Fuck. Did you?"

"Nope. I've gotta do another russe, so do you mind running out?"

"Let me just put this stuff down."

I followed him into the bedroom. The bed was an inviting mess of rumpled sheets. I considered lying down but knew if I did, I wouldn't get up for days. He changed into sweatpants while I explained how my deadline had moved.

"That's a fucking nightmare," he said. "I'm sorry."

"Thanks."

"I'm gonna say something and you're gonna want to argue. Don't."

"What?"

"I'm taking Nicky for the rest of the week."

"But our schedule—"

"Pay me back next week. The next few days, you work. Okay?"

The World's Greatest Stepmom would have said no, but I didn't have the strength to argue, so I just nodded. He smiled.

"Only other thing is your party," I said, fully aware that there were actually ten thousand other things. "Every venue is booked, so we're going to have to host and cater."

"Let's cancel it."

"Nope. I just need to get a shitload of food and booze. And I need to borrow some chairs. Anyway, it's only twenty-four people. My grandmother could feed twenty-four people standing on her head."

He looked like he had a lot of thoughts about that but he kept them to himself. He went to the kitchen and started making coffee. Each tick of the clock hit my skull like a hammer.

"Are you going to get milk or should I?" I said.

"If you could be doing anything right now, what would it be?"

"I'd be face down on a Sardinian beach with a burly Swedish man rubbing oil onto my calves."

Or a burly Swedish woman, I thought. That would work too.

"Assuming Sardinia is out of the question," he said, "you'd probably wanna be working, right?"

"Yeah."

"On what, precisely?"

I gave my notebook another skim. Words jumped out at me—

The will.

The letter.

Succession.

Take over.

César.

"There's a letter Laurent wrote. It could be important but nobody knows where it is except maybe his maître d'."

"So go find him."

"But the russe . . ."

He handed me a cup of coffee—still black, naturally—and the smell set the acid bubbling in my gut.

"If we cancel the party," he said, "you don't have to keep making the russe."

"You're the best fucking dad in New York. A passable fiancé too. You deserve to be celebrated."

"I don't need a party to know you love me, B. Go find your maître d'."

I sagged. He was right, obviously. I had so much on my plate that it was spilling onto the floor. So I'd let the party go. I'd take another crack at World's Greatest Stepmom in 1973. He gave me a pretty serious kiss and I was contemplating sneaking him into the bedroom for a quickie but then I heard a harmonica wheezing out the *Sesame Street* theme and an announcer informing me that the show had been brought to us by the letter L and the number 7 and that meant the kids were about to start bouncing off the walls. It was time for them to be Toru's problem.

So I band-aided my toes and swapped the maxi dress and clogs for, okay, a different maxi dress and clogs. Tonight's garment was orange and red swirls that clashed magnificently with my orange and white scarf. I added orange eyeshadow and tangerine lips. I looked exquisite—I know because Toru said so and the boys agreed. I plunged out of the building and back into Central Park. You'd think I'd have felt exhausted but the setting sun was crisping the city gold and I'd ditched the stroller and the kids were behind me. My whole situation was as deeply fucked as it had been that morning, but I felt lighter than helium and there was nothing in New York that could hold me down.

César the maître d' was a prick when I met him, yeah, but that was mostly an act put on to impress the snobs. In reality he was, well . . . it's hard to say. I know he looked like a bulldog—five feet in every direction, a Gallic cube. His eyebrows were small shrubs, teased toward the heavens—either to buy himself an extra half inch or because looking like a demon made it easier to intimidate unworthy guests. In the years I'd been going to Laurent's, he was always at his lectern—tux pressed, flower in his lapel. He held the door; he called cabs; he doled out tables. He was cold to strangers and fawning to friends but I'm not fool enough to think a smile meant I knew him. He took no vacation; he had no day off besides Monday, when Laurent's was closed. So when I needed to find him, I went to the restaurant. It wasn't that I expected him to be there—it's that I couldn't imagine him anywhere else.

The windows were draped black. The famous awning was in tatters from people clipping souvenirs. There were flowers all over the front, most already wilted. I was about to cross the street when the front door opened and out stepped Jean-Louis, the head waiter. In the twenty years since I'd first watched him serve orange duck, he hadn't aged. He had the same jet-black flattop, the same tailored mustache, the same startling posture, the same mammoth hands. His skin was leather, his teeth bleached white, his outfit a green-and-red-checked jacket over a black turtleneck and black slacks. Not many men could put on a turtleneck without looking foolish. Jean-Louis managed to look cool.

You're probably figuring I dashed over to interrogate him, but he wasn't the kind of guy you ambushed. I'd spoken to him hundreds of times, watched him carve roast chickens and flambé all manner of flambéables, but he'd never smiled at me and he'd never asked my name. All I knew was that he was good with a knife and handy with fire and I figured he was just as comfortable deboning a person as a leg of lamb. So all that made him a useful suspect, yeah, but as far as I knew, he had no motive and I doubted the French military taught their paratroopers to make aspic, although they're French, so who knows?

Or maybe that's all bullshit. Maybe he just scared the hell out of me. Either way, I was looking for César—Jean-Louis could wait. So I inspected the flaking gray bark of the nearest tree while he locked the restaurant and slipped down the block and was gone.

The spare key was where I'd left it. I moved through the dining room without turning on the lights. Oddly, I felt no apprehension—as though I was certain that everything terrible that might happen here was already in the past.

"César?"

No answer. No surprise. So I went downstairs. The stockpot had been scrubbed and dried. Whatever litter the cops left behind had been thrown away. I rested my palm on Laurent's door and waited for the courage to open it.

It didn't come.

I opened it anyway.

The air was so thick with stale blood that for a second I couldn't breathe, but I got it together enough to turn on the bare bulb that hung over Laurent's little metal desk. I thought light would help. Like always, I was wrong. Somebody had taken a crack at cleaning up but the whole room was sticky with two-day-old gore. The body had been on the floor when Donati first came in here, but the bloodstains on the desk and chair suggested he'd been killed sitting up and left there for a while. That the killer cut his throat, got the stock going, then tipped the body onto the floor, took the cleaver, and—

I snapped my collar over my nose and took a long breath. The stench of sweaty polyester and faltering deodorant was enough to drive the smell of blood from my nose. My stomach settled. I quit looking at the blood.

Shelves over the desk sagged beneath decades of files. I grabbed a fistful. I found book reviews from 1962. An article about the Beatles coming to Shea Stadium. Receipts for beef bought in 1955 stuffed into a *Playbill* for the '68 revival of *West Side Story*. The kind of shit we save because it feels weird to throw away—junk to burden the ones we leave behind.

The filing cabinet was locked. The desk was not. The first drawer held a couple of old phone books and a mostly empty pint of Seagram's. The second was all papers. On top was a bundle of family photos. I flipped through them, recognizing no one, save for one shot of an alarmingly young Laurent bouncing a baby who must have been Henri. With them was a woman who had coiffed hair, a long dress, and a flat smile. I figured it was Henri's mother, who'd died during the Occupation. Once when he was drunk he'd told me that a Vichy cop had shot her in the head. He never said why.

Below the pictures were a bundle of pay stubs. The salaries were shit, of course—less than a hundred bucks a week, which even with tips was tough to make work in Manhattan. I had to go back four months to find a stub for César. There was no address listed and no indication of why Laurent had stopped paying him. There was nothing else of note in the drawer—no missing letter, no filing cabinet key.

I was combing through another fistful of miscellany when the kitchen light flicked on.

"Shit," I muttered, which didn't help anything, so I dove under Laurent's desk, pulled in the chair, and tucked myself into a little ball like Nicky does when we're playing hide-and-seek. Hopefully I wouldn't be so easy to find. I figured it was either Jean-Louis, who would break my neck, or Detective Donati, who'd throw me in jail. Either way, it would make it hard for me to hit my deadline.

Except it was neither of those assholes. It was a woman. She had bare knees and shiny yellow boots and I could just see the fringe dangling from her key-lime dress. She bent over the filing cabinet. The drawer thunked open. Papers rustled. The drawer thunked closed.

She shifted. She sighed.

I tried not to exhale.

And then she left.

Bernice Black, hide-and-seek champion of the Upper West Side, still undefeated.

I crouched by the door, feeling ridiculous but kind of James Bondy at the same time. When the kitchen light switched off, I counted to five before popping up. She hadn't locked the filing cabinet, so I pulled open the top drawer and found no file on César. Could be there'd never been one. Could be she'd swiped it. In any case, I wanted to know who she was.

So I bolted out the back door, ran down a particularly rat-infested alley and up a flight of rusted stairs that took me back to the street. I looked this way and that way and this way again and was about to give up when I caught a flash of yellow boot rounding the corner onto Fifth. I took off after her and didn't slow down until I was close. She had thick, shaggy hair—short on top and long in the back, like Jane Fonda's mugshot—and I didn't have to see her face to know who she was.

C.J. the bartender and, more important, Laurent's supposed squeeze.

Let's see—what did I know about C.J.? She made an excellent martini but her old-fashioneds were too sweet. She spent service with a smile frozen on her round, pretty face and responded to every order with the same mechanical nod. She was undeniably cute—big brown eyes, full lips—but her work clothes neutralized her good looks. I'd always imagined her as a beautiful marionette, controlled by invisible strings that stretched up to the ceiling, but if she was schtupping the boss she must have had a whole lot going on behind her mask.

The green dress and yellow boots made her easy to track. I followed her up Fifth and down the steps to the BMT. Toru would lose his shit if he knew I was getting on the subway this close to dark but she'd stolen something from that filing cabinet, and anyway, it's not like Toru had to know. She shouldered through the turnstile just as a train screeched into the station. I rummaged in my purse but couldn't find a token. The train doors opened. A few dazed tourists stumbled out. I scanned the floor for a dropped token and spotted nothing but cigar butts and wadded newspaper and half-chewed food. The conductor barked something unintelligible and C.J. got on the train and the doors prepared to close. I summoned all my youthful spirit, got a running start, and vaulted over the turnstile.

I hadn't done it since high school and I'm not gonna pretend it wasn't fun. I soared like a goddamn bird; my feet slammed into the tile and they skidded but I didn't fall. A distinctly cop-like voice shouted, "God damn it, lady!" and you bet your ass I did not turn around. I sprinted across the platform and threw myself through the doors just as they clamped shut. We pulled out of the station, and just like that, I got away with my crime.

The car was sodden with piss, which wasn't pleasant but at least cleared my nostrils of the stench of blood. Breathing through my mouth, projecting the dead-eyed misery that is a New Yorker's only defense against muggers, I leaned on the connecting door, staring through grime and graffiti into the next car, where I could just see the yellow boots. We rumbled downtown. I was afraid she was going to lead me all the way to Brooklyn—I did *not* need another trip to Brooklyn—but at Second Avenue she moved.

I exited onto an impossibly long platform. Aside from a few men dozing on benches, C.J. and I were the only people there. Her heels echoed off the tile as she stomped east. I followed as casually as I could, knowing I was screwed if she caught a glimpse of me, but she was a woman on a mission and didn't turn around as she vanished up the steps.

I pounded up to the landing and shoved through the turnstiles. No C.J. I ran out of the station, emerging beside a hellish little park, and spun around, seeing nothing. But then—bang—I spotted the boots on the south side of the street. I skipped across Houston, dodging cabs and trucks and dickheads from New

Jersey, and pursued her into the barren darkness of the Lower East Side.

It was a neighborhood I visited occasionally for smoked fish or appetizers or serious Chinese. I knew it vaguely during the day but at night it was a labyrinth. We passed boarded-up storefronts and yawning alleys and tenement doorways where addicts slept like stacked corpses. Every few yards I heard footsteps but I didn't see anybody when I turned around. I figured I should hang back from C.J., but those boots were the only light in the whole neighborhood, so with every block I got closer until I was just a couple doorways behind.

If I get killed, I thought, Toru's gonna kill me.

She turned onto, I don't know, Rivington Street? When I came around the shuttered deli on the corner, she wasn't there. I was about to call her name when I remembered that's a no-no when you're following someone, so instead I paced, feeling more exposed with every step. On my second circuit I caught the eye of a man in a doorway, a skinny white dude in a cutoff T-shirt who was smoking and staring and humming to himself. He raised his hand and headed my way. A streetlight caught his face. He was vampire pale.

"Whatcha need?" he said. His words were friendly. His tone was not.

"I'm looking for my friend."

"That's funny, y'know, that's really funny, because I'm looking for a friend too."

He smiled. It was fearsome. He reached out a hand and was about to grab my wrist when the door behind me opened. Music and light spilled out, hot enough to burn his skin. I didn't even look where I was going—I just dove inside.

Twelve

I smelled onion, celery, and bell pepper.

Cajun food. Suddenly I felt at home.

The ceiling was low, the lighting uneven. A dozen mismatched tables were scattered across a floor that rolled like the Atlantic. There was a beat-up tiled counter and a very open kitchen where a muscular man and woman in matching tank tops stirred pots and flung pans. For a second I was pissed—I'd gone through all this just to watch C.J. eat?—but then I realized she was heading for the stage—a rough orange platform in the corner with just enough room for a barstool. It'd be a minute before the show started, so I figured I deserved something to eat.

The woman in the tank top—a Black lady of about fifty-five with deep lines on either side of her unimpressed smile—met me at the cash register. Behind her was a chalkboard that gave the whole menu.

GUMBO Z'HERBES

BLACKENED REDFISH

RED BEANS & RICE

Above it was the restaurant's name: Remoulade.

I ordered the gumbo and, because I'm a dope, pronounced it the way it was spelled. She said it back like "Gumbo zab."

"What's the zab?"

"Greens."

"No andouille?"

"We don't cook meat. Fish sometimes, but never meat."

She asked about sides and I said cornbread and a minute later I was at an incredibly wobbly unfinished table with a bowl of steaming greens swimming in yellow broth. I had modest hopes as I took my first bite and it blew right past them. I tried the cornbread—it was a little dry, a little crumbly. I went back to the gumbo. Sweet, spicy, luscious—like swallowing a swamp. Couldn't believe there was no meat in it. Quite a thing.

There was a couple across from me—stoned, sexy, playing slaps. He was white, with a horribly shaggy haircut and a limp mustache, wearing dark black aviators and a cheetah-print shirt and a leather jacket covered with cigarette burns. She was Black, in a white denim jacket and a two-toned shirt, both collars popped, with a loose prep school tie. I'd never seen two people look so relaxed without falling down.

C.J. waved for the cook to dim the lights. She looked different up there—her wax smile swapped for an easy smirk—and I was trying to figure out what she'd seen in a plump, middle-aged French chef when she started reading her first poem and I remembered that not every rumor is true.

"I eat pussy for breakfast," she said. The crowd chuckled. I may have blushed.

"Not because it's packed with vitamins.

"Not because it's low in sugar, low in cholesterol, low in every kind of fat.

"Not because I like the jingle, not because the mascot's cute.

"Not because you get a free decoder ring in every specially marked box."

If you think she didn't wring every ounce out of *box*, reader, you are mistaken. She waited until the laughter died down. She was looser now, milking every word.

"Not because it's made crunchy to stay crunchy.

"Not because it's ideal for breakfast in bed.

"I eat pussy for breakfast because when you find the honest-to-god best part of waking up, you might as well have it to start every day."

She read two more poems after that. I couldn't tell if they were good, precisely, but they were as hot as the gumbo. By the time she was done I was sweating and I don't think it was from the food.

When she finished, a husband-and-wife folk duo who looked like half-melted candles took the stage. C.J. stepped down, pulled a beer from the cooler, wiped it down, and pulled the tab. The cashier passed around a floppy blue felt hat. I dropped in five bucks and went to pester the poet.

"You work at Laurent's," I said. She snorted, flicking her hair back even though it was too short to actually get in her eyes.

"Yeah, I've seen you around. Gladys something?"

"Bernice Black."

"Oh. The one that found him."

"Yeah."

"I'd say I'm sorry but that'd be a lie. Because if it hadn't been you, it probably would've been me."

The folk duo launched into a ponderous "Sloop John B." C.J. pulled on her beer. The pale brown skin of her neck bobbed hypnotically. She gave a look like, *Why the fuck are you still here?*

"I'm trying to figure out who killed him," I said, "and people keep mentioning this letter he wrote to César."

"Doesn't ring a bell."

"I heard you witnessed it."

"That'd be another lie."

Frustration rose in my throat. I swallowed it.

"Any idea who he wanted to take over the restaurant after he was gone?"

"Listen, lady, I just worked there. I liked it because the hours beat catering and tourists tip pretty good when they're playing high class. But I ignored the bullshit. Everybody knows the minute I have enough saved, I'm gone."

"Where to?"

"Berlin. New York is dangerous and expensive and that's a shitty combination. I wanna go someplace where I can afford to be weird." Another long sip of beer. She wiped her mouth on the back of her hand. "Hold on a second. Did you follow me here?"

"Maybe."

"Why?"

It was not a friendly question. I stared at the pressed-tin ceiling, looking for a way to make what I was going to say next sound polite. I came up empty.

"People say you were fucking him."

Her fist closed on her beer.

"You believe that? Even after you heard my poetry?"

"Some people eat pussy for breakfast and cock in the afternoon."

"Yeah, well, not me. So if you're done spouting bullshit, I'd like you to—"

"Why'd you go by the restaurant?"

"Who says I did?"

"You snuck in. You went down to Laurent's office and you opened his filing cabinet and you took something out."

"You're a grade-A creep, you know that?"

"What'd you take, C.J.? You can tell me or you can tell the police."

Her fist leapt forward faster than I could see. She yanked on my dress. Stitches tore. She smelled like Camels.

"You know me when I'm uptown," she said. "That means you don't know me at all. This neighborhood, this restaurant—they're where I come to be me. You don't get to infect that with your rich bitch bullshit."

She let go. I stepped back, keeping my mouth tight to stop it from quivering.

"I get it," I said.

"Shut up."

"I do. I really do, because that's what Laurent's was for me. And somebody went in there on Monday morning and killed my best friend."

"Your best friend, huh?"

"Why's that funny?"

"I wasn't fucking him but I talked to him a lot. So I know he never wrote any letter about who he wanted to take over the restaurant because he was planning on sticking around until the sun burns out. And I know he wasn't your best friend because I never heard him mention your name."

That hurt and she knew it. I wanted to smack her but I try not to hit more than one person a week and the fight with Stones put me at my quota. So instead I decided to throw my weight around.

"You know what I do for a living?" I said.

"Bother lesbians?"

"I write about food for the *Sentinel* magazine. Six hundred and two thousand people see my column every goddamned week. And if you don't tell me what you stole from that filing cabinet, I will inform all of them that the best restaurant in New York is a vegetarian Cajun joint named Remoulade."

"Fuck you."

"There'll be a line around the block. Socialites in turbans and kaftans; Wall Street dudes in three-piece suits. Even if you're lucky enough to get a table, this place will never feel like yours again."

Her eyes held on mine, unblinking and cold, until she reached into her bag. She set a manila envelope on the counter. It was unmarked save for the letters D.C. in Laurent's handwriting.

"Know what D.C. stands for?"

"I know a first grader who'd say Detective Comics but somehow I doubt that's what you mean."

She chewed on the inside of her cheek, then said, "D.C. stands for David Clarke. Remember him?"

Sure. He'd been a regular. He'd written a couple of scandalous, thinly veiled novels about the premier bitches of New York society in the early fifties, then coasted on his reputation until he died of a heart attack at the Met Opera in '69.

"They were friends?"

"They weren't just friends, stupid. They were neighbors for twenty years. Nobody ever asked about the connecting door."

She slid over the folder. I unwrapped the string. Inside were love letters written in confident, halfway legible script. Most were more than ten years old. I skimmed, spotting names that were famous when I was in college, accounts of excellent meals at restaurants long closed. None of the details meant anything but they sketched out a love like pressed flowers—beautiful and dead. The only thing I saw that seemed to mean anything was a postscript to a letter dated the week Kennedy got shot, in which David asked Laurent: *Don't you think it's time to forgive the boy for the omelette incident?*

The boy. I wondered if that was Henri.

"Laurent asked you to remove these from his files?" I said.

"He told me they were there. This is what he meant."

"Can I hang on to them?"

"Fuck no. When I'm done here, I'm burning them in the gutter. People like us have to be discreet."

"I had no idea he was gay."

"Not many did." Her face softened, like she'd decided that I was too stupid to be a threat. "I didn't even know until after David died. Laurent needed someone to sit with him after service and watch him get drunk. I didn't mind."

"He was lucky to have you."

She didn't respond. Either flattery was wasted on her or I didn't know what she wanted to hear.

"Since you're so agreeable," I said, "perhaps you could answer a couple of questions?"

"Get me another beer."

I got her the beer and I got myself one too. A Schaefer. It was cold and flavorless and exactly what I needed.

"Where were you Monday between twelve and two?"

"I spent the night at a friend's place downtown. I stayed for lunch. Call her if you don't believe me—Spalding 7-3677."

"What'd you do the rest of the day?"

"Bullshit. The bank, the supermarket. Laundry."

"And who do you think killed Laurent?"

She took a long drink.

"Could be anybody."

"Think you could narrow that down?"

"How about his kid?"

My back stiffened. It made me a dipshit, but I still felt protective of Henri.

"He has an alibi," I said.

"A good one?"

He said he'd been serving lunch at his restaurant. He'd given no one to confirm it. It was airtight—if he was telling the truth. I shrugged.

"And Jean-Louis is an obvious suspect," she said, "because he's definitely done it before, but I don't know. Him and the old man had some kind of bond. Macho shit. I think Jean-Louis would cut his own dick off before he'd hurt Laurent. Of course, if you made him angry . . ."

"What about César?"

"Maybe. They were old friends or enemies or, I don't know, some kind of combo. But lately they weren't even speaking, which made service really fucking awkward."

"Any idea why?"

"Nope."

"Did Laurent shoot heroin?"

That froze her from toes to scalp. I tried not to look smug but I didn't try hard.

"Why do you ask?" she said.

"There was some by his body. A lot of it, apparently. I'm not really hip to that kind of thing."

"It wasn't his."

"Whose was it?"

She nodded at the floppy blue hat.

"You tip?"

"I'm not a monster."

"How much?"

"Five."

"Make it twenty and I'll fill you in."

A crumpled twenty was all I had left. I was saving it for a cab, but in that moment I'd have let any number of muggers slit my throat to learn what C.J. was holding back. I dropped in the bill. It felt silly to make change from an old hat, so I left the five alone. C.J. emptied the hat onto the counter, faced the bills, and squished them down the side of her boot.

"It's César's."

"You're kidding."

"Because he doesn't look like a junkie?"

"Because he's a middle-aged maître d'."

"Heroin's very democratic. You heard his story?"

I shook my head.

"César was one of the Butter Boys. Got out of France fifteen minutes before the Nazis rolled in, landed in New York arm in arm with his best friend Laurent. They opened restaurants across the street from each other. Laurent's thrived. César's flopped. The older waiters said Laurent ran him out of business and gave him the maître d' gig out of, I don't know, guilt or something."

"No shit."

I'd never imagined that César could cook. All the time I'd known him, the only thing he'd ever made was a very strange dish he called "three-day spinach," for which he simmered spinach in cream for a full seventy-two hours until it quite literally melted in your mouth. He did it every year for Laurent's Christmas party—it was very gross and very good at the same time.

"What does that have to do with heroin?"

"His whole life was about sucking up to people who were bitter, arrogant, and entitled. Smack was the only way he could put up with their shit."

I wanted her to be lying. But her voice was steady and her eyes were locked on mine. The folk duo plodded into a cover of "Blueberries for Breakfast" that was somehow even more repellent than the original. I killed my beer and tried to think.

"It wasn't just César," said C.J. "Half the staff were junkies. He turned them all on. Sometimes they tried it once and that was it. Sometimes they got wrecked."

"Like French Vic?"

She nodded.

"Vic took to it like a fish to water. Bottomed out in six months and they had to send him back to France. It's a shame because he's a sweetheart. I hear lately he's clean."

I could've told her he wasn't, but it wouldn't have helped anybody, so I kept my mouth shut.

"But Laurent never touched it?"

"Nope."

"Then why did he have it in his office?"

"Laurent held on to everybody's stash, kinda to help them keep it in check, but mostly as a form of control. Very hard for someone to quit a job, to ask for a raise, to show up late, to bitch about long hours, if their boss has their habit in his hands."

I felt like there was cold water slipping down my back. I tried to find words to defend Laurent but all I came up with was:

"You're fucking with me."

"I'm not."

"He wouldn't do that. Laurent loved helping people. If someone had an addiction, he'd get them treatment. He wouldn't use it for leverage."

"Let me guess—he gave you madeleines."

"What?"

"Every time you paid the check, he'd palm you one of those shitty little cakes, right?"

"What's your point?"

"I bet you thought that was just between you, right? Yeah, well, he did the same routine with every reporter that came through the door. Same with politicians, actors, agents, crooks—anybody who he thought he could use. They weren't even made in-house. He bought them by the case."

That floor was slanted, and I suddenly felt like I was going to slide right off. I tightened my grip on the bar. C.J. smirked, enjoying twisting the knife.

"You were friends with front-of-house Laurent. Schmoozing, smiling, giggling, flirting. Back of house he was a tyrant. You want to keep a restaurant alive in New York, that's kinda what it takes." She lit a cigarette. "Anyway, César is a junkie. Jean-Louis is a psychopath. Don't fuck with them, you understand?"

"I'll do my best."

The folk singers crashed through their finale. The man asked the crowd, "Who wants to hear one more?" and was answered with a silence that truly hurt. They shuffled off the stage. C.J. killed her second beer.

"I'm doing a few more poems," she said. It did not sound like an invitation to stick around.

"Do you know where César lives?"

"No."

"Any idea where I can find him?"

"He's a movie nut. If he's not working he's usually at the Crusade."

"I don't know it."

"It's one of those old-time palaces west of Times Square."

"A porno house?"

"Sometimes. But also French movies, Swedish movies. Y'know—shit you have to read."

Before I could ask any more dumb questions, she headed for the stage. In the dim yellow light, she looked at home.

By the door was a little wire basket holding copies of that week's *St. Mark's Arch*, whose cover posed the question nobody had been asking: "McGovern v. Nixon—Who's a Better Lay?" I grabbed one and went to my table, where my gumbo was cold and the fuckable couple had fallen asleep. I flipped to the movie listings, where films with nudity were marked with little drawings of the body parts the audience could expect to see. That night the Crusade was playing the *Decameron*, followed by a double feature of *Grand Prick* and *Country Hooker*. The doodles promised tits and dicks and bush and ass. What ex-chef could resist?

Thirteen

It was good I hadn't bothered to save cab fare because there wasn't a cab for miles. So I headed for the F on streets that were even more empty than they had been before, clutching my purse and feeling white and bourgeois and pathetic and afraid. I'd spent so much time laughing at tourists who feared my city, but as the restaurant vanished all I could think was New Yorkers are putting up with five murders a day and had we hit our quota or was there room for one more?

Once again, I heard footsteps. Once again, nobody there. So I kept walking, one block and then another, as time stretched into an endless paranoid blur, like the last time I'd made the mistake of smoking dope.

Dope. An appropriate word. As in, how could Bernice be such a dope to believe Laurent was as cuddly as he made himself out to be? I'd hurled myself into this story to save my career, yeah, but also to honor his memory. If that memory was bullshit, I could quit—impossible—or I could treat Laurent like the subject of any other article and print every truth I could find, no matter how vile. That was the professional approach. It would also be a hell of a lot easier said than done.

Of course, all the ethics in the world wouldn't mean a thing if I got killed on my way home. I was walking as fast as I could without breaking into a sprint and the train still seemed miles away. I saw movement in every shadow, rustling in every alley, and the idea of taking the train from one bad neighborhood to another was starting to feel like suicide. I'd taken a judo class a couple of years before, after a friend of mine got mugged and went nuts for self-defense, and I tried to remember what they'd taught me about taking down an armed man, but all I'd retained was that it's hard to throw people and it hurts to get thrown. I was sweating again, not from poetry and not from gumbo, and then I turned onto Allen Street and I'd taken two steps when—

"Bernice Black!"

I yelped. I couldn't help it. And I felt like an absolute goddamned fool when the woman who'd yelled my name started to laugh.

"What the hell are you doing downtown?"

It was Liza, aka Susan Gullett, dressed for a night out. She was wearing heavy leather boots that looked like she'd stolen them from a Civil War soldier, a puke-green velvet suit, and one of those flat-brimmed hats that Catholic priests sometimes wear. She stomped down the sidewalk like the city belonged to her.

"Work," I said, wishing there were a smoker nearby so I could throttle him and take his cigarettes. "Vegetarian Cajun."

"Remoulade?" she said, a little impressed. "How'd you like it?"

"Hit or miss. But when it hit, it hit hard."

Susan nodded. I felt the way I did the time Toru and I went to

France, on the rare occasions when my high school French actually worked. It was like I'd cracked a secret code. She was just as cute as she'd been outside of Cœur but less frantic, and I was starting to think I'd been wrong about the flirting until she said: "Come with me."

"Why?"

"I know an incredibly dirty bar around the corner whose owner made the mistake of letting the *Arch* run a tab. Let me buy you somewhere between one and four drinks."

"Again . . . to what end?"

"We're doing a little something on Laurent Tirel. I hear you are too. So I want to get you drunk and plug you for information. Sound good?"

Her lips were parted just enough for me to see the gap in her front teeth. She took a step toward me and a realization exploded across my brain like lightning.

She means it.

She doesn't give a damn about Laurent. She's probably not even writing about him. She wants to buy me a drink and take me back to her apartment and take off my clothes and kiss my lips and my neck and my breasts and my chest and my hips and—

And if I wanted, I could let her.

"Laurent Tirel was born in Calais in 1904," I said. "His father was named Henri. The first thing he ever learned to cook was hard-boiled eggs, and during the war he—"

"That's press release shit. I want the dirt."

"Like what?"

"Like is it true they found his head in a big lump of Jell-O?"

My mouth went dry. I'd been a good little reporter and I'd kept that nugget to myself, which meant she either got it from the police or—

She'd heard it from the killer.

"Who told you that?"

"We're competitors, Ms. Black. I protect my sources. Now, if you'd let me buy you a drink, we'd be friends. Friends I tell everything."

"It wasn't . . . it wasn't Henri, was it?"

She shrugged, her eyes cutting me full of so many holes, I'd make a passable colander.

"Was it French Vic? Was it César?"

"I'm not saying, not out here. I think we've got a lot we could do for each other—a lot of information we could share. But we can skip the bar if you're shy being seen with a . . ."

"A what?"

"Newspaper editor."

She sounded out the words molasses slow. By then we were pretty close together. Her neck smelled like clean sheets drying in the sun.

"Because you know," she said, "I've got a nice little apartment on Tompkins Square. You should see the view in the morning."

I stepped backward. This was too much, way too much, and I'd already been kidnapped that week and the cat was shitting everywhere and Peter's project was a mess and all I could say was "I have to get to the train."

"I'll walk you. It's not safe for a girl on her own."

She grinned. I tried to match her expression. I'm sure I looked deranged.

But we started walking and my heart quit doing its impression of Gene Krupa. We were close—not touching, but close—in a way that felt familiar and sane. For a little while, it was just like being on a walk with an old friend. The streetlights shone a little brighter. The sidewalks were not quite so long. It was easy, suddenly, to talk. I realized I didn't know anything about her except that she was cute and smoked Winstons and thought Minnie Anglade was a bitch, so I asked her to fill in the gaps. She said she was born in the suburbs of Philadelphia, where the biggest thrill was sneaking into the city to make out with greasy boys and, when she was lucky, dance in the background on local TV. She got hooked on journalism at Sarah Lawrence, then followed a twisting path from Bronxville to Copenhagen to the Lower East Side. She'd planned to be the first woman to run the *Clarion*. She found she was a lot more comfortable downtown.

"Why were you so surprised to see me below Fourteenth Street?" I said.

"I thought you didn't eat nothing but old-school French. We don't have that down here."

"Would you believe I eat everything? Had a cover story last month about all the new places opening up in Chinatown. Cantonese restaurants serving stuff I'd never even heard of. Before that I was in Brooklyn comparing Italian and Middle Eastern bakeries. Last year I spent a month running all over Queens eating Thai. The gumbo z'herbes at Remoulade has me thinking I should do something about the new vegetarian."

"But French shit is your favorite."

"I guess so."

"Because of Laurent?"

"It wasn't just him. It was . . . the restaurant was special."

"Sell me on it, because I never saw the appeal."

I thought for half a block, composing my words as carefully as I would my next lede.

"It's like stepping through a portal. When César opens that door, the city's not dying. There's no piss on the sidewalk. You can walk down the block without getting shot. You're not even in

New York anymore. You're in Paris with Hemingway and Gertrude Stein—or in a stateroom on the *Normandie*, crashing across the Atlantic. All my favorite memories are tied up in food, so one bite at Laurent's still makes me feel like I did the first time I had it, when I was nineteen."

"I'm glad, then."

"About what?"

"That every time you taste gumbo z'herbes you'll be back in the night that Susan Gullett held your hand."

And her fingers wrapped around mine. They were cool and firm, and when they squeezed, I squeezed back. I held her hand as tight as I could, and suddenly the dark was no longer a threat—it was security, as impenetrable as covers pulled over your head. Nobody was watching us. Nobody fucking cared. We were behind a Chinese restaurant and the air smelled like crab rangoon—sweet and crisp and fried.

"So I heard something," she said.

"Yeah?"

"Is it true you've been bringing your kid to interviews?"

I should have been embarrassed but there was no malice in her voice, just amusement so gentle I couldn't help but laugh.

"Well, he's not my kid. He's, uh, well, he'll be my stepson eventually—maybe fall? We're thinking fall." I waited for her to react. She didn't. I blathered on. "And why shouldn't he tag along? It's not like I can afford a sitter."

"I just, I don't think I ever met a writer who was so damn determined. Like, as an editor I plan the fuck out of stuff because otherwise the paper would never come out, but once I'm out the door, I don't know . . . I surrender to chaos."

"How many writers do you know who have kids?"

"Basically none."

"So there you go. I'm an aspiring stepmom and a reporter and a writer and that means I've got at least three full-time jobs. Also my cat is a surprising amount of work. The only way I can handle all of it and still have time to sleep is to make the most of every fucking minute."

We reached a corner where the stop sign had been bent in half by a crashed car. We ducked under the steel, shoes crunching on broken glass, and she did not release my hand. We passed an alley where there was a sound like steel girders being sawn in half but then a door swung open and drunks poured out and I realized it was music.

"So what would happen if you let go?" she said. "If you gave in to chaos once in a while?"

"I'm afraid . . ." I paused, trying to find a way to tell the truth without sounding like a fool. "My entire life would fall apart."

"And we wouldn't want that."

"No."

After that we were pretty much quiet until we got back to the train. She let go of my hand. My palm was hot and clammy and nothing had ever felt so fine. She leaned against the railing, face green in the subway light.

"See you uptown, Bernice Black."

I didn't say anything because what was there to say? I just cupped her cheek and plunged in my face so fast our teeth clicked. I felt her chest stiffen and at first I was afraid she was going to pull back or slap me or laugh but then she relaxed against my body and kissed me back.

It was quite pleasantly like getting shot in the head. Like I really felt my brains explode across the sidewalk. I felt the little park catch fire, smelled the concrete melt, heard the streetlights burst—all from the heat between our chests.

I took a breath.

I pressed a hand against the small of her back.

I kissed her again.

This time it was different. Less frantic. And for the first time in maybe my whole life I was still. My brain went dark. Language left me. I *breeeeeeeeeathed*. For a few seconds, I just felt like—

Bernice.

When we finally knocked it off, I pulled back and Susan was smiling again.

"Well," she said.

"Yeah."

A pause. Because I can't stand silence, I asked a stupid question.

"What are you wearing? I mean your perfume, it smells like soap but cleaner than soap, like cleaner than clean, like—"

"I don't know."

"You don't know the name of your own perfume?"

"I steal it from our photo editor. I'll ask."

"Thanks. I mean, just . . . thanks."

We didn't say anything else. I floated down the steps. I was still out of subway tokens but who needs a subway token when their feet don't touch the ground? I took a running jump over the turnstile and the train was right there on the platform like it was waiting for me.

So maybe you're thinking, *Now our girl is screwed. She had her moment and now she's gonna get smacked down for the sin of being happy.*

But the joke's on you, sucker, because nothing happened at all.

The train was clean and rapist-free. The lights worked and the only smell was Susan's perfume echoing off my skin. It wasn't until we cruised past Bryant Park that I remembered I was supposed to be staking out the lobby of a Hell's Kitchen porno theater looking for César Lerond.

"Fuck it," I said. "Fuck it!"

Neither of the car's other passengers looked my way. New York is good for that kind of thing. I flipped through my notebook until I found the latest draft of my reporting plan. I tore it into confetti and sent it tumbling out the window. Let the track fires come. Let the city burn. César could wait until whenever the fuck I found the time.

By the time I got home it was after ten and everybody was asleep. Not just my family—the building, the block, the town. On the whole planet, in fact, I was the only person who was really awake. Toru had chucked most of the kids' toys into the cardboard rocket ship. The living room was as close to tidy as it ever got. It was almost like living alone.

My mind was going eighty miles per hour and sleep was out of the question, so just for the sake of hearing somebody else's voice I called Ambrose. His service said he was at Quint's, so I called there and they brought the phone to his table and I had to practically shout to make myself heard over the geriatric roar.

"Did you ever hear of the omelette incident?"

"Sounds like an airport thriller."

"Something to do with Laurent and Henri."

Ambrose chuckled. He chewed on something—it crunched like a French fry. Quint's has very good fries.

"Their particular psychodrama is one I've always tried to avoid."

"I'll ask Henri tomorrow. I have to go by Près to taste his aspic."

"'To taste his aspic.' If I didn't know you better, I'd think that was a euphemism. How goes the great jelly hunt?"

"I ran all over town today. Didn't find anything."

"I'm sure Henri will deliver. He lacks imagination but his technique is unimpeachable. You're at home?"

"Yeah."

"Heading to bed?"

"Soon. Why?"

"Oh, I'm dining alone. No matter how I try to pretend that a table for one isn't depressing, well, sometimes it is. Couldn't I tempt you with steak tartare?"

I had the phone wedged between ear and shoulder so I could rub my feet, which looked straight from a World War I trench. I wasn't sure I'd make it to bed, much less to the East Side.

"I can't. I'm sorry."

"Nothing to apologize for. Let's speak tomorrow, though, because . . ."

"What?"

The velvet went out of his voice.

"I told you yesterday that I was afraid someone's been following me. Well, it's ridiculous, you know, and I didn't really believe it, but when I got back to my studio last night after dinner, the lock had been forced and the door was hanging open."

"Christ. Had anything been stolen?"

"Nothing was disturbed. It felt like a message. 'Look how easy it would be. Look what we can do.'"

"Are you okay?"

He tried to laugh.

"I'm probably imagining things. What would my analyst say . . . cultivating dangerous fantasies in order to exaggerate my own importance."

"Normally I'd agree with him. But after Laurent . . . Is there anywhere else you can sleep tonight?"

"Another glass of Chianti and I'll be dozing in my booth. Really, I shouldn't have said anything. I'm fine."

"You're sure?"

"As silver."

I could tell he was smiling but there was fear in his voice and it made my stomach churn.

"Take a cab, will you?" I said.

"It's ten blocks."

"I mean it. I don't want to lose another friend."

We said our goodbyes and I hung up the phone and poured a large glass of scotch that did nothing to quiet my mind. I'd spent two days piling up motives and alibis until I had far more than I could use. I could have spent a year on this story. When I woke up in the morning—assuming I ever fell asleep—I'd have just over forty-eight hours to go.

"Yeesh."

A second glass of scotch took the edge off enough that I was able to get in bed but it was still a couple hours before I fell asleep. As I drifted off, feeling the warmth of Toru's body, listening to his gentle snores, something clicked.

The way I felt kissing Susan was undeniable.

Which meant I was going to have to let Toru know about everything I'd squeezed into the thirty-two-ounce jar.

And I would.

I absolutely would.

Eventually.

That thought scared me so much that I hardly bothered asking the big question: How did Susan know what the killer had done to Laurent's head?

Fourteen

• Thursday •

Toru, the saint, let me sleep through breakfast *and* school drop-off, which meant I was firmly passed out when he shook me awake to announce, "Your kidnapper's on the phone."

I took the receiver and felt the haze of sleep scraped off by Tiny Tommy's exquisite Brooklyn accent.

"Need to see you at the place," he mumbled.

"What?"

"Said I need to see you at the place." Still mumbling, but faster now.

"I don't speak conspirator. Be more clear."

Toru slid a mug of coffee into my free hand. Still black but better than nothing. I mouthed, "Thank you."

"The place *where we eat duck*. Where the thing happened the other day."

"Oh. That place. Why?"

"Another thing happened. You better take a look."

Another thing.

If he couldn't say it on the phone it was probably criminal. Could be fire. Robbery. Assault. But as the final remnants of last night's joy melted into a queasy mess, I was certain there was another body at the other end of that phone line and all I could think was—

Not Ambrose.

Not Henri.

I'd have killed for a shower but there was no time. I yanked another maxi dress out of my closet—I was long on maxi dresses that year, sue me—and whipped it over my head. It was long and soft and covered with tangled green and white lines that looked like a cloud of Nicky's Spider-Man farts. I took another pull on my coffee.

"You're not really going to see that bastard?" said Toru.

"Tommy's okay."

"He's a murderer."

"But he didn't kill Laurent. I don't think."

"Phenomenal. Go have breakfast with somebody who probably only kills people you don't know. What do you think—should I fish your body out of the river or wait for you at the morgue?"

I pushed into the living room, where Nicky was turning the couch into a fort and *Hazel* was blaring on the TV. I yanked open the fridge and gave the cream a shake. Still lumpo. Toru showed off his scowl.

"Nicky told me you found a dead man in a bathtub."

"He wasn't dead. He was sleeping. Maybe stoned."

"Oh."

I killed my coffee and found my clogs. They were by the front door, where I'd kicked them off back when I was buzzing from

Susan a few thousand years before. Toru emerged from the kitchen, scowl replaced with a "let's be nice" smile. I tried to match him but the coffee had hit my stomach like a sledgehammer, and Christ, I was worried about whatever was waiting at Laurent's.

"When you're done with our favorite murderer," he said, "what's your plan for the day?"

"I don't have one."

His eyebrow raised.

"Who are you and what have you done with Bernice Black?"

"I genuinely have no idea."

"Well, don't forget dinner."

"I always remember dinner."

"I mean at Elma's. That's tonight."

Darkness descended upon the city. Pits of flame opened in the sidewalk, belching sulfurous fire. Milkshakes melted. Lox spoiled. Macy's closed and took Gimbels with it and every decent consignment shop above Canal Street died at the same time. But none of that horror matched the prospect of spending three hours in Elma Zumwalt's leopard-and-ivy dining room, watching our hostess stupefy herself on vodka stingers while we choked down hot spiced beef.

"Do we have to?" I said.

"Listen, she's your friend."

"God, she is, isn't she?"

"But if you want to skip it . . ."

He let that hang. He wanted to flake and god knows I did too but it had been hell getting a sitter and we'd canceled the last two times. I shook my head.

"We're stuck," I said. "Who knows? Maybe a few hours away from the story will clear my head."

"Can we at least get really drunk?"

"But of course."

He squeezed my shoulders and kissed me about fifteen percent harder than normal. I kissed him right back and it wasn't forced—I loved this guy bad. When we'd finished that nauseating display of affection, I noticed his eyes were bloodshot and it occurred to me I probably wasn't the only one whose nerves were ragged.

"I love you," I said. "And I'm being careful out there. I swear."

"Good. Because the kids need you and I need you too."

I nodded and smiled. I was rotting from the inside out, and Christ, it was a relief to leave.

A half hour later I was shoulder to shoulder with Tiny Tommy and his gunmen in the alley behind Laurent's. Tommy was dressed for tennis, knees angry red in the brisk morning air. Blue was in his leather coat; Stones wore a green corduroy suit, four sizes too big. Tommy lit a cigar and I sucked in the smoke in hopes that it would mask the smell.

"Ready?" he said.

"No."

Didn't matter. Blue flipped the dumpster lid. The stench got worse. I saw a body sticky with blood, crawling with maggots and flies. There was a yawning gash across the throat. The head was tilted back, the tendons of the neck exposed as clearly as in a biology textbook. Rejecting several million years of evolutionary desire to run from death, I leaned in to see the face.

Not Henri.

Not Ambrose.

César.

There were eggshells in his hair and coffee grounds glued to the blood on his face. Rodents had nibbled away chunks from his cheeks, his neck, his palms.

"Collection truck found him," said Tommy. "Poor motherfucker."

"Close it," I said. "Jesus Christ close it!"

Blue closed it. Tommy kept talking but I was reeling—coffee and guilt churning in my gut. Even I, a newcomer to the field of dead-body appreciation, could tell César had been dead for days, but it felt like my fault. Like if I'd gone looking for him the night before—instead of goofing off being *happy*—he wouldn't be rotting in a dumpster. I knew that didn't make sense but I'm Catholic enough that there's nothing I can't feel guilty about. I tore open the fire door and spent a while panting and sweating and somehow managing to not throw up.

Tommy came inside.

"Why on *earth* did you think I'd want to see that?" I said.

"It's a scoop, isn't it? I'm doing you a favor here, trying to say thanks."

"Thanks for what?"

"The heads-up about the cops. Homicide pulled me in after you and me ate, sweated all that nice Burgundy right out of my pores, but thanks to you I knew what was coming. They bought my alibi, they let me go."

"What do you mean, they 'bought' it? It's true, isn't it? You were making soufflé?"

"Oh yeah, of course. Absolutely true."

He smirked like a kid who'd written a dirty word on the bathroom wall. I shook my head.

"I need water. Let's go upstairs."

I'd have sat anywhere but Tommy had standards, I guess,

because he led me to Olympus and pulled out Grace Kelly's chair. I'd never sat up here before. The view made the dining room look small.

Stones gave me water. I drank until the ice clinked against my teeth. He topped it up. I couldn't tell if he was embarrassed to see the woman who'd kicked his ass or if Tommy had told him to play nice. I didn't really care.

"He's been dead a few days," I said. "Right?"

Tommy dragged on his cigar.

"Yeah. Sure."

"So he could have died before Laurent or after. Maybe he walked in on the murder and so the killer did him too. No time to do anything clever with the body—just killed him and dumped him and hoped nobody noticed."

"Or Laurent killed César and somebody else killed Laurent for revenge. Or the killer was here for César all along and Laurent caught him and that's why he died. Or—"

"Shut up. I've got enough theories."

Tommy wasn't used to women telling him to shut up. He looked like he liked it.

"What do you want us to do with the stiff?"

"Call the police!"

"I'd rather they didn't know I was here."

"So have Blue do it. Or the driver who found the body. Tell them to make a big show of being cooperative. And if you're not here, then neither am I. I don't think it's good if Donati considers us friends."

"Sure."

I scribbled down some impressions of the crime scene. My stomach lurched. I breathed.

"Was there a cleaver in the dumpster?" I said.

"Not that we saw."

"Did your boys search the body?"

"I told them not to do anything that might leave fingerprints."

I flipped through my notes, straining to tie this mess together.

"There's supposed to be a letter that Laurent wrote to César naming a successor," I said. "Have Stones look through his pockets and see if it's there. If he's worried about fingerprints, there are cleaning gloves under the waiter's station."

"Why me?" said Stones.

"Because you're an asshole."

"Fuck that. I don't take orders from chicks who—"

Tommy raised a finger. In a week of menace, it was somehow the most frightening thing I'd seen.

Stones sulked out. I clicked my pen.

"Laurent ever say anything to you about a possible successor?" I said.

"Nah. His whole life was the job. That makes it impossible to walk away. My uncle was like that and it killed him. That's why I play tennis, why I cook. You don't have a life outside of work, you don't have a life at all."

"So wise! You should teach seminars on personal growth. You ever hear a story about Laurent and something going wrong with an omelette?"

"What could go wrong with an omelette?"

We pondered that question for a few minutes, getting nowhere. Stones returned, stripped to his undershirt, blood on his elbows and garbage in his hair. Humiliation suited him.

"That was *horrible*," he said.

"No letter?"

"Fucking of course not."

"Language, asshole," said Tommy.

"I apologize, madam," said Stones, digging into his pocket. "This was all I found."

He slapped down a roll of mints, a battered leather wallet, and a key with a flimsy rubber key chain that read, HOTEL CHANTAL. 694 NINTH AVENUE. ROOM #303. In the wallet I found César's ID, a couple of photos of a girl who could have been his daughter, seven dollars in cash, and a ticket stub for *The Garden of the Finzi-Continis* on Monday—murder day—at two P.M.

"So Laurent died first," I murmured.

"You want the cops should have these too?" said Tommy.

"The wallet and the mints are theirs."

"And the key, I just leave it on the table where anything could happen?"

"Yeah."

He left. I took the key, downed my ice water, and hit the street.

Westward ho—across the scalp of Times Square, where fuck shops and fifth-rate burlesque hung like dandruff. Tiptoeing past needles and condoms and glass shards and shit, I made my way to Forty-Eighth and Ninth—a grubby little block like every other one in Hell's Kitchen. The Chantal was a grimy brick pile perched atop a taxi dispatcher. I stepped up pockmarked marble steps and banged on the whitewashed steel.

The buzzer buzzed and I entered one of the darkest rooms I'd ever been in, a lobby whose sole features were a sagging sofa, a shredded tile floor, and the steel cage that held the front desk clerk. She was a young woman in sunglasses that covered most of her face, wearing thigh-high boots and hot pants and smoking a skinny cigar. I'd put together an elaborate lie about being César's daughter who'd come from France to see her papa—I was going to do the accent and everything—but she was gawking at *Cosmopolitan* and didn't look at me as I headed up the stairs.

If you're thinking the third floor was high enough to clear the taxi fumes, you're wrong. The air in César's room coated my tongue like chalk. The scenery was grim: a sagging mattress, peeling paint, a view of an airshaft, and no decoration but magazine pictures of Sainte-Chapelle and Invalides that he'd pasted onto the concrete walls. But the bed was made and the walls were scrubbed. The shelves held fresh herbs growing in water and stacks of canned food from foreign climes. I grabbed a tin of somon, which I'm pretty sure meant salmon in what I'm pretty sure was Turkish. A hot plate sat in the corner, right on the floor, holding a pan of César's three-day spinach. It looked fermented. I left it alone.

In the closet I found two pressed tuxedos, frayed polo shirts and chinos and sport coats, all very Kennedy administration. The side table held a Gideon Bible whose near-total underlining suggested César was a big fan of god. There were cigarettes and condoms, heroin and syringes and a half-pint of gin, plus letters from a daughter in Nantes and photos of grinning grandkids. None of them matched the girl in César's wallet. Beside that was a crumpled receipt from Laurent for a $500 advance on future salary—which was, presumably, the reason he hadn't been getting paid. It wasn't hard to guess what the money was for.

The only thing I wasn't expecting was the piggy bank.

It was a big ugly bastard the size of my head, perched on the sill to prop open the airshaft window. Years of polluted air had left its peppermint swirls a smoky gray. It looked like something an uncle would give to a nephew he hated. I tugged it out and gave it a shake. No quarters rattled. No dimes clinked. There was no sound at all.

I squinted into the slot. There was paper in there, blue and lined, with GUEST CHECK on the top. There was writing but I couldn't make out the words. I rolled Piggy over. His belly was smooth ceramic. No way in but the hard way.

For some reason, breaking a dead man's piggy bank felt like more of a violation than rifling his drawers and stealing his somon. But I'd come this far, I figured, so why not go all the way? I was about to smash it when someone pounded on the door.

"Open up!"

The voice was coarse, the accent French. It wasn't Henri and it wasn't Vic and since most of the other French guys I knew were dead, that made it Jean-Louis. I froze. He banged some more.

"I see the light, asshole. Open up *now*."

I couldn't think of anything constructive to say, so I kept my mouth closed and backed away. He slammed his foot against the door so hard the city shook. It stayed shut. Barely.

I tucked Piggy under my arm and looked for an exit. There was nothing but the airshaft, and come on, even I wasn't stupid enough to think that was a good idea.

He kicked again. Wood splintered.

On the floor beside the hot plate, there was a little cutting board and a chef's knife whose steel was mottled with age. An image popped into my head from my women's self-defense class: the instructor thumping her fist and repeating, "Never pick up a weapon unless you're good enough to stop your opponent from taking it away." I left the knife alone.

A third kick. The frame ruptured. The door dangled by a splinter.

I cradled the ceramic pig.

Jean-Louis slammed his shoulder into the wood. The door slapped onto the ground. He took one step and I brought poor little Piggy down on his head. It exploded into forty-five million pieces and his legs turned to jelly. He cracked his shoulder on the bedframe and puddled on the floor. I kicked him in the face and ran. My self-defense instructor would have been so proud.

I got halfway down the hallway before I realized I'd forgotten to grab the paper that had been inside.

"God damn it," I said, which accomplished nothing. "God fucking damn it."

I remember one time when I was in high school and me and Bobbie went into Manhattan to play tourist in Central Park. We were coming home on the express and we pulled into Times Square and we saw the local across the platform.

"That'll take us to Union Street," said Bobbie, dragging me off our train.

"But the express goes over the bridge."

"But I hate walking from Pacific."

"But I like going over the bridge!"

She pulled and I pulled, and wouldn't you know it, before we could make up our minds, both trains zoomed away.

That's how I felt in that hallway, caught between the extreme good sense of running and my desperate need to see that guest check. Before the train doors closed, I ran back to César's room.

Jean-Louis was dazed but conscious, bleeding from the temple and rolling on the floor trying to wipe splintered ceramic from his eyes. I couldn't see the check. I looked under the chair; I glanced under the bed. No dice.

"Putain!"

He got halfway up, groaning horribly, then slumped onto his ass. My guts turned to cement as I realized he was between me and the door. He flicked up his fingers. The guest check was crumpled in his hand.

"Give it to me," I said.

"Or what?"

"Or I scream rape."

He smiled in an altogether unappealing way.

"What makes you think anyone in this hotel cares about rape?"

He unfolded the check and read it. He smiled harder.

"What's it say?"

"Maybe I'll let you have it if you tell me why the fuck you're snooping around."

"And then you'll let me go?"

A nasty laugh trickled out of his lips as he braced himself against the doorframe and tried to stand. He was wearing leatherette driving gloves and it wasn't hard to imagine how they'd feel closing around my neck. I was out of options. I grabbed the knife.

It was heavier than it looked—like a sledgehammer, maybe, or a Cadillac. I aimed it at his throat. He stopped moving.

"Hand it over," I said, "and get the fuck out of my way."

His eyes flicked up at me, gray as the harbor. He didn't argue; he didn't curse. He snapped out his hand and grabbed my wrist so tight I thought the bones would break.

It's what I figured he'd do.

I ripped my arm backward, dragging him up until our faces were level, until I could smell the tar on his breath, until my knee was three inches from his crotch.

I slammed my knee into his testicles as hard as I could. They crunched like wrapping paper. He let go.

I tore the guest check out of his fist, vaulted over his crumpling body, and sprinted down the hall. This time I didn't stop. I tore around the corner and down the steps and I'd gotten to the second landing before I noticed the knife was still in my hand. I dropped it and kept running—out the stairwell and past the clerk and back into the street.

I didn't stop until I hit Times Square. My lungs were on fire and my legs were too. I was beneath a marquee advertising a double feature of *Biker's Orgy of Pain* and *Teenage Anal Eruptions,* both of which I think starred Doris Day? I wanted to sit but god knows there weren't any benches and even if there had been, they probably would have been irredeemably soiled. So I leaned on the old stage door and took a few deep breaths and when I'd halfway stopped shaking I looked at the slip of paper that had almost gotten me killed.

Fifteen

The two people who needed to see it were Oswald Blount and Henri. It would have been polite to show them separately, probably, but it would be messier to do it together and mess was what this story needed. So I called Henri and told him to meet me at Oswald's office. He didn't want to come but I guess I sounded like the kind of woman who bashes paratroopers with piggy banks because he didn't say no. While I waited for him, I grabbed coffee and an egg sandwich at the Koffee King on Forty-Third and Broadway. The coffee tasted like soggy cardboard and the sandwich was sweaty with grease but it smoothed me out a little. My head was throbbing and my stomach was on fire but I was fine, I swear. This was day three on this story and I'd already incapacitated two men. When I'd smacked Stones and his gun down to the Brooklyn sidewalk, it took hours for my hands to quit shaking. After whatever the *fuck* that was with Jean-Louis, I felt numb and I couldn't decide if that was good or bad.

Fuck it. Forty-eight hours left.

I took a final swig of my coffee and tossed it into the trash can on the corner. It tipped over and trickled out through the can's mesh, joining the scummy river that was slowly eroding Times Square. I hustled down to an anonymous building on Forty-Third and took an extremely rickety freight elevator to the seventh floor, where Oswald Blount Theatrical Management had its global headquarters. The ceilings were high; the floors were rough. The only light came from a scum-streaked window at the end of the hall. I peeked down at the street, expecting that from here the city would look clean, but nope—Broadway's filth was visible from space.

I'd been waiting maybe five minutes when the elevator slammed open. Henri stomped out, wearing chef's pants and a stained white T-shirt that fully exhibited his softening frame. He was carrying a tote from the Met and smelled like bitterness and gin.

"What the hell am I doing here?" he said. "We open for lunch in fifteen minutes and I called my night guy to cover but he was hungover, so he sent his cousin and his cousin is an okay cook but he sweats everywhere and tells the most disgusting stories and—"

"César is dead."

He swayed like a house of cards.

"You're . . . you're kidding."

"I saw the body. I smelled his blood. Now, come on—we've gotta talk to Mr. Blount."

He didn't move. He was frozen against the wall, hand pressed to his forehead, eyes closed, breathing wet. He did not seem to understand that I had no time for slow men.

"What's the problem?"

"I can't go in there."

This was no different from coaxing Nicky through a tantrum. I breathed. Scrounging up my last wisps of patience, I asked in my gentlest voice: "Why not?"

"Blount's going to make fun of me. He's such a bully, Bernice, such a greedy piece of shit. He doesn't even care that Dad is dead."

"Yeah, well, this is a meeting you have to take."

"Why?"

"I found your dad's will."

I held up the guest check. I let him see it just long enough to spot the handwriting.

"Is Oswald gonna like it?" he said hungrily.

"Definitely not."

A nauseous grin spread across Henri's face. He tore open the office door and marched inside. I followed him into what had to be the world's smallest waiting room. There was a metal-and-chrome couch, a painting that was somehow both abstract *and* pornographic, deep shag carpeting, and a narrow window overlooking the street.

"Do you have an appointment?" said the receptionist, an intensely handsome young Black man whose headshot, framed and propped up beside his Selectric, identified him as Danny Clarke. He sat inside a little cubby that I guessed was a converted coat closet, behind a desk that had been cut in half and wedged into the doorframe.

"I don't need an appointment to speak to that fucking rat," said Henri.

"What my colleague means," I said, "is that we require only a few minutes of the great man's time."

"Mr. Blount is in a meeting."

I could hear a woman talking in Oswald's office. I couldn't

make out what she was saying but she had the mellow diction of a Broadway veteran. It could have been Uta Hagen. I didn't care.

"I'm going to open that door," I said. "You can try to stop me but it'll be next week before you get out from behind that desk."

"Damn it," said Danny. "Fine."

Henri and I went inside. The office was only slightly larger than the waiting room. One wall was covered with cabinets and little drawers. The other was filled with posters for shows featuring Oswald's clients—*Fiddler* and *The Odd Couple, The Killing of Sister George* and a revival of something called *Ready, Willing & Mable.* The only furniture was a desk and a leather love seat where Oswald was lying with his knees pressed against his chest and a tape player running on the floor.

"You are a tiny little ball," said the woman on the tape, who was definitely not Uta Hagen.

"I am a tiny little ball," said Oswald, voice muffled by the throw pillow that covered his face.

"No, you're not," said Henri, knocking the pillow away. "You're a tiny little prick."

Oswald scrambled up, face red and hair wild. He was fully dressed—tight jeans and a ribbed sweater with laces across the throat and about a foot of fringe dangling from the arms—but he couldn't have been more embarrassed if we'd caught him stark naked. He retreated behind his heavy wooden desk, which was far too large for the narrow room, and screamed: "Danny! We talked about this!"

"I'm sorry, Mr. Blount!"

"You are a tiny little ball," whispered the tape player. I turned the woman off.

"Goddamned idiot," said Oswald.

"Don't blame Danny," I said. "It's not his fault I'm a pain in the ass."

"Well, what the hell are you doing here?"

"I've got Laurent's will."

The news hit him as hard as it had Henri. He dropped into his chair, smoothed down his hair, and cleared his throat several times. Then he lifted the silver lid off a dish of Kraft butter mints and crammed a fistful into his mouth.

"Whatever's on there is meaningless," he mumbled around the mints, "legally speaking. Even if Laurent wanted Junior to take his place, it's my name on the deed."

"The restaurant world would never forgive you," said Henri, "if you ignored Dad's final request."

"The fuck do I care about 'the restaurant world'? Bunch of freeloaders and addicts and drunks. I'm here to feed tourists. That's all that counts."

Henri slammed his fist against a shelf. Awards shook. He turned my way.

"You know he stole Dad's recipes?"

"The fuck are you talking about?" said Oswald.

"They were in the office. A wooden box with a brass latch, full of three-by-fives. Some in his handwriting. Some in my mother's. Some in my fucking grandmother's. I went looking for them yesterday. They're gone."

"I wanted a recipe, I'd look in a cookbook. And I've tasted your dad's. They're only okay."

Henri lunged for Oswald, sending his executive desk set clattering to the floor. Oswald scooted out of Henri's grasp. Henri was about to climb on top of the desk when I yanked him away.

I snarled, "Do you guys think you look sexy when you're

fighting? Because you don't. It's like watching a baker slap together two wads of dough."

"He started it," mumbled Oswald.

"Do you idiots want to hear the will or don't you?" They nodded. "Then sit down. If either of you move, I swear to god, I'll make you regret it."

They sat, both of them trying to hide how hard they were breathing. Henri looked triumphant. Oswald looked scared. I took the guest check out of my pocket. I allowed myself to breathe.

"Dear César," I read. "My food is tired and so am I. This year, I retire. On Bastille Day, perhaps—a day of freedom for our country and for me. When I'm gone, no matter what Oswald Blount says—"

"I'm telling you, this shit means nothing," said Oswald.

"No matter what Oswald Blount says, the restaurant goes with me."

There was a painful silence before Henri croaked, "What?" and Oswald said, "Oh my *god*."

"Burn it down if you have to," I concluded. "I want no successor. The place is Laurent's. Without Laurent, it must die."

Oswald's laughter ran through Henri like a buzzsaw. Henri wobbled to his feet, groaning horribly, and worked his mouth until he was able to croak out: "If the restaurant is closing—"

"Who the fuck said the restaurant is closing? That letter is moving but doesn't mean shit. I'll get us open again before the end of the month."

"At least . . . please . . . the recipes."

"I don't have 'em and I don't need 'em. I'm gonna have the best chef in New York City. His name, in case you weren't aware, is French Vic Anglade."

I expected Henri to go for Oswald's throat but he just stood there for a little while, staring at his scuffed shoes. He mumbled, "I have to go. We're out of veal stock."

He stumbled out of the room. Oswald must have wanted more of a confrontation, because when the door creaked shut he pelted it with a fistful of butter mints. They clattered off the door and sank noiselessly into the carpet. I was disappointed too. I'd brought Henri here to see how he reacted to his father's letter. I'd expected him to get angry, to let something slip. Watching him crumple like that just left me feeling like shit. Oswald opened a cabinet and yanked a cork out of a bottle so old that its dust had dust and slopped a few fingers into a glass. He drained it, refilled it, and poured a matching one for me. I didn't drink.

"Don't give me that look," he said. "I own the restaurant and I own the name and I'm under no obligation to shut it down just because a dead man said so."

"Even if it makes you look callous?"

"In my industry, 'callous' is a compliment. I'm gonna let everyone know that the great artist wanted his masterpiece destroyed but that I'm keeping it open in his honor."

"You're so terribly noble."

Either he couldn't hear the sarcasm or he just didn't care. He smiled so big it looked like it hurt.

"Gotta tell you, kid, this murder is working out very well for me."

I flicked my fingernail against the glass and watched the drink ripple.

"Oswald, I think you owe me a favor."

"Anything, of course, my god."

"You're opening Laurent's tomorrow night."

"Why?"

"Because I'm having a party. Twenty-four guests—well, maybe a handful more—at eight o'clock. Naturally, you're invited too."

"That sounds delightful, baby, but I doubt Vic will be available on such short notice."

"I'll find someone to cook. You just open the doors."

I sipped my drink. It was port. Sweet and fruity and vinegary at the same time, with a hint of—

Oh *shit.*

The same sweet something I'd been smelling in the aspic. I tried to keep my poker face as I said, "So what are we drinking?"

"An 1888 port from some burg in nowhere France. It was the most expensive shit in Laurent's cellar, so when I bought the place I helped myself to a bottle. Honestly I think it tastes like Night Train but what are you gonna do?"

"Where'd Laurent keep it?"

"Locked up under the bar. Only him and the bartender—whatshername . . . C.J.—had a key. Oh shit! That reminds me!"

"Yeah?"

"Oh, you're gonna love this, baby. I'm gonna blow your little mind."

"Try me."

"I know, I know, you think I'm a blowhard. But this is on the level. See, I didn't take those fucking recipes but I did go by Laurent's yesterday to have a little poke around. I found something so incredible, I don't even know if you can cope."

"Hand it over or fuck off."

"Say please."

I held up my middle finger. Cackling, he slid open his top drawer and pulled out . . .

Something. Seriously it was just . . . something. I wish I could be more specific but whatever the hell it was, I had no idea.

He tossed it on his desk and waited for me to be impressed. I leaned close, inspecting a little wad of brown fur that looked an awful lot like a mangled rat. I gave it a poke. It didn't seem like it had ever been alive.

"Don't you know a scoop when you see it?" he said.

"What is it?"

"A bloodstained toupee!"

I leaned closer. He wasn't wrong. Tangled curls sprouted from a mesh, the edge of which was streaked red, like somebody had used it as a rag to wipe blood from their face.

Ew.

I took another swallow of the port. I didn't know from Night Train but I'd had Manischewitz and it wasn't far off. Something about Oswald's handful of matted wig made me want to cry.

All I could say was: "Uh . . . wow."

"It was in Laurent's office, jammed up between his desk and the wall. Cops must have missed it. Didn't belong to him, so I figured, I dunno, maybe your killer is missing a rug? Anyway, consider it my gift to you. Take it! I mean it! It's yours!"

I've never been one to refuse a gift, so I drained my glass, wrapped the toupee in a bunch of tissues, and dropped it into my purse.

"Take good care of that, girlie. It's gonna crack this thing wide open. And when you win the award for, I dunno, news lady of the year, remember to thank old Ozzie Blount."

He picked up his phone, which I guess meant the meeting was over. I passed through the waiting room. Danny stared like I was salmonella. When I reached the hallway and found Henri sitting on the floor, I felt as low as a bug. His tote was open. Between his legs sat a silver bowl full of ice and a plate of tomatoes in aspic. He smeared some of it into his mouth.

"Get up," I said.

He kicked the bowl toward me.

"This is why I'm out of stock. You should at least have a bite."

So I dug my fingers through the softening jelly and popped a slice of tomato into my mouth. The flavor was nice but the texture was slimy and there was no hint of pepper or nutmeg or Oswald's '88 port.

"Well?" he said.

"It's fine."

"Just fine?"

"Just fine."

"You know, you've got a real knack for ruining my life."

"On your feet. You're a grown man and you've got lunch to prep. I'll walk you partway."

He got up. I handed him the aspic. He dropped it on the floor. The plate shattered and the aspic splattered and inside the walls the rats got ready to feast. He followed me to the elevator.

While it clanged up the shaft I asked, "What was the omelette incident?"

"The what?"

"Something with your dad."

"Oh Christ. *That.* I can't believe he even remembered it. It was fifteen years ago maybe, at night after service, and Dad was hungry and he wanted an omelette, so I made a big one for us to share, classic, y'know, with just eggs and chives, and it was fucking perfect because I can cook omelettes in my sleep. So I put it on a plate and poured a couple glasses of Cab and it would've been a nice father-son moment except he thought he saw this little brown spot."

The elevator arrived. Henri wrenched open the doors.

"And I said 'it's nothing' because it was *nothing*, the omelette was pale yellow—like the sun behind fog—but he said it was burned and he flipped the plate over and walked out without a word."

"Jesus."

"That was when I knew I'd have to quit."

We rode to the street. When we hit bottom I asked, "Did you kill him?"

He didn't flinch. Just shook his head.

"I used to think I wanted to. I blamed him for everything, y'know? I could've had a nice, sensible job; I always liked numbers. I could've been an accountant. Show up every day at the same time. Take some numbers from here, move 'em over there. Get paid. Go home. Feels like . . . peace. But the way he raised me I could've never been anything but a cook."

We cut over to Sixth, where the crowds were thinner, and walked in near silence all the way to Central Park. My pity washed away, leaving behind the most intense frustration I'd ever felt. Several times I dipped my hand into my purse and twisted the toupee in my fist. I'd put in so much agony, so much work, and all it had gotten me was a literal piece of trash. What a fucking joke. I felt a little more bitter about it with every step, so there was real acid in my voice when we stopped at the statue of Bolívar and I said: "Do me a favor. Close your eyes."

He thought for a second, then spoke. "Kiss me and I slap you."

"You wish."

His eyes shut. I stretched the hairpiece like it was cellophane and hovered it over his head. What remained of his hair was chestnut, thin and soft. The toupee's coarse curls were closer to oak. It didn't match what he was working with today, but it was a dead ringer for the way he'd styled it when we met.

I was about to drop the thing on his scalp to see if it fit but he popped an eye open, saw what I was doing, and smacked my wrist away.

"What the hell?" he shouted. Birds startled. Tourists stared.

"Oswald found it at your dad's. It might be the killer's. I just wanted to make sure."

He pulled Parliaments from his pocket. Funny, I thought, that the whole scene in Oswald's office hadn't made him want to light up, but the hairpiece did.

"I'm not sure what offends me more. That you think I killed my father or that you think I'm vain enough to wear a rug."

"That's not a denial."

"Get the fuck out of here."

"You can't throw me out of Central Park."

"Go!"

I didn't. Instead I twirled the hairpiece on my index finger until he bellowed, "You are impossible!" and stomped away. I was getting somewhere.

Maybe.

The rug was his.

Or it was somebody else's.

It was the key to the whole murder.

Or it was meaningless.

I'd figure it out. But first I had to see a man about a flag.

Sixteen

I got to Peter's school as the bell rang and plunged into a schoolyard flooded with children driven frantic by seven hours of pretending to learn. I sliced a path through six football games and a free throw contest and somehow managed not to get hit in the head. Clearly, my luck was turning around.

Toru was already there—he's never, ever late—gabbing with the moms who refused to learn my name. Nicky was terrorizing the older children. Peter was staring at the cracks in the ground. When Toru spotted me, he cocked his head.

"Everything okay?"

"I was in the neighborhood. How's Peter?"

"The other kids presented their projects today. He had to sit and watch."

"That's a fucking crime."

"Maybe grab him ice cream on the way home?"

"Lemme take care of one thing first."

I marched on the land of Rigor. Mr. Salas leaned on the wall, chatting with the other teachers, laughing like he hadn't shattered a young boy's heart. I got in his face and literally backed him up against the wall. I was close enough to smell his breath.

Baloney.

I hate baloney.

"You're accepting Peter's project or what?" I said.

He smiled blandly.

"My decision is final."

"I'm not saying he should get an A. But he deserves a chance to present."

"It would hardly be fair to the other children."

"The other children can fuck off."

Nervous laughter bubbled up from the assembled teachers. Mr. Salas drew a patronizing breath.

"Miss Black, profanity has no place here."

"I've had an interesting week, Mr. Salas. Do you want to hear about it?"

"I can't see what bearing—"

"One of my dearest friends was decapitated. I found the head."

The laughter died. Salas ran his tongue over his lips.

"I'm sorry to hear that."

"This morning I found a corpse in a dumpster, throat cut, gnawed on by rats. Another friend of mine."

Sweat inched down his sideburns.

"As distressing as that is—"

"And a few hours ago, I brained a man with a piggy bank and held a knife to his throat."

He gulped. Honest to god gulped. It was beautiful.

"What does any of that have to do with me?"

"Nothing at all."

I pulled the crumpled flag of Andorra from my purse. I tucked it into the pocket of his shirt.

"Peter presents tomorrow?" I said.

"Miss Black . . ."

"I'm sorry, that wasn't a question. Peter presents. Tomorrow."

"Yes, of course. First thing."

I patted the sap's cheek and left him alone. I strutted past the gaggle of moms over to Peter and squeezed his shoulder and said, "Mr. Salas admitted that he was wrong. He's accepting your project after all."

Peter didn't quite hear me. I repeated myself and he stared like it was too good to be true and so I said it one more time and he flung himself forward, slamming into me hard enough to empty my lungs. I found myself spinning just so we wouldn't topple over.

I put him down and he literally jumped up and down with joy. I told him, "Go bother your brother, okay?" and he whooped and disappeared, ready to bother the whole damn world. I couldn't quit smiling. I looked at Toru and he was grinning pretty big too.

"How the hell did you make that happen?" he said.

"I told Salas we were having a tough week. I guess he took pity is all."

Toru looked at me like I was a god. I didn't dispute it.

"Let's grab ice cream at the deli on the way home," I said. "And milk and cream for the charlotte russe."

His brow furrowed.

"Is the party un-canceled?"

"As of, oh, thirty minutes ago."

"Where?"

"Still Laurent's."

"But Laurent's is closed."

"I took care of that."

"Who's cooking?"

"Somebody besides me."

"How is any of that possible?"

"I am very, very good."

He looked a little terrified but didn't argue, which was probably the right call. When the kids got sick of running in circles, we walked home and—miracle of miracles—remembered to hit the deli on the way.

My triumph dulled only slightly when we got off the elevator and discovered Detective Donati pounding on our door. I said hello and I guess he wasn't expecting that because he yelped, then slumped on the wall clutching his gut. He had on the same suit as the other day—different tie, though—and looked like he'd spent most of the week being run back and forth through a mimeo machine.

"B.B.," said Nicky. "Who is that melting man?"

So I introduced everybody and told him to come inside. He shook his head.

"My lieutenant wants me downtown so he can yell at me for a while."

"Don't be an idiot. We're having charlotte russe."

"What's that?"

"The food of the gods," said Toru.

Donati didn't say yes and he didn't say no but when I opened the door he followed like a dying dog. Peter took his hat and coat and Nicky tried to swipe his badge. I got the boys set up watching TV and Toru retreated to the bedroom to chug through some writing. While the oven got warm, I sat Donati at the counter in front of my most recent practice russe. He stared like he was going to cry.

"Dig in," I said. "I need the bowl."

"César is dead."

I leaned on the fridge, arms crossed, trying to look shocked.

"God. That's . . . just . . . wow."

"Don't give me that bull—" He glanced at the kids. "That bull. You were spotted entering the restaurant not long after the garbage guys found the body."

"You think I killed him?"

"Naw. This kind of brutality, there's no question this was a Mob hit. He got killed seven, eight hours after Laurent. Was in that dumpster close to three days. It was really gross."

"So how come your guys didn't find him?"

"Oh no. Oh no. I'm gonna get enough of that guff from the brass—I do not need it from you. We got three different murder calls the morning Laurent was killed, okay, so we were stretched latex thin and we did the best we could." He gave the counter a feeble slap. "But my analyst is on my butt to be more open with my feelings and right now I'm feeling upset—no, I'm feeling hurt—that you visited the crime scene and didn't think to give me a call."

"Maybe I didn't know it was a crime scene. Maybe it doesn't matter." These suggestions left him dizzy. I nudged the big bowl of creamy sugar slop. "Eat. It'll help."

"So after we bagged up César, I went over to Ninth Ave to look at his hotel room and it was a wreck. There was busted-up porcelain or something all over the ground and blood, and I wanted to ask if you knew anything about that, okay?"

"Eat."

His head dropped into his hands.

"Everybody's gonna yell at me."

Nicky climbed onto the stool beside Donati. He grabbed a fistful of the russe and smeared it into his mouth, then patted some of the gloop onto Donati's shoulder.

"Try it—you'll like it."

It was a perfect imitation of the guy in the Alka-Seltzer ad—kid's a born entertainer, I'm telling you—and it got Donati to taste a little off the tip of the spoon. His jaw relaxed and his eyes shone. He took a real bite. Then a bigger one. Then he went nuts, slopping it into his mouth like he was plastering over a hole. So I cooked and he ate, as steady as Mike Mulligan and his steam shovel. He dug out most of the bowl. When he was done, he slumped, born again.

I handed him coffee—now with milk!—and said, "So what'd you want to ask me?"

"Forget it. Just forget it." He scratched his head and smiled a sleepy smile. "Only, please, don't cause any more ruckus, okay? This case is a mess and honestly I can't take any more strain."

I nodded solemnly.

"You've been talking to people up and down Laurent's block," I said. "Any of them see anything interesting?"

"Like what?"

"Like a guy with dark brown curls going into the restaurant on Monday morning? Kinda fake-looking dark brown curls?"

"Not that I heard." He stared at me, trying to decide how suspicious he should be, but then another wave of sugar hit and he let it go. "Just leave it alone, wouldja?"

"I'll do my best."

He retrieved his hat and coat from the corner where Peter had dumped them, said his goodbyes, and got out of there. I set the empty russe bowl into the sink, squirted it with soap, and let it soak while I fixed the kids a box of Kraft. While they ate I finished the new charlotte russe and gave it a taste. It was good—better than the first, probably the best I'd ever made. But it wasn't a hundred percent. I knew just the man to ask why.

I got to Carnegie Hall a little while before curtain. Gowns and suits milled around the entrance; the lobby glowed like a welcoming cave. I slid around to the side door, took the elevator to the private residences, and walked down a warped hallway that smelled sharply of lemon. I let myself in without knocking and was walloped by an invisible fist of melted fat. It wasn't a large room but the north wall was all windows and that made it feel huge. Nearly all of it was given over to the kitchen, where half a dozen Upper East Side debs toiled at hot plates. The furniture was all dark wood and the floor was Moroccan tile. In the far corner, a small area was blocked off by purple velvet curtains—Ambrose's private room.

Ambrose stood at his electric range. His collar was starched, his manner easy, but I saw agony behind his soft brown eyes.

"Hollandaise is nothing to fear," he said. "Even if it made your mothers quake in their aprons. Our double boilers are hot. The water simmers. We add our egg yolks and beat until smooth. As so."

The room filled with the clacks of panicked whisking and the intoxicating odor of brunch.

"Lemon juice," said Ambrose, tipping in a tablespoon with hands that shook so slightly only I could see. "Our melted butter, our hot water. A touch of cayenne and a pinch of salt. Very good. Keep mixing . . . yes. Lovely, ladies. Disarm your stoves and pour. You have all just made a beautiful chicken hollandaise. Have a bite and . . ."

He spotted me as the debs showered their chicken with yellow sludge. He was dressed as nattily as ever—a spotless white shirt, sharply creased green trousers, an apron covered in yellow half-moons. But it was the first time I'd ever seen him without necktie or cravat and that wasn't a good sign. I held up my hands, telling him to take his time, but he was eager for the interruption.

"Just a moment, girls, while I confer with my colleague," he said. "Taste your sauce. Nibble your chicken. Compare notes. And remember Ambrose's maxim—"

As one, the girls recited: "If it tastes good, the calories don't count."

Ambrose's bedroom was like the inside of one of Nicky's forts—I couldn't decide if it was cozy or claustrophobic. An enormous sleigh bed that he'd inherited from his mother filled the floor. A smudged display case hung crooked on the wall, showing off Ambrose's medals from World War II—a Purple Heart and two I didn't recognize. To one side was a rack of suits, arranged by color, and a pair of soft green chairs that he'd bought from the Plaza, with wings high enough that two people could whisper and still be heard. I sat him down and handed him a bowl of that afternoon's russe. He didn't ask what it was. Just gave it a taste and smacked his lips.

"It's excellent, Bernard."

"Fuck you. You think I came here for empty compliments? That russe is goddamned good and I know it, but it's not perfect and I need the best palate in New York to tell me why. Take another bite, Clendenon, then open fire."

He ate. Not desperately, like Donati, but with scientific precision. While he did that I took down the medal case, huffed on the glass, and scrubbed it clean with the cuff of my dress. I hung it back up and nudged it straight. By the time Ambrose set the bowl aside, his hands weren't shaking anymore.

"The texture is off," he said.

"Yeah."

"Are these fresh ladyfingers or bought?"

"Fresh, obviously. Could it be the custard?"

"Absolutely not. The custard is featherlight." He stared into space, tugging at the skin that hung slack beneath his jaw. He clapped his hands together. "I know! It's the whipped cream, Bernard. It's ever so slightly grainy."

I swept the last of the russe into my mouth. The bastard was right.

"God damn. I over-whipped it."

"Happens to everyone. Next time you'll nail it to the wall. Now, was that really what brought you here or is there something greater than charlotte russe on your mind?"

I smirked. Old bastard knew me too well.

"You heard about César?" I said.

"The bodies are really piling up, aren't they?"

He was trying to be arch but his cheeks were pale and his voice strained. I'd never seen him so close to crying. I smiled, strictly to humor him, and said, "Want to see something vile?"

"Always."

I pulled the toupee out of my bag. Some of the curls were knotted; others had lost their spring. I smiled like it wasn't embarrassing.

"Recovered at the crime scene. I don't suppose it belongs to you?"

Laughter rumbled out of his chest. He rubbed his shiny dome.

"I started balding in high school. The battle was lost by the time I turned twenty-five. I've never found a hairpiece that made me look like less of a fool."

He draped the toupee across his head. It fit like a yarmulke on a watermelon.

"What do you think? Is this the new Ambrose Clendenon?"

"Perhaps not."

He handed back the toupee and slumped in the chair.

"I should say, Bernard, I'm grateful you're here."

"What's wrong?"

His good humor faded. He lit a particularly delicious-looking cigarette and contemplated its smoke.

"I took your advice last night. Didn't walk home. But it took a while to find a cab and while I was waiting I noticed a man in a town car staring like I was a chicken he wanted to purchase, pluck, and fry."

"What kind of town car?"

"How should I know? It was maroon—an awful color—and when I finally landed a taxi it followed me all the way home. It parked across the street. When I woke this morning the car was gone but there was a man leaning against a loading dock, smoking with hideous intensity, who followed me to the luncheonette where I had my breakfast, then trailed me right back home."

"Same guy?"

"I can't say."

"Curly hair, bright blue eyes?"

"I didn't see his eyes but he had the curls. And he was wearing a long leather coat, the same color as the town car from the night before. For all I know, he's still out there. It's idiotic but I haven't left home all day."

I wrote it all down. That was definitely Blue's coat, but this felt wrong.

"There's something you're not telling me. About your relationship with Tiny Tommy, or what happened to Laurent or—I don't know. Something."

"You're wrong."

"Constantly. But not about this."

He jammed his cigarette into the remains of the russe, spent a moment drumming his knees, then lit another.

"We've been friends for a while, Bernard—"

"Which makes it stupid to lie."

"Fine." His voice dropped. Thanks to the magic acoustics of the Plaza chairs, it was like he was whispering right in my ears. "Tiny Tommy really is a student of mine. He's quite promising, if you can believe that, and a genius with a knife. I *have* taught him to make mushroom and leek soufflé. But we weren't together Monday morning."

"Then where were you?"

"Paying a visit to my attorney."

"Why?"

"A personal matter. Well, professional. Well, personal and professional but—"

"God damn it!" I slapped my leg. Quite a lot harder than I meant to, actually—it really hurt. "I've got, fuck, less than two days on this deadline and now you tell me one of the most important things I've turned up—Tiny Tommy's alibi—is bullshit. You really fucked me here. The least you can do is say why."

Ambrose collapsed in on himself. His suit pooled around him. He looked haggard. I wondered how much weight he'd lost. Guys his age were like cats—they hid illness. My dad, the stubborn bastard, was the same way.

"I've been offered a job," he said.

"You say that like it's a death sentence."

"It would be a major change at a time in my life when change is terrifying. I canceled on Tiny Tommy to consult with my lawyers, to learn if it would be a conflict to accept the offer while continuing to write my column at the *Sentinel*."

"What's the job?"

"You know the pleasure I take helping chefs refine their menus?"

"Sure."

"Well, Rockford Shanklin has offered me an absolute stinking fortune to help him narrow his vision for Number 5. I'd be a formal partner."

"He needs the help."

"And I need a purpose. It would be a chance, you see, to prove I can do more than taste and complain."

His voice had gone as low as a dry creek. The sight of him, shrunken and sad, switched off my anger. I'd never seen Ambrose yearn. Hell, I'd never seen him admit he had any problems more serious than undercooked fish. He wanted this more than anything and I wanted it for him too.

"You're going to take it?"

"My attorney said it would be unethical to take the job while continuing at the *Sentinel*, and I've had that column so long that losing it would be like cutting off a leg. I don't know."

"You remember that first time you took me out to eat?"

"Greenspan's Dairy. Borscht and buttermilk."

"And a knish the size of two fists, swimming in mushroom gravy. You asked how I liked working at the *Sentinel* and I said it was wonderful and you knew I was full of shit. You helped me admit that I got palpitations every time I walked into the office because I was certain the whole staff could tell I was a stupid, scared little fake. You told me—"

"That everyone in New York, especially those of us said to have found success, is stupid, fake, and scared. That all it takes to be a professional is to act like one."

"I figure that if this job scares the hell out of you, that means it's probably a good idea."

Before he could respond to my excellent advice, a waxy blonde in a Liberty-print dress poked through the curtains and said, "Oh! There's a whole little room back here!"

Ambrose rose, cheer bolted back in place. He wrapped his hands around hers and said, "Yes, Miss Tyler?"

"You know that thing that keeps happening to my sauces?"

"I do."

"It happened again."

He smiled, a portrait of patience.

"Ambrose will help."

He followed her out of the bedroom. I glanced around, looking for something to entertain me while he solved her sauce. There was a book splayed open on Ambrose's dresser—*Famous English Cookery*. I tried to read a recipe for black pudding but between the phrases *hog casings* and *dried pigs' blood* my interest waned. I was setting the book back down when I noticed, hidden in a nest of wrinkled cravats, a mostly empty bottle of Obetrol, the same diet pills that kept the pounds off Elma Zumwalt and her chums at Atmosphere. That explained the weight loss. Perhaps the paranoia too. Or maybe the son of a bitch was just sad.

I tucked the pills back where I'd found them and returned to the kitchen, where Ambrose was showing the blonde how to repair a broken hollandaise by whisking in hot water. When he finished, the class applauded, and both he and the blonde basked in their approval. I tugged off my scarf, bought at a thrift store and made of supposedly "authentic post-war parachute silk," and tied it around his neck. It looked better on him than it did on me.

"There's the new Ambrose Clendenon," I said.

"Thank you, Bernard."

"I didn't know a fucking thing about restaurants when I took this job, you know that?"

"But you learned."

"Yeah. You can do this, man. Rocky Shanklin needs somebody to rein him in. You're the only man for the job."

"Perhaps. But it's impossible. I'm simply too old to start something new." A smile flickered across his face. "But there is one way you could help—assuming you have the time."

"I certainly don't. Ask anyway."

"Rockford called earlier. Said Vic's bagged the job at Laurent's and they're having a little party at Number 5 to celebrate."

"A party, really? César and Laurent are barely cold."

"It is a bit close to dancing on their graves, I agree. Rockford is a genius at cooking—not at tact—and he and Vic's relationship with Laurent was hardly reverential. But he swore it would be a quiet little gathering and he's going to be giving me a very hard sell to join his team and I'd love to have you there for support."

"I'm supposed to go to a dinner at Elma Zumwalt's."

"Then I've saved you a fate worse than death."

"Her hot spiced beef is that bad, huh?"

"Like gnawing on asphalt. And all your favorite suspects will be there. Perhaps you'll find a match for that disgusting toupee!"

Now, there's an idea. If all you've got is a bloodstained toupee, you might as well use it. I thought for a moment and then realized there was absolutely nothing to think about. Forced to choose between Elma Zumwalt and a room of could-be killers, the killers win every time. Anyway, it was worth it just to preserve Ambrose's smile.

So while he made the rounds nibbling on everyone's chicken, I gave Toru a call.

"I was wondering," I said, "if instead of going to Elma's tonight, could we—"

"Yes. Whatever it is, absolutely. Let's go."

Seventeen

It was not a quiet little gathering.

By the time Toru and I pushed through the plastic flaps at Number 5, everyone was drunk and most of them were stoned. Candles and tripod work lights provided shadows out of a Dracula movie. Ratty rugs covered the floor and bolts of felt dangled over the holes in the walls. The tables, pushed into the center of the room, were heaped with a dizzying array of food. The bathtub was full of ice, canned beer, and bottled liquor. Boxes of crayons had been emptied in front of Nicky's farting Spider-Man and everyone was adding to the mural.

Twenty or thirty chefs and hangers-on stumbled around. I recognized Bev and Denis from Quint's, Glenn Christian from Linda II, Sarah Perch and Preston Greene, who'd just taken over the Red Wall, and this French-Canadian bastard named Serge. That's it. Just Serge. They had speakers blasting what I think was Jefferson Airplane and a sideboard covered with ramekins full of drugs, some of which I recognized—I'm hip enough to know rolled joints, quaaludes, and cocaine by sight—and others that were a brightly colored mystery.

"Probably we should eat and take drugs," said Toru.

"Go to town. I'm on the clock."

He helped himself to a joint and a book of Number 5 matches. Call me a stuffed shirt, but I really think a restaurant should finish its floor before they start printing matchbooks. He grabbed a vaguely clean plate and piled it with roast chicken, onion rings, smoked trout mousse, shucked oysters, champagne-braised sausages, and a beautifully bloody filet mignon.

"What's your plan?" he said, ladling rich brown sauce over the whole plate.

I found myself too embarrassed to explain the toupee, so I kept it simple.

"I don't have too much going on this week. Got your birthday party tomorrow and I'm filing the most important story of my life the day after that, so tonight I just need to find the killer, hand him to the cops, and maybe knock out a draft if I've got the time."

"Easy."

"Yeah. Bernice Black, American detective—stirring up shit and seeing what happens."

"Never thought I'd say this, babe, but sloppy looks good on you."

He gave me a kiss that I think he'd have stretched into heavy petting if I hadn't pushed him away.

"Get stoned. Eat."

"Yes, ma'am."

He parked himself on one of the loose banquettes, dragged on his joint, and settled down to feast, as happy a man as ever lived. I grabbed a pint of cognac and waded into the fray. I felt like Cinderella's prince, except instead of a glass slipper I had a bloody wad of fake hair.

Rocky was the center of attention, naturally. He was leaning on the wall, his alarmingly well-defined chest shimmering with sweat. His Viking curls were piled on his head and he had his tongue down the throat of a young woman wearing a white gown whose hem was stained black by the floor. Vic sat beside them, champagne between his legs, a neat line of stitches across his forehead, wearing the same Hendrix shirt and smiling like he'd been gorging on Halloween candy. Either one of those bastards could have killed Laurent and I was done letting them jerk me around.

I took a long pull of cognac. I felt like a rottweiler, a prize-fighter, an ICBM. I was going to grab them by the hair and shake loose the truth.

Except right then something happened that knocked the wind out of my chest. I'm not exaggerating—it felt just like falling off the monkey bars and suddenly your lungs are concrete and breath won't come. What I'm trying to say is, Susan Gullett was at the top of the stairs.

She was wearing a sheer white peasant dress—yards of skirt and way off the shoulders, as Audrey Hepburn once said. She'd done her makeup bright green, like a woodland elf, and as she stepped down those not-quite-trustworthy steps, adrenaline flooded my mouth.

I spun around and got as close to the wall as I could without French-kissing it. Someone had drawn a picture of a fish with a top hat and mustache. A speech bubble said, *Frankie the Fish Likes It Salty*. I stared at Frankie as I sucked in useless air, wishing Mr. Salas were there to give me a pep talk on the virtues of

Intensity and Rigor. I couldn't figure out why I felt so stupidly afraid.

Before I could find the answer, hot breath flooded my ear.

"Do you have any idea how rich I am?"

It wasn't Susan. Her voice wasn't that wet, that male, and I seriously doubted she was rich. It was Shipley Merritt, Rocky's backer, who I guess was bankrolling this bacchanal. His curls were bouncing, his lips were moist, and he was wearing a Harvard blazer and no shirt. I shoved him back. He swiveled his hips until his pants slipped off, revealing an alarming lack of underwear.

This is my penis, this is my penis.

It was cuter when Nicky did it.

"If I put pâté on my cock," he said, "will you suck it off?"

I looked around—nobody seemed to think this was odd. More important, Susan was nowhere to be seen, which meant I could halfway remember my halfway plan. I fluttered my eyelashes and laughed like he was as cute as he thought.

"Can I pull your hair first?" I said. "Before you get too excited, I mean the hair on your head."

"Whatever works, baby. I love a girl who likes it rough."

"Then you'll really like me."

I wrapped my fingers through his slimy orphan Annie curls. I yanked like I was starting a boat motor and he fell, spluttering, to his knees.

"It's real," I said. "Congratulations."

I left him writhing and scanned for Susan. The steps, buffet, and banquettes were all clear but no matter which way I looked, I felt her eyes boring holes in my back. I knew I was being ridiculous. I wasn't going to run from her. I'd say hello. I'd be adult. I'd—

A hand closed on my elbow and I leapt out of my skin but it was a false alarm named Minnie Anglade. She'd frosted her hair. Her eyes were swimming in orange and her dress was an extravaganza of sequins, like somebody tore off a piece of the sun. She looked like she always looked. Mad.

"You promised me a write-up," she said.

"I don't have time—"

"Every day this week, I'm checking the paper. Every day this week, I'm disappointed. I don't like to be disappointed."

"When my column runs—which isn't until Sunday, okay?—I promise Cœur will feature prominently."

Especially, I thought, if your husband killed Laurent and César.

"Good. Because otherwise, you stay banned."

"That would be a shame. I'm looking forward to seeing how things change over there after Vic goes to Laurent's."

She pulled her shoulders just a little bit straighter and sneered like Norma Desmond.

"Victor is going nowhere."

"Then what are we celebrating?"

"Oh, I'll let him have his fun now. But my husband's obligations are to Cœur and to me. I would kill him, Miss Black, before I let him leave."

She spun away. I spun her back. Her eyebrows went so high, they looked like mountaineers preparing to scale her hair.

"Something I've always wondered, Minnie—is that a wig?"

"That's a disgusting question."

"What about your husband? Does he wear a toupee?"

She leaned close. Her foundation was cakey. It smelled like hot rubber.

"My husband is an addict. He is tacky. He is impotent. He is a fool. I accept these sad facts—they are my cross to bear. But I would not tolerate a bald man."

She shoved past me and made for the buffet. I pushed into the crowd, still heading for Vic and Rocky, and found myself blocked by a herd of men with sideburns and comb-overs whose Nehru jackets failed to disguise their guts. I pulled on the cognac and tried to figure out when I started to hate parties. In my early twenties they were a chance to dress fancy and swill martinis, to argue with half-loathed acquaintances about Kennedy and Goldwater, Kubrick and Coltrane. But we got older and the nation exploded and our idea of fun became hopelessly tame. A lot of people older than me—particularly the white men—couldn't take it. They grew beards and swapped wives and hid coke in their breast pockets. A party was no longer an opportunity to act like our parents—it was an excuse to be kids. As someone who channeled her neurosis into healthier pursuits—like lesbian fantasies and brawling with gangsters—the spectacle made me sick.

Or maybe that was the cognac. Because the bottle was half gone and so was I. I didn't set it down. Vic and Rocky had gotten lost in the crowd and Susan still hadn't reappeared. Which wasn't anything to worry about because it's not like I wanted to talk to her. I didn't care at all. I was being an adult, okay, and I was keeping my wits and I was . . .

What the hell, I thought, is wrong with Ambrose?

He was squeezed under the stairs with his back to the crowd. His scarf was sopping with sweat, what remained of his hair was on end, and he was methodically crushing vol-au-vents in his fist and setting them back on the tray. Obetrol, baby. The perfect pill for anybody who wants to be as skinny as a garden snake and as twitchy as a rat.

"Are you all right?" I said.

"I'm on the verge of soiling myself. Tiny Tommy and the man in the red leather jacket. They're *here*."

He pointed through the gaps in the steps. I could just make out a pair of shiny black shoes and the shimmering stripe of a tuxedo pant. I took a slow breath. Ambrose was wearing me out but two of his friends had died that week and that'll make anybody skittish. I figured I'd take one more crack at calming him down.

"You said yourself the guy loves food," I said. "He's here to eat. That's all."

"Don't be naïve, Bernard. He's here for me."

"To do *what*? Drown you in the bisque?"

"To send a message. Christ, he knows I've been talking to you. When that story runs, if there's even a hint that I sold him out, they'll find me bobbing in the Buttermilk Channel. I'd never ask you not to publish, of course, I know what it means to you, but—"

"Nobody will know you told me a thing."

"Thank you."

I rested a hand on his shoulder. Through the wrinkled silk of his shirt, I could feel every quaking bone.

"What if I told you everything is fine?" I said.

"Is it?"

"Maybe! Maybe I've unearthed a key piece of evidence that's gonna lead me straight to Laurent's killer. Maybe the men who are following you actually want to be your best friends. Maybe inflation will end and meat will get cheaper and Vietnam will solve itself all on its own. It's possible, isn't it?"

He smiled weakly.

"But hardly likely. I know I'm a silly old fool, Bernard, but I'm desperate for your help."

"So what do you want me to do?"

"Talk to him! Make him trust me. Get him to leave me alone."

I didn't have the time. I mean, not remotely. But friendship is not always convenient, and anyway, I had a couple of questions to ask our local representative of the New York Mob, so I said okay and patted Ambrose's head and his hands more or less stopped shaking. I rounded the stairs and caught up with Tommy and Blue at the bathtub bar.

"Absolute goddamned mess," muttered Tommy. His tux was neatly tailored; his bow tie a drooping pair of elephant's ears. He'd slicked down his hair and re-upped his noxious cologne. He looked like an angry tater tot.

"Come to a cocktail party," said Blue, "you expect a fucking cocktail."

"Pour some gin. We'll pretend it's martinis."

I wedged between them and nearly choked on the stench of chemically engineered masculinity. Tommy gave a thin smile. Blue handed him a glass of halfway-cold gin.

"Eat," I said. "The food's not bad."

"Who cares? I mean, yeah, it tastes good and that's beautiful, but is this the scene now? Drug-addled idiots with their pants down past their cocks, acting like they're geniuses just because they know how to work a stove?"

"It's certainly not something I could handle every night."

He settled onto a banquette. He sipped. His scowl settled deeper onto his nut-brown face. I wondered what Emily Post would say about the most graceful way to accuse a mobster of murder.

"You get it, Black, that's why I like you. You remember Laurent's when it was really Laurent's, when people dressed to the nines, when Yul Brynner and J. Edgar Hoover were up on Olympus, when you had to really be somebody to even get in the front door. It wasn't just going out to eat, y'know? It was like . . . ah, Christ, I'm gonna get weepy . . . it was like you could touch the stars."

"That was a long time ago."

"Feels like yesterday." He drew in a breath. "Well, these burn-outs can't have Laurent's. That restaurant owes me a bundle and if Oswald tries to put French Vic in the kitchen, I'm calling it in."

"What's wrong with Vic?"

"He's got a habit. I don't let any of my closest associates touch horse and I intend to be very close to whoever's cooking at Laurent's. Besides, he can't cook potatoes. Every time I'm at Cœur, they're either raw or charred. It's an embarrassment."

"How d'you feel about Henri?"

"I don't think he has the temperament for it. But maybe he could convince me. Is he around? He and I should have a talk."

He started to get up. I grabbed his wrist. His arm was like rebar.

"Wait," I said, and found my mouth had gone dry.

"Why?"

"Because you weren't with Ambrose when Laurent got killed."

Once again he gave me that naughty-boy smile.

"Ambrose tell you that?"

"Ambrose backed you to the hilt. But I talked to his neighbors, his doorman, and the guy who sweeps outside Carnegie Hall and none of them saw you."

I wasn't prepared for the special terror of lying to this man. He stared at me so hard, I felt like he was inspecting the inside of my soul, where a big neon sign was flashing BULLSHIT! BULLSHIT! BULLSHIT!

"People make mistakes," he said. I couldn't tell if he was talking about my witnesses or me. I guess that was the idea.

"People do. I don't. Where were you Monday afternoon?"

"Off the record?"

"No."

"Let's say I was . . . around."

"Around where?"

"Just around."

This answer was so stupid, I forgot how afraid I was. I told him: "That's the worst alibi I've ever heard. It's not even an alibi. It's not even bullshit. It's nothing."

"Yeah, well. More detail would be dangerous."

Blue set down a couple of plates of fancy crackers surrounded by little plops of mousse and pâté and dip. I dredged a cracker through some warm crab sludge and said, "So forget Monday. Tell me what this asshole has been doing outside of Carnegie Hall."

"You think I'm an asshole?" said Blue, genuine hurt in his voice.

"I think you followed Ambrose Clendenon home from Quint's last night and you sat on him all day. What for?"

"There wasn't . . . I mean he wasn't . . . I mean I didn't . . . ah, hell."

"What Blue is struggling to communicate," Tommy said, "is that I asked him to keep an eye on Ambrose. After what happened to César—"

"This started *before* we found César," I said.

"So after what happened to Laurent, I wanted to make sure he was safe is all."

"And if you scared him into confirming your alibi, that's just a bonus?"

He spread a minute amount of mousse on a cracker. The knife twirled in his hand.

"I don't think I could forgive myself if something happened to Ambrose."

"You could've just talked to him. You didn't have to break into his apartment."

The knife stopped.

"We didn't go near his apartment."

"Then who did?"

"Don't you read your own paper? The city's dangerous. Probably just a break-in. You can't lay that on me."

"Tommy, you're not ten percent as cute as you think. I don't know precisely what you've been doing but I do know it's scaring Ambrose to death. The cops love you for this murder—for César too—and the last thing you want is for me to call Donati and tell him your alibi is junk."

"Is that a threat?"

"No. This is a threat: Back off Ambrose or I'll tell the whole goddamned city that you wear a toupee."

He squeezed the knife until his knuckles went white and his face turned even more orange.

"Where did you get that hateful lie?"

"I have my sources."

"This is your doormen? Your fucking street sweeper? Tell me who said that so I can puree their balls."

"Just leave Ambrose alone."

"Touch my hair."

"No."

"Touch my fucking hair. Blue, grab her wrist and make her touch my hair."

Blue reached for my wrist. Acting like this wasn't exactly what I was looking for, I dug my index finger into Tommy's do. It was soft like melting plastic. I kept pushing until I felt scalp.

"It's real," I said.

"Damn straight."

"You'll let Ambrose breathe?"

"Sure."

I was about to exhale when I spotted Susan, elbow deep in the bathtub full of liquor. She pulled out a fifth of vodka. Water twisted down her reddened arm. I allowed myself to stare. Her eyes found mine. Her lips parted. I stood up so fast I almost flipped the table.

"I have to go to the kitchen."

If Tommy and Blue said anything, I couldn't hear it over the hammering of my heart. I slammed into the crowd, bobbing and weaving until I shoved through the kitchen door.

The air was thick with sweat, profanity, and smoke. Ambrose was in the corner, alternating nips on a cigarette and bites of something that looked like salmon mousse. Henri was hunched over the stove, deeply surly, wearing what looked like the same chef's pants and undershirt I'd seen him in earlier that day. French Vic was hanging on his shoulder, absolutely wrecked, mumbling in his ear.

"I'm gonna make your daddy proud, I swear to you, you understand?"

"Get off me."

"I always admired him. I mean from when I was a boy, you know, he was an idol to me, an icon, a god."

"Shut up."

Henri gave a vicious shrug but failed to dislodge Vic. A door swung open and Rocky ambled in carrying another case of liquor. He slammed down the case and ripped open a bottle and guzzled until I thought I might be sick. He let off a belch that shook the ceiling tiles, then wrapped Ambrose into a bear hug and said, "My man."

"I heard you offered him a job," I said.

"Hush!" said Ambrose, straining admirably to extract himself from Rocky's grasp. Beads of sweat like cooling wax studded his face and scalp. Rocky pinched his cheek.

"This adorable old bastard," said Rocky. "I'd do anything to get him on my team."

"Why?"

"He's the first person I ever cooked for that doesn't just suck my dick. I mean I can fix him a plate of something really crazy, something nobody ever even dreamed of before—and he'll tell me to fuck off and do it again."

"I'd like to think I phrase my criticism a bit more gently than that," said Ambrose, blushing all the way down to his collar.

"Like this morning I woke up, and bang, I had *the* idea—the one that I've been waiting for—the one that's gonna put Number 5 on the map, that's gonna change American cooking forever. And I called Ambrose, because lately I always call Ambrose, and I said two words."

"Chicken potpie," said Ambrose.

"My three favorite things. That's all the restaurant serves, get it? Fried chicken. Homemade pie. And this exceptionally potent grass I buy from my cousin upstate. Chicken potpie."

"That certainly qualifies as an idea," I said. "What did Ambrose say?"

"What nobody else would have the balls to tell me."

"That selling grass is illegal?"

"Who gives a shit? We'd figure that out. But he said—how did you phrase it, Ambrose?"

"I told him it was stupid."

Rocky smacked his hands together and gave a little yelp.

"Stupid! So fucking stupid! Would've taken me six months to figure that out. But Ambrose knew just like that. Or, like, try this."

He pulled a terrine from the fridge, sliced off a hunk, and slid it across the counter. It smelled alarmingly good.

"I wanted to make an American terrine. Like, embarrassingly American. Ground turkey and cranberry sauce and Milwaukee bratwurst and cornbread stuffing. Ambrose told me to shut the fuck up."

"Again," said Ambrose, "not in those words."

"So I dialed it back to just the turkey and the bratwurst. It's American, yeah, but not Yankee doodle dandy. Have a bite."

I ate. I wanted to think it was stupid but either I was drunk or it was amazing or—probably—both. Rocky saw my satisfaction and snapped his fingers to celebrate.

"He's good," I told Ambrose. "A total dope but still pretty good."

"You're right."

"So take the job! What've you got to lose?"

"Only everything."

"And who needs that?"

Rocky carved off a healthy chunk of terrine and slid it to Ambrose, who chewed and blinked and chewed some more. He leaned over and whispered, "But what about Tiny Tommy?"

"Sorted."

Standing up straight, Ambrose took the rag off Rocky's shoulder and wiped his forehead dry. He took another bite of the terrine. When he spoke, he sounded twenty years younger.

"You really think it's a good idea?"

"Probably not," I answered. "But it sounds like a hell of a lot of fun."

He took a third bite. Closed his eyes. Savored it.

And then he said: "Okay."

Rocky swept him up and spun him around and kissed him loudly on the mouth—a hug almost as good as Peter's. Ambrose was laughing so hard that he forgot how much he hated being touched. Drinks were poured and toasts were made, and we were opening another bottle when Henri punched Vic in the shoulder, then screamed "Asshole!" and stormed out through the back door. There was a moment of awkwardness. Ambrose stared at his shoes. Vic slumped against Rocky, laughter bubbling up from his chest.

"You know, in France we have a word for men like Henri," he said.

"What is it?" said Rocky.

"Dickhead."

At that, even Ambrose laughed. I pushed through the door and found Henri in the alley, pacing and smoking and stomping on trash.

"I don't remember you picking so many fights," I said.

"Yeah, well, I'm at the end of my rope. Dad's restaurant is my birthright. They stole it from me."

I looked down and was pleased to find the cognac still gripped in my fist. I took a long drink, cursing the men whose bullshit consumed so much of my time.

"That's what you and Vic were bickering over in there?"

"I asked him not to take the job. To tell Oswald it should go to me. You know what he said? 'But it's my dream.'"

He aimed a Bruce Lee kick at a trash can and shouted, "It was my dream first!" The can toppled. A family of rats bolted out.

"Feel better?" I said.

"No."

"So maybe try letting go, huh? You're better off without it, man. Only an idiot signs up to be captain of a sinking ship."

"I know, I know." He slumped onto the pavement and squeezed his jaw with both hands. "Dad's place is fucked. Près is fucked too. But if I could choose between them, I'd take the one that feels like home."

"You could talk to Tiny Tommy."

He looked up at me with wet, red eyes.

"The garbage guy?" he said.

"He's got leverage over Oswald. Kiss his ass a little."

"I'm not gonna beg. Not for what's mine."

"You think you're gonna get what you want stomping around an alley yelling at rats?"

He spit at the ground. It landed on his shoe. I squeezed the toupee in my fist. I still wanted him to try it on, but what was the point? Poor bastard didn't fit anywhere—not even a toupee.

Eighteen

The next thing I remember, I was back in the dining room, a glass of Tiny Tommy's gin in one hand and half a baguette in the other, gnawing the bread like a squirrel. A couple of the lights had gotten kicked over, so the room was darker, sticky with spilled booze, and foggy with hard drugs and lust. I'd seen at least one couple slip under the stairs to fuck and public fornicators are like roaches—if you see one, there's a dozen more just out of sight.

I was on the banquette next to Toru, pressing my head against the wall so that the room wouldn't spin. He was absolutely wasted—on booze, on pot, but mostly on food.

"They just kept feeding me. I told them to stop—or maybe I said, 'Don't stop'?—and I didn't even know what I was putting in my mouth, B, but it was so, so good. There was this shrimp thing? Or maybe cauliflower? When you've finished charlotte russe you're learning it next."

His head rolled onto his shoulder. His eyes tried valiantly to focus.

"This is better than Elma Zumwalt's."

I patted his cheek, took his plate, and picked over the remains. The individual dishes could no longer be distinguished—it had a Jackson Pollock thing going on—but it was excellent mush. Every cook in New York put something on that plate. It was a holy thing.

The banquette sagged under Oswald Blount, who was as drunk as a man can be without falling down.

"I'm a fucking genius."

"Then why are you wearing that tie?"

"Do you know how hard it is to poach a chef from his own restaurant? Vic's the hottest hash slinger in Manhattan and he's gonna be all mine."

"You're sure his wife is gonna let him go?"

He swiveled his head toward me, tongue lolling like a bulldog's.

"Lady, I'm the adultery king of Midtown. I don't give a shit about wives."

He grabbed a fistful of food off my plate and was licking it off his fingers when a shadow fell across his lap. He looked up to discover a skyscraper named Blue.

"Mr. Motisi would like to see you," he said. At first I thought he was talking to me—but nope, this particular summons was directed at Oswald Blount.

"Who the shit is Mr. Martini?" said Oswald.

Blue jabbed a thumb at Tiny Tommy, who was at a table by himself, tearing into a brace of lobster.

"Tell him to go fuck a hole in the ground," said Oswald.

"Mr. Motisi thought you might feel that way. He asked me to

inform you that your restaurant is rather heavily in his debt, which means you come to him."

"Oh yeah?" Oswald tried to stand up. The table got in his way. He tried again and, with Blue's help, made it to his feet. "I'll tell that orange bastard who owes who."

"Be careful," I said. "He's dangerous."

"So am I."

"No, I mean it, Oswald. Don't fuck around."

"I'm just gonna talk to the man. Explain things. But if he gets tough I'm gonna jam his elbows up his ass."

And with that bit of foolhardy bravado, he was gone. I probably should have gone with him but at that point standing was doubtful and walking was out of the question. If Oswald Blount wanted to make a fool of himself, who was I to get in his way?

I closed my eyes and felt my heart thumping and tried to convince myself that, like I'd told Ambrose, maybe everything was fine. Yeah, I was fully screwed and had been ever since I made my bargain with Judy, but if you take an impossible assignment there's no shame in falling short. Which was good because I had three notebooks full of color and a gut full of cognac and not much else.

Only this didn't mean I was giving up!

I thumped my fist to emphasize my not-giving-upness. Toru startled, then settled back down.

No, there would be no giving up for me. Not even a little bit. Tomorrow I was going to wake up and drink a gallon of water and eat a dozen fried eggs and I was going to *work*. I'd turn my three notebooks full of color into a beautiful story about an industry in mourning, with a lot of wit and a lot of dirt, and even if I didn't reveal the killer at the end, it would still be a nice piece and we'd be first to it and sometimes being first is almost as good as . . .

My train of thought derailed as another weight settled onto the banquette. Without looking I knew it couldn't be Oswald because Oswald smelled like money and sweat and the person beside me smelled cleaner than clean.

So here's something I haven't mentioned and which probably doesn't mean anything at all: All of my sexual fantasies take place in restaurants. Even when I was a kid daydreaming about Gene Kelly's thighs—seriously, see *The Pirate*—the floor he was pinning me to was the black and white tile at Angelo's on Third Ave. As I got older my tastes in imaginary sexual partners broadened and the restaurants where we screwed became more luxe. Big surprise, most of the time it was Laurent's. In my head, there'd be lilacs and larkspurs on the tables and napkins folded just so and nobody in there but me and, y'know, whoever. We'd fuck on the banquette, leather squeaking beneath our bodies, or on a starched white tablecloth or on the plush red carpet.

And I never told my analyst because I knew he'd turn it into this whole thing, when the simple fact is that I like to imagine screwing in restaurants because I think they're the most beautiful places on earth. The way I figure, a nice restaurant done up for service is like a Broadway theater all ready for showtime, except the chairs aren't torture and there's plenty to eat and you can go to the bathroom whenever you want. What could be more romantic than that?

Anyway, I bring this up so that when I say Susan's appearance made me wish everybody else in that restaurant would disappear, you understand what was on my mind.

"How you doing," she said, setting down a plate of little fried somethings. She popped one in her mouth and smirked as she chewed. I was stuck between her and Toru and the table. There was nowhere to run and I was sweating like spoiled cheese.

"Susan Gullett, let me introduce my *husband*," I said, putting the word in 52-point font. "Toru Komatsu, Susan Gullett."

"I'd shake your hand," said Toru, "but I'm all buttery. I don't suppose you brought me dessert?"

"Nope."

"I like you anyway."

The new best friends then spent a few hundred years discussing, I don't know, the weather or baseball or the atomic weight of plutonium or the Guatemalan civil war. Screaming static filled my ears and it was all I could do to scan for blood-red words like *kissing* or *smooching* or *Frenching* or *necking* or just plain *lesbian*. But then Toru's half of the conversation became punctuated with exaggerated yawns and suddenly he was asleep and Susan and I were dangerously close to being alone.

Across the room, Oswald leaned over Tommy's table. They traded whispers that turned into shouts that turned into snarls. Every eye turned toward them. Susan scooted a little closer to me. Nobody was watching us and even if they had been, what would they see? Two women talking while one of their men dozed on the banquette. What could be more innocent?

"So about last night," she said, smiling like a goddamned imp.

"No comment."

"Not about *that*, you goof. I mean have you reconsidered filling me in about Laurent? Because we've got our little story running tomorrow and I'd like to hear what you know."

"It seems like you know plenty."

Tommy thumped a finger into Oswald's chest hair. Oswald closed his fists on Tommy's lobsters and squeezed until they burst. A hush went over the room. I probably should stop them before they kill each other, I thought, but Ms. Chaos was rubbing her knee against mine in a way that made me genuinely worry my leg might catch fire. I was outside my body and that makes it hard to walk across a room.

"Is it true Laurent's recipe box was stolen?" she said.

"Who told you that?"

"I don't give up sources."

"The same person who mentioned the aspic?"

She shrugged. It was incredibly fucking cute.

"I told you—I only spill to friends."

Tommy seized Oswald's collar and dragged him across the table. I really, really needed to get over there but Susan's hand had made its way to my knee and it had me stuck to the banquette like a railroad spike. Oswald was screaming and his face was claret and I'd have gone to help except . . .

Except let's be honest—it wasn't her hand that had me locked down and it wasn't some imaginary railroad spike.

It was me.

"Are you sure you don't want to be friends?" she said.

Doing this next to Toru was completely insane. But Toru was a million miles away, cruising on a cloud of dope and shrimp. Adrenaline had my mouth tasting like a chemical spill and my heart pounding hard enough to crack a rib. I should have shoved her off but I'd wanted this my whole fucking life, I was realizing, and when something you've always wanted grabs your knee it's hard to say no.

Tommy flipped Oswald onto his back. A couple of the less-wasted chefs made like they were going to intervene. Blue stood up—he'd been eating soup this entire time—and they stepped off. Tommy pulled back his hand like he was going to thrash Oswald.

"Listen, man—" said Oswald.

Tommy gave Oswald the lightest possible slap. All the fear went out of the room. Everybody laughed. Tommy pulled back for another smack and I tore my eyes off him and let them go where they wanted. I inspected the soft curve of Susan's jaw. The way the tip of her nose pulled down when she smiled. The dark fuzz on the edge of her eyebrow. Her soft mop of brown hair. It could be a wig, I thought. If I touched it, I'd know.

"What does it take to be your friend?" I said.

Her hand crept up my leg as steady as floodwater. The laughter around Tommy's table was petering out and I could hear Oswald struggling for help under the steady *tap-tap-tap* of gentle, humiliating slaps. A snore rattled out of Toru's chest. I tried to tell myself there was nothing wrong with just letting him sleep. A single dad deserves a nap.

"We do what friends do. Get a drink. Try not to talk about work."

"What else is there to talk about?"

"Anything. We. Like."

Her hand stopped. Halfway up—high enough to be suspicious, too low to give me what I needed. Tommy shoved Oswald off the table. Butter, cutlery, and bits of lobster rained down on him. What the hell, I thought. I grabbed Susan's hand. I kept it moving up.

And up.

And up.

And then her hand brushed my underwear and every light in the place went out. Folks screamed, as you can imagine—the hysterical shriek of drunks who weren't sure if this was terror or fun. And then I felt fingers on my cheeks and breath on my lips and Susan kissed me very, very hard.

This time the world didn't melt. My head didn't explode. It just felt perfectly, unquestionably, inescapably—

Safe.

It didn't last. The door to the kitchen swung wide and Rocky Shanklin stood there, silhouetted by the glowing range, locks glowing like burning wheat.

"Who wants dessert?"

A cheer rang out. Toru sat straight up, eyes blinking without seeing, and muttered, "Dessert?" My mouth clenched so hard I almost bit off my tongue. I smacked Susan's hand away from my leg. Her breath tickled my ear as she said, "Enjoy your present."

She got up. The lights came back on. I wanted to go after her more than anything but Toru was stirring, so I just watched her all the way up the stairs. She never looked back. I looked down and saw a black and gold box adorned with interlocking male and female symbols.

Alyssa Ashley. Musk.

"What the fuck do I look like? A waiter?" shouted Rocky, hands making streaks in a massive silver tureen. "Come and get your fucking chocolate mousse!"

His guests streamed toward him—everyone except for Oswald, who was just now picking himself up from the floor, and Tiny Tommy, who had disappeared. Toru got up and I tried to follow him but my knees were weak from liquor and other things. I collapsed into the squeaking banquette.

"No sweat," said Toru. "I'll get two plates."

"Remember—"

"Extra whipped cream. I'm the world's greatest fiancé. Think I'd forget?"

Oh god, I thought. And I'm the world's scummiest scum. He swayed away. I tried to swallow my guilt but it didn't go down easy. I nudged open the little box and tipped out the perfume. I unscrewed the cap and breathed deep. I got baby powder, cut grass, freshly washed hair. I got Susan. And then a cloud of Carolina tobacco washed it all away. Henri plopped into the nearest chair, cigarette dangling, mouth puckered with rage. I shoved the perfume back into the box and snapped: "What do you want now?"

"The balls on that bastard."

"What balls? Which bastard?"

"Rockford fucking Shanklin. Dishing up chocolate mousse—my father's *signature*—before Dad's body is even cold."

"Lots of people make chocolate mousse."

"Rockford, Christ. What kind of name is that anyway?"

"He's from Louisiana."

"Doesn't talk like it."

"Do I talk like I'm from Brooklyn? Do you talk like you're French? We're New Yorkers, end of story."

"Well, I can't wait to taste this shit."

"I'm sure it will be vile."

Toru returned with two plates piled with airy whipped chocolate, clean and pure and cold. My hunger roared back and I felt certain that if I didn't eat that mousse as soon as possible, I would die. But instead of setting down the plates, Toru scowled.

"Aw shit," he said. "The whipped cream."

"It's fine, baby."

"I fixed you one with, like, a mountain of whipped cream. I set it down to get spoons . . . I must have taken the wrong one. I'll be right back."

"Don't take a goddamned step. I want that chocolate and I want it now."

"You sure?"

I grabbed the plate. I ate. The mousse was soft as a whisper, the chocolate so powerful it made my hands shake. I took another bite and when the cocoa wave broke I caught a dim echo of mint. I opened my eyes. I hadn't even realized they were closed.

This was one of the best things I'd ever tasted.

And I was pretty sure I'd had it before.

"It can't be that good," said Henri.

"It is."

He took my plate, gobbled up a bite, and turned fire-engine red.

"That pig," he said.

"Kinda familiar, huh?"

"That fucking pig!"

"Can I have my plate back now?"

He slammed the plate so hard it cracked, scattering mousse across the bare white table. He got up violently; his chair clattered to the floor. I scooped up one last bite—doing a decent enough job of avoiding the shards—and went after Henri. He marched toward Rocky, who stood over the tureen like a hunter with a prize kill. Rocky was about to say hi when Henri seized the tureen and clamped it onto Rocky's head.

It takes a lot to shock a crowd that stuffed with quaaludes and chocolate, but, reader, they gasped. Chocolate splattered across Rocky's chin, chest, floor. Rocky tilted the bowl off his head. Crash. He looked like a child who'd had a hell of a lot of fun losing a mud fight. He licked mousse off his lips and smiled.

"Brother. What gives?"

"That's my dad's mousse."

"'Scuse me?"

"You stole it, you dirtbag, you killed him and you fucking stole it."

"You think I killed him for chocolate *mousse*?"

"I don't know why you killed him but—"

"It's a family recipe, friend."

"Bullshit."

"Swear to god! My mother used to make it, first Sunday of every month. We'd eat it after church. That's, like, my whole childhood, and you dumped it all over the floor."

"Fuck. Your. Mother."

I reached for Henri but I was too drunk or too slow or, I don't know, too something. He planted both hands on Rocky's chest and shoved. Rocky tumbled down into the moussey mess. Henri kicked him and kicked him and then kicked him again, just for fun. I tried to stop him but he was very angry and sort of strong. Finally I pushed him clear enough that Rocky was able to get to his feet, spluttering, nose bleeding, his cool finally gone.

"You bourgeois prick!"

"Show me the card."

"What are you talking about?"

"Show me where your mother wrote that down. Show me the card or I'll know you killed my dad."

Rocky planted his feet and loosened his shoulders.

"Where I come from, a man who says a thing like that is liable to get punched in the jaw."

"Go ahead."

Rocky raised his fists. Henri did the same. They locked eyes for one long second and then Henri took a step forward and Rocky shifted his weight like he was going to throw a punch but instead he spun on his heels and ran the fuck away. Henri tried to grab him by the neck but I was pulling him back, so he couldn't quite reach.

He did, however, grab a fistful of Rocky's hair.

And those golden locks?

That chocolate-sodden Viking mane?

It popped right off.

Henri gawked at it—the whole blond do hanging limp in his hands. I pointed at Rocky, whose dome shone like a bare bulb. What hair he had was matted and brown, almost pubic in the way it clung to his acne-scarred scalp.

"You're bald!" I shouted. "You're bald!"

Yeah, it's not a polite thing to yell at someone. But it had been an odd night—an odd week!—and I guess my etiquette failed me sometime around the second murder. I scrambled over the table, kicking a plate of calf's brain fritters, a bowl of blanched string beans, and the rest of that gorgeous terrine. I lunged at Rocky like a football tackle, sending both of us crashing to the ground, every type of food imaginable raining on our heads. He wiggled under me—I smacked his face as hard as I could and shouted, "Don't get up!"

He looked scared. Neat. I tore open my purse with my teeth—I swear, my goddamned *teeth*—showering him with scraps of paper and loose makeup and stale bits of kaiser roll that I'd stashed for Nicky like a month prior. I finally got my hands on the toupee—that fucking toupee—and wrestled it onto Rocky's wiggling head.

It fit. I mean *perfect,* okay, and the color matched every squiggly hair. I'd never seen anything like it. It almost looked real. I had done it, god damn it, and that seemed to justify everything. My grief about Laurent and guilt about Susan didn't vanish but in that moment they shrank into something I thought I could maybe live with. I had the killer and that meant I had my story and that meant everything was, from a certain perspective, A-OK.

"Tell me everything," I said.

"Get off."

"Did you kill him?"

"I can explain, okay? Just get off my balls and let me talk."

But he never got the chance. Because before he could open his mouth, Minnie Anglade shrieked like a runaway train.

"He's dead! He's dead, you monsters, he's dead!"

"What are you talking about?" howled Oswald.

She answered with the kind of scream that cracks crystal. And we all looked her way and we saw Vic, the poor bastard, flopped across the table, face buried in a plate of mousse.

Mousse absolutely heaped with whipped cream.

The mousse that was meant for me.

Nineteen

• Friday •

Funny thing is, he wasn't—dead, I mean. At least not yet. By the time I pushed past Minnie—who was howling like a fire alarm—there was warmth in his skin and breath on his lips and his eyes were half open too.

I grabbed the nearest glass of water and snapped at Rocky, "Salt! Salt, god damn it, salt!" He finally got the message and threw a shaker my way. I dumped the whole thing into the glass and tipped it into Vic's mouth. He coughed and he spluttered but I rubbed his throat and I made sure he got most of it down. He threw up chocolate all over the place—on the table, on his wife, on me—and settled into a fog that was not quite sleep.

Someone pressed a napkin into my hand. It was Toru, the mensch, looking impressed and horrified all at once.

So the records kept spinning and the room did too. People sobbed and shrieked and collapsed in anguish and Toru and I held hands—a kind of prayer, I guess, that this idiot wouldn't die.

He was still breathing when the ambulance showed up. Still breathing when they dragged him out on the stretcher. Still breathing, I guess, when they loosed their sirens and roared toward Roosevelt Hospital. The police rounded up everybody but Tiny Tommy and Blue, who were long gone, and Toru, who got sent home because, as Donati said, "I know where you live and being married to her is punishment enough."

So I don't know how many hours later—it was morning, I guess, and Ringling Brothers were parading elephants through my skull—I was sitting on a brutally uncomfortable bench at police headquarters in a room that stank of stale smoke with a heavy undercurrent of dried vomit, which, in fairness to the NYPD, was mostly coming from me. They'd questioned me until I was hoarse but every time I asked to leave Donati said, "Just a little bit longer." I was staring at my hands, trying to use my mangled manicure to distract me from nagging visions of myself dead on Rocky Shanklin's filthy floor.

Right then it was Minnie's turn in the interrogation room and I was alone with a disconsolate Rockford Shanklin. He was coming down from at least three different things and he kept emitting these irritating little moans. I'd taken the toupee off him while we waited for the police and slipped it back into my purse. He was still covered in blood and chocolate and random food and he wouldn't stop twisting that damn blond wig in his hands. All his swagger had seeped out. Even his voice had gone thin. He was not so cute anymore.

"So what the fuck happened?" I said for the third or fourth time.

"I'm waiting for my lawyer."

"Your lawyer can protect you from the cops, dipshit, but not from me."

"Huh?"

I smacked my notepad. He curled into a sad little ball.

"Vic survived the poison in his whipped cream," I hissed. "I'm a lot smaller than him. You know what happens if I eat it? It hits me faster and harder and I drop dead in your pathetic excuse for a restaurant."

"I didn't poison the whipped cream!"

"Who did?"

"I don't know! The place was a scene, man, it could have been anybody."

"Then tell me how your toupee ended up stained with my friend's blood."

"I have the right to avoid self-incrimination, you know. That's, like, the Third Amendment."

"And I have the right to tell Donati that when I got to Laurent's on Monday, I saw Rockford fucking Shanklin sneaking out the back door clutching a cleaver."

"But that's lying."

"I don't care!"

"I'm telling you, I didn't kill him. I'm, like, a creature of love."

"Then explain this."

I jammed the toupee under his nose. Between the dried blood and the accumulated crumbs that filled my purse, it had gotten pretty vile. He retched but didn't puke and finally croaked out: "Would you believe he was dead when I got there?"

"Convince me. Quickly. Because if you don't, when Donati comes back I give him the toupee. I'm not a lawyer but that seems like enough to convict you for murder."

"Okay. But just . . . put that thing away."

I folded the toupee as neatly as I could and stowed it in my purse. He tugged his blond wig back onto his head. It was matted with chocolate and he couldn't get it on quite straight. It had been sexy before but now it just looked like a wig.

"What were you doing at Laurent's?" I said, notepad in hand.

"I, well . . . Christ, this is embarrassing. I needed help with my chocolate mousse."

"I thought it was your mother's recipe."

"It was! She really did make it the first Sunday of every month. And I wanted it on the menu, you know, like, to honor her? But it turns out all of her recipes are kind of shit. The mousse kept coming out watery."

"Did you ask Ambrose for help?"

"Of course. He told me not to bother—that chocolate mousse was Laurent's signature and I'd be an idiot to challenge him on it. I guess I'm not very good at taking advice, huh? I thought if I went by the restaurant Laurent and I could use the mousse to kinda bury the hatchet. It, uh, it didn't work out that way."

A pair of uniformed cops brushed past us and entered the interrogation room. They handed Donati something in a plastic bag. He stared at Rocky hungrily. I shifted so Rocky could only see me. The arm of the bench was sticky, like the kids had been here eating jelly.

"Why switch wigs?"

"The one you found—that's my incognito piece. I wear it when I'm buying, y'know, pharmaceuticals or when I'm any place where I don't want to be seen."

"Like the restaurant of a tired old hack."

He whimpered some more.

"I was gonna apologize to him about that. I loved Laurent's, y'know? When I gave that interview I was just trying to stir up shit. Get publicity."

"It was still a lousy thing to say. Why'd you leave the toupee behind?"

"Well, and this is the part I'm worried the police aren't going to believe . . . I sort of took it off to do some cooking and I guess I never put it back on."

I asked the next question slowly. "What were you cooking?"

"An, uh . . . an aspic."

If he thought I was going to jump up and down shouting *Eureka*, he was disappointed. I just wrote it down. I'd been a reporter long enough to know how to keep a straight face.

"Step back a second," I said, like this was the most ordinary conversation in the world. "Take me through this from the minute you showed up at Laurent's. What time was it?"

"Afternoon."

"More specific?"

"I'm not the kind of person who thinks about time."

"Phenomenal. How'd you get in?"

"The front door was unlocked. The lights were off. I went downstairs. I could smell somebody was making stock. The kitchen was empty and there was a big pot of it cooling on the stove. The office door was open and that's where I saw them. Laurent's body was at his desk—he looked dead, man, like deader than anything I'd ever seen—and somebody was on their hands and knees holding fistfuls of kitchen rags, trying to sop up the blood."

Rocky's voice had dropped to a thin whisper. His eyes were locked on the cracked tile between his feet. He did not see me scribbling down every word he said.

"Did you see their face?" I asked.

He chuckled. It sounded like it hurt.

"Oh yeah. We had a whole little talk."

"Somebody you knew?"

"Uh-huh. She's very recognizable."

My voice was steady as I asked, "It was a woman?"

"One of, um, one of the most famous women in the world."

"Who?"

"And that was what surprised me, y'know, because when you see her in pictures she's not usually covered in blood."

"What's her name, Rocky?"

"Elizabeth."

I wrote it down. Underlined it twice.

"Elizabeth who?"

"Two. Or, I guess, the Second. Elizabeth the Second."

I set my pen down. I swallowed a scream.

"You saw the Queen of England in Laurent's office, on her hands and knees, cleaning up blood?"

"You see why I was surprised."

"Rocky? When all of this happened were you, by any chance, really fucking high?"

He hid his face in his wig, moaning like Nicky when he colors outside the lines. I wanted to hit him but my temples were throbbing and my tailbone was aching and I felt like my stomach had never been so empty before. I just wanted to get this done.

"Oh god. My analyst is right. I'm a catastrophe. It was a nice day, all right, and when I saw how blue the sky was I figured I'd celebrate with a tab of acid but it didn't hit, so I took some more and I was still feeling pretty straight when I went over to Laurent's, but now that I say all of this out loud I'm thinking that maybe, yeah, I was out of my fucking skull."

"Christ. Okay, walk me through your conversation with the queen."

His eyes lit up. Drug freaks love recounting a trip. None of them seem to realize that it's the most boring topic in the world.

"She was not happy to see me," he said. "Gave me a lot of, 'What on earth are you doing here?' in that fancy accent of hers. I told her about the mousse and she said to get the fuck out and I asked what's up with Laurent and she said get the fuck out, so I asked about the veal stock and she said something about aspic and I was like, okay, aspic I understand."

Uniformed police were collecting around the interrogation room like dust bunnies. I needed him to finish this before he got taken away.

"Sure, sure, sure," I said. "What happened next?"

"I told her to get out, that I'd handle the aspic and I guess I was screaming pretty loud because she bolted. But before she left she muttered something I couldn't quite hear but it sounded like, 'Off with his head,' which as you know is a very queenly thing to say, and that started ping-ponging around in my head and sounding more and more like an order and when the queen gives an order you don't say no, so . . ."

He trailed off like he wanted me to finish the thought.

"You've gotta say it," I said. "Not me."

"I cut off his head and encased it in aspic."

"Fuck, man."

"I know, I know, I'm disgusting. But in that moment I really felt like it was him or me and he was already dead, so what's the harm? He was meat. French meat. I told myself it'd be just like breaking down a pig."

"How'd you take off his head?"

He gulped like he was going to throw up.

"The cleaver was already on his desk. I knocked his body out of the chair and just, y'know . . . went to town. It got pretty hairy. At some point I guess I used the toupee to wipe my face, then I saw how much blood was on it and I just tossed it."

"What happened to the cleaver?"

"I don't know. When I was done with it, I dropped it."

"Why the aspic?"

"The stock was right there. It seemed natural, y'know, like what he would have wanted? I was there most of the afternoon, I guess, because when I finally left the sun was getting ready to go down. But I finished the aspic. Prettiest one I ever did."

"Yeah."

His eyes were red and gunky. His shirt was soaked with come-down sweat. He looked scared, little kid scared, not of the cops but of the possibility that I might not believe him.

"I don't know," I said. "It'd make a lot more sense if you'd killed him."

"I'm sorry. I just . . . didn't."

I rapped pen against pad.

"How'd you solve the mousse?" I said.

"Oh, Ambrose came through. When he heard about Laurent, he told me he thought it would be appropriate as, like, a tribute. Said mine was bland because my mother was skimping on chocolate. He was right."

"He always is. You didn't take the recipe box?"

"This is the first I heard of any fucking recipe box. If Henri thought I stole his dad's mousse, I don't know what to tell you. Chocolate mousses are either good or bad, y'know? The good ones all basically taste the same."

"Did you tell any of this to Susan Gullett?"

But before he could answer, a hand closed on his shoulder. Rocky looked up to find Detective Donati, still wearing the suit with charlotte russe on the shoulder, looking as close to fierce as he could get.

"The heck are you two talking about?"

"Cooking," whimpered Rocky.

"This clod say anything incriminating?" Donati asked me, a nauseating twinkle in his eye. "If he did, better tell us. This could be the last chance for you and me to be friends."

All I had to do was hand over the toupee, hang Rocky out to dry, and write the story of the drug-addled upstart who killed a legend. After I filed I could sleep for a week, and god, I wanted that bad. But the toupee stayed in my purse.

"Strictly small talk," I said.

"Doesn't matter," said Donati. "He's still under arrest."

Donati yanked Rocky up hard enough to rip his collar. Rocky shot me a look of pathetic gratitude as he was dragged toward the interrogation room. Minnie Anglade stood by the door, her face like a pizza left out in the rain. She spit in Rocky's face. The loogie slapped against his skin. He didn't even bother to wipe it off. The exchange made Donati smile. I called his name and he sauntered over like John Wayne with a head injury.

"You can go now."

"I'd love to. But Rocky didn't kill Laurent."

"Don't be an idiot."

"I'm telling you—he made the aspic. He cut off the head. But Laurent was dead when he got there."

"So who killed him?"

I glanced at my notes. Elizabeth II. If that was Rocky's story, better it come from him than me.

So I said: "I don't know. Yet. But I don't even see how you can hold him. You don't have any evidence connecting him to Laurent's."

Donati nodded at the nearest uniform. It was Adam-12, as blandly handsome and unresponsive as ever. He lifted the evidence bag. It held a wood-handled cleaver, matching the knife set at Laurent's butcher's station. It was crusty with blood.

"Where'd you find it?" I said.

"Embedded in a cutting board at Rocky's restaurant, hung up on the wall like a dang trophy. Not where I'd stash a murder weapon but I guess geniuses are different from you and me. Now, will you please get out of my way?"

"That knife was planted."

"The heck are you talking about?"

"I was at his restaurant on Wednesday afternoon. I saw the cleaver in the cutting board. Its handle was steel."

He pressed the heel of his hand against his forehead. Whatever he was trying to accomplish, it didn't help.

"Why would Rocky kill Laurent?" I said.

"Smack! The lab at Roosevelt called two hours ago. Victor Anglade's blood was half poison, half heroin. Maybe he and Rocky heard Laurent was holding and they killed him for the stash."

"And then left it behind?"

"César showed up while they were in the middle of prepping their aspic. They cut his throat, chucked him in the dumpster, and ran. Then at last night's party, Rocky sees Vic getting tanked, decides he can't be trusted, and decides to take him out."

"The poisoned mousse was meant for me."

"I have no reason to believe that."

"Well, what kind of poison was it?"

"Potassium bromate. Hair salons use it. It's an essential ingredient, apparently, in a permanent wave."

I pointed at the man in the interrogation room, who'd melted across the cold steel table. His wig lay like a mangled animal on the floor.

"Does that look like a man who's giving himself home perms?"

"I'm gonna find out. I had the boys pull the infamous aspic out of the evidence fridge. We're gonna confront him with it. Between guilt and the hangover and what I read as a naturally nervous disposition, I bet he cracks like an egg." He rubbed his head some more. Then he sort of smiled. "That reminds me. You see the papers?"

"I've been busy."

"C'mere. I got something, oh boy, you're just gonna love it."

He waved me over to a desk covered with the morning papers. The tabloids were open to the racing tips; the broadsheets had been divested of their sports sections and tossed aside. The only untouched paper was slim and colorful and extremely downtown. The *Arch.* He snatched it up and clutched it to his chest.

"I know you've been running all over town playing detective, thinking you're on the fast track to a Pulitzer." I'd never seen him so pleased with himself. It was disgusting. "And all that even though I told you it was unethical for you to be on this story."

"So what?"

"So maybe you should've listened to me. Because the burnouts on St. Mark's beat you to the punch."

He dropped the paper on the table. The cover was upside down, so it took me a second to realize that I was looking at a rather crude drawing of a decapitated head floating in a Jell-O mold, surrounded by chunks of what I guess were supposed to be marshmallows, with a chef's hat perched on top.

The headline read, "Nightmare in Aspic: How Grandma's Favorite Truffle-Slinger Got His Head Chopped Off—And What It Means for the Future of Restaurants in New York."

Christ.

I tasted blood.

A little story my ass. She'd scooped my guts out and dumped them on the fucking cover.

I'd have been hurt if we were friends.

When the static in my ears faded, I realized Donati had been talking this whole time.

"So this here is why I don't care what you say about Rocky Shanklin or French Vic or any other freaking thing. You told this Gullett broad about the aspic. You told her *everything*."

I tried to tell him that I'd managed to keep that to myself, despite all her wheedling, but my throat was too dry. I took a sip of the nearest cup of cold coffee and had another go.

"Why would I spill to my competition?"

"Because you're a dope, what do I care? All I know is, this murder is wrapped and nobody even yelled at me. Get out of my station before I start yelling at you."

"Yeah. Yeah, that'd probably be a good idea."

I got as far as the stairs before I noticed that the *Arch* was still clenched in my hands. I tore it open, flipping past bawdy horoscopes and horny personal ads, past a column about the budget crisis at the sanitation department and a roundup of all the new Off-Broadway plays that featured fucking onstage. When I finally got to Susan's article, well, it was what you'd expect.

A beautiful story about an industry in mourning.

A lot of color.

A lot of dirt.

She had everything but the killer. And even if I hadn't given her as much as Donati thought, there's no question that some of it was from me.

"Entering this restaurant is like stepping through a portal. When César, the iron-faced maître d', opens the door for you, you can pretend the city's not dying. That there's no piss on the sidewalk. That you could walk down the block without getting shot. Suddenly you're in Paris with Hemingway and Gertrude Stein or in a stateroom on the *Normandie,* steaming across the Atlantic. It's a stupid fantasy, sure, reactionary and bourgeois, but some people have nothing else."

Getting scooped always hurts but I was a big girl and I could take it. That wasn't the reason I felt tears gathering at the corners of my eyes. I felt so low that Donati was starting to make sense. This had always been a Mob hit—the aspic really was just frippery. I didn't belong here. I didn't know shit.

Come on, Bernice.

It's not like you really liked her.

Get it together.

It's not like those kisses meant anything.

God damn it, girl! You are too hungry for this shit. Get some food in your stomach and go from there.

I plodded down a grand flight of marble steps, following the scent of stale rolls and hot coffee, figuring that at the very least, the NYPD owed me breakfast. Homicide's sad excuse for a kitchenette was wedged into a weird little room with tall ceilings and peeling paint and a rusted metal grate over a window that was too grimy to let in light. The walls were papered with pornography. I grabbed a hunk of dry wood masquerading as a Danish and chewed. I poured a cup of bubbling sludge and, figuring it might be drinkable if I drowned it in milk, pulled open the fridge.

For the second time that week, I found a head.

Only this time it was the same head in the same aspic. It had melted a little bit on the way downtown and looked like a sand castle after it's taken hits from a couple of waves. Laurent's eyes had gone glassy and his mouth had drooped into a frown. He had every right to be disappointed, I thought. I had around twenty-four hours left and I didn't have anything that hadn't already been printed in the fucking *St. Mark's Arch.*

Fucking Susan Gullett. She was better than I'd realized. She was quick, sneaky, and ruthless—and she'd gotten the story without anybody trying to kill her. She was a better reporter than me, but I needed the answer more than she did. And I knew food. That was the only advantage I had left.

So I choked down my nausea and grabbed a spoon.

I crouched in front of the fridge.

I closed my eyes. I scooped up the tiniest bit of aspic and slid it into my mouth.

It was disgusting.

I mean, anything with a human head inside of it is going to be vile, but this also happened to taste like shit. There was the black pepper and the nutmeg and the port and pimento and all of that was fine, but there was also enough salt to pickle my tongue. I spit it into the garbage and spent a while rinsing my mouth with scalding coffee. And then I headed back upstairs. Adam-12 tried to stop me from barging into interrogation but I made like I was gonna chuck the coffee at his pretty square face and he flinched long enough for me to get through the door.

Donati and Rocky were staring at each other like two people on the world's grimmest blind date. As soon as he saw me, Donati started shouting, "Out! Out! Out!" but I was loud enough to make Rocky hear my question—the only question left that mattered.

"Did you taste the aspic?"

"Of course I did."

Adam-12 wrapped his arms around my waist. He picked me up and dragged me across the room. I jammed my feet into the doorframe. He pulled as hard as he could.

I screamed: "How did it taste?"

"Kinda salty but I was high. I thought it was fucking great."

My grip broke. Adam-12 wrenched me out of the doorway and tossed my bruised behind onto a bench. Donati got right in my face. His breath smelled like garlic bagel. He shrieked, "I wish I had a dungeon to lock you up in."

"Later. Rocky isn't your guy. You're looking for Queen Elizabeth."

"You're deranged."

"So what? I'm also correct. When Rocky showed up at Laurent's, there was a body in the office and veal stock on the stove. Rocky used the stock to make aspic, but he didn't prep it, and he was way too high to notice that it tasted like shit."

"So what?"

"So why did somebody go to the trouble of making the world's most perfect veal stock and then dump in so much salt that it tastes like the water at Coney Island? Answer that and we'll find the killer."

His eyes looked like a pair of boiled eggs that he was trying to squeeze out of his skull. His chest heaved.

"Hold on . . . Hold on . . . Hold on . . ."

"I'm holding."

"You *tasted* it?"

"Just the teensiest little bite."

So help me, dear reader, I tried not to laugh. But he was so angry and the whole situation was so undeniably sick and once I started giggling, man, I just couldn't stop.

"Shut up," said Donati. "Shut up!"

I tried, I swear to god, but that just made it worse. So, doing his best Colonel Klink, he bellowed: "Get her out of here!"

His men obliged. They hoisted me off the bench and out of the office and I figured they'd put me down somewhere around the hallway but they carried me flight after flight and I was howling the whole time. They set me down—quite gently, I might add—on Centre Street between a pile of garbage and a second pile of garbage. I laughed until my sides split and my jaw ached and my neck was wet with tears because, god damn it, I'd been right from the start. This wasn't about garbage or debt or heroin. This wasn't about jealousy or succession or toupees. This murder had always been about food and that meant there was no son of a bitch on earth who could solve it but me.

When I finally quit laughing I grabbed two bacon and egg sandwiches from the deli and headed for the train.

I had a party to plan.

Twenty

An hour later I'd swapped my vomit-encrusted dress for a red blouse and high slacks. The oven was hot and so was I. I had a whisk in my hand and the phone wedged against my shoulder and I was yelling at Shipley Merritt to get the hell out of bed.

"I don't give a shit how hungover you are. Get up and get dressed and get down to Centre Street to bail Rocky out of jail."

"Who is this?" he asked for the fifth or sixth time.

"Bernice Black. I'm a restaurant critic and you're in the business and that means you do what I say."

"But . . . but why?"

"I don't like innocent men rotting in jail. And anyway, I'm throwing a party and Rocky's a riot. Tell him not to show up too high, yeah? I'll have questions."

He was still jabbering when I hung up. I glanced at the oven and confirmed my ladyfingers were not quite brown, then started piling up all the stuff I'd need for the rest of the russe—milk and cream and sugar and Harveys Bristol Cream. I was rummaging for the gelatin when Toru appeared in a set of lime-green pajamas, fresh from putting Nicky down for his nap. He squeezed into the kitchen, poured me coffee, and spoke in the voice he used to try to talk the children down from tantrums.

"Do you mind sitting down?"

"Where the fuck is the gelatin?"

"I don't know."

"It should be with the baking stuff but it's not with the baking stuff. Did I put it somewhere else after I made the last practice russe? Did I run out?"

"Stop it."

"Did the kids put it somewhere? Did *you*?"

"Stop!"

I quit moving. Well, on the outside. Inside my heart was pounding and my brain was spinning and every limb was vibrating under a stream of tiny lightning strikes.

"I'm not throwing a party without dessert."

"I mean you have to stop *all of this*. You're manic."

"You say manic. I say . . . productive."

He pressed my palm into the counter's peeling imitation tile. His hand felt cool and the tile did too. I don't think I'd ever seen his eyes so red.

"Somebody nearly died last night because he ate a plate of food that was meant for you. If I weren't so blessedly absent-minded, if I hadn't lost track of your plate, the kids and I would be alone."

This cut me in half. I mean it was all I'd been thinking but it sounded even worse out loud. To keep myself from crying, I retrieved my hand and continued opening drawers. I found the gelatin wedged against the back of the silverware drawer. Did Nicky do that, I wondered, or was it me?

"You're right," I said. "You're absolutely right. But there's a man in jail who is going to go down for murder—a drug-addled twerp, yeah, but not a killer—unless I sort this out."

"Fuck him. You're the only one I care about."

"Then let me do my work."

"No."

"What do you mean, 'no'?"

I looked at him. The big living room window was right over his shoulder and the light made me squint, so I couldn't see his face as he croaked: "I mean quit the story or . . ."

"Or what? You've obviously been rehearsing this, Toru. Spit it out."

"Or I don't want you in the apartment with the kids."

"You're kicking me out?"

He chewed his lip.

"I'm saying that right now, being near you doesn't feel safe. Drop the story or just . . . leave."

An ultimatum, I thought. How interesting. How unlike him. It was a bit like glancing at your chest and noticing a gaping hole where your heart used to be. His apartment no longer felt like home.

He said my name a few more times. I think anyway. I couldn't hear him over the ringing in my ears. I crinkled the gelatin packet, mouth feeling like I'd dumped a pound of the stuff down my throat, and considered his offer. I'd always wondered how it would feel to throw myself off a cliff.

Time to find out.

"Okay."

"Thank you. Wait. Okay to what?"

I slipped into the living room, which had returned to its customary state of chaos, and opened the overstuffed hall closet. I pushed through boots, coats, sheets, quilts, children's artwork, and empty suitcases until I found the big canvas bag we used on our very occasional trips to the beach. I brought it to the kitchen and shoveled in the junk for the russe. Toru stared.

"What are you doing?" he said.

"Packing. Obviously. Grab my typewriter?"

"B."

"Paper too. I've got a deadline."

"You're not serious."

"Of course I am. I can't work without paper."

The egg timer went off. I pulled on the oven mitt and retrieved the ladyfingers from the oven. A perfect golden brown. In a just world they'd get a half hour to cool, but that wasn't in the cards. I dumped them into a Ziploc bag, leaving it open so that the steam wouldn't make them mushy. I ran water over the mold until it was cool enough to touch and chucked it in the bag.

"Are you sleeping with someone?"

It was a deafening question that he asked in a whisper, a concession to the child trying to sleep in the next room.

"Where do you get that?" I said.

"It's the only reason I can think for you to walk out."

"The answer is yes. I'm fucking a guy named Toru Komatsu."

"I meant somebody else."

"No."

I packed the bag, then repacked it when I realized I'd put the ladyfingers on the bottom. If they got squished I was through.

"What about Henri? You went outside with him last night. I smelled the cigarette smoke on you when you came back in."

"I quit smoking three months ago. I quit making it with other people the day we got serious. Is there anything else you want to know?"

"Have you been thinking about anybody else?"

That froze me. I tasted Susan's lips. I felt her hand squeeze my thigh. I took a slug of the Bristol Cream. It tasted repellently like Christmas.

"There's nobody. Nothing."

"Then there's no reason for you to leave."

"Except that I have to finish this story. Like have to have to or I'll lose my fucking mind. And if you don't want me to do it here, I can do it somewhere else."

"Are we still getting married?"

"We'll figure that out after I file."

He sat at the table in the living room, limp, shot through the heart. At that point his eyes were faucets and I guess I was crying too.

"You'll pick up Peter?" I said. "I know it's my day but I have to find someplace to spend the night and anyway if I talk to Mr. Salas again this week he'll probably file charges."

"Put your shit down. Please. I was bluffing."

"No shit. But part of you meant it, and anyway, you're right. It's safer. I'd feel like a dope if I got any of you killed."

I forced a sad little smile. He was too limp to smile back. And then, without even really understanding how I'd gotten there, I was in the doorway clutching my typewriter and half the kitchen. Nicky was murmuring in his bedroom and I knew that if I didn't get out of there now I never would.

"Where are you going?" he said.

"I'll tell you tonight."

"What's tonight?"

"Your party, stupid. Eight o'clock at Laurent's. Come hungry, yeah?"

He didn't answer. Didn't move. Just watched me walk out the door. I sobbed all the way down the hallway and in the elevator too, but I got it together before I hit the street. Deep in my mixed-up brain, I grabbed another empty jar, dumped in the whole morning, and labeled it "Left the Fiancé, Took the Bristol Cream." The shelf was getting pretty crowded. When this was over, if I wasn't dead, I'd have to clean it off.

There's more than one way to make a charlotte russe.

Some people make it so stiff it stands up on its own and serve it as a dome covered in dainty little whatsits. Others mortar it with whipped cream, so it's more of a cake. Sensible people, like yours truly, serve it like a trifle—ladyfingers cradling the glop—which looks like an absolute mess unless you've got a really gorgeous serving bowl. So when I hauled my whole goddamned life into Laurent's kitchen, the first thing I did was raid the crystal. I found a glittering bowl the size of a small swimming pool.

"I guess I'm doubling the recipe."

I opened the door to Laurent's office, parked my typewriter on the least bloody corner of his desk, and dragged out his phone. The cord stretched just far enough that I'd be able to cook and talk at the same time. That was essential, not just because I had calls to make but because I knew that if my mouth and hands weren't both occupied, I'd really fall apart.

The kitchen was spotless—who had been cleaning up in here? Jean-Louis?—but I fixed that by dumping my entire bag across the counter. My ladyfingers were squashed to shit. Sigh. So I pulled out bowls, turned on the oven—quite a feat, like starting a battleship—and got cranking on a second batch.

While the oven got hot, I worked the phone. I started with Toru's friends from college and publishing and California—the people he'd actually be happy to see. Most of them already had plans but I cajoled and guilted and outright threatened until all of them agreed to be there at eight. I got the ladyfingers in the oven. The air thickened with the smell of tiny cakes. The place almost felt alive.

I pulled in a deep breath and started on my people. The first call was easy.

"I'm doing dinner tonight and—"

"Yes," said Ambrose.

"Don't care what it's for?"

"Last night you put new life into me. Whatever you said to Tiny Tommy, it worked. Nobody followed me home; no one was lurking on my corner when I woke up. If you need me, Bernard, I'll go to the ends of the earth. Or, well . . . Fourteenth Street."

"That's the sweetest thing I've ever heard. Fourteenth Street won't be necessary—it's Laurent's at eight."

"Divine."

I hung up, gritted my teeth, and dialed Elma Zumwalt. I thought she was going to be screaming at me for missing her dinner but as soon as she heard my voice she gasped like a kid on Christmas.

"Is it true, darling? Oh, don't tell me, don't tell me, don't tell me, but is it true?"

I swear, I could smell her perfume through the phone.

"Is what true?"

"One of my little birds was on Eighty-Sixth this morning and spotted an increasingly notorious restaurant critic storming out of her apartment building, red-eyed and packed for singledom. Can you confirm?"

"It's hard to say, Elma."

"Then where are you? Tell!"

I sighed. Elma was like a toddler—when she felt like a game, everybody had to play.

"I'm shacked up with my lover in a grubby little apartment downtown. Dust bunnies the size of Grace Church. Flying roaches imported from South Carolina. You'd be sick."

"Oh, ha ha ha, darling. But where are you really? The Plaza? The Hyperion? The Savoy? Last year all the divorcées-to-be wintered in a kind of magnificent drunken hive at the Carlyle, they had the filthiest parties, but most of them have gone back to their husbands, poor things."

"I weep for them."

"Now, about this lover, darling—you may have intended that as a joke but I detected the sweaty tang of truth. Has this lothario a name?"

"Let's say . . . Susan."

"Oh, ha ha ha. Now, why are you calling? I'm sure you're not ready to start man-hunting yet but do know my Rolodex bulges with the rich, bald, and tasteless."

"It's about a party—"

"The nerve! Inviting me out after you shamelessly skirted my little affair last night."

"I—"

"Joking, joking, you missed nothing, the beef was latex and the orange flavor tasted like children's cough syrup. But as much as I'd love to, you know I have plans."

"That's a shame, Elma, because I was really counting on you."

"You were? For *what*? Don't say food, good god, I'm done cooking until New Year's Eve."

"I need something to wear."

Silence. I thought the line had gone dead but it turned out Elma had been struck dumb by joy. Finally she spoke, with a sob in her voice.

"I have been waiting so long to hear those words."

"Nothing too fancy."

"Of course not."

"And I'm gonna be on my feet all night, so comfortable, yeah?"

"I have just the thing. Oh, Bernie, you've made me the happiest girl on East Seventy-Fifth!"

We hung up. The whole time we'd been talking, I'd worked on my russe. I beat the yolks and whipped in the sugar. I scalded my milk, tempered the eggs, and beat it all together. I sprinkled in gelatin, stirring like it was any old custard until it began to clot. I tossed in a pinch of salt—I could hear Laurent bellowing, "We must always have salt!"—and then killed the stove and let the whole thing cool. My prep was paying off, I guess, because I hardly glanced at the recipe. My hands knew what to do.

I pulled my legs onto the counter and had Information get me the number for the *Arch*. Susan was out, but I told her alarmingly mellow assistant that she was not invited to my party.

"Hold on, man," he mumbled. "You're calling to tell Gullett *not* to come to your party?"

"That's right."

"That's pretty cold."

"She deserves worse. She knows why."

My nose twitched. My toast was burning.

"What party is it?"

"What?"

"Well, it's Friday night, yeah? So there must be thousands of parties happening in New York tonight. How will Gullett know which one to avoid?"

"She's allowed at any party not hosted by Bernice Black."

"Got it."

"Which is happening at Laurent's restaurant."

"Yeah, okay—"

"At eight o'clock."

I hung up the phone and remembered I wasn't making toast. I leapt off the counter and tore open the oven.

"Shit, shit, shit!"

I grabbed the ladyfingers, singed my fingers, found a rag, and yanked them free. Turns out those restaurant ovens don't fuck around—they were charred. I bashed the mold against the counter until they tumbled out, shoveled them into the trash, and started again. Once they were in, I popped into Laurent's office and flipped through his Rolodex. He had the number of every fish, meat, poultry, and veg dealer in the boroughs, but none of his staff. So I called Henri.

"Can you get in touch with C.J. and Jean-Louis?" I said.

"Leave me alone."

"Absolutely not. I'm having a party at your dad's place tonight. A birthday for my hubby, a wake for Laurent. You're cooking dinner for, let's say . . . twenty-four. Oh, and remember that kid you met the other day? He and his brother might be there. Do something simple for them. Talk to Rocky if you need tips."

"There are so many reasons why I am not doing this for you."

"The pantry is stocked, the fridge is full, and all the corpses have been removed—"

"That's my father you're speaking about—"

"And it's my fiancé's party! You think you're a cook? You think you're good enough to take over Laurent's? Oswald will be there tonight. Prove it!"

"What happened to staying off the sinking ship?"

"What happened to home?"

I slammed down the receiver before he could answer. And realized I hadn't gotten an answer about C.J. and Jean-Louis. Whatever—there were other ways. First I checked my ladyfingers—golden but not brown. Two more minutes. Next up, whipped cream. I dumped my two quarts of whipping cream into a big silver bowl, pulled out my little green mixer, and realized, fuck, I'd left the beaters at home. The dessert station had a huge electric mixer, but either it had blown a fuse or I was too thick to figure out how to turn it on. All that was left was the old-fashioned way—the hand beater hanging like a battle-ax on the wall.

I wanted to curse but there wasn't time. I climbed back onto the counter and started mixing, feeling like a kid cooking with Dad while Mom was at church. I was just getting into a rhythm when I remembered—

"Fuck! The ladyfingers!"

I ripped them out of the oven. They were absolutely goddamned perfect. While they cooled, I got back to beating. My arms ached, then burned. The cream stayed liquid. I had a long way to go.

To pass the time, I called Verucchio, in Williamsburg. The waiter who answered sounded even more weary than me. I asked for Thomas Motisi, and a few centuries later, Tommy came to the phone. Still beating the cream, I told him I needed a favor.

"I'm throwing a party tonight and there's a couple of friends I don't have time to get hold of. C.J. Corrales and Jean-Louis Lacaze."

"I know 'em."

"Oh! And Minnie Anglade. I need her too. Can you make sure they come?"

"How sure? *Extremely* sure?"

"Just 'sure' oughta do it."

"And what do I get in return? Because I tell you, Miss Black, you don't want to be owing me a favor."

"One sec."

I jogged over to the walk-in freezer. After a minute's rummaging and cursing, I found about fifty pounds of frozen duck. As Oswald Blount would say: bingo.

I told Tiny Tommy: "Three words. Caneton à l'orange."

"Ma'am, that's good enough for me."

"Oh, and bring a bunch of those little pencils that golfers use."

"Okay."

I hung up the phone, glad people no longer questioned me when I asked for something weird. My arms were seizing now, my shoulders little balls of magma, but stopping wasn't an option, so I beat and I beat and nearly an hour later, I had—

A bowl of thick soup.

"Don't cry, B," I grunted, trying to get my arms going again. "Just keep your hands turning."

So I pushed through the pain, even though it was useless, and I was trying to figure out if I had time to get down to the Bowery and buy some goddamned beaters when the back door swung open and Jean-Louis floated in like Dracula in avocado slacks.

I raised the mixer.

"One more step and I won't just crush your balls, I'll whip them to stiff peaks."

He raised his hands. I think it was supposed to be a friendly gesture but he was still wearing those leatherette driving gloves, and I don't know, they just looked murderous.

"What do you want?" I said.

"An Italian friend called. Told me I was working a party tonight. Said it like I didn't have a choice."

"You're early."

"I wanted to . . . Well, I was raised to understand that if you cause a woman to come after you with a knife, you may owe her an apology. Or better yet, help with her whipped cream."

He attempted a smile. It made him look like a jack-o'-lantern but I guess it was genuine, and anyway, I was out of gas. Every joint screamed as I let the beater go. He gave the cream a look of concern. Before he could say anything I said, "I don't want any feedback. Just whip it till it's stiff."

He gave a sharp nod—the man understood how to follow orders—and said, "What about the egg whites?"

"The same. If you know how to turn on the electric mixer you might—"

He whipped off his tiki shirt. His arms looked like the cables on the Brooklyn Bridge. Forget the mixer—he could have thickened the cream with a glare.

"You're tired," he said. It wasn't a question. "Lie down somewhere. I'll do the egg whites just before you need them. The cream I'll put it in the fridge when I'm done."

I left him to it. I was about to pass out at one of the downstairs tables when I remembered there was something else I needed to do. I hustled upstairs, grabbed a garbage bag, and went table to table, seizing paper daisies by the fistful. They crunched like death as I stuffed them into the trash. For the first time in a decade, I could breathe. I went back downstairs and flopped onto the most secluded banquette. The *click-click-click* of the hand mixer sang me to sleep.

Twenty-one

I figured I was dreaming because Susan was there, smiling like we were gearing up for a lazy Sunday in bed. But then I felt the drool, sticky on my cheek, and the wicked crick in my neck and realized this was no fantasy. My voice was thick with sleep as I said, "What the fuck is going on?"

"I heard you were having a party."

"I am. At eight."

"It's eight-fifteen. Everybody's upstairs."

She was in a blue suit with a floppy baker's boy cap, a bolero jacket, and mammoth trousers. She was grinning and her hair was tucked behind her ears. She helped me up—her hands were warm in a way I couldn't fully engage with at that moment. I tried to rub sense into my temples.

"What about my fiancé?"

"You say 'fiancé' like it's a venereal disease."

"Have you seen him or not?"

"Not."

That was bad—that was really fucking bad—but there were about eight million things I had to handle before I could deal with him.

"I need C.J. making drinks."

"She's on it."

"I have to get Henri set up in the kitchen."

"He was born in this kitchen. Come on, Black—everything is fine."

It was adorable that she thought I'd trust her word. I shoved through the swinging doors and for a moment my addled brain thought Laurent had come back to life because in his whites and cap, Henri looked so, so much like the old man. Freed from the confines of Près du Parc, Henri was a wild bear—movement fluid, jaw unclenched. He spritzed a final something onto the last platter of hors d'oeuvres and nodded at Jean-Louis, who clapped. A pair of waiters emerged from the shadows and swept the plates away. I reached for a bite but the waiter spun out of my reach. Henri wiped his brow, took half a breath, and switched his attention to a cauldron of bubbling brown sauce.

"How's the duck?" I said.

"What duck?"

"I was gonna tell you when you got here but I was asleep. You've gotta make caneton à l'orange."

"You're saying this now? I've got chickens roasting and the hors d'oeuvres are already out and you want caneton à l'orange for twenty-four?"

"Twenty-five," said Susan. "I crashed."

I figured Henri would scream. But he just stirred his sauce and stared at the ceiling, mind racing through some fundamental kitchen math.

"I don't have the recipe; I don't have the time."

"So make it up. Now's your chance to pioneer, I don't know, caneton à l'orange au fils."

He looked like he wanted it. But he shook his head.

"Impossible."

"It's not for me. It's for Tommy Motisi."

"Who the hell is Tommy Motisi?"

"Garbage pickup."

He blinked a couple of times and then it clicked. He flicked off his burner and said, "Fuck the chickens. I'll get the duck."

"Good boy. I'm gonna go find my fiancé. Grab me when it's time to assemble the russe."

Next stop, dining room. Susan and I were halfway up the stairs when I remembered I was mad at her. I backed her against the railing. She smirked like she'd been waiting for this. I was turned on and I was wounded and I didn't want to let her see either thing.

"You should fire your assistant," I said. "I told him you were *not* invited. I guess nobody at your sleazy little rag knows how to listen."

"Rich isn't my assistant—he's my publisher. He said you sounded like you were, y'know . . ."

"I don't."

"Winking."

She leaned on the railing, perfectly at home. I couldn't understand how someone could look so balanced while standing on two different steps.

"Your story fucked me five different ways," I said. "I staked my career on this and you—"

"Got there first? Listen, I know getting scooped hurts but just because I think you're neat doesn't mean I'm going to quit doing my job. I'm a professional. I thought you were too."

"The only people who knew about the aspic were me, Rocky Shanklin, the cops, and the killer. I didn't tell you about it. So who did?"

She answered by fluttering her eyelashes.

"I know you think you want me to give up my sources, Miss Black, but if I did would you still respect me in the morning?"

"If you're not here to help, then why the hell did you come?"

She dropped the coy act and took a second to think. As angry as I was, I knew I wanted the answer to be, *I'm here for you, Bernice, and nothing else.* But that's not what she said.

"My story was good but it didn't have the ending. I think yours will. I wanna be here when you get it. And anyway, I've been hearing so much about this damn restaurant—I had to see it for myself. You gonna throw me out or let me stay?"

I was torn between a desire to kiss her and shove her down the stairs. Because I am sensible, refined, and mature, I did neither.

"Stick around," I said. "I'd like you to see how professional I can be."

And then I went to find Toru, like I should have been doing all along. I was stepping through the door at the top of the stairs when a perfumed missile named Elma Zumwalt slammed into my chest and swept me into the powder room. She shoved me onto the toilet. It shook. So did I.

"What the fuck!"

"You look like you got scraped off a cab's back seat. Some friend I'd be if I let your guests see you in this state. Now, you'd better pee. You won't get another chance."

Elma had gone full drag queen. Her wig scraped the ceiling; her eyeshadow stretched to her ears; her earrings had enough bulk to anchor an ocean liner. She whipped a garment bag off her shoulder and tugged open the zipper. A galaxy poured forth—

champagne tulle dripping with purple and green sequins. It had a slit to the knee, pointed shoulders, and a collar that would choke me if I laughed. She was absolutely right—once I got into it, there'd be no getting out.

"That's not a dress," I said. "It's an implement of torture."

"It's Bob Mackie and don't waste my time."

A makeup bag slammed onto the counter and before I really understood what was happening, my jaw was clamped in her fist and a brush was tickling my cheek.

"I—"

"Shhhh!"

Trying to pull away only made her squeeze harder, so I let her get on with it. She had a steady hand and a sharp eye. I'd never seen her so calm. When she'd finished, she opened the door and barked at Susan, "Get our girl a cup of coffee."

"I don't take orders from—"

"Do you have a name, darling?"

"Susan Gullett."

"Have you ever thrown a party, Susan Gullett? A grown-up party, I mean—not just a half dozen longhairs smoking dope and grooving to *Sgt. Pepper*? I speak of evening wear, catering, flowers, music, and lights."

Susan, fighting a smile, shook her head.

"Then you haven't the faintest idea of the pressure a hostess feels. This is the biggest night of Bernie's life. Don't fuck it up."

Susan's mouth opened, then closed. She left.

I snuck a peek in the mirror. I was expecting clown makeup but Elma had a surprisingly light hand. I didn't look like I was wearing anything—I just looked less tired.

"Are you taking off those trousers," she said, "or am I doing it for you?"

"Elma, it's a beautiful dress. It's not me."

"That's the whole idea. So I take it you're balling the girl in the floppy cap?"

"Excuse me?"

"You said his name was Susan. I thought you were joking—"

"I was—"

"You weren't."

She patted my hand. I should have been frightened—she was the last person in New York you wanted keeping a secret—but her gaze was steady and her touch was firm.

"It doesn't bother me. My philosophy is that life is too short to refuse pleasure. If you want her, get her."

It took me a second to realize she wasn't joking. I shivered, trying to absorb the strange realization that Elma Zumwalt, of all people, understood me. Either she had hidden depths or my problems weren't as complicated as I'd thought. Either way, I was grateful.

"And I suppose that starts with putting on your dress?" I said.

"There's a reason no one ever said 'fuck-me slacks.'"

I took off the pants. She admired her shoes while I peed, then helped me into Mackie's beautiful monstrosity. It was heavy, it was uncomfortable, and the sequins stabbed my legs every time I moved, but when she zipped it up I felt like a knight wearing chain mail, strong enough to punch through a wall. Elma was trying to make sense of my hair when my coffee arrived. I took one sip—Elma wouldn't allow any more—and when I handed back the cup I caught Susan glancing at my calf and I had to concede that, fuck, Elma knew her stuff. But my hair was a lost cause. So she jammed down a jeweled headband, strapped me into a pair of purple suede pumps, and informed me that, at last, I was ready for my party.

The dining room was pregnant with cigarette smoke and perfume. Tables had been pushed together and laid for a banquet; nearly all of my friends and enemies were there. Jean-Louis's waiters were dipping around like a pair of barn swallows. Tiny Tommy was charming the hell out of Toru's friends. C.J. was pouring Oswald an old-fashioned. Even Rocky was there, up on Olympus with Ambrose, washed and changed and wearing a white jumpsuit and his luxuriant blond wig, which he'd either replaced or somehow scrubbed clean. Everyone was in evening wear. Like the restaurant, they looked as beautiful as they ever had. I'd been proud of myself for hanging with the crowd at Number 5—even if it did end with me covered in vomit and hauled off to jail—but god, this was better. A waiter drifted past. I nearly got an hors d'oeuvre but he twisted away at the last second and disappeared.

"Have you seen Toru?" I asked Elma.

"Coast is clear."

"No, I actually want to talk to him."

"Sure you do, dear." She squeezed my shoulder. The sequins dimpled her palm. "Don't spill on the gown. Cost the late Mr. Zumwalt over two grand."

And with that, she melted into the crowd.

"So what's the plan?" said Susan, her lighter's flame casting her eyes into shadow.

"There isn't one."

"No shit?"

"I've done everything I can. Gonna let the killer come to me."

"And if they don't?"

"My life is fucked. No big deal."

She dragged on her cigarette, lipstick staining the filter purple.

"Something I wanted to tell you," she said. My heart beat hard enough to rattle Elma's sequins.

"Yeah?"

"It's kinda stupid, but—"

Before she could finish her stupid thought, she was interrupted by five hundred pounds of Italian muscle. It was Stones and Blue, clearing a path for Tiny Tommy, who glided in carrying a pair of cocktails. He handed me one—I thought it was a martini but it turned out to be a Gibson—and gave Susan a stare so hostile, it could strip paint.

"Susan Gullett," she said. "*St. Mark's Arch.*"

Tommy grinned like a dead man.

"Could you give us a minute?" she said.

Tommy kept grinning. After an uncomfortable few seconds she said, "Well . . . never mind," and headed for the bar. It wasn't easy watching her go.

"She was about to tell me something important," I said.

"Thankfully, I don't care. We gotta talk about poison. Now, I wasn't at last night's orgy at Number 5—"

"You goddamned were."

"He goddamned was not," said Blue, with a finality I didn't want to argue with. "And me neither."

"Thank you, Blue," said Tommy. "My point is that although I did not attend the party in question, I understand it broke up rather abruptly when somebody pumped a load of potassium bromate into French Vic's whipped cream."

I nodded, wondering how he knew the poison's name. Maybe the police told him. Maybe he had other ways.

"So I'm looking forward to dinner but I have no urge to be poisoned," he said.

"Neither do I."

"Then if it's all right, I'm gonna send Stones down to the kitchen to keep an eye on your chef. He's gonna taste everything before it goes out. If he dies, Blue puts a bullet in your chef's ear. Does that sound fair?"

"Henri would hate that. Go right ahead."

"Why me?" said Stones. He was blotchy, skin orange in some places, green in others, and pale all over. I almost felt sorry for him except I actually didn't at all. Tiny Tommy clapped him on the cheek.

"Like the lady said yesterday—because you're an asshole. Don't sweat it, kid. Maybe you'll die tonight but you're gonna eat better than you ever have."

Stones started to argue but Tommy pursed his lips and that sent him on his way.

I pointed at the bar, where Oswald had barricaded himself behind an old-fashioned and three piles of napkins. There was a bruise shaped like Staten Island on his cheek.

"You and Oswald need to work your shit out," I said.

"What do you care?"

"I shouldn't. Except that if you don't, this place shuts down and turns into—what? Some third-rate steak house? Another Midtown diet pit? I've said goodbye to enough. I don't want to lose this."

"Yeah. Neither do I."

"So talk to him, wouldja?"

"Okay. But it's not because you're pretty and it's not because you've been a good sport with the cops. This is a personal favor, from me to you, because I happen to like the way you write."

And they say an English degree is useless. I made for the bar and he and Blue followed. When Oswald saw us, he sank as far into his chair as the upholstery allowed.

"Back off, you lunatic," he said. "What you did last night was assault."

"Hey, man," said Tommy, "you interfered with my lobster. What's a guy supposed to do?"

"Expect a letter from my attorney. You are banned from this restaurant, you are banned from *Fiddler,* you are—"

"Okay, okay, okay," I said, hands raised like a cop directing traffic. "You both have colossal, eye-catching dicks. But you've also got a problem. Tommy, you'll never see a penny of the money Oswald owes you if the restaurant closes down. And Oswald, if you piss off your garbage collectors, this place will be dead in a week and you will be too."

Tommy smiled at Oswald like a hungry shark. Oswald looked like he wanted to hide under his chair. He mumbled, "Maybe you're right."

"Then it's time to break bread." I grabbed a bowl of pub mix from behind the bar. They reached into it and came up gripping the same little pretzel. There was a moment of tension and then Oswald let go. Tommy smiled. That seemed like a good start. "I'll let you knuckleheads figure out the money side of it. Let's see if you can do it without hitting each other. And since Vic is out of commission, you'll also need a chef. How about Henri?"

"Eh," said Tommy.

"Fuck that guy," said Oswald. "Spent his whole life riding Daddy's coattails. He'll never cook in this restaurant again."

"Funny you say that because he's cooking here right now. Don't get pissy. Just try the duck. If it melts in your mouth—and I guarantee it will—give him a six-month tryout."

I got out of there before either of them could say no. While they chomped on pub mix, I slunk down the bar, where C.J. was pouring Manhattans for Toru's friends, all of whom looked alarmingly normal next to my collection of weirdos. I drained the Gibson, found that cocktail onions were less disgusting than I remembered, and ordered another.

I told C.J.: "Thanks for coming in."

"As if I had a choice. Your buddy called me up and asked, 'Whaddaya like better? The carrot or the stick?' I said carrot and he told me he'd give me five hundred bucks for one night's work. Something about his tone told me I shouldn't say no."

"Well, still. Thanks."

She poured. Ice shards drifted across the drink's surface. I took a sip and they were gone.

"I'm sorry about César," I said. "And, uh, well . . . everything."

"Me too."

"If Oswald manages to keep the place open, will you stick around?"

"I've been here too long already. Berlin calls. When we're done tonight, I'm taking my five hundred dollars to the airport and I am gone."

I nodded, wondering what it would be like to just go places, to walk away from work and family and fear. I couldn't picture it. She poured herself a vodka shot and took an imperceptible sip.

"I was wondering," I said. "In addition to lifting love letters from the safe, did you happen to walk out of here carrying a little wooden box with a brass latch?"

"What was in it?"

"Laurent's recipes."

And that's when C.J. did something I'd never seen her do at Laurent's. She laughed.

"Lady, I don't cook. I get other people to do it for me."

She left me alone with my gin. I risked a glance at the clock. My deadline was in fifteen hours. I'd need to slow down on the cocktails or I'd be in no shape to write tomorrow.

Of course, that's assuming I had anything to write at all.

Minnie Anglade settled onto the stool beside me, holding a glass of milk on the rocks and a shot glass full of something clear. She downed the shot and sipped the milk and didn't look like she enjoyed either one. Her clothes were the same as the night before, only rumpled, and everything about her called to mind a deflating balloon.

"How is he?" I said.

"He'd be dead, they said, if you hadn't made him throw up. I owe you thanks. My husband is hardly perfect, but I prefer him alive."

"My pleasure. Thanks for coming tonight."

"A man with a gun told me I didn't have a choice."

She tugged a flask from her purse and refilled the shot glass. It was quickly empty again.

"You don't need to worry about poison," I said. "We've got a professional tasting everything before it goes out."

"I'm not eating. I'm here to sulk and get sauced. When your hoodlums give permission, I shall leave. Goodbye."

She sulked away. It was hard to imagine someone so small cutting a grown man's throat. But she certainly had the willpower and I had to admit it would be funny to see her get convicted and then find a way to decide that killing him was my fault.

I was raising my cocktail to my lips when Elma snatched it out of my hands. Before I could complain she'd disappeared into the crowd. I wondered where Toru was, what the kids were doing.

I was considering calling them when a scream came from Olympus—not of terror but of sheer indignation.

"It will never work!"

Ambrose slapped the table and shouted it again, then pointed at me and yelled, "Bernard! Your opinion is required!" So I crossed to Olympus, where Rocky was scribbling in a composition notebook and Ambrose had a cigarette hanging from his mouth and a glass of bourbon clenched in his fist.

"Rocky," I said. "Bullwinkle. How can I help?"

"I've yoked myself to a lunatic," said Ambrose. "And it is your fault."

"You quit the *Sentinel*?"

"Gave notice this morning."

"That's amazing."

He grinned.

"Didn't think I'd go through with it? Well, they were giddy. Gave the impression that they'd been struggling to get rid of me and I'd saved them the trouble. So, boats burned, I stand on the rocky shores of Number 5, where I find my new partner has decided to stake everything on—how did you describe this madness?"

"French," smirked Rocky. "American style."

"What's it mean?" I said.

"Brace yourself, Bernard. It's even more foolish than 'chicken potpie.'"

Rocky spun the notebook. It was labeled: *Menu! (The Good One. For Real).* I skimmed. I saw lamb with baby beans, chicken soufflé with morels, a salad with beef and rice.

"Remember that terrine you tasted last night?" said Rocky. "That's what I'm going for. French classics with an American spin. Light and assertive and surprising, with a menu that changes every day."

"Which is impossible," said Ambrose.

"Not if you market every morning! It's how they're doing it in France. We could do it here too."

"When was the last time you were awake in the morning? And it doesn't count if you never went to sleep."

"So I'll get a bedtime. I'll buy an alarm clock. I'll cut my intake of heavy drugs down by, I don't know, seven percent. We could make this work."

"But what would be the point?"

"My time in jail changed my perspective—"

"You were there less than a day!"

"So what? Being inside, a guy has time to think. Everything I've come up with since I started Number 5, it's all bullshit. It's phony. By summer I could be on trial for murder, you know? Hell, I could be dead! I don't want to die cooking crap."

"Very noble. But insane. Please, Bernard, tell him—he's shooting for the moon."

Ambrose was annoyed, yeah, but he was loving it. I read the menu a second time. A third. My stomach growled.

"If you could pull this off—"

"I fucking could," said Rocky.

"I mean . . . I'd eat it."

"You'd eat anything," said Ambrose.

"I won't dispute that. As a matter of fact, I'd like to eat something now."

And because sometimes the universe is kind to good little restaurant critics, my prayers were answered. Jean-Louis's waiters appeared with steaming tureens of soup. I sniffed. Leek and potato, so fragrant I basically jumped out of my chair. Toru still wasn't there but there was at least one murderer in the room and it didn't seem prudent to force them to wait. I headed for the table. Susan sat beside me and I didn't tell her to go.

"How's your story?" she said, draping a napkin across her lap. "Has the killer come to you?"

"He will."

Or she, I thought.

But we ate the soup and nobody slipped. And then came the duck and it was brilliant—cooked just to the point of tenderness, in a sauce lighter than anything Laurent ever turned out, with a citrus flavor so sharp it was like eating Florida—and everyone was charming and respectful and nobody seemed like a murderer at all. The duck cast a spell—ending arguments, turning enemies into friends. Oswald and Tommy reached an accord. Ambrose and Rocky quit arguing about the menu. Minnie Anglade almost smiled and Elma nearly started to make sense. It would have been lovely if I could only forget the bloodstains downstairs.

"All right," said Susan. "I get it."

"Get what?"

"The butter, the cream, the ambiance, the crystal and the candles and the silver and the waiters tromping around like soldiers. With light like this, everybody's better looking. With food like this, nobody's mean. It's like it . . . it takes the edge off the world."

I didn't answer her. Probably I wiped my mouth or speared another piece of duck. It's a shame I didn't do anything to mark the moment because that, folks, was when I really fell for her. The candles got a little more shimmery—or maybe my eyes were watering?—and it's possible I was about to make an even greater fool of myself when Henri poked his head out of the stairwell and shouted, "Black! Get your ass down here!" I dabbed my mouth, smoothed my sequins, and stood up smiling, even though I had no fiancé and no killer and was pretty much absolutely doomed.

"'Scuse me, folks," I said. "I have to go finish making the greatest dessert in the whole damn world."

I got up. Stones pulled out my chair—I was glad to see he'd finally learned some manners—while Oswald and Tommy showered Henri with extremely profane compliments about the duck. Henri blushed like a dopey kid and I was actually happy for him, since he was trapped in the same nightmarish week as I was. When I left the dining room I felt a clammy kind of worry tickling my stomach, but I ignored it and it probably would have stayed ignored if I hadn't found Toru waiting at the bottom of the stairs.

Twenty-two

He was at the mayor's table, unshaven and unwashed, staring at an untouched plate of food. He'd gotten dressed, at least, in cream slacks and a striped shirt I'd gotten him for Christmas the year before. Across the room, Jean-Louis was staring at the ceiling while his waiters shared a copy of *Silver Surfer*. They didn't seem interested in me. Toru kicked out a chair. I sat, shredded a little of his duck breast, and munched. There was so much stress pumping my veins, my arms felt like they were on fire. The Gibsons had torn through me and I was dying to pee but I didn't have time for another argument and god knows I'd die before I let him see how upset I was, so my voice was steady when I said: "I guess you snuck in the back?"

"I banged on the back door until Henri took pity."

"Why not come upstairs? See your friends?"

"Because I'm not as good a liar as you. I didn't know how to explain to them that I have no idea why my fiancée left."

"You know *precisely* why."

"I told you I was bluffing. I asked you to stay."

"After you asked me to leave!" I took a deep, pointless breath and said, "I'm sorry, I have to go finish dessert."

"We're not done talking."

"Right now we are."

I made it all the way to the kitchen door without screaming or sobbing. I told you, I'm very good at crossing a restaurant floor. But Toru was quicker. He spread his arms and blocked the doorway.

"Do you understand that I'm working right now?" I said. "We can continue this endless conversation when I'm done."

"I can't wait that long."

"Just what is it you want to know?"

"The truth. Whatever the hell it might be."

"Yeah?"

"I can handle it."

Fuck it. Fine.

"I'm bisexual."

It hit him like a knife in the neck. It was suddenly very easy to get through the door.

The kitchen was a spectacular mess. Twelve beautifully roasted chickens steamed on the counter. Dishes overflowed from the sink and the range was splattered with Henri's discarded brown sauce. All I cared about was my serving dish, which was right where I'd left it, glittering in the kitchen's harsh light. I lined the edges with the ladyfingers, fitting them as carefully as Nicky built block castles. It wasn't easy. My hands were shaking and I was on the verge of throwing up.

"So bisexual," said Toru, "just what does that mean?"

I knew that voice. Polite, reasonable, flying with rage. I hated when he talked to me like that. It was supposed to be calming but it just made me want to get under his skin. I needed him to admit how angry he was—because if he got pissed off, maybe I wouldn't feel so goddamned bad.

"It means I like sleeping with men and women."

"Have you slept with any of them? Women, I mean? Or men for that matter?"

"No."

I scraped custard into the bowl. It was fucking heavy but there was absolutely no way I was asking Toru to help.

"Then how do you know?" he said.

"Because I know, okay? Because I've spent the last year trying very hard not to know and just about split my head."

"But if you haven't—"

"Let's say you spent your whole life eating chicken, all right? And you liked it so much that you didn't think you'd ever want anything else. But then one day you saw a steak, and man, you didn't have to taste it to know how good it would be."

"Why do I have to be the chicken?"

"Fine, you're the steak, just—who cares!"

Don't cry, B, don't cry. I smeared the last of the custard over the ladyfingers, then folded in my freshly beaten egg whites. I tried to focus on how pretty it looked—yellow streaked with white, a field dusted with snow.

"What does your analyst say?"

Anger pulsed from my fingertips. There was nothing I hated more than when somebody asked for my analyst's opinion, like he was the expert and I was just some poor idiot trapped in my own broken brain.

"He mocked me. I fired him. I don't have to prove a thing. I'm bisexual, the end."

He thumped his fingers. Instead of telling him to shut up, I opened the fridge, which was still mercifully head-free, and grabbed the vat of whipped cream. I had the strangest urge to jam my head into it and scream but that probably wouldn't have helped anything, so instead I scraped it into the piping bag and guided it onto the russe, spiraling from the outside in. No matter how deep I breathed, my hands would not stop shaking.

"So I know you're pissed," I said. "I'll never make it as World's Greatest Stepmom. I'm out all night and I sleep through school drop-off. I feed the cat pâté until she shits on Peter's project. I get bored at the playground and I can't help cursing in front of the kids."

"Have I ever complained about any of that?"

"And now, to top it all off, I'm half gay. Well, maybe more than half. Or less. It depends on the day. Anyway, you've got every right to yell."

The kitchen door opened. Jean-Louis poked his head in and said, "It is time."

"Fuck off!" I shouted, and clever fellow, he did. My hand slipped and I screwed up part of the whipped cream. I wiped it off with my pinkie and started again. I popped the stray bit into my mouth. It tasted how it was supposed to. At least this much I got right.

"If you feel guilty," he said, "that's coming from you, not me."

"Well, of course I feel guilty! I feel guilty for wanting something new and embarrassed for feeling guilty and pathetic for feeling embarrassed. When I'm working I feel guilty for not being with the kids, when I'm with the kids I feel guilty because I'd rather be at work. I feel guilty because I kissed Susan Gullett and I feel abominable because more than anything in the world, I want to kiss her again—"

"Just stop!"

He pelted a spoon into the sink. It clanged around. I flinched, which screwed up another little mound of whipped cream, so I wiped that off and did it again. I was going to make this perfect if it killed me. At this rate, it probably would.

"Who the fuck is Susan Gullett?" said Toru, his voice back to scary-quiet.

"A reporter. An editor, actually. She's upstairs."

"The woman from last night?"

"That'd be the one."

Jean-Louis popped his head in again, suggesting he wasn't quite as clever as I'd thought.

"The guests are restless," he said.

Toru bellowed at him—

"Get out!"

I'd never heard him shout like that. I'd never seen him so red. Not your problem, I thought. *Focus on your piping, B. You're almost done.*

While Toru's chest heaved, I smeared on the last dollop of cream, twisting my hands for a final flourish. For a civilian, I'd done okay. I'd have liked to celebrate but he was still staring.

"What?" I said.

"I'm glad you feel guilty."

"Oh yeah?"

"You've been deceptive. You've been reckless."

"I've been busy!"

I smacked the piping bag onto the counter. It splorped whipped cream everywhere, including on my dress. Ah shit, I thought. Elma's gonna kill me. I shredded a rag trying to clean the sequins. I think I got most of it off. When I looked up his face was a few shades less red. He moved like he was going to hug me. I nudged him away.

"I'm sorry," I said. "Not for being who I am. But for how long it took to tell you. It's been hard."

"Just tell me what you want, B."

"To date women."

"That's a big fucking ask."

"I've tried not to say it. Every way I know. It didn't work."

He squeezed the bridge of his nose, wincing like I was an oncoming sinus headache. I drummed the counter until he mumbled: "I gotta think about it."

"Take as long as you want. Now, are you coming or what? There's a killer upstairs expecting dessert."

I was trembling too much to heft my vat of sugary glop, so I let Toru carry it upstairs. When we stepped into the dining room our friends clapped—for the dessert, for the birthday boy, and I guess a little bit for me. Elma got up so he could have her chair. I stayed on my feet.

The room was wrecked. Chairs shoved back, feet on tables, cigarettes burning or drowned in empty wineglasses. Everyone slouched like they'd had their batteries yanked out. Normally I hated public speaking but I felt loose—there was nothing left to fear except maybe getting killed—so I dove in.

"Shitty week, huh?" They chuckled. "Laurent and César dead. Vic nearly there too. We're hurt, all of us, in ways that will take years of very expensive analysis to unravel. So I wanted to give you a gift."

I nodded at the russe, whipped perfection gleaming in the candlelight. My mouth would have watered if I'd had any saliva left.

"Meet the charlotte russe. It's the best dessert in the world and I make it perfectly. At least I think I do. I don't know for sure because nobody can judge their own work—that, I like to tell myself, is what critics are for."

Further chuckles. Jean-Louis and his waiters handed out golf pencils and slips of paper. Susan gave me a look like, *What the fuck are you doing?* I shrugged because, frankly, I had no idea.

"So for the first and I swear to god last time, I want you to judge me. Eat a little. Write a little. Be brutal—god knows I am—and write your name on the thing because I don't get to publish anonymously and neither do you."

"Do I get a taste?" asked Henri, his toque unbuttoned, a brandy dangling from his fingertips, long legs swinging off a barstool. I'd never seen him so relaxed.

"Of course. You and Stones and C.J. too—you earned it. Come on, folks, make room."

The waiters circled the table, dishing up russe on plates that cost more than everything in my kitchen. Minnie Anglade tried to refuse but Jean-Louis insisted and even she didn't have the nerve to contradict him. Once everyone had been served, I took a bite and everyone followed my lead. I chewed and thought and chewed and swallowed and then thought a little more.

It was just right.

In the candlelight, my guests' skin shone like wax. Some of them looked happy, some uneasy, some outright distressed. Tiny Tommy ate like a conveyor belt—bite after bite after bite—while Oswald took two bites, closed his eyes, and sank back into his chair. Ambrose ate almost nothing off his plate but kept sneaking nibbles from everyone else's. Henri hardly touched his, preferring to drink instead. At one point Rocky gave a meaningful grunt. Heads turned his way, eager to hear what the professional thought, but he kept mum.

"Bernice," said Toru—softly, like I was a doll that would break if he spoke too loud.

"On the paper, dear," I said. "Oh, and happy birthday."

"Thanks."

I was too nervous and full of piss to eat any more, so I sat as straight as I could and closed my eyes. It sounds grotesque but I love the noise of people eating, when conversation is traded for the clink of forks, the smack of lips, and—if the host did their job—little *mms* and *ahhs*. Their not-quite-silence gave me strength.

After five minutes, I asked them to record their thoughts. The waiters collected the slips and topped up the wine while I skimmed. The responses were what I'd expected. My palms tingled. I was on the verge of doing something brilliant—if I was right—or catastrophically cruel. Even though my bladder was bursting, I needed a few more minutes to think.

"The feedback is fascinating," I said, "thank you. Even those who I'm sure would love to stab a critic were uncommonly fair. I want to ponder this a little bit before I respond. Jean-Louis, open a few bottles of champagne and give our guests some cheese, huh?"

I took a few steps. I stopped.

"Oh, Ambrose, you mind coming with me? I could stand a second opinion."

He smoothed his hair and pushed back from the table. The week had taken its toll. His cheeks were hollow, his suit baggy, his lips tight. But nobody had ever been more at home in a restaurant. With easy theatricality, he waved an arm at the wreckage and said: "Might I bring my drink?"

"As long as you've got one for me."

He sloshed wine into two empty glasses and followed me down

the stairs. His newly gaunt frame was still heavy enough to make the stairs creak—a nice reminder that even though he was older than me, Ambrose had more than enough strength to break my neck.

I hoped it wouldn't come to that. But when we entered the kitchen I made a point of noting every knife.

"You've done it, Bernard, you've done it. A perfect party, a perfect russe—and all under the specter of death. I am awed."

My mouth was dry and the wine didn't help. I talked slow.

"I used to live for your compliments."

"What do you mean?"

"I was a kid when I met you and Laurent—dumb and hungry and credulous. I've grown up a lot since then but when you talk, man, it's like snapping a finger and I'm a nineteen-year-old know-nothing from Brooklyn who's terrified of being found out. Whatever you said, I took for gospel. Even when it sounded like bullshit."

He lit a cigarette. His hair, face, collar, and kerchief were all the color of dirty linen.

"I don't think either of us is drunk enough for this brand of honesty."

"Then drink up. Because it's going to get a lot more raw."

His wine left a red smear across his upper lip.

"What is it, Bernard?"

"First tell me about the russe."

"You have my notes."

"Come on, Ambrose. You built a life judging other people's food. How about mine?"

His posture stiffened. A soldier ready for debrief.

"The whipped cream was perfect. The ladyfingers soft but not soggy. And the texture of the custard was sublime."

"But how did it taste?"

"Lovely."

"That word doesn't mean anything."

"Sweet! Creamy! Everything a russe should be." His chest swelled. "Have I missed something? When you apply yourself, you're a very good cook. I don't know what else to say."

I held the little stack of papers.

"Read them."

"I have no interest in what a bunch of half-drunk nitwits—"

I slammed the papers onto the counter, which clanged in a most satisfying way. Ambrose, for perhaps the first time in his life, shut up.

"Read them, you fucking fraud." I smacked the metal. "Read."

His smile quivering, Ambrose drained his wine, shifted his cigarette to his left hand, and started to read.

"Your onetime beloved, Henri, said it 'tastes like boiled sock.' Oswald Blount calls it 'like snorting rotten eggs.' 'Real bad,' says Rockford Shanklin, while C.J. the bartender has given us a doodle of a defecating dog. I'm shocked."

"I'm not."

"I feel like the victim of a practical joke. What's going on?"

"I'm a busy woman, okay? Two kids, a full-time job, a murder investigation. When the cream spoils, I don't always remember to throw it away. It can live in my fridge for weeks, getting sour and lumpy, and sometimes I bring it to Fifty-Fourth Street and use it to make a dessert."

"I don't—"

"The russe was disgusting, Ambrose. It looked perfect but it tasted like cold death. Everybody noticed but you."

"Perhaps I exaggerated to spare your feelings—"

"You've never spared a feeling in your life. It's your palate, Ambrose. Something's wrong with it. And that's why Laurent is dead."

He raised a shaking hand and growled, "I don't have to take this . . . this nonsense!"

He stomped toward the door. I let him get halfway before I said in a deeply calm voice, "Yes, you do."

He whipped around.

"Why?"

"Because this is the fairest hearing you'll ever get. Aside from the man whose throat you cut, I'm your best friend in New York. I've loved you for years. I loved him too. I want—no, I *need* there to be a good reason for Laurent's death. Tell me what's wrong and maybe I'll understand."

"My palate is ironclad."

"Ambrose—"

"The best in New York! That's what they say, isn't it? Give me something to taste."

He wrenched a drumstick off one of the roasted chickens. Flecks of meat sprayed from his mouth.

"Butter! Rosemary! Pepper and white wine, too much garlic and not enough salt!"

He flung the drumstick at the floor. It rolled under the counter, a gift for the rats. His chest heaved.

"My palate is *fine*."

"I tried the aspic, Ambrose."

"What aspic?"

"The one with Laurent's head in it. I stole a bite right out of the NYPD fridge. Nobody in New York could have made an aspic that pretty except for Laurent and you. Problem was, it tasted like seawater. Like it was made for or by someone whose sense of taste had gone haywire. I've watched you eat a lot this week. At Cœur, at your cooking class, at Number 5. A lot of the time I disagreed with you—disagreed sharply, like we were eating different food—but I kept my mouth shut because I never learned how to tell Ambrose Clendenon he's wrong."

"You're imagining things."

"I am *sick* of you telling me what to think!" I took an unhelpful breath. "At Cœur, you got specific about texture but never flavor. Even when you were mocking Elma's spiced beef—a shitty thing to do to a student, by the way—you talked about how it felt, not tasted. And at your cooking class, you smoked two cigarettes before critique, which you'd never have done if you were serious about tasting the food. So all that shit made me think there was something wrong and I wrecked the russe to make sure. What is going on?"

He slumped against the counter and lit another cigarette. He looked like a wet towel tossed on the floor. I had loved this man for so long. I wondered how long it would take that love to die.

"A smarter man would call his attorney," he said.

"You don't need a lawyer. You need confession. This is your last chance."

He took a meaningful drag and tried to grin.

"I was in a taxi. I never used to take them, of course. Cabs are for tourists. New Yorkers walk. But I got mugged twice last year and it's supposed to be safer taking cabs."

Christ, I needed to pee. And I was tired and thirsty and most of all I had a deadline. But if I pressed him he'd clam up, so I just got out my notepad and wrote.

"It was last year, the tail end of winter. The streets were black slush and I was late for a reservation at Quint's. I caught a cab. We were racing down Lexington when a woman rumbled into the crosswalk with a stroller. The hack slammed on the brakes—my face slammed into the bulletproof glass."

I remembered. The bruises had been horrible. He'd told me he'd slipped getting out of the tub. I'd brought him tomato soup.

"For three days, I was seeing stars. When they cleared, I found I couldn't taste anything at all. I could feel food on my tongue, could recognize hot or cold, soft or hard, but everything was as flavorless as plain water. The doctors said it should fix itself. It did not. My livelihood, my passion, my reason for being—all lost with one tap of the brakes. And the last thing I ever tasted was an Automat grilled cheese."

"What the fuck does that have to do with Laurent?"

He opened cabinets at random until he found brandy. He filled his wineglass with liquor. He didn't even pretend to taste it—he just dumped it down his throat.

"It should have been the end of me. A food critic with no sense of taste is little more than a well-dressed compost bin. But the cruelest thing was, nobody noticed. I'd eat, I'd spout nonsense, and everyone nodded their heads. So the accident didn't just steal my future—it made me understand that everything I'd ever said, everything I'd written, had all been pointless. In 1954, I ate a lovely bouillabaisse. I wrote a lovely paragraph. Who cares?"

It looked like he might cry but he got himself under control. That was for the best. One self-pitying tear, I thought, and I'd smack him across the jaw.

"Was this when you started taking the Obetrol?"

"Saw the bottle, did you? I've been practically living on those little orange lovelies. I like how they numb my appetite. Eating without tasting is agony. And they do lend a wonderful sense of purpose, even to a life as suddenly pointless as mine. With them it's almost pleasant, living a lie."

"They make you jittery? Paranoid?"

"Like stuffing your underwear with fire ants."

He downed more brandy. His cheeks glowed red. I shifted, trying to find a position that eased the ache in my feet, my calves, my bladder. Nothing helped.

"So Laurent knew something was wrong?" I said.

"He was arrogant and vain and not nearly as good as he thought he was, but Laurent was no fool."

"How did he work it out?"

"I was here for lunch. It was slow—lately it always was—so he brought me a bottle of sauvignon blanc and joined me while I ate chicken fricassee. He said I seemed unwell, that I was gulping when I used to chew. I tried to play it off but he was smart, the bastard, just like you. Peppered me with questions about the dish. I said the truffles had never been so flavorful, the chicken never so tender. He said the chicken was overcooked and that he hadn't been using truffles for six months—that he couldn't afford them anymore. I tried to make it into a joke but he was disturbed. A good friend would have pressed me into a confession. He'd have offered consolation. Help. But as I'm sure you've learned, Laurent was no one's friend. He decided it would be more amusing to lay a trap. As a matter of fact, it was a bit like yours."

It felt like an accusation but I didn't react—I just kept scribbling. My handwriting was far past legible. My muscles, still sore from my battle with the beater, quivered.

"The aspic," I said.

"He played on my vanity. Called to say he'd lost the feel for his aspic. That he needed the master's touch. I came by on Monday around lunchtime. The restaurant was dark. Laurent's stock was reducing on the stove, nearly ready to use. He gave me a taste and I told him the truth—it was perfection. Firm enough to set, but not rubbery. Rich and smooth and easy on the tongue. I had no way to know he'd enhanced it with a pound of table salt."

"Once he caught you, what'd he say?"

"He laughed in my face. Demanded I write him a feature—a profile of Laurent Tirel, the timeless genius, whose food was better now than it ever had been before. I called him washed-up, overrated, a disgrace to France. I told him I'd rather hang up my pen than write one word praising him. So he called the press. By which I mean you."

A shiver cut through me. Where had I been Monday at lunchtime? At home, probably. Making ham sandwiches for me and Nicky. If Laurent tried to call me, it didn't go through.

"I didn't mean to do it," said Ambrose. "I just stood in the kitchen, smelling that stock, feeling its fat congealing on my tongue, and I heard him chuckling to himself as he sat in his office. The grinding of the phone as each number dialed went through me like a dentist's drill. And then suddenly the knife was in my hand and I walked into his office and . . ."

He choked out a sob.

"Finish," I said. "I don't care if it hurts to say. It should hurt."

"And I killed him."

"How?"

"I cut his throat."

"Why?"

"Because he gave me no other choice. If my secret got out, it would mean the end of the *Sentinel*. The end of my flirtation with Number 5. I'd have been out on the street."

"That's better than being a killer!"

"I know that now. I've been an absolute wreck ever since. I keep seeing his eyes, you know, wide and accusing, sick with betrayal. I can still feel the knife in my hand. The weight of it plunging into his throat. The heat of the blood as it splashed across my wrist. At first I thought I could live with it but it's worse every day. I'm coming apart."

And he looked at me with the same eyes he'd given me the night before in his studio—that stare like a sick old dog who just wants to be held one more time before he dies. I flipped to a fresh page.

"What happened next?"

"Nothing good. The instant Laurent stopped quivering, the adrenaline and the Obetrol abandoned me. I crashed. I was sobbing in the kitchen, frantically washing my hands, when Rocky floated through the door. Stars, Bernard, you've never seen someone so high. He kept asking daft questions and calling me 'Your Highness,' and no matter what I said, he just wouldn't go. And then he asked about the stock and I told him it was for aspic and those glassy eyes of his lit up and he said I could leave, that he'd finish the aspic and clean everything up. I ran. I guess I thought that if someone found him there, with the body and everything, that he might take the blame for me."

"You'd have let that happen?"

"I'm not proud of it. But yes, I think I would have. I stayed away for most of the day. Taught a class—I don't remember a second of it—and walked the streets and finally came back here, expecting the building to be infested with police. But it was just as quiet as before. Rocky was gone. Laurent's body, sans head, lay on the office floor. I found the aspic in the fridge. I was trying to figure out how to get rid of it, to make it all go away, when César arrived, sweaty and quaking and dope sick. I tried to get rid of him but he was intent on going into Laurent's office and as soon as he opened the door and started screaming, well—"

"You cut his throat and threw him in the dumpster."

"God, I'm sorry. I really am."

"I don't care. Tell me what happened."

"I see it in images. I was out of my head with pills and fear. I've no idea how I muscled him into that dumpster but I suppose I did because suddenly I was in my apartment. I tried to sleep and of course it was impossible—my heart was flying and every siren sounded like the police coming to drag me away. But they never came."

He slumped against the counter.

I let him take another belt of brandy and then asked: "Were Tiny Tommy's boys really following you around?"

"Yes."

"And the break-in at your apartment?"

"A lie. A rather pathetic attempt to throw you off my scent."

"Same reason you planted the knife at Number 5?"

"Indeed."

"What about French Vic?"

A sneer flashed across his face. It was gone in an instant, replaced by the same look of wretchedness he'd been wearing since his story began, but it lingered in my vision like a bolt of lightning. Some part of him, I realized, had enjoyed this.

"You said you'd found something that would lead you straight to Laurent's killer," he said.

"I was joking."

"I couldn't be sure. I'd spotted some bromate in Rocky's

pantry. I use it in bread-baking classes—it does wonders for oven spring but eat it straight and it's nasty stuff. I stirred it right into your whipped cream."

"For fuck's sake."

He stared at his shoes.

"Not that it matters, but I only used enough to make you sick."

Only enough to make me sick. As though murder were a charming new recipe he was tinkering with. As though he had any way, while cranked up on speed and paranoia, to know just the right dose for me.

"Vic's doctors said it was more than enough to kill anybody."

"Well, that wasn't my intent!" He took a pained breath. "I didn't want to kill you. The point was to slow you down, to give me time, to . . . Christ. I don't know. Does any of this make sense?"

"Yeah. But it's still fucking vile."

I closed my notebook. Through the ceiling, I heard chairs shifting. My guests were antsy. It was time to bring in Donati and friends.

But the phone wasn't where I'd left it. Someone had returned it to Laurent's desk. I made for the office, walking backward until it started to feel silly. Ambrose was focused on his cigarette and his drink. He didn't care about me now and I don't think he ever really had. I left the office door open and kept an ear on him as I dialed Homicide. Ambrose didn't make a sound.

A desk sergeant told me Donati had gone home. I told him I'd wrung a confession out of the man who killed Laurent Tirel, and none of that seemed to mean much to him but I said *murder* enough times that he got the point. I was giving him the address when a thump came from the kitchen. I dropped the phone and bolted back in there and found Ambrose lying on his side, clutching a chef's knife and carving his wrist like a Thanksgiving turkey.

I kicked the knife out of his hand. It slid under the range. He tried to get up but he slipped in the blood. I grabbed a washcloth and squatted beside him and squeezed his wrist until his eyes bulged. He tried to get away and I smacked him in the face as hard as I could.

"Let me die, damn you, let me die. You owe me this much."

"I don't owe you a fucking thing."

For a while we were quiet. Then he snorted like he'd thought of something funny. I didn't ask him what it was—I'd heard enough of his jokes to last ten lifetimes—but he told me anyway.

"My condition will do me one favor. The prison food won't taste so bad."

I didn't laugh. I didn't look. I just kept holding that washcloth until the cops showed up.

Twenty-three

• Saturday •

I handed Ambrose over to a pair of uniformed pricks who were functionally identical to Adam-12. Toru was waiting on the other side of the swinging doors, looking dazed, like a succession of bombs had just exploded in his face.

"Ambrose killed Laurent?"

"Yep. Which means I need to get to work."

I swept toward the stairs. He followed.

"We were in the middle of a pretty serious fight."

"You talk. I'll listen."

"I can't talk if you don't stand still."

"Then wait until I'm done!"

At the top of the stairs, I screamed "Elma!" until she popped her head around the corner. I dragged her into the bathroom, slammed the door, and said, "Get me out of this straitjacket."

"Did you get whipped cream on my dress?"

"Now!"

She peeled me like a shrimp and I didn't wait for her to leave before I availed myself of the facilities. I don't think anyone in history has ever enjoyed peeing more. While I pulled my street clothes back on, Elma stared at me, cigarette hanging from her lip like Marlon Brando.

"This evening has been an absolute scream," she said.

"Thanks for the dress."

"It did the trick. That reporter of yours looked like she was trying to swallow you with her eyes."

I didn't say anything but I'm not gonna pretend that didn't feel good. In the dining room, cops swarmed like termites. They were reading Ambrose his rights and all my friends were yelling. Over the din I could just hear Toru shouting.

"I need to talk to you!"

And I'd have obliged, I swear, except Donati was bearing down like a torpedo and there was nowhere for me to run. So I yelled back, "Just one second!" as Donati clamped my wrist and dragged me toward the bar. I didn't even fight him. I flipped open my notebook and gave him the whole goddamned tale.

Before I knew it, it was three A.M. Everybody was gone but me and Donati, his photographer, and Toru. The detective had filled two notepads. Every time I thought he was done, another question popped into his head. When the pub mix ran out, my patience did too.

"I've got a deadline, god damn it. Can I leave?"

"Not yet."

"You've got your killer. What the hell else is there to say?"

We were still up at the bar. The lights were on full blast. The air stank of cigarette smoke and duck fat, of spilled wine and a rancid charlotte russe that I was absolutely not going to clean up. Toru was up on Olympus, dozing in Princess Grace's chair. The photographer wandered around, capturing every thread in every napkin, every smear on every glass. Donati's eyes were bleary, his cheeks puffy. He looked as tired as I felt.

"I wanted to say, uh . . . well, I guess I'm a little bit sorry."

"What for?"

"You know the uniform who was with me when you found the body?"

"Adam-12?"

He giggled. I didn't know cops could giggle, but there you go.

"Yeah," he said. "Only his right name is Kriter. Apparently he's been, uh, intimate with one of the ad sales people down at the *St. Mark's Arch*. So some of the details in their story that I thought came from you, uh, well, it's possible they came from us. He's in real hot water and I just wanted to apologize for, uh . . ."

"Throwing me out of police headquarters?"

"Yeah."

He stared at his shoes. I was tempted to pat him on the head.

"Thanks, Detective. I'd love to spend a few hours chewing you out but instead how about you let me go do my goddamned job?"

"Yeah, uh, yeah. Go ahead. And thanks, I guess, for the help."

So I grabbed the nearest wine bottle and was rinsing it in the bar sink when Toru came my way. He looked like somebody had been working him over with a meat tenderizer.

"Why are you still here?" I said.

"Donati wanted you chaperoned. Said he was afraid you'd find another murder to get involved with on the way home. I think he was worried about you. I guess I am too."

"Thank you. Really."

He caught a glimpse of himself in the mirror and spent a second trying to smear his hair back into place.

Without looking at me he said: "I dozed off thinking about what life would be like without you. It seemed awful. So the answer is okay."

"Okay?"

"To the whole, y'know, women thing. Okay."

Well, how about that? Okay. I didn't say anything. I just felt warm all over, so much blood rushing through my head that I thought it might pop off and float away like a balloon.

"You're a good sport," I said. "Thank you."

"We gotta talk about it, though. Like probably a lot? So are you coming home or what?"

Home. Didn't that sound lovely? But I had to say—

"Not yet."

I grabbed a pot of moderately scummy coffee off the back of the bar and, as tidily as my exhausted hands could manage, poured it into the wine bottle. I fished a cork out of the garbage and jammed it in.

"I'll be back after I file."

"Can't you write at the apartment?"

"On Saturday morning? With the TV blaring and the kids screaming and the cat puking all over my notes? No thanks."

"But where are you going?"

No time for silly questions. I kissed him softly, then popped open the register and grabbed a few twenties, just for walking-around money and because, damn it, this restaurant owed me one.

"I love you," I said. "You get that, right?"

"I love you too."

"Good. I'll call you tomorrow. Uh, or rather later today."

I grabbed my typewriter and plunged into the street. I made for the avenue, figuring that if anyone tried to mug me, I'd give him a Smith Corona to the jaw. The deli on the corner was back in business despite the Ford-shaped hole in the wall, so I ducked inside and ordered:

A bacon, egg, and cheese.

A sausage, egg, and cheese.

A pastrami, egg, and cheese.

Which steamed in their wrappers as I stuffed them into my bag. I stood on the corner and scanned for a cab. All of them were off duty but boy, I did not care. I stood in the street and got in the way of one of them and he almost ran me over but the second time I tried it worked great. The cabbie was horrified to see me out by myself and said he was happy to take me wherever I wanted to go, but he pulled a face when I told him—

"The Hotel Chantal."

Ninth Avenue looked even grimmer at night—like a city getting walloped by the plague. I thumped on the Chantal's door and got buzzed in quick. The girl in the thigh-highs was gone, replaced by a guy with curly eyebrows, coarse gray stubble, and nose hair as thick as the woods in Central Park. Think Ed Asner but without the raw sex appeal. I pounded up the stairs and let myself in.

César's apartment smelled like old spinach and NYPD aftershave. The remains of the piggy bank were still scattered across the floor. I'd have rather gone anywhere else but I needed someplace quiet and god knows nobody in this building gave a damn whether I lived or died.

I tried to open the window but it had a guard on it that stopped it after three inches. This was where chaos brought me—the kind of hotel where people come to kill themselves. Well, I had no time for melancholy. I dumped coffee into César's only cup—blue and white Japanese china, covered with unblinking golden eyes—took a pull, and opened the Smith Corona. A little piece of wood tumbled out—the missing camel from Nicky's peg puzzle. I gave it a kiss and held back some tears and said: "We'll get you home soon."

In all the excitement of my first visit here I'd failed to notice that while César's room boasted a singularly uncomfortable wooden chair, there was no table and no desk, so I set the typewriter on the chair and sat on the floor.

"My back is gonna be fucked," I muttered. The pale blue beast hummed gently. I ground out a few sentences of garbage, cranked up the paper, and started again. After three false starts and a few more gulps of coffee, the words started to flow. The typewriter, loud as a machine gun, made my head pound and my eyes ache. My downstairs neighbor thumped on the ceiling and the guy next door screamed some truly inventive profanity but I just let it be part of the rhythm. I'd come through hell, motherfuckers, and it was time to tell the tale.

Naturally I started with the head. Then I jumped back, laid the tension on thick as I could, gave a few words about what Laurent's meant to the city—taking pains to drop some of the old boldface names—then shifted to César's shithole apartment so we could get to know our second victim as well as we knew the first. And then I danced across Midtown, from Cœur to Près to Number 5. I showed the restaurant world in mourning. I described every beautiful dish. I bled all over those goddamned pages and I swear to god it was good enough to make marble cry.

I came of age in the humorless, strike-threatened newsrooms

of the early 1960s, when the first person was strictly outlawed and we were all told that "you had to earn the 'I,'" but I'd almost been poisoned, god damn it, and if that didn't earn the *I*, nothing ever would. So I was there but I wasn't the hero because this story's only hero was food. Delicious and repulsive, overpriced and cheap, old-fashioned and new. I sold it so hard you could feel the salt on your tongue.

The only time I hesitated was when I got to the end, when it was time to explain Ambrose's involvement. He'd told his story like it was a tragedy, and I figured he'd wanted me to parrot him, just like I always had. It would have been easy. I decided, stomach churning, to tell the truth instead. And that was that Ambrose, as much as Laurent, had made me who I was. He'd taught me how to charm a maître d', how to fake it like I knew about wine, how to pan a crummy restaurant without crushing the chef's spirit. I let the readers know that he'd broken my heart and that my feelings about him didn't mean a thing. I wrapped up by saying that I'd always figured anybody who'd take another person's life was a selfish son of a bitch. Now that I'd finally met a killer, I was sure.

And when it was finished I started again because I'd never let anybody read my first drafts and there was no way in hell I was going to start now. And that's when the magic happened, man, the magic that only reporters know—the magic called deadline. Words tumbled like water from a burst pipe. Time slowed. Notepaper spread across the floor until the room looked like it'd been hit by a blizzard. Sandwiches were devoured. Coffee was swilled—lukewarm sludge so foul and delicious it made me want to cry. And a long week of misery turned into something that might not have been art but which was probably worth a read.

Finally it was eleven o'clock. I had a solid second draft and I should have taken thirty minutes to read it out loud but come on, folks, there just wasn't time.

I headed downtown.

I proofed it on the train, marking typos and smoothing awkward sentences, pruning adverbs and tweaking adjectives until every description was dangerously sharp. This was my favorite part of writing, when the bones were there and the skin was too and nothing remained but to make it pretty. It's what I'd lived for ever since I first read Strunk and White, and I was only sorry it didn't last.

Except actually it lasted a little longer than I needed it to, because the RR was late showing up and slow as cold syrup getting downtown. It dawdled in every station and stopped in every tunnel. The lights kept flickering and I was on the verge of screaming but I was New Yorker enough not to let the strain show except for the frantic bouncing of my leg. I finally got aboveground and ran like a goddamned fool for the *Sentinel*, where I just about got shot for trying to blow through security. I sprinted up the stairs—fuck those ancient elevators—and dashed through the city room and was panting like a dying horse when I barged into Judy's office and saw I had three minutes to spare.

"Here's your goddamned cover."

Judy took a long breath and stared with exquisite dissatisfaction at the WeightWatchers cards in her hand. She held them up like a birthday party magician. I closed my eyes and chose a chicken Kiev that looked like baked asphalt. Her face fell even lower than before.

"I oughta jump out the window now," she said.

"Assuming it's not jammed. You gonna read this or what?"

"Sorry. Give it here."

She stubbed out her cigarette and lit another and put her feet up and started to read. Oh, baby, it was agony. Watching somebody read my writing was like surgery without anesthesia and this was closer to my heart than anything I'd ever done. I forced myself to stare out the window and contemplate the birds. I tried not to worry about the fact that Judy wasn't making notes, which was either very, very good or very fucking bad.

Finally she set it down. She walked around the desk, opened the office door, and yelled: "Go ahead."

She sat down and wiped her glasses on the hem of her two-toned blouse. There was a potted orchid behind her that hadn't been there on Tuesday but which was already starting to die.

"What do you mean, 'go ahead'?" I said. "They can't print it if they don't have it."

"You're smart. You should work in newspapers."

"Then what's your cover?"

"I had everybody put together memories of the magazine, just in case this didn't come through."

I tried to swallow but my throat was far too dry.

"But I did come through."

"B.B. . . ."

"What's wrong with it?"

"It's good, B.B. It's very good. But it's new journalism shit. Drugs and fucking and the first person all over everywhere. It's not the *Sentinel* magazine."

"You think I was going to 'this reporter . . .' my whole way through?"

"You're right. It wouldn't have helped. You're hanging out with mobsters and you're calling prominent chefs heroin addicts and that's all before you accuse one of the longest-tenured *Sentinel* employees of two and a half murders."

"He confessed."

"According to you. Between Legal and fact-checking, it would take a month to get this vetted and we've got three hours. It's a no. A very firm no."

There was a lot I wanted to say but it all sounded pathetic, so I kept my mouth shut. I tried to pretend it didn't hurt, but come on. I was shattered. I wasn't even craving one of Judy's cigarettes—that's how beaten I felt.

"So I'm out on my ass?" I said.

"It happens. Stings like hell, but it happens."

"You owe me better than that."

She rubbed her neck like there were a couple of walnuts stuck in there.

"You're right. It's a story. I mean, a hell of a story. It's too good to throw away."

"So what are you going to do with it?"

She squeezed tighter. The walnuts weren't going anywhere.

"After the magazine's put to bed, I could maybe walk the story over to the city room."

"If it's too personal for the magazine, how's it gonna work in the regular paper?"

"They'll rewrite it. Kill the first person. Rip out anything we can't verify. It'll be painful but it'll run."

"What about my byline?"

"You get an 'Additional Reporting By' plus the freelance rate. I can't promise you anything more."

Freelance. Because I wasn't staff anymore.

"What is the freelance rate these days?" I said.

"I don't know. Twenty-five, fifty bucks."

I laughed because what the fuck else was I going to do?

"I almost got poisoned. For fifty bucks."

She groaned like this really hurt. I was glad. It hurt me more.

"You think there's any chance the paper gives me a job?" I said.

"That'll be up to the city room." She put her hand on mine. "It's awful. I know. You're a sharp reporter and a hell of a writer and I wish I could do, I don't know, more."

It was a shitty offer. A truly shitty offer. But it was also the only one I had. I took my hand back and ran it across my story as softly as you'd caress a kitten's back. It had felt red hot an hour before but soon it would be ice cold. It needed a home or it would be deader than dead.

"Thanks," I said. "But hell no."

So next thing I knew, I was in the middle of the Brooklyn Bridge. It was one of those days you get in early spring that was right on the edge between breezy and cold. The river glittered like sapphire and the skyline looked brand new. A tugboat tootled by. I twisted my story in my hands. I thought about dropping it, watching it flutter down to the river and disappear.

But nah. That'd be a stupid thing to do.

So I walked.

I angled north off the bridge, past the hideous bulk of the future police headquarters, past the Tombs, where Ambrose was probably learning that even for a man with no sense of taste, prison food tastes like shit. I entered Chinatown, where I grabbed dumplings for strength and water to soothe my pounding head, and cruised up Broadway, where the concrete glitters like false gold. I kept on past Canal and Broome, past Houston and Bond.

All the way to Eighth Street.

All the way to St. Mark's.

The offices of the *Arch* occupied a four-story building whose front door really had a marble arch, how about that? I climbed the stoop and entered a foyer plastered with flyers for bands I'd never heard of and shitty-sounding plays and every kind of protest. I saw one "Rally to Save Brooklyn from Manhattan" and I'd have written down the date except it was already way too late. A propped-open door led me to a long, dark room that stank of ink and pot and patchouli and B.O. Every chair was occupied. Every surface was covered with papers and ferns and ashtrays that hadn't been emptied since the Johnson administration. Every reporter, regardless of sex, wore the same floral shirt and had the same flaccid hair. I was deeply out of my element and I did not care.

I wove through a warren of scratched desks and sagging couches until I reached a door on which someone had used permanent marker to scrawl, EDITOR IN CHIEF. I let myself in. It was a small room. A cone of opium incense burned on the sill of a window that overlooked an incredibly grim courtyard. Susan was hunched over her desk muttering into the phone. Her hair was pushed back over her ears and she was wearing a belted cobalt jumpsuit patterned with bright yellow stars. I disconnected her call. She grinned.

"That was my dentist. Do you know how hard it is to get a dentist appointment in this town?"

"I've got something for you that's even better than a dentist appointment."

"Oh yeah?"

"And in return, all I want is a job."

I dropped the story on her desk. She eyed it like it was a loaded gun.

"Sure it's safe for me to read that?"

"Would you want it if it were?"

She snatched it up and read it quickly. Laughed at all the right places. And when she spoke, oddly, I felt no fear at all.

"It's good."

"I've heard it called 'very good.' You'll print it?"

"We already ran something pretty extensive on the Tirel murder."

"This is better."

"Arguably."

"And it's got the ending."

She pulled a jar of mixed nuts out of her desk drawer. Popped a cashew into her mouth and chewed.

"What happened to the *Sentinel*?"

"It's not *them*."

"But is it us?"

I shrugged.

"Print it or don't. I don't give a shit."

You probably think I was bluffing. In that moment, I was honestly too tired to care.

Susan ate another cashew. A third. Finally she held up her hands.

"I guess we have space next week."

"I want the cover."

"Of course you do."

"And a staff role."

She cackled.

"Do you know how tight my budget is?"

"You're gonna find room. Not as a favor but because you know my work and you know I'm very fucking good."

She propped her feet on the desk. They were bare and just a little dirty. Her toes wiggled.

"It's a tough call," she said. "I'm just not sure you'd fit in at our *sleazy little rag*."

"Okay, okay. I'm sorry I said that. I was being a jackass. Also I was more tired than I'd ever been in my entire life? Anyway, yeah, if I was pissed it was because you were doing your job. You're a terrific reporter—better than me—and I think I've got a lot to learn here. That's why I want to come."

"No other reason?"

She batted her eyelashes like Betty Boop. I hardly swooned.

"None."

"We'll have to shift the desks around, but yeah. B. B. Black, welcome to downtown."

And that's how my new life began.

The pay was shit—she wasn't kidding about the budget—and the hours were punishing but it quickly became the most interesting job I'd ever had. She let me cover everything—not just restaurants but anything even remotely connected to food. I wrote about the rats at the Plaza and the strike at the Rikers cafeteria. I broke the story about how the chef at Gracie Mansion got fired because he refused to cook the mayor's steak well done. I interviewed hot-dog vendors and fishing boat captains, elite caterers and professional butlers and a guy who won an award for "World's Shittiest Pizza." I kept my eyes on the kings and queens of the restaurant world, of course, because I never got sick of fine dining on the company tab, but I made sure my readers knew

Midtown was not the only place to eat. I made friends with the kids in the newsroom—most of whom were actually far more square than me, it turned out—and even got used to the smell.

Shit, what else? They convicted Ambrose of both murders—they couldn't prove the attempted poisoning—and sent him up to Sing Sing, where he got a job supervising the prison kitchen. Carnegie Hall took over his studio as a rehearsal space—the musicians loved it, said it always smelled like butter—and I never spoke to him again.

It would be a lie to say I never missed him. I did, basically every time I went out to eat. Whenever I was confronted with overdressed salad or undercooked meat, I'd hear him tutting in my head. I spent a while trying to silence that voice but eventually I learned to live with it. When a person becomes a part of you, there's no way to cut them out without losing a lot of yourself.

Vic recovered. I guess that potassium bromate really was good for oven spring because he bounced right back—shuttered his restaurant, placated his wife, kicked his habit, and joined Rocky as the sous at Number 5, whose menus Ambrose approved from prison and which quickly became the hottest ticket in town. The farting Spider-Man mural became notorious, even more so than the concept, which started as French-American but changed whenever Rocky got bored.

Henri took over at Laurent's, where he had the backing of Oswald and Tiny Tommy and every good citizen who'd ever had a craving for orange duck. He ditched the stroganoff and went back to cooking his dad's original menu, only lighter and bolder and a little more now. He tossed the fake flowers and tattered curtains, tore down Olympus, and replaced the wall of half-forgotten celebrities with a series of choice nudes painted by his sister. You won't see a fleet of limos parked outside on Friday night but people who give a damn call it the best French place in Midtown. Best of all, Henri seems happier than I've ever seen him. He brought his dad's place back from the dead and that's a pretty neat trick.

C.J. kept her word and left New York behind. That summer she sent me a postcard of the Brandenburg Gate that read, *Berlin is weird as hell. I love it. Tell Tommy thanks for the cash.* Jean-Louis quit too and was never heard from again—until the next year, when he appeared at the bottom of the bestseller list with a cookbook called *Classic French Cooking the Paratrooper Way,* which contained thirty-six recipes that, Henri swore, were identical to the ones that disappeared after his dad died. Henri considered suing him but you can't copyright recipes, and anyway, Jean-Louis remained a scary son of a bitch.

And me and Toru, well, we had a long talk and a lot of tears and we agreed to stay together no matter how tough the whole "dating other people" thing turned out to be. It was beautiful, absolutely beautiful, and we lived happily ever after.

For six months.

At which point the entire thing collapsed in a heap of resentment and jealousy and contempt because it turns out that swinging is a lot harder than it looks. We fought and we cried and we broke up and got back together and then broke up for good. I dragged my whole ragged life to a funky little one-bedroom on East Fifth, an easy subway ride to my old life and a short walk to my new one. Toru kept the apartment and the hi-fi and all the nice furniture, of course, but I got the cat that shits everywhere, so who can really say who came out ahead?

All right, so it hurt. It hurt bad. But a girl can't have everything, can she? I miss the kids like crazy and I miss him too but the path we were on wasn't right for me, so I'm glad I turned around when I still could. There's no shortcut to being grown-up and I'm not so sure I even want to grow up anyway, at least not the way I thought I was supposed to. I tell myself it wasn't worth losing my mind to become the World's Greatest Stepmom, that I'm happier without him, that I'm better off doing my own thing. Some nights it actually feels true.

For now, I've got Manhattan and I've got my job. Susan and I are getting pretty chummy and I'm still not smoking and I've finally got the space I need to figure out this whole "Who am I?" thing. Until I do, well, I've got reservations seven nights a week. I'll never go hungry. As far as I'm concerned, that's the most anybody could ask.

Photo of the author © Gianna Reddick

W. M. AKERS is a novelist, playwright, and game designer. He is the author of the mystery novels *Critical Hit, Westside,* and *Westside Saints*; the creator of the bestselling games *Deadball: Baseball With Dice* and *Comrades: A Revolutionary RPG*; and the curator of the history newsletter *Strange Times*. He lives in Philadelphia but hasn't traded in his Mets cap yet.

wmakers.net

ouijum